BLACKFLAME

CRADLE : VOLUME THREE

WILL WIGHT

HIDDEN GNOME PUBLISHING

BLACKFLAME

Copyright © 2017 Hidden Gnome Publishing

Book and cover design by Patrick Foster Design
Cover illustration by Kevin Mazutinec

ISBN 978-1-959001-22-5 (5x8 TRADE EDITION)

www.WillWight.com

HIDDEN GNOME PUBLISHING

To the nameless minions who give their lives in my books to make the heroes look better.

We will always forget you.

CHAPTER ONE

INFORMATION REQUESTED: THE PATH OF BLACK FLAME.

[WARNING: SIGNIFICANT DEVIATIONS DETECTED. REPORT ACCURACY COMPROMISED. RECOMMEND RENEWED CONTACT WITH ITERATION 110 TO RESTORE FUNCTIONALITY.]

BEGINNING REPORT...

For over five centuries, the Blackflame family held their empire by virtue of unstoppable force. Before facing a single Blackflame sacred artist, an entire sect would surrender.

All across the Empire's lands, rebel strongholds and rival Schools were burned in dark fire. None stood against the Blackflames because none dared; to be suspected of insurrection was to be destroyed.

The Path of the Unstained Shield excels in protection, the Path of a Thousand Hands in versatility. The Path of the Cloud Hammer is respected for mobility and force, the Path of Silver Grace for its elegance. The many Paths of the Redflower family grow food and bring rain throughout the Empire, and the Path of Jade Eyes is unmatched in healing.

The Path of Black Flame was stolen from ancient dragons. It is the art of pure destruction.

But mortal humans are not suited for the power of dragons. Slowly, the Blackflame family declined, their minds and bodies eroded by the destructive power of their sacred arts. Eventually, even the citizens at the heart of the Empire thought of the imperial family as symbols and legends.

More and more of the day-to-day workings of the Empire were left to the Blackflames' traditional servants: the Naru clan. They became the face of the Blackflame Empire, with their loyal reputation and shining emerald wings, and the people grew to know and trust them.

Fifty years ago, when the Blackflame family had faded to ashes and myths, the Naru quietly ascended the throne.

The first Naru clan empress has since moved into private seclusion, and her son now rules the Empire.

As for the Blackflame family themselves, most died out decades ago, gradually eaten from the inside out by their own madra. The only remaining Blackflames are **[DATA NOT FOUND]**.

If their family and their Path are revived, the consequences could be—

CONNECTION SEVERED.

RESTORING CONNECTION...

CONNECTION FAILURE.

[ARCHIVED INFORMATION REGARDING CRADLE REMAINS ACCESSIBLE, BUT ANALYSIS OF CURRENT CONDITIONS AND PROJECTIONS INTO THE FUTURE WILL BE DISABLED UNTIL CONTACT WITH ITERATION 110 IS RESTORED.]

REPORT COMPLETE.

Goldsteel tongs poised, Lindon knelt over the carcass of a twisted wolf.

The dreadbeast looked as though it had been subjected to dissection and decay already, its skin bloody red with spots of diseased black, but it had looked that way even before death. It was cobbled together from mismatched parts, a botched and diseased creation.

He might have passed out from the smell if not for the perfume-soaked cloth wrapped over the lower half of his face, and even so he tried to breathe through his mouth.

Lindon had already made his incision down the ribs of the creature, pinning flaps of skin back to get a look inside. He'd had to saw through a layer of meat and tendons, and his gloved hands were speckled with foul blood.

Now he tried not to choke on perfumed air as he took a deep breath to steady himself.

Fisher Gesha loomed over him, a disapproving presence. Gesha was possibly the oldest person he'd ever seen, like a shriveled pile of wrinkles packed into a sacred artist's robes. Her gray hair was tied into a tight bun on the top of her head, and eight legs of mechanical Forged madra stuck out of the bottom of her robes, lifting her high enough to see over his shoulder.

"Carefully, now, carefully," she directed. "You hit the binding at the wrong angle, you'll chip it like a teacup."

Lindon dipped his head slightly in lieu of an apology, then slid his hand into the wound.

Back home, he'd helped his father clean meat from a hunt, but *this* body had started to rot even before its death, and Lindon struggled not to gag.

He could only get two fingers past the ribs, but they quickly ran into a mass of sharp, solid edges, as though someone had glued broken glass into a fist-sized bundle of shards. He hardly brushed the binding with his fingers for fear of shattering it.

He withdrew his hand most of the way, holding open the incision.

"In a Remnant, the binding would be easier to remove," Fisher Gesha told him, still watching from the side with hands clasped behind her back. "No muscle to cut through, hm? Simple, simple, simple to remove. But dreadbeasts keep their souls in their bodies, nasty little things, so they leave no Remnants. Their techniques grow in them like this, alongside their organs."

She was trying to cram as many lessons into him as she could before Eithan took him away, so that the Underlord couldn't say she'd been neglecting his education. While Lindon appreciated the effort, it was something of a distraction to have to listen when he was trying to remove a delicate piece of Forged madra from a corpse.

Inserting his tongs, he got a solid grip on the binding. Madra could react unpredictably with physical objects, but goldsteel was a unique substance. His tongs looked like ordinary gold until the light caught them, and then they flashed pure white.

Goldsteel could get a firm grip on virtually any kind of madra, which was why it was often used for Soulsmith tools and defenses against hostile Remnants. He held the binding firmly in place, careful not to squeeze too hard and shatter it.

Then he slid two fingers back into the dreadbeast, next to the trapped binding. He pinched a bundle of slick muscle.

And, cycling madra to Enforce his fingers, he tore it away from the binding. It was like pulling apart warm bread.

He would never have been able to tear meat so easily only a week ago, before advancing to Iron. And the dreadbeast was dead, so it was no longer Enforcing itself with its own madra supply.

After he had ripped free every connection from the binding to the surrounding body—and tilted his tongs a few degrees in every direction, to make sure it could move freely—he gradually slid the binding out.

It was a ball of jagged spikes, the yellow of its material barely visible beneath blood and bits of tissue.

He wasn't sure how the madra of such a binding would interact with the physical body, but he still winced at the sight. This had been *inside* a living creature. It must have caused agony every time the beast moved.

Then again, the binding may not have Forged itself into existence until the wolf died. And it wasn't as though Lindon cared for the suffering of a dreadbeast anyway.

He dropped the blood-soaked binding onto a tray that Fisher Gesha had prepared for the purpose, then something caught his eye. He turned back to the wolf's body, inserting the tongs once again.

There was a glimmer of something *behind* the wet space where the binding had once rested, a speck of white too bright and clean to be bone. He pushed some of the muscle away, though he found himself leaning at an awkward angle to get around the ribs.

The white object was a tiny spiral no bigger than his thumbnail, but it was warped out of shape, like a half-melted wax seashell. The white was speckled with a rainbow of other colors—and, of course, drenched in blood—but he reached the tongs in for it.

At the first touch, the binding dissolved like chalk in rain.

Fisher Gesha smacked him on the side of the head. Before his advancement to Iron, she might well have killed him.

"You don't touch madra you know nothing about," she warned, shaking a finger at him. "Very dangerous."

Lindon bobbed his head to indicate he'd heard her, but he couldn't just leave it alone. "But honored Fisher, I believe I saw one of those before."

In fact, he suspected he had one in his pack. His white spiral binding was large and pristine, whereas the one in the dreadbeast had been small and shot through with other colors, but he thought they may be the same crystallized technique. The same technique that had gone into the Jai Ancestor's Spear, allowing it to steal madra.

She slapped him again, on the other side of the head this time.

"You've seen one? I have seen a *thousand*. Spent my life hunting these woods, you think there are surprises here for me?" She jabbed a finger in the direction of the corpse. "When a dreadbeast eats an animal, the meat goes to its stomach. When it eats a Remnant, the madra goes *there*."

Lindon brightened. "If this can steal and process madra, like the Ancestor's Spear does, doesn't that make this a treasure? Every dreadbeast has the material for a new spear!"

He was working himself up with every word, envisioning himself standing in an arena against Jai Long with a white spear of his own. And a core bursting with stolen madra.

Gesha brushed her hands off on the front of her robes, though she hadn't touched anything. "In my grandmother's day, they tried such a thing. Used those bindings to make weapons and take power from the ones they killed. But it did to men the same things it did to...them. Everyone who used such weapons became monsters, hideous and deformed." She shuddered. "If we could make the spear of the Jai ancestor ourselves, why would we prize it so highly, hm?"

Clearly, she didn't know what he'd taken from the Soulsmith foundry at the top of the Transcendent Ruins. "But Fisher Gesha...I have the notes from the ones who *made* the spear." He watched her as he spoke, anticipating her shock.

Without changing expression, she reached into the pocket of her outer robe and pulled out a wooden document case. "You mean these notes? Yes, you left them out the other night. These are ancient, you should be more careful with them."

He would have reached for them if not for the gore on his hands. "I'm sorry, I was overeager."

"Mm. These are brilliant; they will provide you with years of study and inspiration." She tucked them back into her pocket. "Someday. First, you must learn the basics."

Disappointment tightened into panic—he had wanted to use knowledge of the spear as a trump card against Jai Long. "If I may speak openly, honored Fisher: I was hoping to create a weapon according to those notes."

"If an infant wishes to forge a sword of his own, should his interest be encouraged? Hm? No. I will return these to you when you have learned to stand on your own feet as a Soulsmith, and not before."

Lindon wanted to argue, but he was unlikely to earn anything more than another hit on the head. And the smell was getting worse every second he knelt over the dreadbeast's corpse.

Reluctantly, he let the topic slip away.

He dropped the tongs onto the tray next to the one binding they had secured, then staggered away to take a deep breath. They had left their belongings many paces away, to avoid the mess and stench—Lindon's carried in a bulky pack that he normally wore on his back, and Gesha's in a sealed chest of polished wood.

Lindon stopped to remove his bloody gloves and rinse his hands at a station he had set up for this exact purpose. With a wisp of his spirit, he activated a blocky blue construct that he'd nailed to a tree.

Blue liquid trickled from the box, madra Forged into water by a binding inside. Not real water, but anything would do to wash off this tainted blood.

It was only a crude device, barely worth calling a construct at all, as Gesha had repeatedly reminded him. But it worked, and water madra was common here in the Desolate Wilds, as the disciples of the Purelake School outnumbered most everyone else in the region.

Given that most of the nearby trees were at least spotted with black corruption if not entirely black, and the wildlife seemed to share the affliction, Lindon could see why pure water might be a valuable enough commodity to support a powerful School of the sacred arts.

When he'd cleaned his hands, Gesha had already rinsed off the binding and stripped away the extra muscle, leaving the Forged madra exposed: a spiked crystal of yellow madra, streaked with layers of deep red and pale orange.

Most other Forged madra tended to be one solid color,

but this chaotic blend seemed to suit the dreadbeasts. They gave off a riot of conflicting auras, as though different powers warred within them.

Lindon thanked Fisher Gesha as he reached for the tray. "Are you sure you want to guide me so far? Rinsing a binding for me, that could be considered holding my hand."

It was only intended as a light joke. Those had been Eithan's words when he sent Lindon out to train his Soulsmithing with Gesha: "Don't guide him too far, if you wouldn't mind. I don't need someone who can't walk without his hand held."

Thus far, Gesha had taken the Underlord's instructions seriously, refusing to even carry her own trunk out into the forest and making Lindon haul it himself. But she'd seemed to relax as they'd hunted over the last two days, so he thought a small joke might ease the remaining tension.

Apparently he'd judged wrong.

Her face darkened, and she shoved the tray at him with enough force that he stumbled back. Despite her age, she was still a Highgold, and he was only an Iron.

"You want to report me to the Underlord, hm? You want to waste his time? Well, see if I help you any further!" She turned to shout at the air, as though she suspected Eithan was hiding close by and listening. "Not a finger more, you see? Not a breath!"

"Forgiveness, honored Fisher, forgiveness. This one intended no offense."

"Offense? No offense, but see if I risk landing in a boiling kettle with the Underlord just to help *you*. If a dreadbeast comes up to nibble your toes, see if *I* pull you out of the fire. 'You told me not to help him,' that's what I'll tell him." In a quieter voice, she added, "...and I told you to stop with 'this one, that one.' *That* is what offends me."

Lindon gave her a shallow bow and then turned to her trunk, throwing it open. On the top level were all her most common Soulsmith's tools save her drudge, on which she stood. The spider-construct had identified the location of the binding in the dreadbeast's body, and it would take much of the guesswork out of building a construct, but he wouldn't have access to a drudge until he built one himself.

The tools all had components of goldsteel or halfsilver, the gold surfaces flashing white and the silver ones embedded with stars. They weren't made entirely from the exotic metals, but there was still enough inside the trunk to count as a fortune back in Sacred Valley. Here, where the materials were even more rare, they might qualify as a sect's treasure. He was lucky the Fishers had allowed Gesha to take them out...although, with Eithan Arelius standing behind Lindon, they may not have had a choice.

Before selecting his tools, he ran his madra through the binding. It drew one of his cores almost dry, using it to launch a technique. A knuckle-sized bolt of golden light blasted from the binding, tore through the leaves and earth, and smacked into the tree, chipping away a piece of bark.

"Striker binding," Gesha said immediately. "Aspects?"

"At least earth," Lindon said. The color reminded him of earth aura, so he went with his instincts. "Maybe force? Some wind? If you could take a look with your drudge, we could know for sure."

"*Not* for sure. A drudge only checks for what you tell it to check for. There is no substitute for experience. Now then, what would you do with this binding?"

A construct, essentially, was a puppet with a single technique embedded in it. The binding was the technique. Scripts could tweak the specifics, but the bulk of a construct's abilities were determined by the power of the dead matter in its shell and the binding at its heart.

Lindon reached into his pack and slid out a book Gesha had given him only three nights before: *The Combination of Spirits.* It was written by hand, rather than printed by construct like most of the books from Sacred Valley, but he found the observations of ancient Soulsmith teachers fascinating. "I haven't had time to study in depth, but I had some inspiration. You see, here it mentions a Striker construct that won't activate until a certain amount of time passes. You could put one circle on an arrowhead—"

"Launcher," Fisher Gesha interrupted. "You think my question did not have a correct answer, hm? It does. The correct answer is: a basic launcher construct."

Lindon hesitated. "I'm sure that would work, but the binding serves the same basic purpose already." A launcher construct was little more than a container with a Striker binding in it.

As far as constructs went, launchers were boring. Nothing of what they did amplified or enhanced the binding's technique in any way. In Lindon's opinion, you might as well just keep a Striker binding in a script-sealed box and take it out when you needed it.

Gesha reached into the pocket of her outer robe and pulled out a second book: *Soulsmithing for Coppers*. On its cover was a picture of a smiling tree holding hands with a friendly-looking Remnant.

"You forgot one of your new books, hm? Lucky I grabbed it before we left."

She tossed it to him, and he forced a smile. "Thank you for correcting my careless oversight, Fisher Gesha."

"Mm. You'll find instructions for a launcher inside."

Lindon peeled open the book, flipping past overly large illustrations of children putting simple constructs together. It was a grating reminder that he had first Forged madra only a few weeks before.

Technically he supposed he was at the level of these children, but he was pushing himself in every other aspect of his sacred arts. Why did he have to start from the beginning only here, as a Soulsmith?

But Gesha's stern gaze did not relent, so he sighed and walked back over to her trunk, removing the claw of an earth-Remnant, which still twitched with life if he held it too close to the ground. It would serve as the ideal body for this weapon.

With a goldsteel scalpel, he split it open, placing the binding within.

He ran his spirit over the loose construction, letting his power drift into the dead matter. With focus and a few deep breaths, he took control of the Remnant pieces.

The claw began to shine again, like it had when it was part of a Remnant. Lindon felt when his spirit filled the dead matter and the binding equally, empowering them both.

Then he fused them together.

The claw shrunk, compressed, and reshaped itself slightly. The binding melded into the substance of the claw, sealed inside so it was all one piece.

And that was all.

Now it was a shining yellow rod tipped with claws, which would launch a blast of rock-hard energy when provided with madra. It wasn't much of a weapon, but it counted as a success nonetheless.

All the Soulsmiths in Sacred Valley had been Forgers because the process of creating a construct was similar to Forging: you take control of power and give it form. Lindon could have re-formed the dead matter to look more like a sword, or a box, or most anything else, but he hadn't bothered. It was just a launcher.

More than Forging ability, Lindon had learned, crafting a construct required compatibility. The power of the Soulsmith soaked into the power of the construct, and some aspects of madra did not blend well. In those cases, the Soulsmithing process could result in a useless product, or a deadly mistake.

Pure madra was compatible with everything, but it was also weak. It added nothing. Fisher Gesha's madra was attractive—as in, it literally pulled objects together—and that meant she could fuse dead matter to bindings with no trouble at all, and her madra was *still* compatible with most everything. There were a few powers she couldn't re-Forge without danger, but she had a drudge to identify exactly when those were present.

Pure madra wasn't the *best* for any given construct—it weakened the original power of the madra like water added to wine. But it did technically work with anything.

Lindon would take any advantage he could get.

Back in Sacred Valley, every Forger thought they knew something about Soulsmithing, because making a construct was fairly easy. But making one safe? One that performed as intended every time, and lasted for as long as possible?

You had to measure the dead matter and the binding precisely to avoid unexpected interaction, handle the materials correctly, dissect the Remnant properly, *and* know how to customize and tweak the functions with scripts afterward.

Unless you were making a launcher.

Gesha nodded approvingly. "You move quickly, and with confidence. This is good. Only another week or two, and we will take further steps."

He tried to keep most of the disappointment out of his voice as he said, "A week?"

Gesha's hand struck like a hawk taking a mouse, slapping him on the back of the head. This time, it really stung. "Keep your eyes on the present, not the future, hm?" Her spider legs shuffled, turning her back on him.

"Your instruction has been invaluable, honored Fisher," Lindon said, although in truth she hadn't taught him much at all before the last few days. It seemed that his endorsement from Eithan had promoted him from 'servant' to 'student.' "I bow to your wisdom."

She reached over her shoulder, resting a hand on the hilt of her hook. Like all the members of the Fisher sect, she carried a giant bladed fishhook as a weapon, sharp on the inside. Hers was plated with goldsteel, and he'd personally seen her dissect all sorts of Remnants with it.

"You wish to run before you can stand up straight," Gesha said firmly. "You do not travel any Path by skipping steps."

He had skipped every step he could, and ever since leaving Sacred Valley, he had succeeded beyond his wildest dreams.

But he didn't say that out loud.

"The honored Fisher is wise."

"Mm. You are blind."

"Yes, Fisher Gesha."

"Oh, you know this?"

"Yes, Fisher Gesha."

"That is strange to me. A man who knows he is blind would be very careful of his surroundings, lest he be taken by surprise."

Something grabbed Lindon's ankle and pulled him off balance.

Before his Iron body, slamming his chin against the hard-packed earth would have blinded him with pain, and perhaps lost him a tooth. Now, he only felt pressure hitting his jaw, and he instantly twisted to see what had snared him.

A line of purple madra stuck to his ankle like spider's silk, stretching back to a figure of purple light lurking in the trees. Like all Remnants, it looked like a collection of brush-strokes, as though someone had painted it into existence. This one was tall and sunken, with inhumanly long limbs and the gaping face of a fish. Its thin, webbed fingers were tipped in claws, and its blank purple eyes were fixed on Lindon.

His heart hammered, and he had to focus to keep his breath even and steady so that his madra didn't slip out of control. Not long ago, he would have panicked at this sudden attack.

But that was before Eithan had locked him in a stone ruin alone for two weeks. Panic could wait until the fight was done.

The spirit was still two dozen yards away, but it already had him. The purple string fastened to his ankle stretched back to the Remnant's outstretched hand.

Lindon filled his hand with madra and struck out, driving an Empty Palm into the string...but the line only quivered. It remained fastened to his ankle, one end stuck as though it had grown out of his skin.

The Remnant made a sound like a bubble popping, and the line started dragging Lindon across the forest floor.

His breath came in ragged gasps, and he was having

more trouble keeping his breathing technique steady. When he tried to grab the string and pull, his hand passed right through the madra.

Gesha was drifting alongside him, the legs of her spider-construct matching his pace. "You think too highly of yourself, and this is what comes. A Jade would have sensed my approach when I returned to camp. A Jade would have felt this fellow coming."

"Honored Fisher," Lindon grunted, straining to reach one of the goldsteel tools that remained on the dirt. "Help me, please!"

"An Iron child in these woods should have no more pride than a mouse, no more courage than a rabbit. But you have your eyes on the future. You stare only at your goal far away, so you miss the traps before your feet."

Mustering all his strength, Lindon Enforced his arms, driving his hands into the soft earth. The Remnant pulled him through the dirt for another moment, plowing two furrows before his momentum stopped.

Gesha stopped as well, still speaking idly. "This is a lesson for all sacred artists, not just Soulsmiths. A snake who tries to swallow an elephant will only choke."

Lindon may have been too preoccupied with the Remnant trying to eat him than with Gesha's instruction, but he couldn't see how her lesson applied to his current situation. Certainly, he should have taken the time to put down some sort of alarm circle around the camp before he started working on his construct. But he didn't see what that had to do with his unauthorized Soulsmith experiments.

And did they have to have this talk *now?* He was face-down in the dirt, clinging desperately to earth with arms outstretched, shoulders aching so badly they were starting to shake.

Out of the corner of his eye, he saw Gesha slowly draw her hook and examine it in the light. Clearly, she was in no rush to help him.

"You are always trying to skip steps, yes? To cheat. This is carelessness, and it will land you in more trouble than this."

"I understand, Fisher Gesha," Lindon gasped. "Please, let me free."

Something grabbed him by the right hip, and then by the back of the neck. More webs, stretching out from the purple Remnant.

"Maybe you do, maybe you don't." Fisher Gesha beckoned with her left hand, and a purple line appeared between her fingers and the Remnant. "One way or the other, do not tell the Underlord I helped you out of danger."

She heaved on her line, and the Remnant was jerked off its feet as though it weighed nothing, tumbling over the ground as her purple string shortened. When it was dragged to her feet, she swept her goldsteel hook through the spirit's neck.

Bright sparks of violet essence sprayed into the air like blood, and the Remnant's head fell away.

The force pulling on Lindon released, and he sagged into the ground, his arms and shoulders crying out in relief. "This one humbly thanks you, Fisher Gesha."

"Not *this one*," she said. "Before we return, tell me what you have learned today."

"I am careless. I overstep myself, leaping forward when I should progress slowly and carefully."

"Mm. So long as you have learned."

He didn't tell her what he had *really* learned.

He would have caught the Remnant's approach if he were Jade. And she, a Highgold, had swatted it like a fly.

That was the real lesson: if you were powerful enough, you could accomplish anything.

CHAPTER TWO

Tears glistened in Jai Chen's eyes as Jai Long held her hand. "Kral died fighting beside me," he told her. "He went quickly and courageously. He died a hero."

"The Underlord...killed him?" his little sister asked. She labored to push her voice out, every breath a fight against the invisible weight on her chest.

Jai Long squeezed her hand a little harder, but restrained himself so as not to hurt her. "A boy he brought with him. Just an Iron."

Jai Chen's eyes opened wide, and her arms fluttered as though she'd tried to raise them. "An Iron?"

"He struck like a coward. From behind, with a stolen weapon. Even another Highgold couldn't have faced Kral and lived."

The tears welled up again, and Jai Chen sniffled. "Young master Kral..." She couldn't seem to choke out the rest of the words.

Jai Long smoothed her bedsheets. "I would have told you before, but I've had many preparations to make."

He reached down, unlatching a scripted case. From within, he produced his surprise: the Ancestor's Spear, a glowing shaft of Forged white madra scratched lightly with lines of script. Jai Chen struggled upwards in bed to get a look, straining to push herself upright.

"From the very top of the Transcendent Ruins," he told her, as she extended hesitant fingers to touch it. She looked at him for permission, and only rested her hand upon it when he nodded.

"It's warm..."

"It draws madra from others into me," Jai Long said, and she jerked her hands back. "No no, you can touch it. It only means I'll become stronger for every clan member I...defeat."

"Then you'll avenge young master Kral?" she asked quietly.

He placed the spear back into its case, latching it back, so the precious madra didn't dissipate. The scripts on the spear prevented madra decay, but the Sandviper Soulsmiths couldn't say by how much. It was always best to be careful—if he lost this weapon, there was no replacement.

"I would have avenged him on the spot, if not for the Underlord." He patted her arm. "But the Arelius family is not entirely without honor. They will allow me to face him in the arena, in one year's time."

Sadness crept over her face, but it took her a few full breaths before she could speak. "Back to the Empire? But we...we..." He waited patiently as she focused on her breathing. "...we were going to *leave*. Do...do you...want to go back?"

Only to butcher them, he thought, but he spoke calmly. "The Jai clan has refiners and Soulsmiths. If I break into their vaults, perhaps I could heal you myself. Even if that doesn't work, I could earn the support of the Naru or the Kotai. Or one of the Schools; they say the pills of the Jade Eyes can even restore the freshly dead."

Her smile was twisted by pain and bitterness. "You don't... think we can...leave?"

He patted her arm to buy himself time to think before he answered. "When I'm finished, there will be no one left to follow us."

The topic had grown much darker than he'd planned, but they talked for an hour afterwards of lighter and happier things: food, gossip, memories of Kral. When her exertions took their toll and she fell asleep, he picked up his case and excused himself.

Leaving her behind him, etched with the scars of his failure. Her body was perfectly healthy, damaged only by years of weakness and isolation. On good days, her smile was so wide and open that it almost made him forget anything was wrong.

Her spirit told the real story.

Despite himself, he swept his spiritual perception over her, lighting her spirit in his mind's eye. For a moment, he took in the wreckage left by the monster that had rampaged through her soul.

Her madra channels, which should have spread throughout her body in clean, even loops, were twisted and broken. Half of the passages were dim, blocked, and the other half too bright as madra built up in the wrong places. Her core was wrapped in a web of cracks, leaking light like a broken lantern.

Enough madra trickled through her ruined spirit that she could just barely move. Even that much was a miracle, the result of healers working day and night for a week after her accident.

The culprit lay coiled in his core even now, the Remnant's madra blending with his own as it gradually dissolved, its memories and sensations lurking at the back of his mind. By the time he reached Truegold, he would have digested it completely.

It was the most total, thorough revenge he could imagine.

He had been exiled from the main branch of the Jai clan because the Remnant was from a different Path, and he'd brought his sister along because she had no one left to support her.

The clan could have restored her. It might have cost

them some rare materials, but they could have done it. They didn't, because she was of no value to them.

Which had shown him the extent of the clan's loyalty. Why should he be loyal in return?

He shut the door of his sister's cabin gently, so as not to wake her, nodding to the Lowgold Sandvipers standing guard on either side. These were warriors he'd selected personally, and they knew they answered to him. They would die at their posts.

Though that loyalty might soon be tested, judging by the green banner flying over the Sandviper camp. Jai Long gripped his case more tightly and looked to one of the guards.

"He's back?"

"His bats landed only minutes ago," the guard confirmed. He exchanged glances with his partner, and Jai Long knew their thoughts as clearly as if they'd spoken aloud.

Would the Sandviper chief blame Jai Long for his son's death?

Jai Long found the newly returned group of Sandvipers clustered around a repurposed stable, a cluster of filthy, fur-clad men and women he could smell halfway down the street. They had been in the Wilds for months, too far to respond to the call of the Transcendent Ruins, and now they had arrived to find the heir to their sect murdered.

Days ago, Jai Long had ordered this stable cleared out and cleaned, prepared to host Sandviper Kral's body. The corpse was preserved by rare medicines, waiting for a mourning father.

The Sandvipers parted to allow Jai Long to pass, though their Goldsigns were not so courteous. The miniature sandviper Remnants on their arms coiled and hissed, reflecting their hosts' anger.

Jai Long pushed open the door and slipped inside, holding his polished spear-case. He was already primed to tear the Ancestor's Spear free in an instant; Gokren was a Truegold, and more than capable of killing Jai Long if he reacted poorly. The weapon might be the difference between defeat and survival.

Gokren, chief of the Sandvipers, was a wiry man with slicked-back gray hair and a pair of short, one-handed spears crossed on his back. He wore furs from chin to toe, with the shed skin of some great snake wrapped around his neck like a scarf.

He was not a tall man, and Jai Long was used to him standing with his spine rigidly straight, looking down an upraised chin as though everyone else stood beneath him.

Now he'd collapsed on the floor like a child, sobbing. He gripped his head in both hands, nails driven into his scalp. His reptilian Goldsign let out a long, crooning cry.

Jai Long let the door slide shut behind him, unaccountably disturbed. Somehow, he had pictured a man of Gokren's power and dignity standing over his son's body with arms folded, demanding recompense from those responsible. Maybe a single tear would roll down his face, or his commanding voice would catch for an instant, as a brief acknowledgement of human grief.

He had never expected Gokren to weep as though an enemy had torn out his own heart.

Jai Long had pushed his feelings aside in favor of action, but now his own grief stirred from where it had settled. Gokren had crumpled at the base of a long table, on which a pile of mismatched furs rested. One of those furs had been flipped back, revealing a pale face and a curtain of dark hair that spilled over the edge of the table.

Sandviper Kral had been the first one to welcome Jai Long when he and his sister had been exiled to the Wilds. He had been the only one to look Jai Long in the eyes instead of staring at the crimson bandages wrapping his face, the only one to visit Jai Chen and tell her stories of the outside world. He was the only one who tried to give two exiles a home.

And there he was, cold on a table.

Because of a spoiled Underlord's whim and the tricks of his pet Iron.

When the anger slipped its bonds and burned through him, hot and hungry, Jai Long's hand tightened on his spear-case until the scripted wood creaked and threatened to crack.

Gokren must have heard, because he turned toward Jai Long for the first time, eyes red and face soaked in tears. His voice scraped out wet and raw: "Tell me. Please."

Jai Long wasn't sure he'd ever heard the Sandviper chief make a request of anyone.

"It was the Arelius Underlord," Jai Long said. Gokren stared blankly at the floor, so that Jai Long wasn't sure if he'd heard. He continued the story anyway. "He approached us in disguise, slipping into the Ruins as a worker. Once inside, he freed himself and his followers, leading them to the prize. He beat us to it by minutes, and we would have surrendered the prize to him if he had only told us his name.

"While I fought his disciple, he distracted Kral so that an Iron *child* could stab him in the back with some kind of hidden weapon. We believe it was developed by the Fisher Soulsmiths, but an Underlord could have any number of tricks."

Jai Long watched Gokren for any reaction, keeping his perception open in case the Truegold prepared an attack out of rage. But Gokren only sat there, watching the ground.

"I would have killed him if the Underlord hadn't revealed himself," Jai Long said. It sounded like an excuse, but it was only the truth. "But he has no affection for the Iron. He allowed me to take a prize from the Ruins, and he gave me a year. At the end of that time, I will meet his Iron in a duel, and he will not interfere."

"...where are they now?" Gokren asked.

"The Fishers are keeping their borders tight, but they should have left days ago," Jai Long said. His information was sadly lacking, but he was confident in his conclusion. The Arelius Underlord had no reason to linger in the Desolate Wilds an hour longer than he had to.

"An Iron," Gokren mumbled. He pressed one hand against his eyes. "My son...an *Iron*. They left him no pride when they killed him."

For his sister, Jai Long had played up Kral's death in battle to make it seem as though he had met a respectable end.
That wouldn't work for Gokren, so Jai Long stayed quiet.

Gokren took a moment to master himself, then rose. He
cast one last glance at Kral's body, brushing hair away from
the pale forehead.

"I know you will avenge him," Gokren said quietly. Jai
Long had come in here expecting a battle, but there was no
fight in this man. At least not directed at *him*. "In a year, you
will take back his honor, and I must only endure."

Gokren straightened, and a shadow of the Sandviper
chief's poise returned. "But I know you will not spend this
time idly. What is your plan?"

Jai Long hadn't been sure how to approach this topic. He
had feared that Gokren might learn about the Ancestor's
Spear from one of the Sandvipers and decide to take it away.
He wasn't worried about that possibility anymore.

Placing the long wooden case on the floor, Jai Long
flipped it open and revealed the shining white weapon.

Gokren clenched and unclenched his fists, watching the
spear. Minutes rolled by as he stared, the acid-green Sandviper on his arm hissing every now and then.

"You're going back to your clan?"

Jai Long said nothing, which was answer enough.

"Will Jai Daishou stop you?"

The Underlord Patriarch of the Jai clan was a legend; with
his own hands, he had built the Jai from a remote clan in
the wilderness to an Imperial power. If he acted, Jai Long's
dreams of revenge would melt like snow in the summer sun.

"To him, propriety is the highest virtue," Jai Long said, bitterness in the words. If the Patriarch had been the slightest bit
flexible, Jai Long and his sister would still belong to the head
family. "Every step must be taken in its proper order, and he
will defend that order to the death. He will not act until his
Highgolds, Truegolds, elites, and Elders have all fallen."

Green light dripped from Gokren's body, half-Forged

madra from the Path of the Sandviper, but he didn't seem to notice. "They will feed themselves to you, one by one."

"And by the time Jai Daishou reveals himself, I will be more than his match." The Underlord had once groomed Jai Long to be his replacement, after all. The Ancestor's Spear would allow him to close the gap on his own.

But Chief Gokren shook his head. "The gulf between Gold and Lord is wider than you imagine. It requires a certain insight that I've never gained." He flexed his hand into a claw. "If it was only a matter of power, I would have broken through long ago. But you may not need to face him. Rumor says he is dying; is this true?"

Reflexively, Jai Long remained quiet. Those were clan matters, and not to be spoken of before outsiders.

That thought was replaced by disgust in an instant. Years away from the main Jai clan, and Jai Long was still keeping their secrets. *How deep their poison sinks.*

"Unless they've discovered a miracle cure, he won't live five more years."

"You only have to avoid him for one. By the time you kill the Iron, you'll have gutted the Jai clan. Then you retreat west, back here, and we'll hide you until the Underlord dies."

Jai Long searched for words, but none came. At best, he had expected the Sandviper chief to berate him for leaving. He'd even come prepared for a fight.

He'd never dared to hope that Gokren would break a long-standing alliance for him. He was tempted to tell the grieving father to reconsider, that he was risking the future of his sect for personal vengeance.

But the truth was, Jai Long needed every ally he could get.

The Sandviper crossed the room and grabbed Jai Long by both shoulders. His grip was painfully tight, his eyes fevered. Jai Long had to suppress the instinct that told him to break the hold and escape.

"You were a brother to my son," Gokren said. "Your enemies are mine."

Jai Long's eyes welled up, but he pressed fists together

and bowed.

Gokren squeezed his arms one more time and then released. "Unless they've fled already, some of those enemies are right here in camp. Let's see if you can't test out that new spear."

He threw the stable doors wide open, and the Sandvipers at the entrance straightened in respect. These were the veterans of their sect, the oldest and most loyal warriors. Kral's death would stain them all. They simmered with suppressed anger, eager for a chance to vent their pain and shame.

"We march with Jai Long against his clan," Gokren announced, tearing one of his short spears free. "Sandvipers! *We hunt.*"

Jai Long was prepared for hateful looks cast his way, for words of hesitation and blame, for the Sandvipers to turn their anger on him.

Once again, he saw how deeply he had misunderstood his allies.

They roared in agreement with their leader's words, their sandviper Goldsigns shrieking to the heavens. They clapped him on the back as they passed him, whispered words of encouragement, or pressed their foreheads against his for an instant before rushing off to battle. Not an instant of hesitation, not a word of blame.

With a new family at his side, Jai Long marched to destroy his old one.

Lindon had to spend one more night in the woods, scripting their camp against Remnants and dreadbeasts and curling up in a crude tent only yards away from Fisher Gesha's. After the day's attack, he had woken with every cracking twig and gust of wind, groping for his launcher construct.

But dawn broke without event, so he and Gesha returned to the Five Factions Alliance camp with the rising sun. He read as they walked, committing simple scripts to memory.

"Put that away and listen to me," Gesha ordered as they approached the camp walls. "You are no longer a Copper with one friend and no enemies. You should learn to conduct yourself as a member of a great family, hm?"

Lindon opened his pack and slid *Soulsmithing for Coppers* inside, resting it beside the Sylvan Riverseed's glass case. "I await your instruction."

Her mouth tightened and guilt flashed across her face. "I did not teach you well before Eithan Arelius took you in." He started to disagree—a polite fiction, because she really *had* been a terrible teacher before the past few days—but she cut him off. "It's true, and I'm not afraid of the truth. You were never my disciple before the Underlord picked you up, no matter what I told you. But I could never treat a member of the Arelius family so disrespectfully as to ignore them."

"Gratitude. Your instruction is appreciated, but I have no voice in the Arelius family. Nothing you say to me will reflect on them."

That wasn't entirely true, and they both knew it; before he was attached to Eithan Arelius, Gesha could have cut his head off in broad daylight and the passersby would have simply stepped around his bleeding trunk. Now, she'd have to answer to an Underlord.

But Eithan didn't have time to listen to Lindon's petty complaints. Lindon wasn't some spoiled noble's son with a doting father; in fact, he wouldn't be surprised if the Underlord cast him out of the family on a whim.

Gesha sighed. "This is a lesson for you, as you travel into the wider world. Reputation is a sacred artist's greatest treasure. If the Underlord hears that I have disrespected *you*, he will take that to mean that I do not respect *him*. You see? The powerful have no mercy for those who step on their reputations."

Their conversation stopped as they passed through the entrance of the guarded wooden wall and into the Alliance camp, walking down hard-packed dirt roads past buildings that had been hurriedly tossed together from raw lumber and bare stone.

They had a few moments before they were alone again, so Lindon had some time to think. Gesha was trying not to say it out loud, but Eithan frightened her. She was terrified that something Lindon said might lead to her execution.

Lindon knew that Fisher Gesha was a Highgold who could twist him into a knot without ever touching him, but she was still a four-foot-tall old woman who could have been his grandmother. His heart softened when he saw her careful and afraid. "I won't carry news back to him, I swear it," Lindon said. "He won't hear anything from me."

She gave him a grateful look, clearly relieved that she hadn't had to spell it out. Then she gave a brief chuckle. "He's an Arelius," she said dryly. "If the rumors are true, then he'll hear about it regardless."

Lindon laughed along, but she seemed half-serious.

That made him consider her fears again. If Eithan was really that dangerous, maybe he should reconsider accepting his invitation.

Then again, this could be the one area where he had more experience than Fisher Gesha.

Eithan may be an Underlord, with a level of power Lindon could scarcely imagine, but he'd seen Suriel with his own eyes. He wasn't sure how far she ranked above an Underlord, but he was certain Eithan couldn't hold a candle to her.

"He hasn't descended from the heavens," Lindon said, smiling slightly. "He can't see everything."

"Not *everything*," Eithan said.

Lindon stumbled back, bumping into a wooden wall at the side of the street. More gracefully, Fisher Gesha hopped down from her spider-construct and sunk to her knees, pressing her forehead against the ground.

All around them, sacred artists of all ages dropped to the dirt as well. At first, only a few had caught sight of Eithan, but more and more people noticed. In only a breath, the

sparse crowd of perhaps two dozen people had all fallen to
their knees with heads bowed. Only Lindon and Eithan remained standing.

This was the Fisher section of the Alliance encampment, so
most of the people were Fishers or their allies, but it was still
disturbing to see all these people recognize Eithan on sight.
Only a few days ago, Eithan had pushed through a bustling
crowd a hundred times this size without interruption.

For his part, Eithan stood in the center of the road as
though he'd waited there all along, though he certainly
hadn't been there a moment before. His yellow hair fell
past his shoulders, and his smile was broad and cheery. He
kept his eyes on Lindon and Gesha, as though the strangers
didn't exist. Today, he wore a teal outer robe embroidered
with golden fish leaping and playing among the waves.

"Your unworthy servant greets the Underlord," Gesha
said, and there was a murmur of agreement through the
crowd.

"Underlord," Lindon said, hurriedly sketching a bow of
his own. "Forgive me, I was...startled."

Eithan brushed that away with a gesture. "There will be
no forgiveness. To the blood pits with you!"

Gesha trembled on her knees, and Lindon laughed awkwardly.

The Underlord looked at them, gauging their reactions,
and eventually shrugged. "Not every joke is appreciated in
its time. Tell me, Soulsmith Gesha, would you mind if I bor-
rowed my little brother here? Feel free to say no, although
of course I will have your corpse mounted on a flagpole for
the slightest defiance."

"The will of the Underlord be done," Gesha said from
the ground, her face still in the dirt. Her shaking had grown
more noticeable.

None of the strangers dared to make a single sound.

Lindon passed a hand over his face. With lowered voice,
he said, "Please, Underlord."

Eithan's eyes widened. "Am I to be condemned because

she takes things too...no, fine, all right." He knelt at Fisher Gesha's side and spoke in a much gentler voice. "I beg your pardon, Soulsmith. Please rise and address me face-to-face." He raised his voice. "All of you, on your feet and on your way."

With the speed of Gold sacred artists, the crowd vanished. It was as though the breeze had blown them all away.

Gesha rose, but she did not face him.

"On my word as an Underlord, you will not be punished for anything you say here or have said today," Eithan said impatiently. "Now follow my instructions, Highgold."

Finally she let out a breath and met his eyes. "Thank you for your mercy, honored Underlord. Tell me how I might serve you."

Eithan looked to Lindon. "You see how much faster it is when I just tell them what to do? It's infuriating. I don't want to phrase everything as a command for the rest of my life."

"It sounds hard on you, Underlord," Lindon said carefully.

"Yes, the endless subservience and instant obedience wear on me. But if you call me anything other than 'Eithan' again, I'll have you sleep in a cave full of bats." He stroked his chin for a moment, considering. "You could call me 'brother' instead, if you preferred. Yes, that would be—"

"Thank you, Eithan," Lindon cut in.

"Hmmm. Well, as I was saying: Fisher Gesha, I must borrow your pupil for an hour or six. I'll return him to you in one or more pieces."

"As you will, Underlord."

"And I had something to ask you as well." Eithan drew himself up and addressed the old Soulsmith with full authority. "You will not be punished for any decision you make here, on my word and the honor of my family. We depart for one of my homes in the Empire very soon, perhaps today. I would be honored to have you accompany Lindon as his Soulsmith tutor, but you are free to decline and stay with your sect. There will be no repercussions of any—"

"I decline," Gesha said instantly. She didn't even look at

Lindon. He hadn't expected any different, but it still stung.

Eithan clapped his hands. "A firm decision! Wonderful. Then, good-bye!"

He extended an arm to shepherd Lindon and turned as though to continue walking down the road, but Gesha had already scurried away. A wooden door slammed shut; Lindon wondered if she'd escaped into a random nearby building.

"For a woman her age, she really is spry. Good for her. Not everyone keeps up with their physical exercises as they get older, and a healthy spirit lives in a healthy body."

Lindon adjusted his pack, hitching it up on his shoulders. "I'd like a chance to bathe before I continue my training, if you don't mind. I've been in the forest for three days, and water is scarce."

Eithan turned to him with an expression of obvious disappointment. "Do you think you'll be able to defeat a Truegold in a year with such halfhearted resolve? How much valuable training time do you plan to waste on *baths?*"

Lindon bowed hurriedly. "Forgiveness, please, I spoke out of turn."

"No, I was pulling your strings again. But you really shouldn't waste soap on yourself yet, you filthy mud-caked animal. After a day of this training, you'll be covered in sweat. And probably some blood."

Eithan considered for another moment as they walked. "In fact, it would be best to expect the blood."

CHAPTER THREE

Eithan led him all the way across the territory of the Five Factions Alliance, the ramshackle encampment that had sprouted up after the Transcendent Ruins rose from the ground. The cobbled-together buildings of stone and lumber leaned up against the base of the Ruins like roots at the foot of a great tree.

Lindon hadn't been back inside since Eithan had rescued him from Jai Long's wrath. He fervently wished never to go back; fifteen days trapped in darkness was enough for a lifetime.

The pyramid dwarfed everything else for miles around, like a mountain made of stacked blocks. Its bottom tier took up more space than the rest of the encampment, and its top tier scraped the clouds. Now that the Soulsmith foundry at the top was open, the scripts powering the Ruin had settled into equilibrium. They no longer had to draw vital aura from miles around; instead, it relied on a steady trickle from its immediate surroundings.

In Lindon's Copper sight, each block of the pyramid looked like a softly yellow-glowing cube of golden lightning. That would be the earth aura in the stone itself; the same power that ran through the ground beneath his feet, just far more concentrated. Whenever he looked down into the earth, he had the dizzying sensation of staring into a yellow ocean filled with glowing, crackling bolts.

Aura empowered the entire world with strokes of color: the wind blew hazy green, the sun's rays were a gold richer than the earth, and the broad lake next to the pyramid shone with vivid blue-green ripples. Each person was a mass of color with vibrant green and bloody red predominating.

It was like staring into a world of fractured rainbows.

Lindon had to close off his senses before his head began to throb. Focusing on any aura gave him information about that aura's aspect, so opening his aura sight was like staring into the sun and reading a hundred books at the same time. A headache followed in seconds.

The thousands of sacred artists who had gathered to explore the benefits of the Ruins had started to drift away as soon as the pyramid stopped drawing in aura. Now, only three days later, half of these newly built buildings were abandoned. The dirt paths leading all over the Alliance encampment were all but empty, not choked with traffic as they had been only half a week before.

But news had already traveled fast. Everyone they spotted on the road bowed at the sight of Eithan, murmuring respect as he passed. Usually seconds before scurrying out of their way, lest the Underlord become displeased.

Eithan continued to ignore everyone, chatting with Lindon and occasionally stopping to sweep dust from a windowsill or snip a branch from a bush with the black iron scissors he seemed to carry everywhere. He never glanced at anyone else, whether they bowed or not, and many of the strangers looked relieved by that fact.

Lindon knew better.

Eithan didn't look at them because he didn't need to.

They finally arrived at the end of Fisher territory, amid a collection of wooden buildings that looked as though they had been built in a day and abandoned just as quickly. A bucket of nails rested on a half-finished fence, and a hand plane sat abandoned in the grass.

Eithan gestured to the biggest building, which smelled of fresh-cut wood and sat in a bed of sawdust and wood chips. "Behold," he said, "your new training hall! The crew started and finished it last night."

It was a barn. Fisher Gesha's foundry looked almost exactly the same, except this one was unpainted.

Why was Eithan having new buildings constructed? Weren't they leaving soon?

"I'm eager to see what's inside," Lindon said diplomatically.

"Are you? That's strange. I designed it to look as uninteresting as possible." Eithan swept up the plane and the bucket of nails, placing them next to a pile of other tools. "I'm sure Yerin's reaction was much more entertaining."

Lindon resisted the urge to apologize, instead approaching the barn.

There was an average-sized door on the side, obviously made for foot traffic, and broad doors in the middle designed for livestock. Although if it was built only a day ago as a training hall, why would there be animals here at all?

After a second's indecision, Lindon hitched up his pack and hauled with both hands on the livestock door.

Yerin sat inside, legs crossed, with a white-bladed sword across her knees. She was roughly Lindon's age, about sixteen, but while Lindon had been raised among the comforts of civilization, Yerin looked like she'd grown up in a never-ending knife fight.

Blades had left their tracks in the pale scars on her face and hands, in the tattered edges of her coal-black sacred artist's robe. She cut her hair with her sword madra, so it ended in absolutely straight lines across her eyes and above her shoulders.

The rope tied around her waist was the red of spilled blood, but Lindon couldn't bear to look directly at it. There was something *alive* about that belt, as though it could slither away at any moment.

Her Goldsign grew from behind her shoulder, a silver arm ending in a blade like a scorpion's stinger. Even seated on the floor in a cycling position, she looked deadly, as though she were poised to dive back into a battle.

She nodded a greeting to Lindon, but addressed Eithan. "Daylight's wasting. Am I going back to cycling, or are we going to start hitting these guys?"

She jerked a thumb behind her, and Lindon took a glance over her shoulder. Except for the beams supporting the roof, the barn was wide open from wall to wall. And filling that space was a circle of eighteen wooden dummies.

They were only crude outlines of men: rough shapes of a head and torso, with boards sticking out like arms. They had no legs, only a single pole driven through the floorboards beneath them.

But what drew Lindon's attention, and made him walk forward for a closer look, were the runes carved into those boards. The dummies had been arranged all around a script-circle the size of the barn, and it was one of the most intricate circles he'd ever seen. There were two lines of script circling the dummies, one on the inside and one on the outside, and the runes were packed small and tight; each symbol was only the size of his thumb. He picked out a rune he recognized here and there, but a circle like this was far beyond him.

A second circle, much smaller, overlapped at the far end of the barn. It was only big enough for a single person to stand inside, and a wooden podium rested in the center. Lindon guessed that those were the controls.

Eithan put his hands on his hips and looked over the eighteen dummies with the smile of a proud father. "Six Soulsmiths worked alongside the carpenters all night for this, and I have to say, I think they did a wonderful job."

Lindon could tell that the runes had been carved quickly, but he was still having trouble accepting that this had been done in *one night*.

"This is a traditional training method from my homeland," Eithan said, walking over to stand by one of the dummies. "I've seen similar setups elsewhere, but I'm partial to this design. Yerin, did your master ever take you through one of these?"

"Master wouldn't let me draw my sword on a wooden man," Yerin said with a shrug. "If it didn't bleed, it wasn't good enough training."

"I suspect that, in a few years, you'll have drawn enough blood to satisfy even your master. No need to start too early."

Yerin looked pleased by the compliment, but Lindon was wondering what exactly the Underlord had planned for them over the next few years.

Eithan moved on. "These dummies are more than wood, you see. They are moved by small constructs inside, and are used to practice basic steps in combat."

Yerin's face fell, her disappointment clear. Lindon perked up.

She might not need such simple instruction, but Lindon was looking forward to his turn in the circle of wooden men. He was lacking in many areas, and hand-to-hand combat was one of them. As an Unsouled, he had been encouraged to practice the simple exercises of the Wei clan, but never trained for a real fight.

Eithan strode over to the podium at the center of the control circle, pointing a finger at Yerin while moving his other hand over the podium. "I know how you feel, but be patient. I'm making a point."

The air between Eithan's hand and the podium rippled. The smaller circle around Eithan lit up white, then the light flowed into the bigger circle. Soon, the entire barn was lit with pale runelight.

Suddenly, one of the wooden dummies spun on its axis. A previously invisible circle of runes lit up on its left arm—green—then in its lower torso—blue—then on its face—white. The lights faded away in seconds.

"Hit the circles as they light up. Simple, isn't it? If you do it correctly, and your strikes carry enough madra, the circles will stay lit instead of dying out. When all three circles on all the dummies remain active at the same time, you have won."

Air rippled between his hand and the controls again, and a deafening chime sounded from all the dummies at once. They each spun in place, and the three circles on their bodies continued to shine instead of dying out.

Eithan stepped away from the controls, though the circles in the floorboards remained lit.

The dummies stayed bright for a handful of seconds, their three rings shining, before finally going dark.

"Yerin, if you wouldn't mind demonstrating for Lindon how the system works, I'd like to see you defeat the dummies. As quickly as possible, please."

Yerin stepped between two of the mannequins, tucking her sword-arm closer to her shoulder so it didn't catch on a wooden head. "I just have to hit them when they light up?"

"In the correct timing. If you miss one, the target will go dark again, and you'll have to start over."

She nodded, approaching a dummy. "How do I start?"

When she stepped closer, a green circle of runes lit on the wooden plank it used as an arm. Before Lindon had fully registered the light, Yerin had already struck it dead-center. The arm swiveled back from the force...

...and the other arm came to life, swinging at the back of her head.

She caught the blow with her left hand, striking at the dummy's torso with her right in the instant the blue circle appeared. The wooden man bowed in the middle to deliver a headbutt, but she sidestepped as though she could see it coming, her sword-arm whipping forward to strike the white circle.

Before the chime sounded, signaling that she'd beaten the first dummy, she was already stepping up to the second.

If Lindon hadn't attained the Iron body, he wouldn't be able to catch her movements. The three strikes would have looked like one motion. He'd seen his clansmen punch through walls and dodge arrows, but he'd never seen anyone move so quickly, so easily.

Not up close, anyway. He'd watched Yerin fight before, but when she was in an actual battle, her movement seemed...rougher. More natural, somehow. This was smooth and practiced, like she was executing a routine for the hundredth time.

"This is her *first try?*" Lindon asked, as Yerin stopped a separate strike with each hand while delivering a kick that lit up a green circle. She'd taken down three dummies already.

"This much is expected," Eithan said, examining his fingernails. "Jai Long could clear this course with his eyes closed."

Lindon slipped his hand into the pocket where Suriel's marble rested—a transparent orb about the size of his thumbnail with a single blue candleflame burning within. Its warmth comforted him, reassured him.

Eithan flashed him a smile. "Don't worry," he said. "The heavens are on your side."

Lindon started. Did Eithan know about Suriel? Lindon wasn't particularly afraid of the story getting out, since no one would believe it anyway, but how had Eithan found out? Had Yerin told him?

Could the Underlord *read minds?*

"...because the heavens sent you to me," Eithan went on. "That's nothing if not a miracle."

Slowly, Lindon let out a breath.

The eighteenth chime sounded, and all the dummies glowed softly. Yerin slid backwards and came to a stop in the center, her breathing a little ragged.

"Fifteen seconds," Eithan announced. "Not bad for your first time. The dummies are set to delay you more than injure you, but after a week or two, you'll go through this like wind through a forest."

"What's the fastest I can get?" Yerin asked.

"Twelve seconds is the minimum the script can handle. When you reach that, I'll have a better one built."

Yerin crossed her arms. "How fast is *yours?*"

"An excellent question. As I said, I grew up on a course very similar to this one, but recently I had the Arelius Soulsmiths build me a course set for two seconds."

She waved a hand at the surrounding dummies. "You could clear this in two seconds, if the script let you?"

Lindon's eyes widened as he tried to picture that, but Yerin looked skeptical.

Eithan laughed. "Couldn't your master do as much?"

"*You* are not my master," she said with confidence.

He'd already moved over to the controls, and the colored circles on the dummies died down as the circle reset. "I am not, and I'm sorry I never got the chance to meet him. There aren't many who know him in the Blackflame Empire, but he has quite the reputation in the outside world."

The outside world. Lindon hadn't even seen the Empire yet, and he was already impatient to reach beyond it. The world Suriel had shown him was impossibly vast, and Eithan had seen more of it than anyone else Lindon had met. That alone was enough to make him thankful he'd joined the Arelius family.

The Underlord gestured to the circle. "Lindon. Pretend that I have given you this task to prove yourself as a new member of my family. Act as though these are not training dummies, but enemies, and I have tasked you with our defense."

Lindon looked past Eithan's smile. There was something hidden in those words, though he wasn't sure what. Nonetheless, he shifted the way he thought about the training circle.

If this were a real life-or-death scenario, he'd need more information.

He walked around the edge, glancing at the dummies. As he'd expected, the target circles weren't invisible; they were simply sketched lightly in the surface of the wood and difficult to make out at a distance. The dummy was ringed with other such scripts, carrying instructions and power from the circle on the floor. He'd have liked to look at the constructs within—even if he couldn't understand how such advanced devices worked, he at least might learn something.

Finally, his steps carried him next to Eithan. "Let me clarify, if you don't mind. As long as I light up the circles on a dummy, I have defeated the enemy?"

"Just so."

Lindon nodded. Then he reached a hand out over the controls and sent madra flowing into a command circle.

There were nine circles engraved on the wooden podium, and it took him a moment to find the one he wanted. The first made some dummies spin around, the second darkened the circle, the third had no reaction he could see, but the fourth worked. Eighteen chimes sounded at once, and all the targets on all the dummies lit up.

"Victory," Lindon said, "for the Arelius family."

He bowed so that Eithan wouldn't hear any disrespect in his words, but Eithan only nodded. "Five seconds. He seems to have beaten you by ten, Yerin."

Yerin's ears reddened noticeably, but her tone was dry. "Well, cheers and celebration for him. Let's have him try it the right way, see if he lasts more than a breath."

Lindon kept the proud smile off his face—this was no time for gloating. "No, that's not necessary, I know I could never keep up with you. And it seems like all the enemies are dead."

A smile did touch his face then, as he glanced at Eithan for signs of approval. Eithan's gaze had gone distant, and he stared into the wall of the barn for a moment before waking with a start.

"Ah, I'm sorry. It seems company is on its way, so we'll have to work faster than I'd planned. Why don't you do as Yerin suggests, Lindon?"

Lindon's smile withered as though it had never been.

Moving hesitantly, his mind working for an escape, Lindon slid his pack to the ground and stepped into the ring. He calmed himself with reason—there was nothing to be nervous about. Of course he wouldn't be able to match Yerin's time, but no one expected him to. She was Lowgold, and he was only Iron. They wanted to see him perform a training exercise, that was all.

A few moments ago he had been excited to give it a try; with a little effort, he called some of that feeling back.

The wide circle of runes on the ground glowed white, giving the dummies a somewhat ghostly cast. He stood in the center of the circle, taking a deep breath. He cycled his madra faster in preparation for battle, running his madra to his limbs, readying the Empty Palm technique.

"Begin," Eithan called, and Lindon stepped forward.

A green circle lit up on the inside of its wooden arm, and he struck it immediately with a low-powered version of the Empty Palm. The full use of the technique would exhaust him quickly, but this was enough to inject madra into a script. The target brightened as he hit it.

Then a second wooden arm smacked him on the back of the head, sending him facedown into the fresh planks.

This is the second time I've been hit in the head today, he thought as he struggled back up to his feet.

Eithan was still grinning, and Yerin wore her own satisfied smile. "Good news!" Eithan said. "You've beaten my time."

Lindon bowed to cover his flushed face. "Your pardon; I have forced you to watch an embarrassing sight."

Eithan leaned his elbows on the control podium. "I said I had a point to make. Yerin, which was the best way to clear the course?"

She gave Lindon a sidelong glance. "I'd still contend that facing it head-on is the best way."

"Why so?" Eithan asked. "Activating the controls accomplished the same result."

"Real enemies don't have control scripts, do they?" She glared at the wooden dummies as though she longed to behead them. "Can't lean for too long on a cheat. The top way, the solid way, is to make yourself strong enough to cut through anything."

She spoke with such ringing confidence that Lindon found himself swaying. That was the path that had led her to powers beyond anything his clansmen had ever dreamed of.

He couldn't pick out anything she said that he disagreed with, but somehow he felt like she was leaving something out.

Lindon inclined his head to her. "You two are the experts, so please correct me if I speak out of turn. But in my humble experience, you cannot wait until you are stronger than your opponent to fight. Sometimes the game is rigged against you, and your only option is to flip the board."

Yerin gave him a blank stare. "You're my prime example. You saw you couldn't make it six feet in this world without a Goldsign, but your clan wouldn't let you train. What did you do? You *walked right off.* You've been fighting against stronger opponents since the day I met you, rigged game or no."

Lindon searched for a response, but none came.

That was exactly what he'd done.

Suriel had shown him that he wouldn't make it anywhere without a certain level of strength, so he'd struck off on his own. He should be the first one in line to agree with Yerin.

But he couldn't. Something about her words gnawed at him.

Eithan hopped over, hooked one arm around Lindon's neck, and dragged him over to Yerin. He threw his other arm over her as well. She looked as uncomfortable as Lindon felt, but Eithan beamed down at them both like a proud father.

"You both have a piece of it, don't you? Yerin, you have to watch yourself so that you don't fall into a rut in your thinking. But Lindon...so do you." He ruffled Lindon's hair, which was uncomfortable and strangely claustrophobic. "In our big, broad world, there's a certain difference in strength that no number of tricks will circumvent. For instance..."

He grinned more broadly. "...at your current stage, the two of you couldn't give me so much as a headache even if you stabbed me in my sleep. Though I know you adore and idolize me, so let's give a more reasonable example: if you want to survive Jai Long in a year, you must learn sacred arts the right way. Even with the full support of the Arelius family, and Jai Long on the run from his clan, you'll at least need to reach Lowgold in a *solid* and *proper* manner so you don't collapse into a pile of jelly when he glances in your general direction."

Lowgold. It was the sweet fruit that dangled out of Lindon's reach.

But he hadn't even reached Jade yet. Once he'd longed for Jade, and now he saw it as nothing more than a moat to be crossed. One of many. Even once he reached Lowgold, he'd still have a long journey to match Jai Long.

"Thank you for the instruction," Lindon said. "I never intended to suggest that I wouldn't work hard. I'll train harder than Jai Long, harder than *anybody*."

"I forget how young you are," Eithan said fondly.

Abruptly he released them, taking a step back and turning to face the door. "We'll resume this discussion soon, because our guest has finally arrived!"

Yerin frowned and put a hand on her sword.

"If you recall," Eithan went on, "you have yet to meet my family."

Lindon *had* wondered where the rest of the Arelius family was. Scouts from the Sandvipers and Fishers had spotted Arelius banners approaching weeks ago, and Lindon had expected to meet them by now.

Eithan extended hands to the doorway as though presenting a prize. "It is an honor and a pleasure to introduce... my brother."

The barn door swung open.

The man standing in the doorway looked perhaps ten years younger than Eithan, putting him just past twenty. His hair was the gold of fresh wheat, which must have been an Arelius family trait, but his was tightly curled. He held himself with grace and poise, standing proudly with one hand on the hilt of the slender sword at his hip. A silver bracer covered his right forearm from his wrist almost to his elbow.

He did not wear the traditional layered robes of a sacred artist, but otherwise it looked like he had the same taste in clothes as Eithan: his shirt and pants were deep blue silk, stitched with intricate silver thread, and looked as though they'd been tailored for him only the night before.

He made eye contact with Yerin, then Lindon, nodding to them both.

Before he could speak, Eithan cried out, "Cassias! Brother! It's been too long!"

Cassias smoothly sidestepped without glancing at the Underlord, and Lindon wondered how often *anyone* managed to dodge Eithan.

"I'm not his brother," Cassias assured them, tilting his chin to say over his shoulder: "I am not your brother."

"Cousin Cassias it is, then!"

"Nor are we cousins, except in the loosest sense. Distant, *distant* relatives, we are."

Eithan didn't seem put off. "Well, we're *like* brothers, anyway. You should have come to see me more than two days ago. Did you have to spend so long playing with the Jai clan at the border?"

Cassias straightened, pivoted on his heel, and addressed his...'brother.'

"You saw what happened at the border, I'm certain. And I have my own questions about what I saw from *you*. If I'm not mistaken, you provoked a Jai clan exile and killed the heir to one of their vassal sects."

"Not me," Eithan said proudly, turning to Lindon. "You'll note that young Lindon, here, was the one who brought down the Sandviper heir."

Lindon felt the attention in the room turn to him, and he almost flinched back. This felt uncomfortably like the Underlord was trying to shift the blame onto *him*. His earlier misgivings about the Arelius family returned in force, but he showed Cassias a smile and a shallow bow.

"I am Wei Shi Lindon, honored Cassias. Please excuse me for any inconvenience my actions may have caused you."

"Not at all, Lindon, not at all!" Cassias said immediately. "I am *more* than aware of what happens when my family's Patriarch gets too...enthusiastic. You were caught up in *his* plans, and it is I who should apologize on his behalf."

To Lindon's astonishment, Cassias bowed deeply. "Forgive *us*, and do not hold this against our family. On my name as an Arelius, I will send protection for you when you return to your home. You need fear no reprisals from the Jai clan or the Sandviper sect."

When you return to your home. Did Cassias not know he was coming back to the Blackflame Empire with them, or was he trying to give Lindon a graceful way out?

Either way, the greedy part of Lindon wondered at the nature of the 'protection' he had mentioned. If Cassias was willing to part with a weapon or a high-grade elixir, Lindon might be better off taking them and making his own way...

Yerin pulled at the ragged edges of her sleeve, shooting glances at Lindon every second or two as though checking his reaction, but Eithan laughed.

"You didn't watch us too closely, I see! Yerin and Lindon are coming with us. I have adopted them as outer members of the Arelius family."

Cassias straightened slowly from his bow, keeping a blank expression fixed on Eithan. "I...see," he said at last. "I apologize, Lindon, I was not...aware." He seemed to be struggling not to say something, his jaw tightening at the end of every sentence. "Did you inform the branch heads, Underlord? Did you receive their permission?"

"Time flows on, and plans must keep pace!"

"Plans," Cassias said, the word falling like a handful of mud.

"Which brings me to another subject," Eithan said, and suddenly his entire demeanor sharpened. Though nothing about him changed visibly, Lindon shuddered, the madra in his body shivering in its cycle. An Underlord stood before them now, not just Eithan. Yerin even took two steps back, gripping her sword—for comfort, Lindon hoped, and not because she thought she might have to use it.

Eithan continued, his voice still pleasant but carrying an underlying edge. "Your encounters with the Jai clan at the border. Explain what happened."

Cassias glanced from Lindon to Yerin. "I would be happy to inform you aboard *Sky's Mercy,* if you'd like to—"

"We're among family here," Eithan said softly. "Say it."

"Very well." Cassias relaxed, folding his arms and leaning up against the barn wall. He seemed more comfortable dealing with a businesslike Underlord than a friendly, playful one. Lindon could relate. "I was not only following you to bring you back. My father sent me with dire news shortly after you left."

"Then the Jai clan has seized our assets," Eithan finished, steepling his hands together.

Cassias' eyebrows lifted. "They have. In Serpent's Grave alone, we've lost the flame garden, three warehouses, the sword hall, and two of our medical contractors. Each time, they claim they're settling a private debt. They've sabotaged two major sanitation projects that I'm aware of, and eight full crews have vanished. We don't know if they were bribed away or...silenced."

Eithan spoke in the same lighthearted, half-joking tone as always, but the shivering sense of danger hadn't evaporated. "That's one city. What about the rest of Jai territory?"

"When I left, the worst of their actions were confined to Serpent's Grave. There have been a few unsanctioned duels between our people and the Jai clan, but nothing worse. Of course, that was a month gone."

"And the other clans?"

"The Naru have admonished the Jai clan for their actions, but the Emperor's support will arrive as soon as a winner is made clear, and not before. The Kotai clan has yet to make a statement, but as long as we keep their streets and sewers clear, they won't even notice."

With every word, Lindon felt less and less prepared for this conversation. He had no idea who the major players were in the Blackflame Empire, no sense for the different clans. Or even the function of the Arelius family; Eithan had introduced himself as a janitor, but Lindon couldn't tell whether that was a joke.

"Where did they stop following you?" Eithan asked.

"Two miles east, one mile north. They were forced to break off pursuit, which allowed me to slip through."

Eithan closed his eyes.

Slowly, his smile brightened before his eyes snapped back open. "That puts a wrinkle in their plan, doesn't it?"

"We have a brief window to leave, and I humbly suggest we take it."

Eithan raised fingers to his chin, staring at something in the far distance, thinking. "Soon. I have to adjust to this new information."

Yerin's arms were folded and her Goldsign quivering. Judging by the look on her face, she wasn't happy about being left out of the conversation either. Lindon didn't want to stress his welcome by asking too many questions, but he strained under the weight of his curiosity.

Finally, Cassias remembered they were there. "The Jai clan was trying to prevent me from returning with the Underlord. They weren't bold enough to openly destroy a cloudship flying the Arelius colors, but they've made my life difficult for the past few weeks. If the Jai warriors down below hadn't called for help, I would not have been able to land."

"Called for help?" Yerin asked. "What's got their feathers rustled?"

"I was too high up to see clearly, but it's strange. It seems they were attacked by one of their own."

CHAPTER FOUR

Sandviper techniques lit up the shadows with an acid-green glow as they tore through a wooden wall, their caustic madra melting straight through the rough lumber planks. Wood hissed as it dissolved, the sound almost loud enough to drown out the pleas for mercy that came from beyond.

When the wall fell to pieces, four Sandvipers walked into the one-room shack. A flash of white light, then green, a scream, and the fur-clad Sandvipers came out carrying a pair of struggling figures.

Both wore sky blue robes and had black hair that shone like metal in the moonlight. One captive had hair close-cropped so that it looked like a tight helmet, but the other's fell in a stream of dark, gleaming iron.

A young man and woman of the Jai clan, cowering for shelter and hoping the attack would pass them by. They might have been brother and sister, or young lovers, or two strangers who happened to duck into the same abandoned house.

Jai Long didn't care. His spiritual sense washed over them, confirming that Stellar Spear madra flowed through them both, sharp as an axe and white as snow at noon.

"Both," he said, and Gokren gestured to the Sandvipers. They snapped collars around the two Jai necks. When they realized the scripted metal cut off their access to madra, the man's eyes bulged, while the woman continued to beg through a mask of tears.

The Sandvipers dragged them away to join the others.

Jai Long had never used the Ancestor's Spear before. He knew only the legends—that the original Matriarch of the Jai clan had used the weapon to steal the power of her foes. As far as he knew, he might be helpless while siphoning madra, and it was safer to experiment on captives rather than opponents.

They had captured eight sacred artists of the Jai clan. Twice that number had escaped, and even more had been killed rather than let themselves be taken.

Half of the Jai clan shelters in the Five Factions Alliance had been reduced to rubble.

Only days ago, when the power of the Transcendent Ruins was at its height, Jai Long and the Sandvipers would never have been able to pull off a raid of this scale. They would have been overwhelmed by sheer numbers.

Since the Ruins had been picked clean, most of the Jai clan had drifted back to their homes. The Sandvipers had *all* stayed, waiting for the return of their Truegold chief.

The chief who now stood with Jai Long as his sect members streamed into homes like a swarm of ants, carrying out Jai stragglers.

Seven lights flared in Jai Long's senses, and his eyes snapped to the sky. Shadows flapped against the stars, carrying shapes against their backs, but Jai Long's spirit told him who they were.

Reinforcements. Somehow, the main branch of the Jai clan had sent backup against him *already.*

Jai Long let his breath out in frustration, but it came through his twisted teeth in a long hiss. *How?* The nearest stronghold of the main family was weeks away by air. But only the main branch had the authority to summon an elder.

Six of the figures were at the peak of Lowgold, but the seventh was a Truegold master. Before Jai Long could see him clearly, the elder swung his spear, and a white beam of light flashed like lightning.

Sandviper Gokren vanished from Jai Long's side in the same instant, and then he was standing next to the beam of light as another Sandviper stumbled away. The elder's technique scorched a line in the dirt instead of skewering the Sandviper through the chest.

As expected of a Truegold. Before Jai Long had even shouted a warning, Gokren had sensed the attack coming, determined the target, and pushed the man aside.

Jai Long hurriedly flipped open his spear case, removing the shining shaft of white light. He tossed the case aside, ready to defend himself. If the elder struck again, he might not be able to protect anyone else, but he could at least survive.

He had half-expected the Jai elder to gloat from up above and then rain techniques down on their heads, but instead the seven figures descended toward the street. As they got closer, Jai Long could make out their mounts: bats the size of horses, with wings like unfurled sails. The sacred beasts were dirty gray-white, but their eyes shone like tiny stars in the dark.

As the Jai landed, Gokren breathed deeply, cycling his madra so steadily that Jai Long could feel it, like a mighty river rushing next to him. The Sandviper chief ran a hand through gray hair, pushing it back even further, then gripped the short spear sticking over his shoulder.

"I'll move the Truegold back," he said quietly. "A pair of my hunters will move with me. You lead the rest, but I don't have anyone here who can stand face-to-face against that pack."

The six Jai clan warriors landed their bats only fifty yards down the road, fanning out to cover their mounts. The elder stood behind them, his spearhead rising higher than the silver helmet of his hair.

These were strangers to Jai Long, people he must have left behind years ago in his exile to this wilderness territory. The Lowgolds all had a few traits in common: black hair that gleamed like polished metal, blue outer robes marked with the star-and-spear emblem of the Jai clan, and tall spears that they held with confidence.

Though they were less advanced than Jai Long by one stage, they would never have been chosen as escorts unless they were competent. And while the Sandvipers specialized in hunting the beasts of the Desolate Wilds, the Jai clan was equipped for battle.

"I need them to harass only," Jai Long said, his voice as low as Gokren's. "Split them up, keep them from crashing on me all at once, and I'll handle them."

Gokren's fingers flickered in a signal, and Jai Long felt the Sandviper powers behind him spreading out.

"Sandviper chief," the elder drawled, ignoring Jai Long entirely. "You've interrupted our business tonight."

Chief Gokren jerked his head toward Jai Long. "Not me."

The elder pushed through his escorts, using the butt of his spear as a walking stick. Jai Long's opinion of the man fell lower. He was grinding his weapon into the dirt with every step—didn't he know what that would do to the wood?

"We'll expect a generous apology for this," the elder said. "Go back to your homes and wait for me there. I will have a word with the exile about his new weapon."

Jai Long swept out his perception, looking for another Stellar Spear presence. This group was too far from home to be alone—they would have brought supplies, and left at least one scout to report their fate if they were attacked.

To his shock, he felt only the dim presence of a few more bats roosting two streets down. Extra pack animals, but no sacred artists.

"Where is your scout?" Jai Long asked.

The elder sneered at Gokren; he still refused to look in Jai Long's direction. "We're in the territory of our branch family. Word of what happens here will reach the Underlord, and the chief knows that."

Gokren was a seething mass of power standing next to him, his Sandviper madra foul and bitter in Jai Long's senses. Despite their battle plan, Jai Long couldn't believe the Sandvipers would actually fight for him. The Jai clan were *his* enemies, not Gokren's.

But if they left him, he would be facing six trained fighters and a Truegold elder. His breath came faster, his madra cycling quicker as he looked for an exit. If he moved quickly enough, he could pull them into the Wilds. Away from Jai Chen, and into terrain where he might be able to fight them one at a time. So long as they didn't get back to their bats.

Gokren moved.

The Path of the Sandvipers had no techniques for speed. In a battle of Truegolds, Gokren would be among the slowest.

But he was still far faster than the Lowgold guards.

His short spear flickered out, launching a green ghost of itself that flew at the Jai clan like an arrow. His second spear was in his left hand, already shining green with another technique.

The elder moved like a ghost, breaking the Forged missile into sparks and knocking Gokren's spear aside before he could reach the average soldiers.

The Sandviper chief ended in a low stance, his spears spread to either side like wings. The Jai elder stood on the defensive: back straight, knees bent, weapon pointed straight as a ruler at Gokren's chest.

"Your life is over," the elder said, almost sadly.

"My life ended three days ago."

After another long moment, the Truegolds vanished. By unspoken agreement, they leaped over the buildings to the left, moving to where their battle wouldn't kill their subordinates. Leaving Jai Long and twenty Sandvipers facing six elite Jai sacred artists.

Jai Long ran forward like a wolf into a pen of sheep.

The fighters of the Jai clan did not flinch. They formed up into a wall, side by side but with enough distance between them that they could fight. One raised a hand-carved whistle to his lips and blew.

The seven bats rose with a screech, blacking out the stars. Their wings sent a gust of wind blowing across Jai Long's face, and with screams like glass shattering, they pounced on the Sandvipers.

Jai Long cursed himself. He had forgotten about the bats.

He cast them out of his mind, even though the battle sounds behind him were horrific. He had his own worries to deal with: he was charging into half a dozen enemies, and it was too late to stop. Even if he was charging alone.

Though he was still a good thirty feet away, the Lowgold bodyguards raised their spears and stabbed in his direction. Six spearheads blazed white as they executed the Jai clan's orthodox Striker technique: the Star Lance.

Lines of finger-thin light blasted toward him, each sharp enough to drill through his skull, but his weapon was already spinning

He spun his spear in both hands, executing a technique of his own: the Serpent's Shadow.

His spearhead trailed ribbons of white light as it spun, and those ribbons came to life, slithering through the air with a will of their own. The Forged snakes raised their heads and hissed, coiling themselves between him and the incoming techniques.

Such was the gift his Remnant had left him.

The Star Lances tore holes in his serpents, breaking off chunks of madra with every impact, but none of the techniques penetrated to Jai Long.

Jai Long didn't wait to see what his enemies would do next. He cycled his madra according to another technique: Flowing Starlight. This was an orthodox Stellar Spear technique, which his Remnant had left largely unaffected.

The Jai clan won their duels through superior speed.

The light-aspect madra circled through his channels faster and faster. Lines of white light slid out from his stomach, covering his skin in glowing, serpentine lines, marking the progress of Flowing Starlight. They looped around his shoulders, spilling up his arms and down his legs.

Power gathered in his limbs along with the lines, and when two knots of madra curled up and ended at his eyes, the world around him slowed.

This technique was a way to gradually prepare the body for handling intense speed. It reinforced and fueled him, finally sparking his senses so that they could keep up with his newly empowered limbs.

Six pairs of eyes narrowed as they realized what he was doing, six spirits revolving just like his, lines of white light spilling out of their robes and flowing onto their limbs as they engaged their own Enforcer techniques to catch up with him. The marks on their skin were a matrix of straight lines, not a nest of twisting serpents as on his, but there would be no functional difference in the technique.

Except that he was a Highgold. They were too slow.

He had been reluctant to test out his spear in battle, but now it seemed he had no choice. Whether he liked it or not, he was about to have his questions answered.

Jai Long closed the thirty-foot gap in a blink, coming in low next to the first enemy. The man had started his own Flowing Starlight technique, so he was fast enough to get the butt of his spear between him and Jai Long. But that was all he could do.

The white spear swerved around his, stabbing him in the lower abdomen. Into his core.

Most sacred artists Jai Long knew would have hesitated to fight someone a stage lower than they were, and even if they were forced into that undesirable position, they would avoid killing their opponent. It was shameful and embarrassing to lower yourself to that level, especially in public.

But Jai Long had no pride he didn't mind losing.

Jai Long's spiritual perception confirmed he'd struck the right target, and he withdrew his spearhead in an instant. The man's madra leaked out visibly, spilling starlight and blood in equal measure, but his spear *should* have stolen some of that power. Had it worked at all? He didn't feel any—

A rush of force slammed into his hand from the spear, flooding his madra channels with white light, and he stumbled in his steps.

This was only a fraction of the victim's full power, but it was enough to make Jai Long feel like his channels were about to burst. The next Lowgold thrust at him even as a second swept at his legs, and off-balance, there wasn't much Jai Long could do to stop them. A spearhead sliced his shoulder, and a shaft of solid wood hammered his shin.

He fell onto the grass, pain flaring, but he still gripped his weapon in one hand. Half a breath of hesitation meant death.

Jai Long flooded his madra into the Serpent's Shadow, sweeping his spear in an arc. He left a burning rainbow of white light between him and his opponents, which came to life as a snake thick as his arm. The living technique slithered to face his opponents, hissing.

The snake seized a spear in its jaws, shearing the weapon in half. The head tumbled away, wooden shaft smoking. A Jai woman brushed her arm against the body of the Serpent's Shadow, and she cried out, blood spraying from the cut—the light was sharper than the edge of a razor.

The other enemies ran to surround him, encircling him and preparing their attacks. They had caught up to him in speed by now, as skilled in the Flowing Starlight technique as he was.

Four spread out to cover him, his Serpent's Shadow fading even as it hissed and lunged and tried to protect him. He watched them through watery eyes, his breath uneven, spirit straining to contain the energy he'd swallowed. The glowing lines on his skin pulsed unsteadily, flickering between too much energy and too little.

Any moment now, the four enemies would coordinate, and he would die. He had to break their cooperation somehow, try to get one of them between him and the other three, to throw off their cooperation. He watched for the slightest opening even as madra thundered through him, burning his thoughts at the edges, distracting him with every breath.

Then the heavens intervened on his behalf.

A Sandviper stumbled away from the bats, blood streaming over her face, but there were four acid-green javelins Forging over her head. Before anyone reacted to her presence, she gestured to one of the Jai clan, and her technique blasted forward.

The Jai fighter saw it, bringing his shining spearhead around, but he was a beat too slow, his attention fixed too fully on Jai Long.

Four green lances pinned the young man to the ground.

Jai Long didn't waste the instant the Sandviper had bought him. He swept his spear in a whirlwind around himself, drawing twisting lines of Serpent's Shadow in the air until he was surrounded by a nest of seething white snakes. The effort of Forging such a huge defense would have usually drained his core, but now it just relieved some of the pressure.

Star Lances cracked on the outside, burning holes in his protection, but none were strong enough to completely break through.

He focused on controlling the storm of madra inside of him, funneling it into his spear, piling the energy into the pale spearhead until it glowed.

This was the second Enforcer technique in the Path of the Stellar Spear: the Star's Edge. It reinforced his weapon rather than his own body. Madra surged according to a rough pattern, fueling the deadly star at the end of his spear. By the time it was so bright he couldn't look directly at the weapon any longer, he could breathe again.

Now, his core was merely full.

Jai Long released his Forger technique, and the cage of white snakes dispersed into essence. Thousands of white pinpricks rose into the sky like a bucketful of glimmering dust falling the wrong way.

With his Flowing Starlight twisting around his skin and the Star's Edge on his spear, Jai Long glowed like the moon fallen to earth. Two of them were pulling bloody spears out of the Sandviper who had distracted them, and the other two were desperately trying to put some distance between them and Jai Long.

Finally in control of himself, Jai Long faced four off-balance enemies.

He finished them all in a second.

The first woman he stabbed in the chest, to see if he had to strike the core dead-on to absorb its powers. Another rush of madra filled him, though not as fully as the first kill had. The second man he sliced in the arm, and if he gained any madra from that, he didn't feel it. He finished him off with a stab straight through the skull. The third took a spearhead to the throat, and the fourth through the belly.

All before the first of the four bodies hit the ground.

Leaving him to deal with his own exploding soul.

White light stormed through his channels, tearing him apart as though he'd swallowed a razor-sharp flame. He tried to vent it from his skin where he could, white light spearing through him and leaving tiny, bleeding cuts with every ray.

It was like getting stabbed by a dozen nails at once, from the inside. He screamed.

Through a haze of pain and tears, he saw the Remnant rise.

Only one. The bodies he'd cut with the Ancestor's Spear remained still and quiet, but the single individual the Sandviper had killed vented its Remnant into the air.

Even through his mind-numbing agony, Jai Long glared at the spirit. His thoughts were strained, fogged, but he still recognized the classic Stellar Spear Remnant. The Remnant he was *supposed* to have bonded.

He could barely see it, half-blind as he was at the moment, but they always looked the same.

It looked like a constellation. Points of bright light formed joints, hands, eyes, and a heart, like stars floating in the air. Thin, faded lines connected those points until the spirit looked like a bent, hulking skeleton torn from the night sky.

The Remnant's roar sounded like the rush of a bonfire.

Jai Long staggered forward, leaving bleeding footprints in the grass behind him. More shards of madra cut through his skin, but he could no longer feel them.

Gokren yelled something to him, but he was beyond hearing.

With no technique, no art, he jammed the Ancestor's Spear into the lines of the Remnant's rib cage.

This power was nothing like what he'd stolen in battle. It flowed into him, still and obedient, a gentle rain instead of a vicious flood. His core drank it up greedily until it strained against its limits, pushing to expand and contain this feast.

Jai Long dropped to the ground, cycling desperately. If it weren't for his long hours of cycling every day, he didn't think he would have made it. His soul moved without his conscious will to guide it, looping in precise patterns as it had done millions of times before.

Every Path had cycling techniques for different purposes: cycling to absorb and process aura from the atmosphere, cycling to use a technique, cycling to restore lost madra, and cycling to refine and control the power you already had. It was that fourth pattern he used now, revolving his madra along with his breath. Faster and more urgently than he ever had before.

The stolen light burned him and tore at him, even as the power from the Remnant threatened to drown him.

He knew nothing but guiding that river, losing himself entirely in the rhythm of the madra spinning within him, processing as much of the power as he could.

He swallowed everything he was able, making it a part of him, stretching his core to its breaking point, but it was like trying to drink a lake one cup at a time. There was more here than he could have handled in a week, and it threatened to tear his soul apart.

He shouted again, thrusting his spearhead into the sky.

A Star Lance thicker than his head rushed out of him,

sending a beacon of white light into the clouds.

The extra madra in his veins dimmed slowly down. When his wounds finally stopped shining, the pain shrunk to manageable levels, and his breath grew too ragged to continue cycling, he let the technique and his weapon drop. He sagged, face-down, into the wet grass.

At some point, the sun had fallen to the horizon. Golden light died as twilight approached.

With a twitch of his head, he could see Gokren standing to his right, arms folded. The Truegold was bloody, missing one spear and leaning all his weight on his left leg, but he didn't look worried. He stood within arm's length of Jai Long, apparently unconcerned about the dangers of standing next to a Highgold blasting uncontrolled madra in every direction. The certainty of an expert.

Jai Long struggled on the ground, reaching for his spear. His madra was completely fresh and full, but his channels had been seared, and he felt as though one more technique would be one too many. But he'd learned years ago that he couldn't assume anyone else would protect him, not even Chief Gokren. If someone else decided to attack, he had to muster up a defense from somewhere.

Gokren clapped him on the back of the head, though the wrappings around Jai Long's hair cushioned the impact. "They're dead. Not the bats—my hunters wrangled them up. All seven of them, and only two of mine. Not bad for a night of work."

He spoke lightly, but there was a steely resolve when he said 'two of mine.' He may have been prepared to lose his followers, but he wasn't happy about it.

Before Jai Long could muster up the strength for a single word, Gokren pulled out his one remaining short spear and tapped the Ancestor's Spear lying on the grass.

"That would work for me, wouldn't it? If I could find some Sandvipers who weren't worth as much as their madra." He bent down, running a finger along the body of the weapon. "It's white, but it isn't Stellar Spear madra, is it...no, it's something else."

Jai Long struggled over to the spear, grabbing it with weak hands and cradling it to his chest. Gokren straightened up and folded his arms again. "Don't go shy on me now, boy. I could take that from you if you were at full strength, and you're not. You think I'm going to turn on you now, after I pulled arms on the Jai clan for you?"

Jai Long felt guilty for a moment, but he didn't loosen his grip on the spear. He'd seen people do worse things out of greed.

Gokren shook his head, but turned away and raised his weapon in one fist. "A *good hunt!*" he roared.

The other Sandvipers cheered. They had gathered without Jai Long noticing, staring at the white spear. It was unlimited power, in their eyes. They could gain weeks of power in minutes.

It was all there for the stealing.

They circled him in a wall of fur-clad bodies, crowding him. He hugged the spear tighter, but despite the fresh madra filling his core and eager to be used, he didn't think he could fight if the heavens descended and ordered him to. His body and spirit felt like twisted-out rags.

Gokren saw him and let out a heavy breath. With one motion, he seized the Ancestor's Spear and wrenched it away.

Jai Long sagged, weak and helpless. This was how it ended. He'd finally begun his revenge against the clan that had rejected him, and now...

Gokren picked up the case, slid the spear inside, buckled it closed, and tossed it to the ground in front of Jai Long.

"Get some sleep," the sect chief said. "We've got a long journey ahead."

CHAPTER FIVE

Lindon hit the rough board that served as the dummy's right arm, then its torso, then the head. The circle was unpowered, the target lifeless. If he fueled the training course, it would knock him over instantly, so he practiced on the dead version first. Once he got the routine down, he could try the real course.

The targets flickered with color when he struck them, as his madra passed through the correct spot. They would have stayed lit had the main circle been powered.

He stepped back, rubbing his knuckles. They didn't hurt, but they *would* have before his Iron body. It was a strange sensation, knowing that his hands should be scraped raw by the rough wood.

From further away, he examined the dummy again, as though watching it could help him somehow.

He just needed to be faster.

Each dummy had a different pattern of strikes and blocks, but he'd gone through all eighteen already, committing them to memory. His mind could keep up, and his body should be fast enough. But he still couldn't quite do it. Only an hour ago, he'd powered the circle again, and the dummy had still knocked him on his face.

The sun had long set, the barn lit by a single flickering candle that was starting to burn down. He could have used a scripted light, but it would have lasted for less time than a candle before needing to be powered again, and he wanted to conserve his madra.

It left the dummies bathed in shadow, lending them a sinister aspect. Only the brief flicker of a scripted light at each of his strikes dispelled the darkness.

Lindon moved forward, running through the three strikes again. He sped up this time, pushing his Iron body to the limit, and missed the third hit. The first two sent light rippling through their tiny runes, and the third remained dark.

He forced himself to slow down, breathe deep, and keep the power cycling steadily through his madra channels.

Cool air rushed in, and a door shut.

Yerin walked inside, only the silver blade over her shoulder and the red belt around her middle standing out against the shadows. "Training hard, or you have a grudge against wood people?"

Lindon hurriedly straightened himself, squaring his shoulders and smoothing his clothes. She'd seen him in worse states, but he didn't want to look like he'd exhausted himself against a bunch of wooden statues.

"Only working out a few things," he said, leaning closer to one of the dummies as though trying to figure out its script.

She eyed him for a moment and then walked inside the circle, plopping down onto the ground. She leaned up against a dummy's support pole and sighed. "I'm the last one to tell you to stop working. Heaven's truth, I just got done with three hours of meditation cycling and two hours of technique practice. But even my master would say you need an easy day every once in a while."

"I've stopped to cycle two or three times," he said, but then he wondered if that were true. "Maybe it was four times. Or...six?" How long had he been here?

He glanced at the candle, which was a half-melted lump

of wax in the middle of the circle. The woman who'd sold it to him had sworn it would burn all night. Perhaps it had.

A break couldn't hurt, so he sat beneath the dummy next to her.

Without a word, she passed him a rag. He nodded his thanks, then began wiping the sweat from his head and neck.

"Trick to an Iron body," Yerin said, "is to recognize when you're tired and when you're not. Gets harder to tell the difference. You'll pick it up after a while, but until you do, you're more than likely to run your feet down to the nubs."

Lindon's eyelids did feel heavy, his arms ached, and his hands were cramped...but those sensations faded almost as quickly as they came. Madra trickled steadily from his core, called by his Bloodforged Iron body to heal his fatigue.

"Is that so?" He looked at his hands, feeling the tight ache in his knuckles drain away with his madra. "Incredible. I really *can't* tell."

"That's how you run into more trouble than you can handle. If you ask me, you've got..." Something shivered through Lindon's spirit, and he recognized the touch of her spiritual sense. "...well, that's a puzzle and a half."

He'd seen Yerin walk into battle with a smile on her face. Now, after scanning him, she was frowning and mumbling to herself, staring at his stomach.

Though he had just toweled off, sweat broke out over his skin again.

Lindon dove into his own soul, almost in a cycling trance, clutching at his core with both hands. "What's wrong? What have I done? Did I cycle too much? Am I dying?"

"You're about a thousand miles from dying," she muttered. "As expected of an Underlord, I guess."

"Eithan? Did Eithan do something to me?"

"He handed you that Iron body, true?" Lindon didn't remember Eithan *handing* him anything, but he guessed it was true enough. "Unless I'm wide of the mark, it looks like it's keeping you fresh. You could work your body until your core's dry."

Lindon had felt the same thing already, but he had assumed it was a function of the Iron body. " my ignorance, but isn't that normal?"

"It's normal for the Undying Lizards of the Bluefire Desert. I hear it's normal for some plants." She jabbed him lightly in the stomach. "*People* get tired sometimes."

New possibilities bloomed in Lindon's imagination, and he had to resist the urge to start taking notes. "As long as I restore my madra, I could keep training? How often should I stop and cycle, do you think?"

"Whoa there, rein it in. If you could work all day and night, you'd be fighting *Eithan* in a year, not one little Jai Long. The spirit needs rest just like your body does. You don't want to strain your madra channels, I'll tell you that one for free."

She clasped her hands together and stretched them over her head. "You're an Iron, not a Remnant; you still need sleep. Food. Your spirit's a weapon, and you've got to keep it clean and polished. But you don't have to worry about pulling a muscle, or collapsing in a heap. I'd kill you for that, if I thought I could take it off your Remnant."

Lindon chuckled uneasily, wiping his face with the towel again. So he could work for longer than most people, but not *too* long. What was the limit? How could he tell? It was easy to know when he was running out of madra, but what did strained madra channels feel like? How much more time was his Iron body buying him, exactly?

Lost in thought, he almost handed the sweaty rag back, but he caught himself at the last minute and tucked it inside his outer robe. He could wash it in the lake in the morning.

Lindon dipped his head in thanks and spoke carefully. "Gratitude. You've given me a lot to think about. But if you'll allow me another question: what are my chances? With Jai Long? Do I have enough time?"

"You've got no time at all," Yerin said immediately. "Sleep or no sleep, if Eithan doesn't have something planned for you, then you're dry leaves to the fire."

The truth of that settled onto him, and Lindon couldn't think of anything to say.

Yerin scratched the side of her neck, and in the dim light, he thought he saw her flush. "I, uh...sorry. Didn't intend to say it like that." She hesitated for another moment. "When I was Iron, my master didn't press me to fight a Highgold in a year's time. That's a rotten gamble, no matter what training he gives you."

Yerin knew he couldn't do it. That he was going to die in a year.

He stared at the dummy across the circle because he didn't want to see the truth on her face.

"I'm not going to gamble," he said quietly. "There are other ways to get to him, before the duel. He eats, he sleeps, just like anybody else. He has enemies. He has a family."

Yerin's Goldsign arched, as though the blade were trying to get a better look at Lindon's face. "Dark plans for an Iron," she said, voice dry. "You want to hold his crippled little sister hostage, do you think? You want to go to his enemies for help instead of Eithan?"

"I don't know enough about him yet," Lindon said, embarrassed. "You know, there's always poison. Ambush."

"There's always poison," she repeated. "Yeah. You could poison his food, then wait until he falls asleep. Put a *different* poison on your knives, so even if he wakes up, he can't..."

She trailed off, blinking rapidly.

Her master. That was what the Jades of the Heaven's Glory School had done to her master.

Lindon fell to his knees, pressing his forehead against the cool wooden floor. "I did not think. I—"

He glanced up and saw that she was holding up a hand for silence. She waited for a few seconds, visibly swallowing a few times, before she spoke. "They were dogs and cowards," she said at last. "Don't think like them. You don't learn to stand against your enemies by crawling in the dirt."

"As you say. I have no excuse."

"You're on the path now, stable and true. In a year, you

won't recognize yourself."

He certainly couldn't disagree with her *now,* not to her face, but he filed his plans away carefully in the back of his mind. Surely Eithan wouldn't mind if he prepared for contingencies.

Lindon had just risen to his feet when the door slammed open, and Eithan marched in, carrying a lantern caging a burning star. It lit the barn like midday, making Lindon wince and shield his eyes.

Eithan saw them and paused, as though he'd just noticed them. "Oh, I'm sorry, I hope I'm not interrupting anything." Before they could respond, he added, "I was just being polite, I heard it all."

Lindon was going to find it hard to relax over the next year, if Eithan listened to every word he ever spoke.

The Underlord walked over to the melted candle and kicked it aside, sending a puff of smoke into the air and chunks of wax tumbling across the floor. He set his lantern in its place at the center of the course, then turned to face them with hands on hips.

"I will be truthful with the two of you: I'm facing a bit of a crisis here."

His demeanor was cheery as ever, but his smile *had* shrunk to nothing more than tightened lips. Maybe this was his serious face.

"We'll do whatever we can to help you, of course," Lindon said, knowing that he could never help an Underlord do anything.

"You made a mess out of something," Yerin said, her tone absolutely confident.

Eithan pointed to Lindon. "I will take you up on that offer, don't worry." Lindon's heart sank.

Now Eithan pointed to Yerin. "That's an uncharitable way to put it, but I can't say you're wrong. You know, I do wish I could tell the future. There are sacred artists out there who can, to varying degrees. It would make planning so much easier. And I don't expect you to understand this, but seeing everything makes surprises *so* much worse. You always feel as though you should have seen them coming."

He sighed, flipping his hair over his shoulder. "That's enough of my problems, so let's talk about *our* problems. The Jai clan has all but declared war on our family."

"All but?" Yerin repeated. "Is it war, or no war?"

"If they declared it openly, the Emperor's forces would cripple the aggressor in a day. But the Skysworn stay out of the petty squabbles between clans. As long as the Jai pretend that's what's happening, the Emperor will stay clear."

Lindon had seen similar situations back in Sacred Valley, as the Wei clashed along the border with the Li, and the Kazan raided them both. He saw the problem immediately.

"They'll claim Jai Long."

Eithan nodded to him. "He and his sister were exiled here so that they could serve the main family without being underfoot and embarrassing. Has to do with his wrapped-up face." Eithan waved a hand vaguely around his own head. "They still won't take him back, but once the duel is over, they can pretend he was one of them all along. He wins? They take credit. He dies? We killed a Jai Highgold, and they'll use it as an excuse for *open* war."

He sighed. "And I thought all I'd have to do was write a letter..."

There was an obvious solution here, but Lindon proposed it carefully. "Not to overstep my bounds, but the situation has changed. Couldn't you tell the Jai clan that you changed your mind?"

Eithan braced one foot on the star-filled lantern and leaned forward. "One's word is the currency of the powerful. Reputation and honor are all that prevent us from slaughtering each other, and keep us operating with some degree of civility. What stops an Underlord from killing everyone weaker? Their reputation. What shields their family from reprisals and attacks? Their reputation. Many experts value their good name more than their life."

A dark pall settled over Lindon. Eithan wouldn't change

his mind about the duel, then. That had been one of Lindon's final hopes.

"Besides, I still have a use for your victory," he said. "Jai Long's defeat will give me leverage, whether the clan claims him or not, so I would still prefer you fight. However, there is another option..." Lindon's dead hope flickered to life again. "...I can allow you to leave the family. Your actions would not reflect on my word if you weren't a subject of the Arelius."

Lindon turned to Yerin, who wore a troubled expression but said nothing. Would she come with him, if he left? She might, if he asked her, but would that be fair to her? He didn't know much about the Arelius family, but he knew they represented both a risk and an opportunity. Yerin could grow there, with the support of a well-connected clan.

For his part, anywhere outside of Sacred Valley was a land of limitless opportunity. The Fishers could advance him past Iron. He had other roads he could take.

But he'd be giving up the chance to be trained personally by an Underlord.

Eithan met his eyes, speaking earnestly. "I'll be as clear as I can: the Arelius family employs hundreds of thousands of people, and their livelihoods will be impacted by the results of this duel. If you stay, I will do whatever I have to so that you win. Even if it kills you."

Lindon leaned against a wooden dummy for support. "Killing me...to *win*. I see. How likely is that to happen, exactly?"

Eithan's smile broadened. "It's my last resort. I have every confidence that I can raise you to victory without destroying your future. I can't say you will enjoy the process, though. And I will catch you every time you try and run away."

Yerin still hadn't said anything since Eithan entered the room. She stood with one hand on her sword and one on the blood-red rope around her waist, as though considering her options.

"If you don't mind," Lindon said, "I'd like some time to

consider."

Eithan straightened, brushing wrinkles out of his turquoise robe. "Perfectly understandable, but I'm afraid we're running short of time as it is. We're leaving at dawn. If you would like to join us, look around the Fisher territory for a tall building with blue clouds surrounding the foundation and Arelius banners hanging from the walls. That is our vehicle out of here, so if it's still there, so are we."

He executed a small, shallow bow in Lindon's direction and then started to walk off. Over his shoulder, he called, "I don't like to make decisions for others, Lindon...but I hope to see you in the morning."

The door swung shut behind him, but it fell into Yerin's hand. She hitched up her red belt as though to distract herself.

She still looked troubled, even as she spoke. "In the sacred arts, you don't want the clear path. You want the rocky one. The strongest aren't the ones who climb the highest mountains, but the ones who choose to do it one-handed and blindfolded."

She hesitated as though to add something else before shaking her head. "But it's a short distance between 'rocky' and 'looking for suicide.' I don't know what you should do. I...I don't know."

Then she left too.

Lindon blinked sleep from bleary eyes, sitting up on the barn floor. The touch of sunlight streaming through the wooden slats warmed him, bright and cheery. He started to cycle his sluggish madra, prodding his body into waking and his mind into thought.

Last night, he'd stayed up after Eithan left, trying to clear his mind and make the right decision. He'd known what the *best* answer was: to stick with the Arelius family. But that didn't make the decision easier.

If he stayed, the Fishers could take him to Truegold.

Truegold. Would that really be his limit?

When he had walked among the Eight-Man Empire, Suriel had said that even ten thousand Gold sacred artists couldn't scratch their armor. How far above Truegold were they?

How far above them was Suriel?

He'd pulled Suriel's marble out of his pocket, and the sight of the steady blue candle-flame inside the glass orb had made up his mind. He'd activated the course, matching his newfound determination against the eighteen animated wooden dummies.

When he joined Eithan and the Arelius family at dawn, he wanted to do it after squeezing out every second of practice he could. Maybe he could produce a miracle, defeat the course, and join Eithan and Yerin with pride.

The dummies had knocked him flat, but he'd gotten up again and again. Eventually he'd stopped to cycle, but meditation had turned to sleep...

Sunlight streamed in through the walls.

He jumped to his feet, the unfamiliar power of his Iron body launching him two feet in the air before he landed.

He was late.

He'd missed them.

Lindon stormed through the door, hoping against hope that they'd decided to wait a few hours for him.

The instant he opened a crack, air blasted him in the face, shoving the door all the way open and slamming it against the frame. The wind was almost strong enough to push him off his feet, Iron body or no, and the light was blinding.

He had to throw up his arm against the all-present light, which surrounded him as though he'd been tossed into the sun.

When his eyes finally adjusted and the gusts slowed for a moment, he squinted into the brightness and saw...not the dusty yard outside the barn. Not the collection of ramshackle buildings making up the Five Factions Alliance.

An endless ocean of sunlit clouds, stretching out beneath him.

Lindon shouted and fell backwards, kicking the door shut, trying to catch his breath. The barn was in the *sky*. In the heavens, maybe? Had Suriel grabbed this whole building and lifted it from the earth?

He grabbed the warm glass marble from his pocket and rubbed it between his hands to comfort himself. As his breath and mind settled, he started to notice details he hadn't before: the floor dipped and sagged beneath him, like he was lying on a boat drifting over a lake. Wind whistled through and around the barn.

Lindon leaned on a wooden dummy to prop himself up, catching his breath and staring at the door as though it might open and drag him out into open air.

Wood creaked, and he turned to see the *back* door swinging open. Eithan stuck his head in, smiling.

"A good morning to you!" he said cheerily. "Come join us for breakfast."

Lindon took a deep breath before answering. "You didn't leave me." He closed his eyes and took another breath. "This one thanks you, honored Underlord."

"I kept an eye on you after I left. I could tell you'd made up your mind, so when you didn't make it on time, I decided to drag you along."

Following the Underlord, Lindon pushed open the back door of the flying barn. It swung open into bright lights and furious wind, but there was another door only a foot or two away. This door was painted dark blue, with a black crescent at eye level, and the frame was all white. The colors of the Arelius family.

Between him and the door was a stretch of dense blue cloud. To the left and right, he saw nothing but endless sky and white fluff. Beneath him, a soft blue carpet.

Lindon hesitated, but Eithan didn't. He was already striding across the cloud with full confidence, his steps pressing down as though he walked across a mattress.

It's a Thousand-Mile Cloud, Lindon reassured himself, *just...bigger.* Big enough to carry two buildings.

If he'd needed an illustration of the Arelius family's wealth and power, this would do.

Eithan held the door for him as Lindon fought the wind to enter.

He stepped into a cozy sitting room, all decorated in Arelius colors. Dark blue chairs and couches were arranged into a half-circle around a fireplace of black metal. A spiral staircase led up to a second story, and a pair of tall, arched windows spilled sunlight into the whole space.

Through an open doorway against the other wall, Lindon saw into a second room, this one surrounded entirely in glass that looked out over the clouds. Cassias stood in the glass room over a podium that looked like the control panel for the training course. As Lindon watched, he spread his hand and injected a pulse of madra speckled with silver. Circles lit up one after another on the polished board.

The house veered to the right, cutting through the clouds like a ship through waves.

Yerin had her legs crossed on one fluffy chair, her hands on her knees and breathing measured. When Lindon crossed the doorway, she cracked her eyes open and gave him a little smile.

"Sharp decision," she said.

"I fell asleep."

Eithan hopped over the polished wooden counter that separated the rest of the room from a wall of brightly colored bottles, then started fixing himself a drink. "This is *Sky's Mercy,* the personal cloudship of the family's Patriarch. It serves us as a mobile base when we need to take our business outside of the usual territory."

Cassias didn't turn from his controls, shouting over his shoulder to Lindon. "We stay as high as we can, for the sake of stealth. Sometimes we must fly lower, when there are dangers in the skies or the vital aura runs low. That's when we risk being spotted."

Lindon took a few more seconds to process the sea of gleaming clouds outside the windows. "The Cloud Hammer School spotted you, then?" They were the ones who had first spread the word of the Arelius family's coming.

"I passed through a group of their disciples cycling up here," Cassias responded. "I'm sure they intended no harm, but there's no such thing as a secret."

The floor rose and dipped slowly, as though the cloud breathed beneath them. At the bar, Eithan was pouring two bottles into a third. He didn't spill a drop.

Lindon turned to the Underlord, imagination wrestling with the possibilities of flying buildings. "You lifted the entire barn off the ground?" If the family could build this, he could only imagine what *other* treasures they were hiding.

"I dropped quite a few scales for the Fisher to build that training facility," Eithan said, flipping the bottles into the air and catching all three. "It would be a waste to just leave it behind. We had to expand the cloud base a bit, but it's well within acceptable limits."

"Not *well* within," Cassias responded, but Eithan pointed to the top of the staircase.

"And look who else came with us! Fisher Gesha, how are you feeling?"

A few hairs had come loose from the old woman's bun, her wrinkled face looked pale, and she rested heavily on the bannister, which was shaped like a serpentine dragon's head. She didn't look as though she had the strength to walk down the stairs, but she was standing on her drudge. The eight long spider legs dragged her down the stairs smoothly, as though she were gliding down.

"I apologize for showing you this sight, Underlord," she panted. When she saw Lindon staring, a drop of acid entered her voice, and she snapped, "Can't stand boats, can I? I stay *off* the water, thank you very much, and sailing on the clouds is just the same as sailing anywhere. Hm? You have something to say?"

Lindon leaned closer to her, more concerned about her

presence than her tone. "Fisher Gesha, did you...*choose* to come along?" He didn't want to say too much, because Cassias and Eithan could hear him perfectly well, but he could too-easily picture Eithan snatching up the Soulsmith on a whim.

She studied him for a moment, then reached up and patted his cheek. "I must look like a disaster, to have an Iron worry about me. No, the Underlord told me to think about it, didn't he? Well, I did. I've lived my life among the Fishers, and it's been a long life. It's about time I see the wider world, perhaps bring something back, hm? A little knowledge, perhaps."

One of the spider legs reached up to poke Lindon in the stomach. "And I can't leave a half-grown cub to stumble around in the wild on its own, can I? No, I can't."

Lindon's throat tightened, and he blinked rapidly. She had stayed with him. He bowed as deeply as he could without going to his knees. "Thank you, Fisher Gesha."

She stayed silent.

When he finally raised his head, she was gone.

One of the tall windows had swung open on its hinges, and Gesha dangled half-out with her head in the rushing wind. She retched, the spider legs stretched out as far as they would go to keep her tall enough to reach the window.

Eithan was sipping something from a shallow bowl. "It can take a few days to adjust, if you have a tender stomach," he said. "But we'll have plenty of time together. It will take a month to reach our destination, which we will put to good use."

Yerin woke from her cycling meditation again, cracking her eyes. "You finally bothering to teach us?"

Eithan hopped up to sit on the bar, taking another drink from his bowl. "The question is, are you ready for me to teach you?" He let that hang for a second as he took another sip, then added, "And the answer is no, you're not ready, so I'm going to spend this month trying to prepare you."

He nodded to Yerin. "First, I'd like you to take turns on

the training course. Yerin, you will try to beat your previous time..."

She rose from her seat, ready to try immediately.

"...using only your Goldsign."

The bladed metal arm hanging over her shoulder twitched. She turned to stare at him in disbelief. "I'd have a better chance of clearing it with my bright smile and winning personality."

Eithan turned to Lindon. "And Lindon—"

"Oy. Hey. Don't ignore me."

"I at least expect you to clear all eighteen dummies after a month. Don't worry about your time, for now. While you're working on that, you can bring your second core up to Iron, and brush up on your Soulsmithing. Fisher?"

Gesha leaned back inside, shutting the window with one hand and dabbing at her mouth with a cloth in the other. When she spoke, her voice had an extra rasp. "You should be able to identify all the properties of the seven basic aspects of Forged madra, as well as their combinations. I have the books with me."

Yerin slapped the flat edge of her bladed Goldsign against the wooden bar. "You want me to fight with this thing? Why don't I just tie a knife to the end of a string and use that?"

Eithan studied her over the rim of his bowl. "You think, perhaps, that I don't know what it takes to reach Highgold?"

"No, that's not..." Yerin's ears started turning red. "I'm the last one who would..."

"You think you know better than I do which exercises will allow you to integrate your Remnant's skills and abilities into your own? If your master left you a more complete training regimen for you to follow after Lowgold, then by all means use that."

Yerin's ears had turned bright red. "I didn't aim to say that, Underlord."

"Hmm." He smiled. "You're young, and I'm unaccustomed to explaining myself. I'll try to be clearer in the future, but do as I tell you."

She kept her eyes on the floor, tilted away from Lindon, but she nodded. "It's not so far apart from what my master used to have me do."

"The only difference," Eithan said, "is that you trusted him. Trust comes with time. And *during* that time, you will clear that course with your Goldsign or I'll tie you to a string and drag you behind the house like a kite."

She straightened and marched for the door.

Lindon started to follow her, but Eithan stopped him. "Before you do your morning cycling, take..." -he reached behind the bar with one hand, balancing his bowl in the other, and rummaged around in a drawer— "Aha! Take this." Eithan tossed Lindon a pill the size of his knuckle. It was smooth, with swirls of blue and white mingled together. "Behold, the Four Corners Rotation Pill."

Yerin stopped with her hand on the door.

"It's a pill to make your madra easier to cycle, and it should help you raise your second core to Iron fairly quickly."

Lindon itched to write the name of the pill down in his notes. He had to record every step of his advancement in *The Path of Twin Stars* manual. Which brought him a moment of panic, as he realized he didn't have his pack with him.

He let out a breath of relief as he spotted his pack—with the manual inside—leaning up against the wall. A polished wood-and-jade chest leaked wisps of red from the closed lid, so he assumed his Thousand-Mile Cloud was inside.

"Use the pill together with your parasite ring," Eithan said, pouring himself another drink. "The effects should complement one another, so that it feels like cycling normally, but you'll see twice the benefit. By the time we land, I hope to be able to take you straight to Jade."

Lindon cradled the pill in both hands as though it was his key into the heavens. It smelled like honey and rainy days, and the only thing stopping Lindon from popping it into his mouth was his desire not to waste a single second of its effect.

Yerin had already turned from the door to look at Eithan. "How far did that lighten your wallet, would you say?"

Eithan shrugged, but Cassias called back, "About five thousand scales, the way they measure them out here."

Fisher Gesha's eyes bulged.

"Well, that's a gem and a half," Yerin said. "You got one for me?"

Eithan waved that away. "It's just a fundamental training pill. Lindon will be taking one of these every day, but I have some more *interesting* supplements for you. Right now, your best advancement material is your master's Remnant."

Yerin grimaced, but accepted it. She would have preferred a pill of her own, Lindon knew, but at least Eithan's reasons were good ones.

Lindon could barely pry his eyes away from the Four Corners Rotation Pill. This was worth more than every year's end gift he'd ever gotten from his parents, and he was supposed to take one every *day*. Eithan was like an endless treasure box.

Cassias stepped away from his controls, walking out of the glass room and toward the Underlord. "I would urge you to remember what happened when you took over the training of our family Coppers."

"Oh, that's nothing to worry about."

Cassias turned to Lindon. "I personally rescued a girl who ran from his training into a place called the Thousand Beast Forest. She survived by hiding from two-headed bears. I found her crouched in a cave, dirty and bleeding, but she begged me to leave her rather than take her back to train."

Lindon moved his gaze from the pill to Eithan and back. "That does seem...harsh. Perhaps she may have been pushed a *little* too hard, don't you think?"

"Don't worry, I don't train my students like that anymore," Eithan said, holding up a bottle to the light. "I was far too lenient before. After weeks of my training, that girl should have been *fighting* those bears. With her fists."

Yerin shrugged and opened the door. The wind grabbed

the tattered edges of her outer robe, making them trail behind her like smoke. Her red rope-belt, tied in a broad bow
behind her, was untouched by the wind.

"If you don't feel like you're going to die when you're
training, then you're doing it wrong," she said, and stepped
outside.

Cassias nodded to her back as though acknowledging the
point, Eithan laughed, and Fisher Gesha gave an approving
grunt.

Lindon swallowed his own misgivings, pushing aside the
sinking feeling in his stomach. This was the attitude of the
strong. He had to focus on that, and not on what he imagined Eithan's training had done to the poor Copper girl.

Popping the blue-and-white pill in his mouth, he followed Yerin.

CHAPTER SIX

Jai Long entered his sister's cabin to find her struggling into a set of sacred artist's robes. She pushed her arm through one sleeve, trembling with effort, and cinched her robe with both hands as though the cloth belt was made of heavy chain.

She dipped her head when she saw him, though she had to grip her wardrobe to stand upright again.

He tried to sound cold, but instead his voice came out with a sigh. "What are you doing?"

"Going...with you." She spoke as firmly as she could, but she was looking at the ground, unable to meet his eyes.

Even before the accident, she'd always been shy. And stubborn at inconvenient times.

"I have four Sandvipers staying behind to take care of you," Jai Long said, gently taking her by the shoulder to lead her back to bed. "You'll have to stay with the Purelake School for a while, in case anyone from the clan comes looking for you."

She remained standing, and he was afraid to put too much pressure on her shoulder. Jai Chen glanced up at him like a guilty puppy.

"We don't...*have* to...go," she said, each breath drawn with difficulty.

He couldn't move her without her cooperation, so he folded his arms. "I've already jumped off the cliff. Six Lowgolds and an elder came to the camp looking for me last night, and none of them left."

She didn't need to know that they'd been looking for him *because* he'd been killing Jai clansmen in their homes. There were no civilians in the Five Factions Alliance; everyone who had come to the Transcendent Ruins had done so to try and pull profit from the jaws of danger. Those were sacred artists and warriors that he'd killed.

Though most of them hadn't died like it.

But he didn't need to tell his sister exactly how dirty his hands were. That didn't matter; she was staying out of it.

"We could...go west," she suggested hopefully.

He started to tell her no, but hesitated. She was referring to a legend. In the mountains to the west of the Desolate Wilds, there was supposed to be a hidden valley that occasionally emerged to trade with the outside. The inhabitants were weak, but protected by a curse.

Jai Chen had been obsessed with the legend since she was a girl. It seemed ideal to her: a hidden safe place.

In *his* experience, there were no safe places. He immediately wondered what terrible dangers lurked in the valley no one entered.

But even if the valley didn't exist, the mountains were at the very western edge of the Blackflame Empire, and no one had actively controlled that border for fifty years. It was so remote that even maps drawn in his father's day hadn't bothered to include it.

The lands west of the Wilds were unknown to him, but they certainly wouldn't have a Jai clan.

"We can hurt the clan if we go east," he said. "We can take revenge for Kral. Do you *really* want to go west instead?"

The day before, he wouldn't have asked her such a question. He wasn't as sure of his course as he had been yesterday.

He had burned to avenge himself on the Jai clan for years,

but now that he had the means, he was starting to realize what a monumental task he'd begun. To abandon it now, before he'd gone too far, had a certain appeal.

If they left, this would end as one minor attack on a branch of the clan. No one would look into it too closely, and in five years, no one would remember he or his sister were ever here.

Jai Chen surveyed the floor, clenching her hands together as she thought. Finally, she straightened her back and spoke with resolve.

"I will...go with you. No...running...away."

He gave her a wry smile, though she couldn't see it. "It will take weeks to get there, and we don't have a cloudship this time. It will be painful, and messy, and you'll hate every inch of the journey."

"If you...hear me...complain," she said, "leave me...behind."

Once she was packed, he carried her outside, where Gokren had a motley collection of flying creatures assembled. Thousand-Mile Clouds, collared Remnants, strange constructs that looked like wide broomsticks, a sacred eagle with feathers like dawn, a hovering leaf wider than a man, a huge levitating cauldron, and two dozen gray-white bats.

Some of the sacred bats had been taken from the Jai clan, but the Sandvipers had a colony of the same breed of bat, and two of their trainers used to work for the Jai clan.

Gokren was supervising the collection of mounts and vehicles. He turned, smoothed back his gray hair with one hand, and eyed Jai Chen. After a moment he gestured to a white Thousand-Mile Cloud.

"Load her up," he said, looking up to Jai Long. "We'll get a canopy rigged to hold off the wind and give her some privacy."

Jai Long bowed his thanks and settled his sister onto the cloud.

By the time he'd finished, the sun was setting, and most of the vehicles had gathered a load of packs and bags. Gokren lit his pipe, holding it between his teeth as he pressed the end of a scripted lighter into the bowl.

"You could fly me there and return," Jai Long said, hating himself with every word. He needed their help; he shouldn't be turning them down. "You don't have to risk their lives for my revenge."

Gokren let out a mouthful of smoke. "I'm not an idiot, son." He paused as though he'd said something profound, letting bluish haze drift skyward. "I don't throw my sect away for nothing."

He took another breath, let it out. "Old powers like the Jai clan are as traditional as they come. After you hit them, they'll send a Highgold after you. When you beat him, it'll be a group of Highgolds next. Then whichever Truegold ranks the lowest, and only *then* will the elders start to move."

If it weren't for the Ancestor's Spear, that plan would eventually work. The clan could afford to slowly drown him in sacred artists.

With the spear, he would feed on whoever they sent. To him, every Jai clan enemy was a treasure chest of scales and elixirs.

"I won't reach Underlord that way," Jai Long said, though Gokren knew that better than he did. If advancing from Gold to the Lord realm was simply a matter of stockpiling power, no one would ever be stuck at Truegold.

"That's true enough, but I think I can get you there." Gokren watched the best of his sect saddling their mounts and preparing to leave their home. "Took me forty years to reach Truegold. I'll never be an Underlord, not in my lifetime...but I understand some things. By the time Jai Daishou moves himself, you'll either be Underlord or the next thing to it."

That was Jai Long's plan, though he had expected it to take years. He had meant to wage a long, secret war against the clan, stealing their madra and slowly advancing. Once he could face Jai Daishou as a fellow Underlord, the game would change.

With Gokren's help, his chances improved dramatically,

and his timeline shot up. He might reach the peak of True-gold before the end of the year.

"It's still a roll of the dice for you," Jai Long pointed out. He had to be honest with anyone willing to risk their life for him.

Gokren removed his pipe, gazing into the bowl as though it would tell him the future. "I might be gambling," he said, "but I'd say I'm backing the favorite."

On the fourth day after they left, *Sky's Mercy* had to duck down to the ground to let the constructs recharge. The house landed in an open field, the blue cloud slowly dying away until both *Sky's Mercy* and the training barn had settled safely onto the grass.

The barn creaked and moaned as it came to a rest, but the main house remained solid and silent. Lindon was glad he'd taken Cassias' advice and stayed out of the barn during the landing process, or he would have feared for his life.

The second they landed, everyone left the cloudship and returned to the wonderful embrace of solid ground.

Eithan allowed Gesha and Lindon to look at the scripts and constructs sustaining the giant Thousand-Mile Cloud. It was intriguingly simple. Only one circle on the bottom of the main house to guide levitation, and four pillars—one at each corner—to produce and control the cloud madra. The controls were more complicated than the actual mechanism for flight.

But the madra involved...

Both of Lindon's cores added together would only add up to a normal Iron sacred artist, but compared to his old self, he was a powerhouse. Even so, he couldn't activate any of the scripts involved if he drained all the madra in his body.

The house drew vital aura from the sky to keep itself

powered, but it could only drain so much while in flight. Cassias activated the collection script, and ribbons of white and green aura—visible only in Lindon's Copper sight—streamed into the four pillars of the house. The only script Lindon had ever seen consume more power was the one that had activated the Transcendent Ruins.

Lindon had peeked inside earlier, and besides the Forged madra devices that produced the cloud, each pillar held a crystal flask the size of his head. The aura ran inside those crystals, condensing and processing into the madra that powered the cloud.

It would take three days to fill up the crystals, Cassias said. He had made it to the Desolate Wilds in a month, but that had been carrying one person. Not five people and an extra building.

If they had to spend three days drawing aura for every three days flying, it would take them twice as long to return.

Eithan assured them that he intended to make it back in a month, but they would still spend one day grounded for every three in the air. No one asked him how he planned to recharge their power reserves—he was the Underlord, so he knew what he was doing.

He spread out a blanket and had a nap in the sun, but the rest of them were expected to spend the day doing chores. Lindon regarded the idea with dread: if he was hauling water or scrubbing floors, then he wasn't training. He wasn't getting any closer to defeating Jai Long.

But just because he wasn't practicing sacred arts didn't mean he couldn't improve.

When he was sent to fill a man-sized wooden tub with water, and then bring it back to *Sky's Mercy* to fill up their reservoir, he refused to Enforce himself with madra.

He didn't know any real Enforcer techniques, but everyone used madra to reinforce their body to some degree. Cycling madra to tired limbs, focusing it to lift something heavy—Lindon had been doing that since he'd learned to walk.

This time, he kept the madra firmly in his core, relying

solely on the strength of his Iron body.

Before he'd carried the tub downhill for two miles, filled it up with water, and carried it two miles back, he'd never appreciated just how heavy water could be. The tub was big enough that he could bathe in it comfortably, big enough that he looked like an ant carrying a grasshopper carcass as he made his way back. Without his Iron body, he would have collapsed halfway up, even *using* his madra.

He arrived red-faced and sweating, limbs shaking, and his breathing disordered. But after ten minutes of letting his Bloodforged Iron body restore his fatigue, he set off again.

This might not improve his sacred arts, but at least he could build his muscles. 'A healthy spirit lives in a healthy body,' as his clan used to say.

After four trips, the reservoir was full, and Gesha was impatiently waiting on him. They needed dead matter for his Soulsmith practice, so Lindon, Yerin, and Gesha went out to track and kill a wild Remnant.

Gesha found her prey within two hours, but Lindon stopped Yerin from killing it. Forcing his trembling hands to be still, he looked down on a giant frog that seemed to be made from blue-green blocks.

"Let me try first," he said, affecting a casual tone.

Fisher Gesha's eyebrows went up.

Yerin put her sword away. "Scream and bleed when you need help."

Lindon learned some valuable lessons that day. First, he learned that the Empty Palm blasted a chunk out of Remnants, who were made of solid madra. That would surely come in useful later.

Second, he saw how strong Remnants were in the outside world.

Yerin was true to her word, blasting the frog into a pile of blocky dead matter the second he screamed and bled. She tied the pieces of the spirit's corpse together and dragged the bundle back, while Fisher Gesha carried Lindon.

His Bloodforged Iron body had restored him enough that

he could walk on his own by the time they reached *Sky's Mercy,* though one of his cores was empty and the other only half-strength.

Back in Sacred Valley, an Iron would be enough to fight anything but a very advanced, intelligent, or strange Remnant. Those were children compared to these.

In the Transcendent Ruins, he had battled Remnants most every day for two weeks...but he hadn't *battled* them, had he? Not really. He had used traps, and script-circles, and ambushes. Even when he'd personally killed a few, he had used weapons, or fought them together with Yerin and Eithan.

Now that he thought of it, this may have been the first Remnant that he'd stood and fought, relying on nothing but his sacred arts. And it had driven a two-inch spike through his calf.

It showed him how far he had to go. As though he needed another reminder.

After they'd brought the Remnant inside, the sun was setting. Eithan finally woke up, stretched, and saw that the stream of aura flowing into the four pillars had slowed to a trickle.

He opened up one of the columns at the corner of the house, revealing that the green-and-white madra swirling inside the crystal flask had only filled it a third of the way. "Good enough," he said. "I'm on a schedule."

Then he carefully rolled up one gilt-edged sleeve and pressed his hand to the collection script, which gathered up aura and distributed it to the four crystals.

The script took in the proper aspects of aura automatically, but it could accept virtually any madra. It would take that madra, purify it, and use it to reinforce the existing cloud madra, but the efficiency was terrible.

Thanks to Fisher Gesha's tutelage, he could calculate exactly how terrible: cloud madra was the best to fill the flasks, twice as much pure madra would achieve the same result, and any other aspect would take four times as much power to generate the cloud and lift both buildings into the air.

Eithan filled all four crystals in seconds. Dark blue clouds popped out of each of the four corners, swelling and lifting both buildings off the ground. The levitation circle on the bottom shone bright, showing that it was at capacity and ready to be used.

The Underlord shook one hand as though it had fallen asleep and then walked inside.

Cassias and Yerin treated this as normal, but Lindon and Fisher Gesha had exchanged astonished—and somewhat fearful—glances before heading in. Gesha had confided in him later that she, a Highgold, would have taken four or five days to fill up the circle.

Lindon wondered how long it would be before *he* could do something like that.

Three days later, Lindon had gained a new appreciation for elixirs.

The Four Corners Rotation Pill doubled the speed at which he cycled his madra and expanded his core, noticeably speeding his advancement. Unlike the orus fruit or the Starlotus bud, it didn't provide much external power, but the cycling effect alone was invaluable.

When he put on his parasite ring, it usually felt like he was hanging weights on his spirit, slowing his cycling but filtering the quality of the madra. With the ring and the pill together, he could cycle at his full normal speed, but his madra would still be filtered. Twice the result for the same effort.

He brought his second core up to Iron by the seventh day, which was actually something of a disappointment.

His Copper core had compressed to a brighter, higher-quality core with ease, matching the second ball of pure madra floating in his spirit. He had confided to Yerin that he'd hoped for a second Iron body, but she'd looked at him as though he wished he'd sprouted a third eye.

"How many bodies do you have? One? Well, there you go, then."

Eithan had been prepared to give him a pill a day, but

thus far it took Lindon two days to process the energy of each pill. In a week, he'd only used three, with a bit of energy left over.

Still, that was fifteen thousand scales. He pictured the Sandviper wagon he'd seen stuffed with boxes of scales back in the Desolate Wilds, and wondered if all of those together had added up to fifteen thousand. How many scales had they mined from the Transcendent Ruins every day? It couldn't be too much more than fifteen thousand, and that was a whole sect of Golds working together.

In the training course, he could clear six of the wooden dummies every time before he messed up: he either missed a step and took a blow or ran out of madra in one of his cores.

That wasn't enough to dampen his enthusiasm, because he was improving. His movements were sharper and faster than they had been the week before, and his madra control was getting better. Every time he struck a target, he had to inject the exact right amount of madra on contact—too little, and the circle wouldn't light up; too much, and the extra energy would be wasted. His Empty Palm was therefore improving by leaps and bounds, as he learned to project his madra more efficiently and precisely.

Cassias and Fisher Gesha praised his progress, but he wasn't satisfied. After the first few days, he'd taken to wearing his parasite ring while training.

The ring was meant to be an aid in cycling to grow his core, not in combat, and it hampered his control over every Empty Palm. It was like trying to practice swordplay with a heavy rock strapped to the end of his blade, and he was tempted to tear the ring off with every strike.

But when he returned to defeating six dummies consistently, even with the parasite ring on, he finally felt as though he was making real progress.

Yerin, in her turns on the course, was frustrated that her progress using only her Goldsign was slower than Lindon's with his entire body. She could only light up four dummies before she was forced to block a blow on her shoulder, or she injected too little madra through the silver limb and a circle failed to light.

She seemed to feel that she had fallen behind Lindon somehow, even though she had literally tied both of her hands behind her back. And she took out her frustration on him, which he felt was hardly fair. Why was it a mark against him that he was finally a little stronger than her *Goldsign?*

His training as a Soulsmith was still in its infancy, though Fisher Gesha tutored him every night before his evening cycling. One night, she spread seven boxes out before him, flipping open their lids and revealing seven different types of Forged madra. They were all in different forms—one a liquid, one a sludge, one a collection of irregular chunks like pebbles, one a quivering pile of glass-like shards—and each a different color.

"These are the seven most common aspects of madra, you see," Fisher Gesha said, pointing to each in turn. "Fire, earth, wind, water, force, blood, and life."

He had studied these aspects before. There were other types of madra that he felt should have been equally common, but these seven were most widespread because they were the easiest types of aura to cultivate. Light aura was everywhere, but it was difficult to convert to madra, and required special techniques to harvest.

The surge of pride Lindon felt when he heard that had surprised even him. His Wei clan practiced a Path of dreams and light, and now it seemed that might be an impressive combination, even by Gold standards.

"You will re-Forge each of these aspects into discs," Fisher Gesha continued. "*Solid* discs, don't just move them into a circle, you hear me? I had a disciple once...troubled girl. Anyway, reshaping madra besides your own is the fundamental skill of a Soulsmith. If you can't do that, you can't do anything. Bring your discs to me, and if I approve them, then we'll try Forging them into needles."

By then, Lindon had grown used to setting extra challenges to push himself, so he decided to skip the discs and dive straight into Forging needles.

Over the next few days, he bent all of his time and effort to the task, eventually succeeding...with six of the seven aspects.

Even water madra could be forced into a solid shape if he focused himself, though it wouldn't stay there, but life... he spent an entire extra day focused on Forging life madra, skipping his training, before he finally gave up and returned to Fisher Gesha in shame.

"It's impossible," she said, eyeing his seventh box. "Life madra on its own is a liquid, and that's the end of it. Even life Remnants are giant blobs of ooze. I didn't tell you because I wanted you to say you couldn't do it, hm? Thought it might get you to think about your limitations."

She looked over the other six needles, which were supposed to have been simple discs. "Doesn't seem to have worked, did it?"

On the night of their eighth day, he was cycling power into his core, using up the last of the Four Corners Rotation Pill before he snatched a few hours of sleep. He breathed evenly in the pattern Eithan had taught him, building up his power one step at a time and slowly pushing the bounds of his core.

After about an hour, he slowly opened his eyes.

...to see Eithan peeking in through a crack in his door.

The first few times Eithan popped up unexpectedly, Lindon's reactions had been entertaining enough that the Underlord kept trying to catch him off guard.

But you could get used to anything if it happened often enough.

"What can I do to serve the Arelius family?" Lindon asked, rising from his bed. Eithan had done so much for him already, the least he could do in return was ignore the Underlord's...quirks.

Eithan kicked the door open and grinned like a child playing a prank. "Cycle! Now!"

Lindon reasoned that Eithan had also earned a measure

of trust, so he dropped to his knees, hands in his lap, and began to cycle. Just as Eithan had shown him in the Transcendent Ruins.

At first, every breath using this cycling technique had felt like trying to inhale water. But he'd grown so used to it over the following weeks that he rarely had to consciously think his way through the technique anymore.

Eithan tapped his fingers together as he waited for Lindon to settle into a cycling rhythm. When Lindon's breathing evened out, Eithan's grin broadened.

"Now," he said, "close your eyes. I'm going to teach you a trick."

I should trust him, Lindon reminded himself. *I owe him.*

Once he'd returned to the position he'd held before he was interrupted, Eithan's voice cut in. "Madra is very responsive to your imagination. It's part of you, just like your thoughts. So as you study more advanced techniques, you'll find that holding a clear mental picture is just as important as moving your madra in certain patterns."

That fit Lindon's experience. As he advanced, his madra was easier to visualize, and he was better able to get the power to do what he wanted without forcing it into a pattern.

"I'm going to teach you a cycling technique. Once you've mastered it, this method will take you to Jade and beyond."

Lindon leaned forward eagerly, eyes squeezed shut, suddenly afraid to miss a word.

"This is a technique for processing your madra, not for battle," Eithan went on. "If you try to fight while cycling like this, you might as well tie your ankles together."

Lindon wondered if he should be taking notes.

"In your mind, focus on your core. Ah, I mean *one* core. Pick one."

The core that had reached Iron first was brighter and more solid than the other, so he focused on it, letting the bright blue-white ball fill his vision as the other one fell behind into irrelevance.

As he breathed, his madra cycled, spinning out from his

core to run out to the rest of his body and then swirling back.

"Your core is made of stone. Picture it as a huge, stone wheel. It's all you can see. It's like a wall of heavy, solid stone."

Lindon focused on that image, superimposing it over the blue-white sun.

"Now, as you exhale and cycle madra through your body, the stone grinds away at the edges of your core. It's heavy, and it rolls slowly, pushing your core outward."

That was harder to hold. Madra usually flew out from his core freely, but he had to slow it down, forcing his core to rotate and running power through it a scant inch at a time.

He felt like he was pushing that stone wheel up a hill with all his strength, all while trying to keep madra from slithering through his grip. If he lost concentration for one second, the strings of madra would escape and the wheel would fall back down, crushing him.

The effort of moving his madra in such an unnatural pattern caused his channels to strain, as his spirit groaned under the effort. Sweat dripped over his eyelids as he concentrated, and each exhalation was agonizingly slow.

"Now, when the madra comes back in, spiraling from your limbs to your core, the stone wheel shifts. It slowly rolls back the other way, grinding your core again."

It was like letting the wheel roll downhill, only to haul it to a stop and pull it back up again. He poured all his madra into the effort, controlling his spirit with every ounce of his concentration.

There was an instant in the middle where he felt like he was manually stopping his own lungs. He gaped like a fish, his lungs frozen as though the stone wheel sat on his own chest, before he finally got it moving the other way.

Eithan waited for him to get himself under control before graciously reminding him that he still had to hold his previous cycling pattern. It took Lindon another half an hour to match the old timing, and by that time his soul felt like he'd pounded it flat. Only minutes of cycling, and he was more exhausted than he would have been after hours of practicing in the dummy course.

But Eithan wasn't finished.

"Once you have a grip on that, you want your wheel to spin as slowly as possible without stopping. Breathing in the same pattern, I want to see how *slowly* you can move your madra, how heavily that wheel turns, how that huge stone wheel is almost stopped and your madra is just *crawling* along.

"Then you exhale, and it goes back the other way."

Only two more minutes, and Lindon began to seriously wonder if he was going to pass out. He couldn't wait for Eithan to leave so that he could take a real breath.

"This technique is called the Heaven and Earth Purification Wheel," Eithan said, and Lindon felt his weight settle onto the end of the bed. "It has a long and fascinating history."

Lindon would have cried, but he couldn't spare the breath.

"I'll spare you the details." Lindon almost let out a sigh of relief. "But to reach Jade, you need to form a spiral in your core. The spinning motion will condense the quality of your madra, increase your receptivity to spiritual forces, speed up madra recovery, help your control...all sorts of benefits. Eventually, the suction force will become strong enough to contain a Remnant."

Though he itched to take notes, Lindon would lose the breathing technique if he so much as opened his eyes. And that would be disrespectful to the Underlord who had gone through the trouble of teaching him a technique.

If only he would *leave*.

"Every Path has their own Jade cycling technique, and it emphasizes certain aspects of the spirit. Some are particularly good at processing aura efficiently, others help you recover your madra in minutes, and so on. It's a deep and varied field. But I selected this technique just for you!"

Lindon tried to thank him, but grunting out a single syllable almost lost him control of the revolving stone wheel.

"The Heaven and Earth Purification Wheel slowly grinds away at your core's borders, focused *entirely* on improving your capacity to contain madra. It does what you tried to do by Forging and swallowing your own scales: it uses temporary power to push at the bonds of your core, expanding your ability to permanently store power. But while swallowing scales loses some energy in the Forging process, this keeps the entire cycle contained, so there's no loss. It's also slow, difficult to practice, and you will feel like you're choking and dying."

Lindon nodded and almost choked.

"But it works with any madra, including pure. If you fill your second core with another Path, this technique will work for that too. And your Path of Twin Stars breaks one normal-sized core into two smaller cores, so without special elixirs or a technique specifically focused on capacity, you'd never get even one of your cores up to its normal size."

Lindon finally lost the technique. His madra slipped out of his control, he gasped as though he were coming up for air, and the power he'd been damming up in his core surged through his body. His eyes snapped open, and he jerked to his feet like a puppet with strings pulled.

Eithan nodded. "That can happen." He rose, brushing his robe off as though preparing to leave. "All cycling methods have tradeoffs, so if after a few days you have objections, I can recommend a different technique. But control can be learned, quality can be improved with elixirs, collecting aura only takes patience, and as for recovery...why would you need to recover madra quickly when you have more than you could ever use?"

Lindon was still trying to recover his breath, but he swiped his sleeve across his sweaty forehead and bowed slightly. "I won't give up, Underlord. I trust your wisdom."

"Underlord isn't my name," Eithan said, before pointing to Lindon's pocket. "You might want to avoid wearing that ring of yours for the time being. This technique is hard enough without hobbling yourself." He touched his forehead and nodded. "Well then. A good night to you."

The door shut behind him.

And then immediately opened again. Eithan poked his head back in. "You're going to keep cycling, aren't you? You're not going to slack off while my back is turned?"

"Your back is never turned," Lindon said, voice dry.

"And don't forget it." Eithan widened his eyes, staring at Lindon intently as he slowly shut the door.

Lindon took a few moments to breathe before sitting down on the bed. He had started to picture the stone wheel before he slipped his hand into his pocket and ran into the cold circle of halfsilver.

Eithan had said not to use the parasite ring, but Lindon was trying to push himself beyond what his teachers required. Then again, the thought of trying that cycling technique with the additional burden of the ring physically made him shudder. It was like wrapping his lungs in bands of iron.

He was pulling his hand out of the pocket, leaving the ring behind, when he brushed past another small object: a slightly warm ball of smooth glass.

Lindon gripped it in his fist, picturing the steady blue candle flame. Jade wasn't his goal. Jai Long wasn't his goal. Even Underlord wasn't his goal.

If Eithan could have saved Sacred Valley, then Suriel would have shown him a vision of Eithan. He had to reach further than Eithan thought possible.

He settled into a cycling position and slipped on his ring.

CHAPTER SEVEN

When the moon rose on their thirty-second night of traveling, Cassias Arelius walked away from the control board of *Sky's Mercy*. The script didn't need constant maintenance, but he felt better with someone watching the sky. If a Three-Horned Eagle rose out of the clouds, they would be in trouble without someone close enough and quick enough to steer out of the way.

Not that any Arelius would miss the approach of a threat like that, even with his eyes closed. His web of madra showed him nothing but clouds and empty air for a quarter-mile around them.

And the Arelius Underlord was aboard. Even the wind couldn't sneak up on Eithan.

"Would you like to take the last shift?" he asked Eithan, who was sprawled out on the couch with a book in hand.

In less than ten hours, they would arrive at Serpent's Grave. If he could have drained his core dry to push *Sky's Mercy* any faster, he would have—his wife and son were waiting for him down there. They'd left their home back in the capital to follow him, and then he'd abandoned them for two months to chase down their delinquent Underlord.

This was his job now, however much it strained him to be away for so long. Eithan was the reason he'd been able to marry Jing in the first place; only an Underlord's word had convinced their families to agree to the match. Even putting up with Eithan for the rest of his life wouldn't be enough to repay that favor.

Though he had taken Cassias' place.

Cassias was born to be Patriarch of the Arelius family. He was a direct descendant of the bloodline, his appearance and conduct were impeccable, and from an early age he had impressed everyone with his skill in the sacred arts.

But none of that had been good enough for Jing's family before Eithan took his side. He'd traded away his position as Patriarch's heir with a smile on his face, but the occasional reminder could still...sting.

Eithan yawned and shut the book. "Nothing but clear sky between us and a safe landing."

A web of invisible power stretched throughout *Sky's Mercy*, bringing Cassias little snippets of information: Fisher Gesha's sheets rustling as she turned, Yerin's eyelids crinkling in a disturbing dream, Lindon's chest rising and falling evenly. There was no privacy when an Arelius was around, but it was polite to act otherwise.

Everyone knew what the Arelius could do, but they didn't know about the limitations. Publicly, the family liked to pretend they had none.

Now that he'd confirmed the outsiders were asleep, Cassias spoke freely. "They can't hear us. Tell me when we're really close enough for you to guide our landing, please."

He'd known Eithan for six years now, and worked closely with him for most of that time. He could tell when the man was bluffing. Usually.

And one of Cassias' first tasks after Eithan's arrival had been to determine the limit of the Underlord's senses.

Stretching, Eithan spoke through another yawn. "My father used to say the First Patriarch could watch over his descendants from another continent. Maybe even from...beyond the grave." Eithan waggled his eyebrows up and down.

"Do you often listen to myths?" Cassias asked lightly.

"Yes. That's the secret to reaching Underlord: studying old tales. That, and bladder health." Eithan headed to the back, to the side of the bar. "If you'll excuse me, the house can fly itself for a moment."

Cassias was left alone in the central room of *Sky's Mercy*. It had been his home for the last two months, and over the course of his life he'd spent even longer inside, but he'd grown up expecting it would belong to him.

Now, it was Eithan's. Cassias was only borrowing it.

Everything in life was a trade.

Before heading upstairs to his own bedroom—there were six aboard *Sky's Mercy*, as well as the washroom, the bar, a training room, and a silent chamber for cycling—he stopped.

Over the month since departing the Desolate Wilds, he'd built up a certain curiosity. Now that the other three were asleep, and the two children had both left the circle of wooden dummies alone, he had a perfect opportunity to indulge that curiosity.

Eithan would know what he was doing, of course, but it was best to operate as though Eithan knew everything. The Underlord could stretch his web to a target miles away, if he was focused on a specific spot, but he saw everything within a hundred yards without even trying.

Cassias pushed the door open, took two steps on cloud through the bitter, cutting wind, and entered the repurposed barn.

Only slanting bars of moonlight cut through the shadows, but Cassias could see all eighteen dummies with his bloodline powers. An arm here, a slice of head there, a piece of a circle, but it was enough for him to fill in the gaps. As he moved, strands of his detection web swept through each of the dummies in turn. It was as though he could run his fingertips over everything in the room, slowly gaining a picture.

He finished in a few seconds, confirming what he'd suspected. Because he knew Eithan was listening, he shook his head and sighed.

"You're *not* trying to kill him?"

When he re-entered *Sky's Mercy,* he found Eithan standing at the control panel. "Of course I'm not," the Underlord responded. "When a mother bird pushes a chick from the nest, is she trying to kill her child?"

"That's a Lowgold course," Cassias said, his tone dry. "I trained on something similar until only a few years ago."

"It should be similar *indeed*. I took the plans from your training room back in the main house."

Cassias cast his web back over to the barn, sweeping his sensations through the dummies. It wasn't as quick or as detailed as it had been when he was standing an arm's length away, but it was still thorough.

With very little surprise, he realized Eithan was telling the truth: the two courses were virtually identical. It would be a relief if he ever caught the man in a lie instead of a half-truth, bluff, or exaggeration.

"You're teaching a child to wrestle by locking him in a closet with a wolf," Cassias said. His tone straddled the line between polite subordinate and stern caretaker.

He had gotten to know Lindon over the last few weeks—the boy was earnest, quick, and almost entirely ignorant about the sacred arts. Cassias didn't want to see him hurt.

Someone had raised him completely disconnected from the real world, and he needed a thorough, solid education. It would take years to prepare him with all the knowledge he needed to face society, especially as a representative of the Arelius family. Their enemies would tear him apart, if he weren't ready.

Eithan seemed determined to cram those skills into him in a matter of months. That wouldn't help him or stretch him; it would burn him up like dry tinder.

"Jai Long is dangerous, even for a Highgold. Best to start Lindon on something as safe as a wolf, wouldn't you say?" Eithan was *sitting* on the control panel, reading his book again as the night sky stretched out the windows behind him. He didn't even bother to face the glass.

"You really want him to fight against a former Jai clan heir? Still?" It wasn't technically proper to question the Underlord, not even in private, but Eithan had never been one to lean on propriety. Besides, dealing with him was a trial that would stretch anyone's manners.

Eithan flipped a page. "You've been watching Lindon and Yerin both. What do you think?"

"Yerin is a treasure vault," Cassias said immediately. "I can't imagine completing a Lowgold training course using a Goldsign like hers, but she almost has it. Her madra is incredibly stable if she really reached Lowgold only a few months ago, and at this rate she could reach Highgold inside a year. She was born for the sword arts."

"Not just born," Eithan said. "Made. And Lindon?"

"He's...talented," Cassias said hesitantly. In truth, he didn't know what to make of Lindon's ability. His mind and attitude were admirable enough, but his spirit...

He had two half-sized cores filled with Iron-quality pure madra, a few *very* interesting trinkets in his pack that Cassias had respected his privacy enough to ignore, and an Iron body that was far beyond his capacity to support.

He knew Eithan must have led Lindon to that particular Iron body, but he didn't know why. Lindon having to carry that body was like a child trying to control an Underlord's weapon; they might be able to flail it around a little, but in the end, it would do more damage to them than to anyone else.

"He's a mess," Eithan said, flipping another page.

"I wouldn't put it *quite* like that," Cassias said, but he was relieved he hadn't had to spell it out.

"His Bloodforged Iron body takes too much madra to sustain, and he's weak as it is. No matter how physically resilient he becomes, he's no more than half a sacred artist." Eithan looked over his shoulder and showed Cassias a grin. "Have I hit the mark?"

Cassias lowered his voice. They were still all sleeping, but this was the sort of subject matter that should be discussed discreetly. "Why train him, then? The branch heads will worship you for bringing home the Sage's apprentice. You don't need a second disciple. And I can name you a dozen sacred artists Lindon's age with twice his skill."

Eithan hopped down, tossing his book onto the control panel. He walked over and threw an arm across Cassias' shoulder. Then he turned so they were both looking out over the night.

"Imagine with me, will you?" Eithan extended his free hand as though presenting a glorious future. "Imagine if he could restore each of those cores to full size and raise them to Lowgold. With pure madra in one, he'd be a unique re-source, and he could still follow a combat Path in the other. That's *two* full cores, so he could bring out the full capabili-ties of the Bloodforged body with energy to spare."

"It's a delightful vision," Cassias said. "He would throw the Lowgold rankings into chaos. In ten or fifteen years, he could grow into a pillar of our Arelius family, and follow me and Jing to the top of the Truegolds."

Cassias shrugged out of Eithan's arm and turned to look him in the eye. "But he won't be ready in a year. Even if he were, he would be no match for the Jai clan exile."

Eithan's eyes sparkled. "But you haven't heard about his second Path."

When Eithan told him, Cassias was speechless for a mo-ment. After a pause, he forced himself to start breathing. The Underlord was just needling him again, to watch him squirm.

"Please don't worry me like that," he said at last. "I almost believed you."

"Then you were almost correct."

The horrifying possibilities of Eithan's plan started to creep into Cassias' mind one by one, but he refused to consider them. "He's not born of the Blackflame line. He couldn't handle the madra."

"Didn't you wonder why I'd given him a top-grade Blood-forged Iron body?"

"But you can't get him the aura though, surely, unless

you've tucked a dragon away...in the..."

He trailed off. Horror dawned on him as he realized where they were going.

Eithan beamed. "Serpent's Grave. We're heading right into the dragon's mouth, as it were."

...that might work.

Heavens help him, but that *might actually work.*

"No," Cassias said, still refusing to acknowledge the truth. "The branch heads will never allow it. The Skysworn will never allow it. The *Emperor* will never allow it!"

"There's an old saying about asking forgiveness rather than permission," Eithan said, "but the essence of it is, 'I'm going to do what I want.'"

Cassias had given up his spot in the family for Eithan. He'd suffered for Eithan's mistakes, taken the heat of the family's anger over Eithan's childish whims, and hauled his family halfway across the Empire to Serpent's Grave...and then left them again, because Eithan had wandered off.

But even he had limits.

His shouts woke Fisher Gesha. She made it to the top of the stairs to see the Underlord with a hand over Cassias' mouth, stopping him from calling out to Lindon.

Cassias hadn't even gotten a chance to draw his sword; Eithan had seen every movement coming, broken his techniques before they formed, broken his stance, and broken the flow of his madra. It had taken him no more effort than scooping up a kitten.

Cassias stopped struggling, his shoulders slumped. There was no standing against an Underlord.

As Lindon and the entire Arelius family would soon realize.

It was their last day before landing in the Blackflame Empire, and Lindon was up early to train. Not earlier than Yer-in, who was sitting with legs crossed outside the circle of wooden dummies at dawn, already cycling.

And now, this was to be his final attempt at the eigh-teen-man course before landing in Serpent's Grave. He slipped the parasite ring into his pocket and cycled his madra, standing in front of the first dummy.

He glanced at Yerin so that she would start counting. She nodded. "Run it."

Lindon moved with a speed born of habit, striking at the targets on the right arm, torso, left arm. Without looking, he raised his forearm to block the counterstrike.

He could hear the bone creak.

The sudden pain was a flash of lightning down his arm, but he'd already moved to the second dummy. The injury cooled just as quickly, his Bloodforged Iron body drawing his madra directly to fuel his recovery.

It had been impossible for him to complete the course. Even if he'd executed each step perfectly, every hit that landed on him took too much of his madra. He'd asked if he could stop the drain, and Eithan had looked at him as though he were crazy. "Can you stop your body from heal-ing? No. That's what bodies do. Yours just does it a little too well."

With two Iron cores and three weeks of training under the Heaven and Earth Purification Wheel, he could barely, just *barely*, finish the eighteenth dummy.

This run went smoothly all the way up to number six-teen, where he placed his foot too wide and didn't have the footing to take the overhead blow. He blocked with both arms crossed, but he was supposed to stay on his feet. This time, thanks to his misstep, he went down to a knee.

He couldn't allow his last attempt to end in a failure.

Lindon slammed the heel of his hand into the dummy's chin, pushing an Empty Palm through the bottom of the cir-cle and into the center. The madra penetrated, even though the hit had been off-center, and the circle glowed.

He lunged for the next dummy, clearing the last two without incident.

As soon as the last bell rung and the last light shone, he draped himself over the wooden frame, panting and sweating. Both his cores were weak and empty, and it would take him half an hour to refill them even under the effects of the pill.

But that wasn't the important part. He looked to Yerin expectantly.

"Twenty-one, by my count." She chuckled at his relief as he sagged off the dummy, collapsing to the floor. "That's more than nothing. I'd have been proud of that at Iron."

"I don't believe you had a course like this when you were Iron," Lindon said, lying on his back and staring up at the ceiling.

"No, I had to fight half a dozen starving wolves with a shaving-razor." She sighed and moved into the center of the ring. "You got a count going?"

He hesitated. "Yerin, we're already there. I don't mean to suggest anything..."

"Start the count," she said, steel in her voice.

He started counting.

She leaned into the first dummy, her Goldsign blurring silver. First target green, second target blue, third target white. One-two-three and she was onto the next one. Even with just the bladed arm, she was faster than Lindon.

Yerin complained that she couldn't make the Goldsign do what she wanted it to. Over and over she said that, until Lindon was sick of hearing it. To him, she always looked in complete control.

She reached the ninth dummy in seven seconds, and this one had a target low in the abdomen—where the core would be, in any sacred artist but Lindon—one in the chest, and one in the center of its head. It was one of Lindon's favorites, because it only moved its arms defensively; it never hit him back.

Yerin struck the lowest circle easily, the second a little slow, and her third blow was knocked aside by a wooden hand.

All the previous eight dummies, which had remained lit until then, dimmed slowly as though the light leaked out of them.

She stood there panting, glaring at her wooden enemy, and Lindon thought the red rope around her waist had brightened from dark red to the pure crimson of fresh blood.

Finally, she screamed, her Goldsign striking forward and taking the dummy's head.

She didn't look at Lindon or excuse herself, dropping to the floor right there and beginning to cycle. Her cheeks and throat were flushed with anger, her scars standing out in stark contrast to her red skin.

Lindon was already walking to a box in the corner, which was filled with replacement heads. They'd picked up some extra wood on one of their landings, and every time Fisher Gesha said he needed practical experience, he hollowed one out and filled it with the simple scripts and basic constructs the dummies needed to function.

The outer scripts and core constructs of each dummy were all unique, but the heads were the same, which fortunately made them easy to replace.

He screwed it on—the original wood was lighter than the replacement, and he would need to carve a target circle onto it. He pulled out a short-bladed knife to start, but Eithan threw open the door.

"Twenty-one seconds is fairly good," Eithan said with a broad smile. "Now, if you'd gotten below twenty seconds, *then* you'd have done something."

Lindon bowed, accepting what little compliment there was. After weeks of working with Eithan, he'd started to realize exactly how high the Underlord's standards were. If he used a technique to blow a hole in the moon, Eithan would ask why he hadn't taken care of the sun, too.

"As for you, Yerin..." She didn't open her eyes at Eithan's words, apparently still cycling, but Lindon was sure she was listening. He'd gotten to know her better over the last few weeks too.

"...you're still trying to get your Remnant to guide you. You're making things harder for yourself."

"He's talking to me," Yerin said stubbornly, eyes still closed. "If I could hear him clear, I'd be two stages stronger by now."

Eithan's smile was filled with pity, as though he looked down on a dying old woman. "No will of your master remains in the Remnant. You're hearing impressions that echo from his remaining memories."

"It's him, so I'm listening."

"The *easiest* way to reach Highgold is to break down your Remnant for power. You are staring at a feast from afar while wondering why you're so hungry. All other paths to Highgold are—"

She bounded to her feet, cutting him off. "I'm not going to bury his voice. You know how much of his teaching I'd be giving up? You think you can make up for that? Are *you* a Sage?"

"If only I were," Eithan said calmly. "It would solve many of my problems."

She stepped forward, glaring up at his chin. "A Sage's Remnant can do things you can't imagine. I'm telling you, he's in there, and he'll get me to Highgold in a snap."

Eithan placed two fingers on her forehead and slowly pushed her back until she was standing an arm's length away. "The path from Lowgold to Highgold is learning to use more than the excess energy your Remnant provides you. You normally break down the Remnant itself for power, digesting its skills and its madra. There are *other* ways past Lowgold, certainly, but this is the most direct path."

Her face reddened even further, her Goldsign drew back as though to strike, but Eithan continued with his tone and smile still friendly. "We have time. Perhaps you'll choose to feed on your master's Remnant, or perhaps you'll find another way. Or you could do neither, and Lindon and I will leave you behind."

Lindon flinched. He had been perfectly happy to stay

out of *that* conversation. For the past four weeks, Yerin had ranted about Eithan's instruction and how he didn't understand her master like *she* did.

Eithan clapped his hands together. "All right! Let's leave your failures and inadequacies aside for the moment. Even now, we are arriving at our destination. You should clean yourselves and join me in the sitting-room, because I suspect you'll want to see this."

Eithan left Lindon and Yerin behind, which suspended them in silence as they toweled off and packed up.

"It's less than easy to keep a Remnant under control," Yerin said after two minutes of quiet.

"I can't even imagine," Lindon said honestly. Someday he would, though. He looked forward to it.

"I *am* trying. My master knows how to reach Highgold without cracking into his Remnant, I just need to hear what he's telling me."

Sometimes Yerin spoke like this when she needed to bounce ideas off Lindon, even when he had no clue what she was talking about. He usually nodded and let her work it out aloud.

But he could tell the difference between needing a sounding board and needing encouragement.

"You're pushing against Highgold, and you're complaining that it's too *slow?*" Lindon asked, exaggerating his surprise. "You're disappointed because you're not a Highgold by...sixteen summers? Seventeen?"

She shrugged. "Thereabouts. The count gets a little thrown off for a while."

"And you're not just a Gold! You were hand-selected by the Sword Sage himself! Compared to Eithan..." He hesitated, because he wasn't sure how powerful the Sword Sage was. He'd never heard of the man until Suriel had mentioned him as Yerin's master.

"He was much stronger than an Underlord," she said quietly.

"Underlords and Sages are *fighting* over you. It wasn't until this year that I could push an eight-year-old Copper off his feet, while you could carve your way through a mountain with a dull spoon."

"I have more than one reason why I can't just drift merrily along," she said, but a smile had started to creep onto her face. "You don't have to polish me up, you know. I'm just venting smoke."

Lindon tucked the parasite ring into his pack, making sure all the pockets were closed and fastened before he hoisted it onto his shoulder. "I'm not 'polishing' anything. The heavens opened up and showed me visions of all the greatest people on the planet, people who can wrestle dragons and strike down armies. Then they brought me to you. You're all so far above me you might as well be stars."

The words hung in the air for a moment before he heard them, and then some heat rose into his cheeks. He didn't look away, though.

Yerin gave him a lopsided smile, and this one sunk into his memory: her smile, the thin scars standing out against her skin, her black hair mussed from training so it didn't look straight anymore.

"That has a sweet sound to it, now you've said it," she said at last. The instant passed, and she turned to open the door onto the screaming wind. "Heavens never came down to show me anything, and that's the truth."

Eithan stopped in his tracks even as the front windows filled with crags of black stone: Shiryu Mountain, the peak where the last of the dragons had gone to die. He'd intended to leave the children to their little moment—they would need to trust each other even more than they trusted him, and trust was always built on small, personal moments—but a phrase caught his ear, carried to him on threads of power.

The heavens opened up and showed me...

He tended to smile by default, but now his grin stretched his lips to the breaking point. He'd wondered. From the first glimpse of that little glass ball in Lindon's pocket, the one with the steady blue flame, he'd wondered. Some of the boy's comments, some of his actions, had made him more and more certain.

And now...now he knew.

The heavens opened up...

Very interesting indeed.

CHAPTER EIGHT

With Cassias actively working at the control panel and Eithan standing proudly in front of the windows, Lindon and Yerin looked down over the city of Serpent's Grave.

"This," Eithan announced, "is the birthplace of the Black-flame Empire. The imperial capital has moved over time, and moved again, but here is where it all began: where the last of the dragons who once ruled this land were finally brought down."

"Dragons?" Yerin asked, unsettled.

"That's where the empire got its name. After the dragons were destroyed, a certain family found a source of their power, ruling for centuries like dragons themselves. That source lies beneath us, although of course it's been all but tapped out over the generations."

Lindon had been raised to believe dragons were myths—or if they did exist, only in the heavens. But Suriel had shown him a dragon beneath the sea.

And besides, *something* had left all those bones.

The black mountain beneath them rose from a desert like the crest of a dark, frozen wave. A vast spine, yellowed with age, twisted and curled around the rock, with a serpentine skull resting at the mountain's foot.

It was the most complete skeleton in Serpent's Grave, but far from the only one. A claw here, a pile of sharpened fangs there. And *Sky's Mercy* had yet to begin its descent—if he could see them from here, what would they look like on the ground?

"Serpent's Grave," Lindon said aloud, and Eithan pointed to him.

"Well named, isn't it? I have to applaud the empire's straightforward naming sense."

The floor fell out from Lindon's feet.

He caught himself on the edge of a table, which was bolted to the floor, and sank into one of the chairs. He'd discovered over the course of the journey that it was best to take a descent sitting down.

Yerin joined him, and Cassias was braced against the control panel with eyes locked on his landing, but Eithan stood with his hands in the pockets of his red-and-gold outer robe. His head was almost pressed against the glass, which reflected his smile.

As they fell lower, Lindon started to make out details among the bones. Dark spots in the bones resolved into holes—windows and doors, through which people streamed. The streets wound around the biggest bones but cut through others, which had been hollowed out or stacked together to make buildings.

Lindon leaned forward in his seat. Over the years, these people had carved a city into a dragon's graveyard. A long, straight bone, sticking out of the earth, was covered in windows and ringed with stairs. A fractured skull had a huge gong mounted in the eye socket. Four claws reached out of the ground with man-sized lanterns dangling from their tips.

The city had even crawled up the mountain, so that the black stone bristled with towers. More bones rose like a thorny crown from the mountain's peak, with palaces nestled between its spikes.

Lindon was overwhelmed at the sight of it all. Sacred Valley had what they called towns and cities, but this city dwarfed his imagination. Even leaving aside the size, he had never heard so much as a *legend* about a city of dragon's bone.

This was the world Suriel had opened for him. His myths didn't even come close.

Sky's Mercy was circling one location: a rib cage, with the gaps between each rib closed by pale stone and mortar. A pair of banners—blue and black and white—flew from the highest peaks, proudly displaying the Arelius crest. Cassias descended until they were almost on top of the bones, then drifted to the end closest to the mountain.

Massive greenhouses stretched in rows behind the buildings, their glass roofs letting in sunlight and allowing Lindon to see the fields of crops growing inside. Scripts shone along the outside walls, and rain fell from one of the ceilings.

The sacred artists here had advanced beyond the need to live off the land. They had bottled up their farmland and taken it with them.

One plot with enough space to hold another enclosed farm had been left empty, little more than a wide square of reddish dirt. Cassias steered them until they floated over that square, and slowly edged down the last few feet.

Eithan turned from the window and walked to the door, hair streaming behind him. "I don't know about you," he said, "but I'm ready to get to work."

Cassias left the controls, running a hand through his yellow curls. He had worn his best today, and he smoothed every crease in his shirt as though worried about leaving the slightest imperfection.

Lindon was wearing a sacred artist's robe in the Arelius colors, but it was weathered from the trip. He wondered if he should have asked for something more presentable, but Yerin was wearing the same tattered black she always did, and she didn't seem concerned.

Eithan threw open the door, revealing a hundred people arranged in ten rows of ten, all clad in blue with the black crescent on their backs. Lindon had a very good view of their backs, as they had all prostrated themselves on the ground with their heads pressed against the reddish dirt.

"The Arelius family greets the Patriarch," they shouted, in a unified voice that shook the ground.

Yerin winced and knuckled her ear. "Wouldn't have turned down a warning."

"Patriarch?" Lindon repeated. Eithan heard him and turned.

"Oh, yes, I'm the head of the family. I expected you to have guessed that by now."

Cassias stepped in front of Eithan, his steel bracer Gold-sign gleaming in the sun. "Number one, step forward and report."

The leftmost servant in the front row, a heavyset woman in her middle years, stepped up and bowed to the Patriarch.

Even *she* was dressed for a festival. Polished blue-and-silver combs held back her gray-streaked hair, her servant's uniform looked perfectly new, and rings glistened on her fingers.

Lindon first thought that even the servants lived like royalty here, but he supposed the Underlord's arrival was a big day. Perhaps this was like an audience with a king.

She didn't make her report in front of everyone, as Lindon had expected. Instead, she moved to whisper in Cassias' ear. After a moment, Cassias turned to address Eithan in a normal tone.

"Since I have been gone, our misfortune has multiplied. Our fourth-ranked crew of lamplighters working on the mountain have returned with severe burns. They refuse to implicate anyone, but they were working on the peak, just outside the palaces of the Jai clan."

Eithan dipped his head, and the servant woman continued whispering in Cassias' ear.

Lindon exchanged glances with Yerin. The whispering was pointless. Eithan could hear everything, and could probably read a list of issues pinned against a wall halfway across the city. The Underlord gave no indication that this bothered him, or was in any way unusual.

He nodded through a few more reports before Cassias said, "We've recently received reports indicating a natural spirit has formed in the sewer."

Eithan looked over in surprise, though he *must* have heard the story at the same time Cassias did. "Have we let the sewers back up so badly, then?"

"It's a life spirit. Apparently the Jai clan had a mishap some weeks back, when their refiners dumped failed elixirs into the same chamber where the Soulsmiths disposed of their dead matter. It was an...unexpected reaction."

Cassias' tone told Lindon exactly how 'unexpected' it had been, but Eithan only nodded again. "Two and a half miles east," the Underlord said. "Just south of the Sandstorm Quarter, directly beneath the fountain shaped like a three-headed dragon."

Cassias turned to the rows of kneeling servants. "Ninety-nine and one hundred," he said. The two people in the back rose to their feet, bowed, and then scurried off.

The woman whispered again. "The paint was beginning to chip outside the Jai clan's second-ranked auction house," Cassias reported. "We repainted overnight, but the new coat was scraped and marred in the morning. The Jai clan reported our painters, but it was our top-ranked crew."

Someone tugged on Lindon's sleeve, and he leaned down to hear what Fisher Gesha had to say. Yerin leaned in next to them, listening.

"You've noticed the ranks, hm? Everything here in the proper Blackflame Empire has its place, numbered and categorized. You always know which restaurant is the best, which public lavatory is the worst, which servant is more useful than another. Everything they do here is about climbing one number higher, you see?"

Yerin huddled closer. "That's a twisty way of doing it."

Gesha hit Lindon on the side of the head. "The opposite of twisty, isn't it? Everything's clearly laid out. Higher-ranked businesses can charge more, the highest-ranked disciples get the best resources, and the top families get more support from the empire."

"What did you mean the *proper* Blackflame Empire?" Lindon asked. "And why did you hit me?"

Gesha hit him again. "Blackflame Empire covers more land than you think. The Emperor holds the title to the Desolate Wilds, only there's nothing he wants out there, so he leaves us to ourselves. The empire stretches past the mountain range to the west of us, but I couldn't tell you just how far, could I?"

Lindon had grown up in the mountain range to the west of the Desolate Wilds, and he could say with confidence that no one there had heard of the Blackflame Empire. It was widely accepted that the land outside Sacred Valley was untamed and barbaric.

Eithan joined their conversation, speaking out one side of his mouth. "The Emperor hasn't been able to hold on to the full scope of its territory for two generations now, though don't let the imperial clan hear you spreading that around. As for the ranking, I'm proud to say that we are the first of the major servant families, subject only to the great clans of the empire. I myself am considered the eleventh strongest of the Underlords." He flashed a smile. "But I'm first in charm!"

Lindon wondered if charm was actually ranked.

Cassias discreetly elbowed Eithan, concluding his report with, "Due to a series of anonymous reports, the Skysworn are currently investigating us for negligence. The Jai clan have publicly proposed that the Redflower family supervise sanitation, with our employees given to their authority. The Redflowers have repeatedly declined."

Eithan straightened himself up and looked over the servants. "I have witnessed the business of the family, and let it be known that I am more than satisfied with our performance. The inner and outer members of the family have honored our name, and our employees have behaved with dedication and loyalty. I could not be more pleased with how this family has conducted itself in my absence."

Cassias stared wide-eyed at Eithan as though he'd never seen him before. The servants all reacted differently: some bowed lower, some raised their heads to gaze on the Underlord, and others shouted loyalty to the Arelius family or insults to the Jai clan.

"We thank you for the honor, Underlord," Cassias said, turning to the servants. "Dismissed."

The servants shouted in unison once more: "The Arelius family thanks the Patriarch." Their voices were surely Enforced, judging by how the shouts made the nearby sand shake. This time, Lindon was prepared for the noise, and he cycled madra to protect his ears.

Though they were dismissed, they stayed on their knees waiting for the Underlord and his entourage to leave. Eithan strode through the rows of prostrate figures, Cassias keeping pace beside him. He beckoned Yerin and Lindon to join them, so Lindon hitched his pack up on his shoulders and followed, his red Thousand-Mile Cloud drifting along behind. Yerin walked with him, and Fisher Gesha scurried behind on her spider legs.

"You conducted yourself with admirable dignity back there," Cassias said to Eithan, as they passed into the giant rib cage. The ceiling between the ribs was painted in murals of a thousand colors, showing sacred artists locked in battle with dragons. The ribs themselves were etched with delicate scripts, though none of them were lit.

Eithan smoothed back his long hair as he walked. "They didn't need a friend today, they needed to know I would solve their problems. I had to inspire confidence."

Cassias looked him up and down. "It's like I've never met you."

"It was nothing much, but feel free to shower me with praise."

They continued chatting even as they entered a vast chamber, but Lindon was absorbed by the noise and motion of the Arelius family in action. Workers in blue-and-black scurried here and there—some of them carrying brooms, others buckets. Some wore blood-spattered aprons, others carried sacks over their shoulders. A fireplace big enough to burn wagons took up a chunk of one wall, with a chimney carved into the bone. Servants separated piles of trash and tossed pieces into the flames.

Half of that same wall was taken up by a long desk with six smiling people behind it, all wearing Arelius badges on their chests. Workers lined up in front of them, only to be pointed in a certain direction; it must be where they received their assignments.

A collection of maps were tacked against the opposite wall, some freshly painted, others yellowed with age. Workers with white signs painted on their uniforms—Lindon took them to be leaders of some kind—looked at the maps and compared them to lists in their hands.

It all reminded Lindon of the bustle surrounding the construction of the Seven-Year Festival, but on another scale entirely. Instead of a hundred Wei clan members working on a dozen jobs over a huge arena, here were a thousand employees of the Arelius family packed into a single room while carrying out hundreds of tasks. This was what they did every day.

Yerin was gripping the sheath of her sword, not its hilt, and eyeing every person they passed. "Is it always this... noisy in here?"

Cassias heard her and turned, walking backwards and holding a hand on the hilt of his thin saber. He leaned the weapon to the side, moving the sheath out of the way of a passing servant without looking. "The empire prides itself on its appearance, and we are the ones who keep it beautiful. We must stay organized. This is only the seventh largest city in the empire, so there are only four central facilities like this one. In Blackflame City itself, there are a dozen, all bigger and busier than what you see around you."

They passed out of the bustling room and into the sun again, which glared at them over the head of a pale stone statue that must have been ninety feet tall. It was rounded and smooth with age, but it depicted a figure with wild hair and torn clothes, eyes furious and teeth bared in a snarl. The statue had a dagger raised as though to strike.

It seemed like an odd likeness to carve outside a janitor's headquarters, but before Lindon could say as much, Eithan pointed to it.

"The family's original Patriarch," he said. "There are legends about him all over the world. Serpent's Grave was one of the first outposts of the Arelius family on this continent. It isn't the headquarters anymore, even in the Blackflame Empire—they've moved to the capital city, to stay close to power—but everyone gathers here once every ten years."

Cassias sighed. "Though that tradition may also be lost to time."

Eithan's smile dimmed. "Yes, well...we'll see in four more years, won't we?"

They walked until they reached the base of the spiraling bone tower Lindon had seen in the distance. Cassias abruptly stopped, polishing the silver bracer on his arm with the corner of his sleeve—it was his Goldsign, but the man cared for it like jewelry. He adjusted his collar, brushed dirt from his pants, checked his sword in its silver sheath, and looked at his reflection in the bracer.

"You look almost as good as I do," Eithan said, waving him on. "Go on. I can handle family business at least as well as you can."

Cassias gave him a doubtful look, but still hurried into the tower.

"His wife and son are in there," Eithan said, which fired Lindon's imagination. Cassias had mentioned his wife half a dozen times over the journey here, calling her the strongest Highgold in the empire, but Lindon had taken that as the praise of a husband.

Now that he knew they rated everything, he wondered if maybe she *was* the strongest Highgold in the Blackflame Empire. And if that were true, where did Cassias rank?

"...so he will be distracted for at least a day or two," Eithan continued. "That's enough about the family business, let's get to what *really* matters."

The doors to the tower swung back open, and Cassias stuck his head out. "I heard that."

Lindon wondered, not for the first time, if there were some way to get the powers of the Arelius bloodline for himself. Cassias had told him no, he had to be born into the family, but Lindon didn't stop wondering.

Eithan must have heard Cassias, but he didn't turn back, guiding their group away from the tower and back toward the main building. "Number one-thirteen," he said, and a man separated himself from the crowd of blue-clad servants around them, going to his knees before the Underlord.

"I want you to prepare Underground Chamber Number Three for entry. Also, take Fisher Gesha to the Soulsmith quarters." He ushered Gesha forward, and she scuttled up to join the servant. Her coffin-sized wooden chest was strapped to her back, dwarfing her, but she carried it as though it were hollow.

"Fisher Gesha is an honored guest from the Desolate Wilds," Eithan said, and the servant glanced up in evident surprise. "However," Eithan continued, "she is to be treated as a guest from anywhere else."

Servant One-Thirteen bowed without a word, letting the Underlord and the rest sweep past him. Fisher Gesha nodded to Lindon, and he saluted her back, fists pressed together.

Lindon had every reason to believe his Soulsmithing lessons were to continue, but separating from a friendly face in this strange city still made him nervous.

Eithan glanced up at the sky, held a hand in the air for no reason that Lindon could tell, and then reversed direction. He took them back out to the base of the First Patriarch's statue, putting one hand on Lindon's shoulder and one hand on Yerin's.

"Are we posing for a portrait?" Lindon asked, seeing no other reason why they should arrange themselves in front of a statue while Arelius servants streamed by.

"Not for a portrait, no," Eithan said, and turned his smile on an old man walking through the crowd.

This man stood tall and straight, though he must have been at least eighty, his white hair flowing down his back. His white robes were intricate and flawless, and like every other set of clothes Lindon had seen since stepping off *Sky's Mercy,* they seemed to have never encountered a single stain or speck of dust.

His face was clean-shaven, and he held his hands behind his back as he came to a stop in front of them. The wind snatched at his sleeves and the hem of his robe, but it didn't touch his hair, which led Lindon to take a closer look.

The pale strands gleamed slightly in the light, and each hair seemed somehow thicker than normal, now that he looked closely. After a second of inspection, he realized what he was seeing: metal wire.

The Goldsign of the Jai clan.

"Jai Daishou!" Eithan said happily. "What brings you down the mountain on this fine autumn morning?"

Jai Daishou kept his gaze fixed on Eithan, never so much as glancing at Lindon or the servants streaming around him. "I was told you would arrive today, and I wanted to offer my greetings in person."

"How generous of you! Please, allow me to introduce the two newest members of my family. This is Yerin, the top-ranked student of the outer family, and Lindon. The second-ranked."

A feather-light touch brushed across Lindon's spirit, and the old man's wrinkles creased into a frown. "Second."

"I ranked them myself! Lindon, Yerin, this is Jai Daishou, the seventh Underlord of the Blackflame Empire."

"And Patriarch of the Jai clan," Jai Daishou added, his frown deepening.

"Ah, that's right. He is also the Patriarch of the third-ranked of the three great clans." Eithan's smile was sunny.

Jai Daishou examined the other Underlord for a long moment. "I don't know if you've heard, but your family's performance in the city has slipped while you've been gone. I can only imagine what it's like over the rest of the empire, without your personal supervision to guide them."

Lindon rubbed sweaty palms on the inside of his pocket, keeping his eyes down lest he attract the Jai Patriarch's attention. Of all the things he had expected to happen when they landed, he had never imagined he would end up between two Underlords in conflict.

He flicked a glance at Yerin, but she was glaring at Jai Daishou openly, arms crossed and Goldsign quivering.

"I'm quite pleased with how the family performed in my absence," Eithan said.

Jai Daishou's attention briefly touched on Lindon and Yerin, and he let out a soft noise of disapproval. "An Underlord should have higher standards."

"Really?" Eithan sounded baffled. "I've always thought my standards were too high. Well, let me know if the Arelius family can help you defend your territory in the upcoming days. Jai Long can be quite a threat...unless, of course, you intend to take action yourself."

That sounded to Lindon like the only genuinely pleasant comment Eithan had made over the whole exchange, but Jai Daishou bristled as though Eithan had insulted his children. "The Highgolds of the Jai clan are more than capable of dealing with an exile."

"I'm relieved to hear it! I knew you wouldn't be forced into action by a single Highgold." The Jai Underlord's face darkened further, but Eithan laughed harder than Lindon thought was appropriate, eventually tapering off and wiping a tear from his eye. "Ah, it's refreshing to have such a friendly conversation."

Jai Daishou had the look of a man about to set a house on fire.

Eithan gave his opposite a shallow bow. "I know it's been brief, but I appreciate you seeking an audience with me so quickly. When I have more time, I'll be happy to pay your

Jai clan a visit in return."

He turned, dragging Yerin and Lindon with him, and started walking away before Jai Daishou had a chance to say anything. Lindon couldn't stop himself from glancing back, to see how the enemy Underlord would take the insult.

The Jai Patriarch folded his hands behind his back again.

Then, suddenly, Lindon's body weighed five times as much. Air rushed from his lungs as his knees slammed into the stone of the courtyard, his head bowing as though a giant palm pressed on his spine.

He gritted his teeth and spent all of his madra to Enforce his body. Even with his full strength, he only lifted his head a fraction.

It wasn't just Lindon. Everyone was on the ground; children cried, splayed out on the stone. A wagon had dumped over, spilling garbage onto the street, and most people he could see were gasping for breath.

Yerin's jaw was set, and she was very deliberately breathing in and out, but she was on her hands and knees just like he was. Even Eithan's knees were bent, his hands held out for balance, his smile gone. The strain showed on his face.

Lindon couldn't take a breath. His mouth gaped, but it was as though the air had turned to stone.

"I have done you honor by speaking to you in person," Jai Daishou said calmly. "Don't spit in my face, Eleven."

Eithan raised his hands and pulled against the air, as though he were trying to pry open an invisible door. He strained for a long moment before, finally, something gave.

The pressure vanished. Lindon gulped down a deep breath. Eithan staggered to lean against the statue of the First Patriarch, red-faced and panting.

Jai Daishou's lip twitched into the first stage of a smile. "You have had a long journey. When you recover, come see me, and I will grant you an audience."

He departed, striding off through the courtyard at his own speed, paying no heed to the servants who scurried out of his way.

When Lindon had recovered himself, he looked to Eithan. In joining the Arelius family, he'd picked up their enemies and rivals as well, and Eithan might not be capable of protecting an Iron from significant threats. Maybe Lindon would be safer if he stayed further away from the Underlord.

But as soon as Jai Daishou rounded a corner far away, Eithan stopped breathing heavily. He straightened his back, smile returning to its place.

When he saw Lindon's concern, he winked. "People here are all so concerned with high rankings. I've always felt that you get more done when you're not in the spotlight, don't you think?"

Yerin rolled her shoulder in its socket. "It's too late to save face. You were hauling like a plow-horse."

Eithan laughed. "I was, wasn't I? Well, maybe I have provoked too strong of an opponent this time." He didn't sound too concerned about the possibility. Reaching into his pocket, he flipped Yerin something that looked like a wooden coin. "Yerin, have one of the servants direct you to the refinery. Show them that token, and ask them for a Purple Feather Elixir."

She brightened immediately. "This will smooth my path to Highgold?"

"Your path to Highgold is very smooth, if only you would listen to me, but this will help you advance your madra base *without* tapping into your Remnant. Cycle as much as you can over the next three or four days, until the pill wears off."

Yerin gripped the token in her fist and ran off without another word.

"What about me?" Lindon asked hopefully. He had received a dozen Four Corners Rotation Pills over the course of the journey, though their effects had begun to fade during the last week or two. But if Eithan had something more powerful in reserve, Lindon wanted a taste of it.

Eithan rubbed his hands together in apparent anticipation. "You and I, Lindon, are headed for my personal favorite room in the entire city: the Arelius family library."

Jai Long hopped down from the back of his bat, sliding down its bristly gray-white fur to the ground. His boots crunched on sand.

All around him, the Sandvipers landed their own mounts. Gokren rode a bat just like his, which had been generously donated by the Jai clan, but the others traveled on Thousand-Mile Clouds of various colors, or flying constructs, or various treasures. Most of their equipment had followed them in a levitating cauldron big enough to stew five men, but it was lagging a day behind.

He ignored the rest of the group, heading straight to a white Thousand-Mile Cloud with a tent erected on it.

Inside, Jai Chen was struggling to sit upright. "Are we... stopping...already?" she asked, her voice soft but threaded with effort.

Jai Long grabbed her by the shoulder, helping her sit up. He wanted to unravel the red bandages around his head and speak to his sister face-to-face, but he needed Sandviper loyalty enough that he didn't want to scare them off.

"We're here," he said, and she lit up. He scooped her out of the tent, pretending not to hear her protests that her hair wasn't straight.

She had suffered the indignities of travel without protest, and now he carried her to look out over the desert. Into the sun, which rose behind a black mountain. At the city of dragon's bone.

This was her first glance of Serpent's Grave in almost ten years, and she covered her mouth and teared up at the sight. Their parents lived in the city somewhere, as did their brothers and sisters.

She smiled at him, wide and open and tinged with grief. Jai Long knew she was glad to be home, despite everything, even if the sight of her birthplace pierced her like a sword.

Behind his mask of bandages, he smiled too.

For very different reasons.

CHAPTER NINE

Lindon had spent much of the past five years working in the Wei clan archives. He was confident he knew what a library was supposed to look like.

But this room, located behind and beneath the bone tower that housed Cassias' family, was just a twenty-foot by twenty-foot square box. It had only one door, and all the walls were pale, yellowed bone. On the ceiling, a few scripted circles glowed with runelight, illuminating every corner.

A small altar of bone rose from the center of the room like an arm, with a claw cupping a ball the size of Lindon's fist. The ball was made of copper plates, and he thought he saw whirring flashes of color between the plates.

All in all, it was nothing like a library.

Eithan waited with hands on hips, clearly anticipating Lindon's reaction.

"Are the books...in the walls?" Lindon finally asked.

The Underlord clicked his tongue. "What are books but a mechanism to store knowledge? If we have something much more efficient available," -Eithan picked up the copper ball— "then why would we need books?"

Lindon peered at the ball. It was a construct of some kind, obviously, but beyond that he couldn't guess. Maybe it would project words onto the wall—some of his mother's White Fox constructs could do as much, crafting images from illusions.

"This is the single most valuable object the entire Arelius family owns," he said, spinning it on the tip of one finger. "Most of us aren't aware of that, but it's true. We primarily use the powers of our bloodline to find areas that need cleaning or maintenance, but as an...unintentional side effect...we also tend to collect other information."

He tossed the ball from hand to hand. "All of that information pertinent to the sacred arts—including secrets about the Paths of our rivals—is stored in here. Some of it also gets copied into dream tablets, scrolls, books, and so forth, but *everything* goes here."

That was intriguing. If they could study the sacred arts of their enemies, they could walk into any battle with the upper hand. If Jai Long's sacred arts were in there...

"How do we get it out?" Lindon asked.

"Well, first, you have to be a blood member of the Arelius family." Eithan continued tossing the ball in his left hand and touched the right against his chest. "Fortunately for you, I am. The original Patriarch left this treasure for his descendants, and they have learned from it and added to it one generation at a time."

"That's incredible. Truly, it's a treasure that I'm honored even to lay my eyes on. But how do we get it—"

Eithan didn't do anything Lindon could see, but the copper plates slowly pushed out from the center of the ball. A light flashed red.

And suddenly a featureless, crimson man stood in the center of the room.

It looked like a Remnant left behind by one of the wooden training dummies: a head without a face, body slender and unremarkable, limbs lifeless and smooth. It was solid red, without details or distinguishing marks.

"Your Path of Twin Stars interests me," Eithan said, spinning the expanded ball in one hand. He muttered something to the orb, and it flashed again.

The red man came to life, crouching on the balls of its feet and raising both hands. It pivoted, driving one hand forward and low, and a pulse of barely-visible madra extended from the blow. An Empty Palm.

Lindon stared at the scarlet mannequin hard enough to burn a hole through it. Never mind looking at his enemy's abilities—if he could study his *own* techniques like this, watching them from the outside in...how much could he learn? He could perfect his every movement.

"There are possibilities for the Path of Twin Stars in the future," Eithan said. "Pure madra is rare enough that it has many advantages, which you've already realized...but it also has quite a few disadvantages."

Another flash, and this time a green man appeared, its hands wreathed in flame. The first figure, the red one, stepped forward to deliver an Empty Palm to its opponent's core...

...and the green figure grabbed it by the face with burning hands. The scarlet head winked out, leaving the red man with bare shoulders.

"As a Path, it has remarkable utility, but it leaves you practically defenseless," Eithan went on. The copper ball flashed red, and the red man stood—whole and alone—in the center of the room once again. "It also happens to be slow to advance, since you can't take in aura while cycling. You must rely on purifying your own madra and increasing it with external factors. Elixirs and such."

Eithan leaned against the wall, smiling, the ball tucked under one arm. "So...I know you're aware of these problems, and you've thought of some possible solutions. What are your thoughts?"

Lindon had assumed Eithan was heading somewhere, and he was still fascinated by the possibilities of the red man and the copper ball. The question left him flat-footed.

"I know I need to develop more techniques, so...if you have some pure madra techniques in there..."

"That's a good line of thinking, and we should come back to that in the future. But we have roughly ten to eleven months before you have to fight Jai Long." Eithan shrugged. "Let's call it ten, to leave some margin for error. Ten months, and you will fight someone so much stronger than you that he may as well be a living dragon, as far as you're concerned. What do you do about that?"

"I need a second Path," Lindon said immediately. "It was one of my first ideas for my second core: you leave one pure, and fill the other with another aspect of madra. But I'm not sure if I can—"

"It's not perfect," Eithan interrupted. "Everyone thinks of learning a second Path at some point, though usually they want to learn another set of techniques compatible with the madra they've already cultivated. You know why that rarely works, don't you?"

"There's only so much time in the day," Lindon said. "And only so many resources you can dedicate to advancement. Instead of ending up twice as powerful, you end up half as skilled in two areas."

"That's all true," Eithan said. "But?"

"But...it's difficult to find someone to train you in two different Paths?"

"That's also true, but it's not what I was getting at. You've explained why learning two Paths is difficult...*but* it isn't impossible. It can be done."

Lindon searched Eithan's face, looking for signs that this was a joke, or a trick, or a setup of some kind. "How?"

"Oh, it's just as you said." He waved the copper ball lazily. "You need to work twice as hard, or spend twice as much time, or have access to twice as many resources, or preferably all three. But I think learning another Path is exactly what you need to do."

The ball flashed, and the green man showed back up, its fists once again surrounded by flame. But this time, the red man took a defensive pose, hands up and protecting its body.

"The Path of Twin Stars has plenty of room to grow," Eithan said, and as the green man drove its fiery fists forward, the red man caught both burning hands in its own.

The fire went out.

The red man followed with a kick to the lower abdomen, the air rippled with colorless madra, and the green man staggered.

That had looked like an Empty Palm executed through a kick. Lindon had tried that on the dummy targets, but his control over his own madra wasn't anywhere close to good enough to execute something like that.

And how could pure madra cancel techniques?

"Would you show that again?" Lindon asked, but both figures vanished. The red man returned to the center of the room a moment later, blank and still.

"You can't take your Path forward until you learn the basics of the sacred arts," Eithan said. "Learn how other Paths work first, and carry those lessons over to the Path of Twin Stars."

Lindon moved his gaze from the motionless red man to Eithan. The Underlord *seemed* to be saying that he could start from step one with a brand new Path and fight Jai Long...in ten months.

Which even Lindon thought was absurd.

"Forgiveness. That sounds too good to be true."

Eithan's smile gleamed. "It's not impossible."

Lindon took a deep breath, his mind whirling with possibilities. "I'll need to spend all my time cycling. Will I have time to learn the techniques properly? Ah, before that, what Path should I learn?"

"That's up to you."

He should have expected Eithan to keep stringing him along, but he didn't even know how to respond. How many Paths were out there? Which could he learn?

His first thought was the Path of the White Fox, but he didn't know if even the Arelius family would have information on Sacred Valley. Or if illusions could defeat Jai Long at all.

"I have many plans," Eithan said, "and many ideas. But I've long believed that it's better for someone to choose their own direction and then accept guidance than to be pushed where I want them to go. Now, I'm willing to show you any sort of Path you like...but I wait for your direction. The world of sacred arts lies open to you. What Path would you like to see?"

"Jai Long's," Lindon said immediately.

Eithan nodded. "Good choice."

The copper plates around the ball spun, and suddenly white light was running in loops through the center of the red man's belly and chest. Lindon could see it as though the figure's flesh had become transparent, and he recognized the patterns: madra channels. It was using an Enforcer technique.

A moment later, straight lines formed on red skin, sliding from the core out to the limbs.

"You're fighting Jai Long," Eithan said. "He was trained in the Path of the Stellar Spear, the signature Path of his clan."

The red man extended one hand, and a red spear fell into its hand. A thrust drove the spear forward, then swept it to the side, fighting an invisible opponent. Spinning the spear, the man moved faster and faster, occasionally blasting a river of white light that splashed harmlessly against the bone wall. As he fought, needles of that same white madra formed over his shoulder, shooting off as soon as they were completed.

An Enforcer technique for speed, a Striker technique to attack, and a Forger technique to defend and cover its movements.

"However, he deviated by bonding a Remnant with subtly different aspects. Now..." The pattern on the scarlet skin changed from straight lines to twisting, serpentine lines. The figure spun its spear just like before, but the spearhead left a trail of white light that hung in the air and came to life.

Like a pale Remnant, the serpent of Forged madra turned to Lindon and opened its jaws in a silent hiss.

The red man traced curls of light through the room, like a man painting on a canvas, until it was surrounded by a spiraling nest of snakes.

"Imbuing Forged madra with temporary life is an advanced technique, far beyond Jai Long. He can only produce this result because he absorbed a Remnant from a Path we'll call...unnatural." Lindon reached up for one of the snakes, to see if the lines of color were illusions or actual Forged madra.

"Treat each snake as though it's made of razor-sharp wire," Eithan said, and Lindon snatched his hand back. "In the fight, I mean. Jai Long will use these to cover his approach—" Suddenly the figure lunged for Lindon, who flattened himself against a wall. The shining white serpents covered the entire room; there was nowhere else for him to go.

"—to block your escape—" Eithan continued, and just as Lindon tried to slide under the light, the red man swept his spear up from the ground and walled him off with white madra.

"—and to corner you for the kill." A snake coiled and snapped at the tip of Lindon's nose.

Though he knew it was a training exercise, Lindon's heart was still hammering. Gingerly, he passed a corner of his sleeve through the light. When it survived unharmed, he tried with a finger.

He felt nothing; no heat, no resistance. With his other hand, he passed through the red man, and once again it was like waving his hand through only air. It *was* just like the Path of the White Fox, then. Forgers could make solid illusions, and Strikers could produce foxfire, but in the end it was all only light and dreams.

He let out a breath he didn't know he'd been holding.

"This isn't even his only technique," Eithan said conversationally. "Just his most common one. If we get you to Lowgold, perhaps your Empty Palm technique could affect him...but he would never allow you that close. In a thousand fights, you would fail a thousand times."

Eithan stopped talking, and all the slithering lights left by Jai Long's techniques vanished. The red man reappeared in its starting position, empty-handed.

Lindon waited for his heart to return to a healthy rhythm before he rose back up the wall to his feet. "So then. I need a second Path that covers for my weaknesses and targets Jai Long's." He hesitated for a moment. "Or...I'm not sure how to ask, but are there any...famous, or especially powerful Paths out there?" The myths and legends of Sacred Valley were filled with tales of unbeatable Paths, so if those really existed, Lindon didn't want to be stuck with a mundane one.

Eithan raised one eyebrow. "You think you need a *special* Path? Are ordinary Paths not good enough to meet your esteemed estimation?"

Lindon ducked his head. "I knew it was childish to ask, excuse me. I only wanted—"

"No, you were right. Powerful Paths, coming right up."

The ball flashed emerald, and the green man reappeared. This time, this one held the spear, and as it twirled the weapon, the spearhead shone like a star. The Path of the Stellar Spear, though Lindon couldn't tell if it was the original version or Jai Long's twisted one.

The red man cupped its hand and gathered a ball of deep purple light. The technique trembled against invisible restraints, as though pushing against the air, and an equally vivid purple sword appeared in his left hand. The weapon crackled and shook, also straining against some unseen bond.

"Path of the Broken Star," Eithan announced. "This Path branched off into the Stellar Spear many generations ago, and the original is far more...potent."

The green man started off defensive, weaving a net of squirming snakes behind, just as Jai Long could do.

The red man disappeared, leaving a violet shadow of Broken Star madra behind. When the scarlet figure reappeared, there was a gap sliced in the barrier and a hole driven through the green man's chest.

"Jai Long might last a little longer than that," Eithan said, "but not too much so. If you mastered the Path of the Broken Star, you'd make a splash throughout the Empire."

The featureless figure still hadn't extinguished its sword, and it buzzed and crackled in the air.

Lindon was tempted to choose this one instantly, but he couldn't pass up the opportunity to see what else was on offer.

"Now, disadvantages: it demands exacting madra control, its techniques are notoriously difficult to apply in real-world situations, and there's only one place to train it: a secret city long lost to the Jai clan."

Lindon felt suddenly cheated. "If we can't find it..."

"It's lost to the *Jai* clan. Not to me. While it would give me great pleasure to see you defeat their heir with the Path they've been desperately hunting for centuries, it *would* take us at least three months to gain access. That leaves you seven months to go from ignorant initiate to skilled sacred artist, and I...well, let's say that you would have the chance to surprise me."

Watching the purple blade, Lindon had to wonder. If there was another way to delay Jai Long or put off this confrontation, maybe he could find the time he needed to learn. It was worth considering.

The red man flickered and reset to the middle of the room, his Forged weapon gone. The green man reappeared, once again spinning Jai Long's spear.

Eithan continued for the better part of an hour. He demonstrated the Path of Crawling Shades, which would turn Lindon's shadow into a symbiotic Remnant of darkness that devoured enemy techniques. He shows off the Path of Twisting Rivers, which used a technique of combined Ruler and Striker disciplines to accelerate Forged water until it sliced through steel.

The Path of the Last Oath was designed *for* and *by* Soulsmiths, and relied on Forging basic constructs on the fly and using them like disposable puppets. With its power, Lindon could counteract Jai Long's shining serpents and bury him beneath the weight of his own improvised minions. The Path of Grasping Sky would allow him to grip Jai

Long with a Ruler technique and then crush his windpipe as a Striker.

Lindon was very intrigued by the possibilities—and by the vast emerald wingspan that came with it—until Eithan told him that the Grasping Sky was the Path of the imperial clan.

Lindon preferred not to make more enemies than necessary, so he reluctantly set that Path aside.

Eithan snapped his fingers as though something had occurred to him. "You know, if Paths of the nobility interest you, I do have one last possibility..."

A dull flash, and the red man reappeared. This time, its hands were swallowed by a substance that looked like black fire, or a thick concentration of inky smoke. The black was streaked with scarlet, so that the figure held two handfuls of dark and bloody rolling flame.

That caught Lindon's interest immediately. The fireballs were intimidating, and this fit his image of a sacred artist: conjuring balls of strange-colored fire. His own clan had used purple foxfire for centuries.

"The Blackflame family united this empire, and ruled it until the Naru took over only five decades ago."

The green man raised his spear, but the red one blasted it apart, a bar of dark fire slicing through emerald flesh. The technique sliced through him like a red-hot blade through snow.

"Their power came from the dragons that originally roamed these lands. It's one part fire to one part pure destruction."

This time, after the green man died, it came back in seconds. It wove a net of twisting serpents in the air with its spearhead.

Black flames ate through the technique, and then the enemy.

"It's not versatile at all, really. It's a potent, violent Path designed for war. Its chief advantage is that it doesn't demand a great degree of control; the main technique involves spraying fire in the general direction of something you want to destroy. Doesn't require much finesse."

The green man appeared again, moving to strike the red man in a blink, but it passed through a curtain of black flames and died once more.

"Children of the Blackflame family were deadly threats even at Copper."

Lindon waited for the hook. He didn't like the rigid nature of the Path much; those techniques were made for blowing things apart, and nothing else. He would prefer something with some subtlety to it, some creativity.

But it did offer him exactly what he was lacking: the ability to break through Jai Long's techniques. And it didn't demand expertise, just a basic competence in Striker techniques.

It appeared to be exactly what he needed.

"There have to be some disadvantages," he said.

"Oh, of course there are. There's a reason why the family lost the Empire and all but died out: this madra eats away at your body as you use it. Blackflames tended to lose their reason in their later years, or else they ended up twisted husks. Their bodies couldn't keep up with their power."

Eithan waited expectantly, and Lindon soon caught on. "But mine..."

"The Bloodforged Iron body is tailor-made to resist corrosive breakdown like this, though it *will* burn through your madra like a bonfire through dry leaves. So you won't be able to rely on that for long."

"Didn't the Blackflame family have bodies like mine?" The resources for Lindon's Bloodforged Iron body had come from a cave in the Desolate Wilds; he had to assume a rich clan from an empire would have the means to do even better.

"They chose their bodies to maximize combat potential, but you? You just need to survive. A real Blackflame disciple might tear you apart head-to-head, but *you* won't lose control of your limbs by the age of sixty. You also have the advantage of a second core, and switching to Blackflame only as needed will minimize the strain. So long as you take the time to cleanse your channels after using Blackflame madra extensively, it shouldn't eat into your lifespan at all."

Then it *was* perfect for him. "Why did you show me those other Paths, if you were going to lead me to this one all along?"

Eithan put on a shocked look. "I am a man of my word. If you decide you want to learn another of these fine Paths, then by all means, I will accept your decision."

Lindon stood, considering. The Grasping Sky was eliminated because of its political implications, the Crawling Shade because it would make Lindon look too sinister to trust. The Last Oath was purely defensive, which wasn't what he needed to win a duel. Broken Star would take too long to find.

"What about Jade Rivers?" Lindon asked.

"Oh, absolutely! Absolutely. As long as you think you can perfectly master a combination Ruler, Striker, Forger technique in the next ten months. And if you think you can evade a Truegold's attacks while taking five seconds to prepare that technique, yes. A fine choice."

Lindon rubbed his forehead and gave in. "The Path of Black Flame, is it?"

"Since the only family ever to use it was the Blackflames, that's what we commonly call it. Either the Blackflame Path or the Path of Black," he exaggerated the pause, "Flame. We like our names simple here."

"Is that family going to come after me for using it?"

"Who cares what they think? They're dead. Mostly."

"...mostly?"

"And I doubt the Imperial clan will be *incredibly* happy about us demonstrating the powers of their predecessor in public, so we're left with that little problem, but that's a minor detail. It isn't illegal to practice the Blackflame Path, unlike the Path of Grasping Sky."

"That was *illegal?*"

"There are only a few places to harvest Blackflame aura in the entire Empire, but to our spectacular good fortune, the Path was created right here in Serpent's Grave!"

Lindon looked around the room. "We can practice here?"

"Not in this exact spot, no. What you're looking for is a location that naturally flows with the aura you'd like to practice. In this case, something that resonates with both fire and destruction. Destruction is one of the most difficult aspects of aura to find and cultivate, but fortunately for us, dragons radiate just as much of that as they do heat."

Seeing the bones of a dragon was one thing, but Eithan seemed to be implying something entirely different.

"Pardon, but it sounds like we're going to see a *real* dragon." It was like learning he was about to feed a lion by hand: a unique experience, but far more terrifying than anything else.

"There's a cave in this very city where the Arelius family has sealed a descendant of the ancient dragons, and that cave is filled with such madra! What luck!"

Lindon finally caught on. "By chance, does that cave happen to be Underground Chamber Number Three?"

Eithan beamed and clapped him on the back. "By now, my servants should have the seals undone and a medical team standing by. After you!"

CHAPTER TEN

Sand blew in waves against a cliff of black stone. A cave mouth opened into the mountain, rough and round, as though it had been chewed into the rock by a worm twice the height of a man. A script encircling the entrance shone scarlet, and though there was no door, a red haze rippled in the air—visible even without Lindon's Copper sight.

"There's a door deeper in, though the servants will have opened that for us," Eithan explained as they approached. A huge stone had been rolled away from the entry, resting now to the side. "We don't want to hold it open for long. You can never be too careful when you're trying to prevent deadly beasts from escaping."

Lindon gripped the straps of his pack tighter, feeling the weight of his halfsilver dagger in his pocket.

Half a dozen sacred artists in various uniforms dropped to their knees as Eithan approached, all of them wearing the colors of the Arelius family. One servant stood apart, outside the haze of the entryway, bowing at the waist.

"The scriptors have undone the prime seals," he said. "Two stand ready to repair the script in the event of a breach, and three of the servants before you are trained healers with madra of blood and life. They lived through the fall of the Blackflames, and they should be able to counteract the Path's powers if you make it outside."

"Exemplary work as always, One-Thirteen," Eithan said, pulling out his iron scissors to snip a stray thread from the servant's outer robe. "Keep it up, and soon I'll have to start using your name. Do you have any—"

He was interrupted by a deep, bass roar that rumbled up from underground. It resonated in Lindon's chest, and he thought he could feel the sand beneath his shoes shaking.

He slipped one hand into his pocket for Suriel's marble, rolling its smooth, warm surface between his fingers.

"Agitated today, is he?" Eithan asked.

"His handlers say that company soothes him," One-Thirteen responded, with a nervous glance behind him. "It seems they haven't had any volunteers since Lady Nakali lost her leg."

"Ah, well, I can't say I blame them. Though the Soulsmiths made her a fine prosthetic, didn't they?"

"No expense was spared, I'm told, although surely she misses her flesh and blood."

"Well, at least she can roast meat on her kneecap now. That should be some comfort." The roar came again, and this time the cave mouth darkened with a red, smoky light. Eithan sighed. "I'm back now, so I'll do my best to relax him. If all goes according to plan, I may have a permanent solution for you."

The servant turned to regard the entry, but Lindon got the impression he was trying to look anywhere but at Eithan. "Underlord, if you don't mind, the handlers wanted me to remind you of the...merciful solution. He has rendered us great service, and it seems honorable to grant him rest. Please pardon my disrespect."

Eithan rolled his shoulders and placed his palm against one of the runes on the side of the doorway. A ripple of almost-visible madra, and the light of the script died. "In this instance, One-Thirteen, I would rather extend grace than mercy."

The haze in the entrance dissipated, and wind billowed out of the tunnel. The air outside had a slight chill to it—though there was no snow in Serpent's Grave, winter was almost upon them—but the breath of the cave felt like it was blowing from the door of a lit oven.

Servants bowed them inside, and as soon as Lindon and Eithan had passed the entrance, the field generated by the script sprang up behind them.

They walked down a long stone tunnel, its sides and floor scraped rough by the passing of ages.

"Who are we going to see?" Lindon asked, because asking *what* they were going to see felt somehow rude.

"We are going to meet Orthos, one of the family's oldest and most stalwart allies." Eithan spoke with a wistful sadness, though his smile lingered. "Long before my time as Patriarch, Orthos served as a liaison between the Arelius and the imperial Blackflame family. Only ten years ago, he overused his power defending us from attack."

Eithan waved a hand. "Defending *them* from attack. Had I been here...Ah, as I was saying, Orthos' own madra overwhelmed his mind. He gave too much of himself for the sake of protecting my family. The branch heads spent a fortune trying to restore him, to their credit, but it was eventually decided to end his misery."

Another roar shook the stone around them, and a ruddy light welled up from deeper in the twisting corridor. This time, Lindon thought he heard pain in it.

"I arrived around that time, and I countermanded the order. I can't say they were wrong for trying to spare him years of suffering, and some within the family think I'm cruel even now to keep him alive. But if there's a chance to restore him, we owe it to him to try until we can try no longer." His voice turned grim. "I've ended lives to avert suffering before, and sometimes it is inevitable. But it's never a decision to make lightly."

Lindon was still curious about Orthos, but a different question took priority. "If you'll allow me a rude question,

I have wondered for some time now: are you not from the Blackflame Empire?"

"Not entirely," Eithan responded easily. "I spent most of my childhood in Blackflame City, as I believe I've told you before, but I was *born* half a world away. The Arelius family is a wide tree, my young adopted brother, with many roots. I've only returned to the Blackflame branch for...six, almost seven years now."

The tunnel was starting to even out, with the red glow becoming slightly brighter. The air seemed to buzz against Lindon's skin, with a slight tingling vibration that he thought would soon grow uncomfortable.

"Incredible that you rose to the head of the family in that time," Lindon said.

Eithan chuckled and adjusted his shimmering red-and-gold collar. "Oh, they couldn't promote me fast enough. Having an Underlord at the head puts them on the same level as the three great clans, so I would improve our standing even if I spent all day drinking peach wine and eating honeydrops. But although I do make a dashing figurehead, I prefer to take more...hands-on control of the family's operations."

Lindon couldn't help a pang of sympathy for the Arelius family elders. Or "branch heads"—whatever they were called here in the Empire. Trying to prop Eithan up as a puppet leader seemed like trying to saddle a whirlwind.

When the tunnel ended, it didn't open up as broadly as Lindon had expected. Instead of a huge room, he found himself at the juncture between five other tunnels, all similar to the first. The ceiling was barely over his head, and the rock looked as though it had been chewed to a sharp edge. The air here sizzled even more strongly than outside, until it felt like insects crawled over every inch of his exposed skin.

The moment they arrived, footsteps like drumbeats approached, along with a sullen glow the color of live embers. Lindon clenched and unclenched his fists, cycling his madra in preparation for a fight, and kept his mind on the dagger in his pocket.

But what good would any of that do against a dragon?

"Bid welcome," Eithan announced, "to the last great descendant of Serpent's Grave."

A massive black shape shouldered its way through the tunnel like a man pushing through a tight doorway. It turned blazing eyes on Lindon: they were inky pools of darkness, those eyes, with a circle of furious red where the iris should be.

The skin of the creature's reptilian head was cracked and leathery, pure black, and clusters of blazing embers burned on its back.

By the light it carried with it, Lindon saw the creature clearly.

"Is this...is this what a dragon looks like?" Lindon whispered.

"A dragon? No, no, I said it was a *descendant* of dragons." Eithan threw out a hand in presentation. "Orthos is clearly a magnificent turtle."

Lindon had wondered if the shadows were playing tricks on his eyes.

Orthos was a massive black turtle, the peak of his shell rising as high as Lindon's head. He was as long as a horse but thrice as wide, and his squat body looked heavy enough to sink a ship. The facets of his shell glowed sullen red around the edges, and black smoke rose from him in hazy waves.

He locked eyes with Lindon, growling like an avalanche. Lindon cycled desperately, pulling his dagger into sweaty hands, ready to dive behind the column in the center of the chamber.

Orthos' mouth dropped open, his jaw gaping so wide it looked unnatural, and smoky red light began to rise up his throat.

"Some days are better than others," Eithan said, stepping between Lindon and the draconic turtle. "He recognizes me on occasion, and will even guide my servants through the tunnels. But other times..."

Black fire billowed out of the turtle's mouth, filling the

walls with oppressive heat and a prickling so sharp it became painful. Lindon's eyes watered, and he pushed himself against the column of stone.

Eithan swiped his hand in a single gesture, blasting the Blackflame madra apart like a gust of wind tearing through a cloud. "Be polite, Orthos. You have a guest."

The light in the turtle's eyes turned orange, like a living flame, and he roared his defiance. Lindon dropped the half-silver dagger to the ground in his haste to clap hands over his ears.

And Eithan moved forward, shoving the sacred beast's mouth closed with both hands. The roar cut off with a snap.

"I know it is difficult," Eithan said, his nose inches away from the turtle's. "But gather yourself and *hear me*. A boy has come to train here. He is one of the family." Orthos struggled, but couldn't escape the implacable grip of the Underlord. "He could help us, do you understand?"

Orthos' eyes finally moved up to Eithan's, and crimson irises dimmed into a look of helpless confusion.

Finally, the turtle growled once, and Eithan released him. "I'm sorry for getting rough. If this works as I intend, you could both learn from one another."

"Bond..." the sacred beast said, in a voice like a rumbling volcano.

Despite Lindon's encounters with Elder Whisper, it still surprised him to hear a six-foot turtle speak.

Evidently that one word exhausted Orthos' energy, because his eyelids fluttered and then slid closed. He sank down onto his belly, letting out a breath like a furnace.

"That's the plan," Eithan said, patting the leathery head. "As I said, Lindon, this place is rich in aura of fire and destruction. I could teach you the Blackflame Path, and you could cycle here, work hard, and eventually grow into a fine sacred artist."

"I am eager to learn," Lindon said. "I know there is no shortcut for work." Ten months wasn't much time, but he was resolved to at least *try* to master sacred arts the orthodox way.

At least until that failed him.

"...instead of all that, I'd like to take a shortcut," Eithan continued.

Lindon let out a sigh of relief.

"Building up aura in your core takes time. You cycle aura every day, a fraction of that aura is converted to madra, and your core slowly transforms to produce madra of that aspect on its own." He waved a hand. "Since we have a deadline, I want you to share madra with my friend here."

"Of course," Lindon said, thinking of the scales he had Forged for Fisher Gesha. "Allow me a few days to gather some."

"I like that attitude, but I think you may have misunderstood me. As I said, Orthos is plagued by a buildup of Blackflame madra in his system, ravaging his mind and his body. We bring him purified madra to cleanse his channels, but it's like sprinkling water on a bonfire. However, if we can *link* your core with his..." Eithan spread his hands. "He gets relief from the burden of his immense power, and you get a piece of that power for yourself. It's a win all around."

Lindon looked to the turtle hesitantly. "Do I just...pour madra into him, or..."

"Even easier than that. There's a contract that humans can make with sacred beasts, and it functions in a similar manner to a soul oath: two spirits binding themselves to one another. It must be mutual, just like an oath. And it's typically done while both the contractor and the contracted beast are young, so the child's madra is pure and the beast's madra has not yet fully developed."

Eithan ran his hand over the smoldering shell, evidently not the slightest bit worried about burning himself. "Orthos is almost three hundred years old. Far from a hatchling, even by the standards of his line. If he were to share his power with a child, the child's body would quite literally explode."

That image did nothing to soothe Lindon's misgivings. "But that's what you want *me* to do?"

Orthos snorted. His eyelids fluttered, and his shell flared red. Eithan snatched his hand away and took a careful step back.

"There are some risks, to be sure. If Orthos is too far gone to consent, the contract will fail. There's the chance that it will work at *first,* but it won't be enough to save him. In that case, you'll still have your Blackflame core, but we'll have to put him down after all. You'll bond his Remnant at Gold."

The turtle slowly rose to his feet, and the temperature in the cave rose another few degrees.

Eithan moved between Lindon and Orthos, shaking out his sleeves in preparation to use some technique. "However, if this works as I hope it will, you won't need his Remnant at all. Instead, when you're ready to break through to Gold, he will use his power to help you bridge that gap."

Lindon wanted to walk forward, but the creature's sheer size, overwhelming heat, and the uncomfortable needle-prickling of destruction aura kept him where he was. "Is this still my choice?"

"Certainly. You have a choice between sharing the power of an ancient dragon-beast or, instead, spending three hours a day in meditative cycling until you can begin to touch the faintest whiff of Blackflame power."

Lindon marched up and placed his hand on the turtle's head.

His madra slipped into the sacred beast with no resistance—an advantage of pure madra. Orthos' madra was black and blood-red twined together, dark and hungry, like a malevolent wildfire. Lindon almost broke contact immediately; the turtle's spirit was so overwhelming and unrestrained that he was sure it would consume his madra instantly.

Black eyes filled with circles of shining red swiveled up, meeting Lindon.

"It's not a complicated technique," Eithan said. "Swear to share your core with him, and to accept his power in return." After another second, he added, "I've found that saying it aloud helps the process. That goes for you, too, Orthos."

"I swear to open my core to you and share my power," Lindon said, though he was ashamed to hear his voice quaver a little. The hand on Orthos' head was starting to get uncomfortably hot.

Orthos' mouth slid open. Thick, inky flames gathered in the back of his throat, streaked with red like blood.

Eithan moved forward. Lindon took a step back, half-lifting his hand away from the sacred beast's head.

"*I swear,*" the turtle thundered, in a voice that slammed into Lindon's ears.

A stream of pure madra flowed from his strongest core, sucked away beyond his control. Lindon stumbled back, releasing his touch, but the bond between their souls did not break. Orthos drank in his power until the core was almost empty.

Then a black-and-red river plunged into Lindon, burning through his madra channels like molten iron through his veins. It didn't hurt nearly as much as he felt it should have; the worst part wasn't pain, it was the feeling that his spirit was burning up. Crisping and blackening like a leaf in a fire. That he was dying, hollowed out.

Everything that was *Lindon* was burning away.

"Heaven and Earth Purification Wheel!" Eithan shouted.

Lindon was still staring at his burning core as though at the stump of his own hand. His mind couldn't process it aside from a sense of numbing horror.

But Eithan's words shook him awake.

He dropped to his knees, picturing the stone wheel, pushing it harder than he ever had before. *Now* came the pain, scorching his soul in a way that was more than merely physical, but the fire helped him as well as hurt. Every rotation of the wheel drew in more Blackflame madra like a spindle gathering thread.

He could hardly breathe, but that didn't bother him now.

All his mind, soul, and will was focused on the heavy stone wheel, churning away.

Either this would work, or the dark fire would burn him to ash.

Eithan watched the two of them with hands on his hips. Orthos and Lindon were both screaming, though he doubted either heard it, and tongues of Blackflame madra leaped around the cave, scorching through Lindon's clothes, leaving grooves in stone. The aura of the place had gone wild, making this cave an oven and steadily devouring anything inside. A Copper who stepped inside this place would have the air scorched from their lungs and their skin crisped and blackened.

So far, the plan was unfolding beautifully.

He picked up Lindon's pack and carried it to the entrance tunnel, where the air was relatively cooler. The books inside wouldn't have lasted much longer without bursting into flames, and the pack itself would have eventually followed.

Without turning his head, Eithan watched the boy and the turtle. They would still be a while. Advancing to Jade usually took some time, after all, even if you had help.

In the meantime, Eithan took the opportunity to flip through Lindon's possessions.

He set aside the books, bandages, medical kit, rune-light, emergency rations, extra clothes, inkwell, spare brushes, blank scrolls, needles, thread, scripted fire-starter, sculptor's chisel, carving-knife, soap, seven purple boundary flags—one broken—and a frying pan, carefully remembering the relative position of each item.

Eithan had seen everything in here already, from the first moment they met, but he didn't want Lindon to know he had interfered with anything. That would spoil the surprise.

Finally, he unearthed what he'd been digging for: the Sylvan Riverseed's case.

It was a box of scripted, reinforced glass, big enough to contain a small cat. A river flowed around the edges, guided by a water-aura script that kept it in motion, but the center of the box was filled by a little grassy island. A finger-sized tree rose from one of the hills, life aura flowing through it in a verdant green web.

Beside the tree stood the Sylvan itself, looking curiously up at Eithan through the lid of its tiny world.

Sylvan Riverseeds were natural spirits—beings like Remnants, only born of accumulated vital aura rather than the death of a sacred artist. They only formed in places where the aura was both extremely strong and in perfect balance. If the aura slanted toward one aspect or another, a different natural spirit would form.

Typically, you would find that balance of aura in the heart of a forest, next to a spring or a river. In such a place, air and earth, heat and cold, life and death all coexisted at the same point in roughly equal amounts.

This spirit looked like a featureless puppet about three inches high, its body the vivid blue of a sunlit lake. It raised a hand to him, and its head split into a wide mouth, like a baby chick begging for food.

Other Sylvans were better suited for different purposes, but Riverseeds were gentle and flexible. They could work with power of virtually any aspect, supplementing and supporting other forces.

Which made them excellent raw materials. They were so malleable that a skilled craftsman could make a Riverseed into a guardian, a weapon, a guide, an elixir, a power source, a drudge, or—in some cultures—a very expensive cocktail.

It was fortunate that Fisher Gesha had never noticed Lindon feeding his pet. There wasn't much a Soulsmith *couldn't* do with a Sylvan Riverseed.

Not the rarest treasure, a Sylvan. But valuable. He had used elixirs made from Riverseed power to help Orthos, though such measures were only temporary. Only a long-standing contract could slowly mitigate the damage that centuries of Blackflame madra had done to his spirit.

Over the weeks since Eithan had adopted Lindon, he'd considered many possible options for the spirit. In the end, he settled on the simplest possible result: he'd leave the Sylvan as it was. Its own pure, gentle powers would balance the corrosive, deadly Blackflame perfectly. No alteration needed.

But perhaps a bit of...enhancement was in order.

If the Sylvan had grown a little faster, Eithan wouldn't need to act at all. But Lindon's scales weren't the most nourishing food.

Eithan ran his thumbs along the glass, tripping a hidden catch and popping open the lid. The Sylvan ran around in circles at the sight, excited, making plopping noises like the drip of water into a pond.

Extending one finger, Eithan conjured a spark of soulfire.

The gray-white flame was half-transparent, like the memory of a flame rather than a flame itself. Unlike a natural blaze, it was perfectly round, spinning slowly and throwing off the occasional flare like a dull, tiny sun.

This was only a fragment of the writhing, spectral gray mass of soulfire that hovered in his spirit, just a few inches above his core. Other Underlords would weave as much soulfire as they could afford, hoarding it against an emergency, but Eithan counted on his ability to make more at a moment's notice. Thanks to the sense provided by his bloodline, he could always find more fuel.

Heat surged against his back, reminding him that time was still ticking on, so without any further hesitation, he flicked the spark into the Riverseed.

Soulfire sunk into the Sylvan's body, and a deeper blue color spread like dye. In an instant, it went from a bright, sunny blue-green to the deep sapphire of the open ocean. The spirit surged and stretched, inflated by the influx of power, growing until its head would scrape the bottom of the glass case's lid. Its hands split into fingers, long blue hair grew from its scalp, and its body flowed into more human curves.

After only a second, the Riverseed panicked.

It flailed its arms, staring in horror at its new fingers. That sight drove it to the far end of the case, jumping into the flowing river. Realizing it was now too big to submerge entirely, it scampered back and huddled under its tree instead.

Eithan chuckled. The enhancement of soulfire was painless and harmless. It could be a bit disconcerting, but in the end, it was nothing but a benefit.

But it did require a certain amount of power for the changes to stabilize. With that in mind, he Forged a scale himself: identical in size to Lindon's, it was a vivid blue-white, and anyone with the least skill in perception could sense its power and density. In the Blackflame Empire, they would call this a superior-grade scale, and it would be worth about ten thousand of Lindon's.

Eithan created it in an instant, letting it drop into the case.

Even huddled under the tree, the Sylvan snapped at food. Its mouth opened wide, and it swallowed the scale in a second, which quickly broke down into nourishing energy.

The transformation surged forward again, the spirit growing even more defined. When the details finally settled, Eithan was somewhat surprised to see what stood there: it was very clearly a tiny woman in a flowing dress, all seemingly formed from azure liquid.

It wasn't unusual for more advanced spirits to start taking on humanoid forms, but Eithan had expected it to look more like *him*. Evidently Lindon had a strong impression that the spirit was female, which had influenced its shape.

She peered up at him with what had been a featureless face a moment before. With one finger, she brushed what looked like hair out of her new-formed eyes and gave him a sharp grin.

Then she straightened up, all of four inches tall, and bowed at the waist.

Eithan inclined his head graciously in return, and shut the lid.

Orthos' spirit felt like a boulder stopping up a volcano: a heavy, steady presence restraining boundless fury. Lindon could feel him even with his eyes shut, could point to the turtle in complete darkness.

But then, he could feel *everything* now.

His body was like a rag that had been squeezed dry, but his spirit soared. Orthos' presence blazed next to him, and the power of the cave surrounded them both like a warm blanket. Pinpoints of energy dotted the caverns for at least a few dozen yards before his perception faded out. Some of those points felt dangerous, even hostile, but some were calm, or else so alien that he couldn't read them at all. He found that he could tell which of the points were stronger and which weaker, just as he could tell which stars were brighter than others.

All of them, it seemed, were weaker than Lindon.

Eithan stood at the entrance to the chamber—Lindon couldn't see him, but he could *feel* him, a steady presence that was strangely blurred. For the first time, he couldn't tell whether the power behind that blur was strong or weak.

Lindon focused on that presence, and his perception flowed out, like a finger he'd reached into the distance. He couldn't hear or see anything this way, not like the Arelius family apparently could, but all the powers of madra and aura were clear to him.

He placed that finger of awareness on Eithan, and the Underlord laughed. Lindon's eyes snapped open; Eithan was standing over him, much closer than Lindon had expected.

"How are you enjoying Jade?" Eithan asked, reaching out a hand to help him stand.

"This is Jade..." Lindon checked his cores. Sure enough, one of his cores was no longer the bright blue of its twin, but a ball of black flames shot through with the occasional flash of red. The Blackflame core rotated slowly without his direction, grinding in rhythm with his breath.

"Barely," Orthos grumbled. The bright circles of red in his black eyes were fixed on Lindon, and a new emotion soaked into Lindon from their bond: arrogance. The turtle took a bite out of the rock as though it were made of cheese, speaking through a mouthful of gravel. "You almost burst under *my* power."

He had, but he was already forgetting the pain: Orthos had taken him another stage higher.

The Patriarch of the Wei clan was only Jade.

Lindon bowed at the waist, speaking with sincerity. "Gratitude, honored Orthos. I am grateful beyond words for the gift of your power, though I am not worthy of even this small fraction."

Orthos' pride flared up, and he stood straighter, until his shell almost scraped the low cavern ceiling. "Yes. You will not lack for rewards in my service."

Eithan patted the turtle's nose, though Orthos jerked back like an affronted child. "Congratulations on your new subordinate, Orthos. If I may remind you: this clarity of yours will not last for long. If you want Lindon to share this burden with you, you should see to his training yourself."

The dragon-turtle snorted, and black flames shot from his nostrils. "My memory is dim, but I remember *you*. You never spoke with proper respect."

Eithan slipped his hands into the pockets of his outer robe. His grin widened. "Do I owe you respect?"

"I do not fear Underlords," Orthos said, words underscored by a growl that shook the earth. "Your advancement means nothing before a dragon's breath."

Eithan drew himself up. "Sir! If this is an issue of respect, we should settle it like proper citizens of the Blackflame Empire. Let a friendly exchange of techniques decide whether you take the reins of Lindon's training, or whether I kneel to you as my master."

Though the Underlord's smile had been wiped away by an expression of haughty dignity, a playful sparkle remained in his eyes.

Orthos' satisfaction radiated through their bond, and his eyes glowed bright. "Trial by combat," he said. "Let it be so."

The temperature spiked again as Eithan and Orthos faced each other, ready to do battle.

Lindon grabbed his pack and ran.

As the battle broke out behind him, his spirit shook with fear and warning...but that didn't stop him from digging around in his pack for his box of badges.

It was time to exchange his iron for jade.

CHAPTER ELEVEN

"Vital aura is the power of the world," Orthos said, limping up the tunnel. His left foreleg wasn't visibly injured, but the pain he felt at every step flashed through Lindon's soul. "Even a hatchling understands this."

Despite the turtle's injury, Lindon still had to hurry to catch up. Based on his limited Jade perception, he would say Orthos' power was comparable to a Truegold, and he had speed to match. "Please excuse my ignorance. I am honored to have a teacher with such power and wisdom."

Orthos' head rose slightly, pleased and proud. "I have never lowered myself to teach Coppers before, but you have latched yourself onto my soul. I should at least treat you like a descendant. Hm. Vital aura. It builds in everything, over time, and can grant great power.

"A stone is a piece of the earth, and it builds earth aura. An ordinary stone has only a mouthful of aura, but as the centuries pass, it grows stronger and stronger. It will continue absorbing power from the earth until it transforms. If left undisturbed, an ordinary rock will grow into a nugget of Titan's Bone: all but unbreakable."

"Forgiveness, but surely *all* stone should be unbreakable by now, if this is only a function of time." Lindon reminded himself to ask Eithan about Titan's Bone.

"Sacred artists have an endless appetite," Orthos grumbled, scooping up a mouthful of rocks nearby and crunching them like candy. "A vein of vital aura piling up in the ground is a treasure trove for earth artists. They will stop at nothing to harvest it for their own advancement. A single candle-flame might be enough for *you* to cycle, but for a true expert, such a weak source is useless. They might as well try eating air."

Orthos lumbered up the path, his emotions growing distant as he drifted into a memory. "Advancement is an endless hunt for greater and greater sources of power. You start by feeding on the aura in candles and campfires, but sooner than you think, you'll be hunting for dragon hearts and sunreaver stones and sacred flames. Always climbing..."

Back in Sacred Valley, the Wei clan had cycled aura at dawn, when the light from Samara's ring and sunlight had intermingled, and when dreams still lingered in their minds. Lindon had never thought of aura as something that could be taken away; light and dreams were not stationary objects that could build up vital aura over time.

The explanation made sense. The Transcendent Ruins had drawn in vital aura from miles around, leaving the surroundings dim and washed-out in his Copper sight. Lindon had thought of that process as something like taking in a breath: the Ruins may have inhaled, but that didn't mean there was any less air outside. Now, he imagined it more like draining a bucket and waiting for rain to fill it back up.

"We cycle aura to trap a portion in our souls, adding to our power," Orthos continued, returning to the present. "It changes the nature of our madra, and over time, it teaches your core to generate madra of that aspect."

That much, Lindon understood. "Is there such thing as pure vital aura? With no aspect?"

Orthos rumbled deep in his throat. "There are more aspects of aura than sparks in a wildfire, but they always take some form. Always. Asking for *pure* aura is like asking for dry water."

"And Ruler techniques?"

"Madra controls aura, and aura controls nature. Water artists can walk on the ocean, call rain, and so on. Earth artists open doors in stone. Force artists can make a feather hit with the power of a collapsing boulder."

Lindon thought he understood. The Path of the White Fox could craft an illusion out of madra, but its Ruler technique affected the mind and eyes directly so that the target *believed* they saw something.

But he was still testing his Blackflame core, running his awareness over it like a child unwilling to release a new toy.

"What use is there for fire aura? Surely you can set things on fire with madra, rather than bothering with a Ruler technique."

Orthos was quiet for a full minute, chewing on the occasional stone. Lindon was considering how best to apologize when the turtle finally spoke.

"For some Paths, this is true. For ours..." One red-and-black eye swiveled to meet Lindon's gaze. "Imagine you have finished a battle. Your breath has driven your enemies before you, and now their corpses lie smoldering on the field. Smoke and flames rise in testament to your power, and courage has left your foes. They flee. You know you cannot catch them all."

A dark, twisted root stuck out from the wall. Suddenly Orthos snapped at it, tearing a length of wood the size of Lindon's arm out of the stone.

He spat it onto the floor, where it burst into smoky, black-streaked flames.

"They trip over the burning bodies of their comrades as they run," Orthos said, "but there is no flight from your fury."

He turned to glare at the floor.

And in a great explosion of heat, the root burst into flames. Lindon had to take a step back; the fire reached the ceiling and filled the tunnel for an instant. It was the healthy orange of a natural flame, not the dark stain of Blackflame, though it was spotted with the odd blotch of black or red.

The fire roared for a second, lapping up the walls as though looking for something else to consume, and then died in an instant.

Of the arm-length root, there was nothing left but ash.

"We called it the Void Dragon's Dance," Orthos said, crushing the ash beneath his paw. "In one moment, the flames devour everything on the battlefield, leaving only smoke and dust."

"As long as there's enough fire around to begin with." Lindon pointed out the distinction automatically, his mind distant. Half of him was overcome with awe at the raw power Orthos described, and couldn't help imagining turning that frightening weapon against Jai Long.

The other half was quiet and subdued, afraid of the deadly possibility locked in his own core.

"Hm. And as long as you have enough time," Orthos added. "Taking control of aura takes time and concentration. You can toss Striker techniques out with every breath, but a widespread Ruler technique takes time to build."

The tunnel had ended, opening onto a chamber with a yellow skeleton curled at the center. Unlike the bones in the city outside, this set was complete: a long serpent's body with four clawed limbs and one reptilian head filled with fangs. A delicate matrix of bones draped over the ribs must once have supported wings.

This dragon's skeleton also wasn't large enough to house a building. It was twice the length of Orthos' body, at most.

But it flickered with black fire. The flames crawled along each bone like worms, occasionally sending up a dull red spark that gave off just enough light to see. Lindon's Jade sense told him the room was filled with power, so he cracked his Copper sight.

He shut the sight again immediately. The dark radiance of destruction and the fiery aura of heat crowded out everything else, so he couldn't even see the power of earth in the rocks beneath. This was a wellspring of Blackflame energy.

"Sit," Orthos commanded, and Lindon scrambled to the ground without hesitation. "Cycle as the Underlord has taught you, but this time, reach to the vital aura around you. You have my power; Blackflame aura will come as you call, and will merge easily with your core." Orthos turned to go, snapping up another rock and swallowing it whole. "Cycle for three days, and then the next stage of your training will begin."

"Thank you for the instruction. Please, stay with me just a moment, until I get the—"

His contracted partner had already left. Lindon could feel the turtle's soul moving swiftly down the corridor.

At least he had packed food. But where, in these dark, broiling tunnels, was he supposed to find water?

Jai Long waited at the end of a dead-end street in Serpent's Grave, Shiryu Mountain looming over him like a titanic gravestone. The shop to his left belonged to the fourteenth-ranked tailor in the city, while to his right, a family ran the ninth-ranked restaurant.

Both buildings were immaculate constructions of newly painted wood, their signs colorful, their lanterns smelling of fresh oil. Even the alley between them was spotless except for a light coating of sand, and he was sure the Arelius family would sweep even that away before dawn. Every stranger who passed the alley's mouth looked like they were on their way to an imperial feast: the women had their hair pinned up and ornamented, their faces painted, while the men wore so many layers of color that they looked armored.

Even their Goldsigns were ornamental. Jai Long saw silver bracers, golden haloes, polished horns, emerald eyes, gleaming tails, and a single pair of broad green wings that marked a member of the imperial Naru clan.

After so long away, Jai Long had almost forgotten. Appearance and rank were everything in the Blackflame Empire. The more of one you had, the less of the other you needed.

With one hand, he tightened the red bandages wrapping his head. The other hand clutched the case for the Ancestor's Spear.

Stellar Spear madra flashed somewhere up the street, and white light bloomed. The crowd he could see through the alley cast disgusted looks backward, speeding along to their destination.

Jai Long flared his madra, cycling it rapidly and signaling Gokren and the Sandvipers that he was about to engage. Then he walked out of the alley.

Some of the passersby sensed the power of a Highgold and gave him curious looks, but they quickly looked away again when they realized he'd covered his face and failed to display any of the hallmarks of a famous faction. Just a nobody.

A few yards down the street, three Lowgolds of the Jai clan were harassing an Arelius street-sweeping crew.

Right on schedule.

The Jai spears were still slung over their backs, so they hadn't managed to provoke a fight yet. Their metallic black hair gleamed in the light of the dying sun.

The blue-clad servants of the Arelius family were huddled against a wall like trapped deer. One of them clutched a broken broom.

"You struck him," a young Jai woman said, pointing to her clansman. "Everyone saw you, just admit it. Say it."

The Arelius family workers scanned the nearby crowd, looking for a way out.

Out of curiosity, Jai Long turned to an old woman standing outside the tailor's shop, holding a bolt of cloth. "Did you see that?"

She looked him up and down, sneering a bit at his face. "You could do better than that, you know. We could weave you a mask that an Underlord would be proud to wear, even on a...*budget.*"

The Jai fighter blasted Stellar Spear madra into the sky again, still demanding something from the Arelius servants.

Jai Long nodded to them. "Did you see what happened there?"

The old woman frowned. "It's as you see. The Arelius family attacked the honorable Jai warrior from behind, breaking a broom over his head."

With a thought, Jai Long quickened his madra again, doing nothing to hide his power. The force of a Highgold echoed up and down the street, and even the Jai clan cut off mid-sentence to turn and look.

"Ah, I believe I was mistaken," the old woman said, bowing until she stared straight down at the bricks of the street. "If I think back, yes, I may have seen the Jai clan corner these Arelius servants unprovoked." She peeked up hesitantly. "Unless...is honorable sir from the Jai clan? I am prepared to swear that the Arelius dogs—"

Jai Long turned and walked toward the Jai clan fighters, slinging his spear case over his shoulder. He wouldn't need to use the Ancestor's Spear after all. The three Jai Lowgolds dipped their heads in his direction.

"Good evening to you, Highgold," the woman said warily. "Are you perhaps from a branch family?"

The white lines of Flowing Starlight began creeping over his skin. The world slowed.

His original plan was to find a team of Jai Lowgolds and kill two of them, capturing their Remnants, and letting the third report him to the Jai clan. As long as no one saw the Ancestor's Spear, they would only send a single Highgold after him next time. If he couldn't let one live, he would use the Spear to drain all of them and eliminate all witnesses.

But there were too many witnesses on the street to eliminate, and plenty to bring word back to the Jai clan that a rogue Highgold was hunting their people. So long as he didn't draw his spear, the clan would hear exactly what he wanted them to.

These Lowgolds might not have been high in the rankings, but they were at least trained. Before the marks of Flowing Starlight were visible, they'd already sensed him, pulling out their spears and assuming aggressive stances.

Too late.

Jai Long thrust both hands out, and a gleaming white snake shot from each palm. A spear would conduct the energy better, but he didn't require the aura of his weapon. The Stellar Spear had no Ruler techniques suited for battle.

The two enemies at his side shouted and thrust out their weapons, the spearheads gleaming like stars, ready to break his serpents.

He'd already moved, gripping the young woman in the center by the throat. White energy flared, and her head tumbled free. Her hair clinked as it struck the street.

The Lowgolds were finding it harder to disperse his snakes than they'd thought, and now he was standing between them. His hands flashed out again, and two more heads rolled.

Only a second had passed, and Jai Long stood in a pool of blood, bodies, and dissipating white madra. One woman lifted her skirts as she passed, though she was well clear of the blood, and gave him a disapproving look. A worker in the restaurant shouted at him for the smell. The old woman outside the tailor's shouted, "And no more than they deserved, sir!"

Traffic didn't stop.

The Arelius workers gave relieved sighs and rose to their feet, but they looked as though he'd saved them from a loudly barking dog.

"Will you be dealing with the Remnants, honored Highgold?" one of the Arelius street-sweepers asked. "Or should we have a crew dispose of them?"

Jai Long pulled some scripted paper seals from his pocket, which he'd prepared for exactly this occasion. He hardly had to stretch out his perception to feel the sources of toxic madra moving toward him: the Sandvipers, here to help him capture the Remnants for later consumption.

"I have men coming," he said, and the servants bowed as they backed up a few steps. One of them had produced scrub-brushes and a bucket; they were already planning to clean the street as soon as he left.

Someone shouted something about the Skysworn, but the white Stellar Spear Remnants had already begun to rise. They each looked different, but they were all thin and bony and looked as though they were sketched on the world in vivid starlight.

He slapped seals on them before they had entirely left their bodies, and by this time, the fur-clad Sandvipers had found their way to the street. They bound the Remnants in scripts and carried them off, taking them three streets over to a wagon they had prepared for exactly this purpose.

As soon as they started walking, the Arelius family closed back in to clean up the mess.

Fate was strange. In ambushing the Jai clan tonight, Jai Long might have done Eithan Arelius a favor.

He started to laugh—the serpentine Remnant had left him with a disturbing laugh, cold and high, like crashing metal.

Around him, the Sandvipers carrying the script-bound Remnants shuddered, but he pretended not to notice.

Yerin dodged the black scissors racing for her face, cycling madra to her limbs to Enforce her speed as much as she could. She still almost took a slash across the cheek, but avoided it, feeling the sharp aura gathered around the blade as it slid past her.

Eithan had overextended for the thrust, leaning onto his right foot to drive the scissors at her. His left arm was tucked behind the small of his back, into the dark blue outer robe that fluttered in the breeze behind him, and he still wore that small, smug smile.

She returned a thrust of her own, punishing his extension, driving the blade at his ribs.

He flared with power as his madra surged, and he vanished. She cut nothing but air. She spun to face him behind her; he hadn't veiled his presence, so she could feel him just as she would feel a bonfire. Simple trick to spin and keep the pressure on.

A thought that wasn't her own floated out from her core: she was making a mistake.

She shouldn't turn and waste that critical instant moving her body; instead, she should channel the Endless Sword through her Goldsign and whip it behind her, covering her movement and giving her enough time to turn.

Without waiting for her permission, her Goldsign obeyed the voice.

The steel-silver arm dangling over her shoulder whipped backwards on its own instinct, against her instructions. It strained to reach Eithan, stealing some of her madra to slash at the air, but she had already begun to turn. Her motion pulled the blade out of line even as it tugged *her* off-balance.

When she righted herself, she stared down the tip of black scissors.

"It's hard enough to quiet one mind," Eithan noted, spinning his scissors around one finger. "All but impossible if you have to work with two."

She ground her teeth, slamming her sword back into its sheath with too much force. Her unwelcome guest squirmed in her core, probing her self-control, looking to use her anger as a crack. It was getting stronger these days; if she didn't advance soon enough, *she'd* be the voice in the back of *its* head.

"*Two* would be sugar and peaches. I'm juggling three."

Eithan flipped his hair over one shoulder. "That's two more than you have to. Your Remnant is not your counselor, it is your resource. You should strip it down and use it for parts."

He didn't understand. He couldn't, even if he knew what

this parasite around her waist really was. It made sure she understood what it wanted, though it didn't use words. It wanted to be *used.*

Better than anybody else, Yerin could tell when something in her head was trying to talk to her.

And her master's Remnant, sealed away in her core, felt the same. He had something to say, so it was on her to listen.

Eithan might know sacred arts up and down. Maybe his advice would be right, for a regular Lowgold with a regular Remnant. But he didn't know what it felt like to carry somebody else's soul around with her.

Unless he wore her skin for a day, he *couldn't* know.

"What have you learned today?" Eithan asked.

"Shouldn't turn when the enemy gets behind me. Should have sent an Endless Sword over my shoulder to keep the pressure on, but I tripped over my own feet trying to turn."

That was the lesson her master was trying to teach her: he'd sent her a message telling her what to do, but she'd been slow to listen.

"Hmm." Eithan flipped his scissors into the air and caught them, all while watching her. "You know, sword artists don't tend to be the philosophical types. Some sacred artists can think their way through bottlenecks and roadblocks in their advancements, but those on sword Paths...they tend to prefer fighting through their problems."

"That's a truth," she muttered.

"Well then, how fortunate for you that you have a teacher who is willing to engage all your preferences and whims." He glanced up at the sun. "We should be right on time, actually. How would you like to take your frustration out on an endless parade of artificial enemies?"

"I think you'll have to race me there."

He began walking across the sandy courtyard where they'd been practicing, still spinning the scissors, and Yerin followed him.

"I've taken the liberty of restoring and preparing the three ancient Trials of the Blackflame family. I think you'll find them...invigorating."

Yerin didn't ask him any questions—he wouldn't tell her anything he didn't want her to know, and anyway, she'd see about these Trials for herself soon enough. But she *was* curious.

Lindon had been gone for three days, learning to cycle this new Path. Eithan's description had been impressive enough that she wanted to see it with her own eyes, but she had her doubts.

On the one side, Lindon was finding it hard enough to progress on his *own* Path. Giving him more to practice was just packing more weight onto an overburdened mule.

On top of that, she'd never trusted fire artists. They never met a problem without trying to burn their way out, which struck her as...crude, if that was the word. Simple. A sword was precise and controlled, but fire just burned everything.

There was another side, though: the Blackflame family had been richer than a nest of dragons. Wouldn't surprise her if they'd left something shiny behind.

They arrived at the base of the black mountain, where a circular hole in the rock was blocked by a copper door and a reddish haze. Golden sand blew against the stone, whipping against her exposed skin.

"Welcome to Underground Chamber Number Three," Eithan said. He gestured to the two attendants in Arelius family uniforms, who quickly began opening the door and undoing the script.

"Hang on there," Yerin said. "This is where Lindon went."

"He's been acclimating to the aura in one of the side chambers, though he should be finished by now. We have to go...deeper."

He wasn't kidding. They walked for an hour, through baking hot tunnels filled with smothering aura, lit only by the occasional red spot smoldering like a bloody ember. Even just sensing the aura would have made her sweat; being down here was like wading through hot mud. Hot mud filled with needles—her skin prickled in the presence of all this destructive aura.

After the hour, their narrow tunnel began angling upwards. "Let's pick up the pace, shall we?" Eithan suggested, and vanished.

Yerin almost stumbled over her own legs in her haste to follow. She poured madra into her Enforcer technique, hurling herself through the dim tunnel, and twice she nearly cracked her skull like an egg on an outcropping.

After a second hour of that, she finally emerged into blinding sunlight. It was enough to stop her like a slap to the face, wincing as her eyes adjusted.

While she was panting and sweating—as much from the oppressive heat as from exertion—Eithan stood cool as a statue in midwinter, leaning against the side of the cave.

"I'm sorry to keep you waiting," he said, and at first Yerin thought he was talking to her.

"Not at all, not at all," Lindon said, and for the first time she noticed he was there, looming head and shoulders over her. He had his bulky brown pack on, both straps, and a black iron medallion showing a hammer.

He stood straight as a spear, staring intently at Eithan.

When she first met him, that stare was rare. Only when he was really interested. But ever since Eithan locked him in the Transcendent Ruins, his eyes had gotten sharper and sharper, like he thought he might miss the one key detail that would lead him to defeat Jai Long.

He gave a shallow bow. "It took me all morning to climb up, and I was glad for the rest."

Yerin swiped at her forehead with a sleeve and tried to slow her breathing. Losing a race to an Underlord was one thing, but she hated to look like she had lost her breath from a little run.

Now that Yerin's eyes had adjusted to the surroundings, she took a look around. They were tucked away in a sort of cleft in the black mountain, open to the sky, but dark rock rose like spires all around them. This miniature valley seemed to stretch for miles, though she couldn't see far over the uneven ground.

Most of it looked blasted and blighted, as though a lightning storm had scrubbed it raw, and the few plants she could see seemed like they'd been dug out of the Blackflame caverns. The grass was black, stringy and tough, and the flowers had dark petals covering dim spots of smoldering red. The bushes were scraggly with glowing red at the edges, as though they had been half-burned and were ready to burst back into flames at any moment.

When she switched to her spiritual sight to glance at the vital aura, the Blackflame power was so thick it choked out everything else. She could barely get a glimpse of life or wind through the overwhelming miasma of black destruction and red heat.

At the other end of the valley stood a free-standing red doorway, just a couple of painted logs with a tiled archway over the top. It was wide enough to admit a team of horses, and dragons of black paint coiled up each support.

Through the doorway, the land was choked with stone columns, so thick they looked like a dense forest. She extended her perception to see if she could sense where the columns ended, but her sense was stopped at the doorway. By some kind of script, she guessed.

"Are there two courses out here?" she asked doubtfully.

"Just the one," Eithan responded. "It's divided into three separate Trials: one for the signature Enforcer technique of the Blackflames, one for their Striker technique, and one for Rulers. Blackflame madra is hard enough to Forge that they never developed an official Forger technique." He cleared his throat. "But yes, to answer the question on both of your minds, you will be taking it together."

She gestured to the red-and-black gate. "We're intended to walk in there together, then?"

Eithan gathered them up with one hand on Lindon's shoulder and one on hers, ushering them closer to the gateway. "These are the ancient Trial grounds for the first generation of Blackflame sacred artists. For centuries, this was how they passed their Path down to their descendants, preserving their legacy.

"Once you enter, the script will seal behind you, and you won't be able to leave until you complete the three Trials." Eithan considered a moment. "Or until you admit defeat, but where's the fun in that? You will find food, water, and shelter here, outside the entrance, and once you've defeated a Trial you can retreat freely. No need to take the same test twice, is there?"

Lindon turned his gaze to the west, and Yerin followed it. In a deep crag, she caught sight of a narrow waterfall. Something scuttled behind it.

"If you don't mind me asking, how long will we be living out here?"

"These Trials have been known to take months, or even as long as two years in some cases." He gave Lindon's shoulder a squeeze. "I trust you won't spend quite so long. And when you emerge, you'll be considered a Blackflame sacred artist in truth."

There was Lindon's goal, all nice and bright and clear, but what about hers? She wasn't likely to dig anything of value out of a course that an Iron could run.

"If you're looking to teach me another Path, I'm happy with the one I've got," she said, words dry. "Lindon can run this maze on his own."

Eithan turned to Lindon. "Orthos was supposed to deliver a package to you."

Lindon hurriedly reached into his pack and pulled out a leather-wrapped bundle, which Eithan took from him. He unrolled it on the ground before Yerin.

Half a dozen fine swords had been strapped to the leather. From the way the aura played over them, they must be sharp as razors—even the Blackflame aura tickling the edges had started to gleam silver.

They were perhaps too sharp to use as weapons, but to gather sword aura? Perfect. "That's a sweet enough gift, but I'm still not seeing why I should stay here. Could just carry these down the mountain."

He waved a hand. "I tried my best, but predicting people's actions is harder than I make it look. Now, you may be wondering what kind of training ground is designed to work for both a Jade and a Lowgold."

Surprised, Yerin's eyes flicked back to Lindon, and she opened her spiritual senses at the same time. Sure enough, he felt like a Jade: his spirit had a weight to it, a gravity, that no Iron could fake. He could actually sense what he was doing now, where before he'd been working blind. On top of that, his core was *packed* with burning, dangerous madra. More than he could have possibly harvested from aura in just a handful of days.

Elixirs. Eithan must have stuffed him full of the good stuff.

He saw her notice, and a little bit of a proud smile touched his lips. Well, he was right to be proud—wasn't long since he'd been happy enough to reach Copper.

Her chest tightened. She *was* glad for him, but...her unwelcome guest was tickling the back of her spirit. If she didn't advance soon, she wouldn't keep ahead of it.

And here Lindon was, hopping from Copper to Jade in three months like nothing. Sure, breaking from Lowgold to Highgold was like smashing through a thick stone wall compared to the rickety wooden gate blocking Iron from Jade, but even so. Why was she the one standing still?

"That's call for cheers and celebration!" Yerin said, forcing a smile. His shoulders straightened, and he brightened until you'd have thought she'd given him a crown.

Eithan beamed along. "Yes, one step closer to survival! Hooray!"

Lindon's smile withered.

"Now then," Eithan continued. "The Blackflames had attendants and even family members on many different Paths, but they all trained together. This course was meant to be passed as a team. I have no doubt that you'll both learn many—"

A dark blue Thousand-Mile Cloud passed over the cliff

towering over them, moving with a speed that left it a blur in the air.

Eithan sighed. "If I had my way, everything would go according to plan, and no one would ever surprise me." That sounded like a pretty rotten future to Yerin.

Cassias knelt on the surface of the blue cloud as it came to rest on the earth, with his right hand pressed against the cloud and his left resting on his sword. The silver bracer on his arm gleamed in the sun, and his curly hair reflected gold.

He faced his Underlord with determination. "Do the branch heads know you've opened this course, Eithan? Does the Naru clan? I thought we'd agreed—"

"Obviously I did *not* agree," Eithan said, steepling his fingers together. "Now, I'd like you to leave before you ruin any of the surprises for our new recruits here."

Lindon was focused like an arrow again, but Yerin was the one to speak. "Let's hear some more about those surprises."

Cassias turned to her, but then Eithan's power flared. He appeared in front of Cassias in a flap of his blue robe, his hand clapped over the other man's mouth.

"That would be cheating, wouldn't it?" he said, shaking his head at Yerin.

Cassias' eyes went flat, and something dangerous stirred in his spirit. He reached for his sword, straining to get enough leverage to draw on Eithan.

It was the first time Yerin had seen a real scrap of steel in him. *That* was the attitude a sword artist should have: if spirits stand in your way, cut them down. If an Underlord stands in your way, well, you do your best to cut him too. Her master would have approved.

Suddenly, Cassias' body shook. All strength leaked from him, and he went limp, sagging to the ground.

Eithan pulled a cloth from his pocket, wiping the hand he'd held against Cassias' mouth. "Now then—"

"Whoa, let's back up a step or two," Yerin said. "He had a message for us. You just want to sweep that away?"

"As I've said before, I'm very good with a broom." He overrode Yerin's objections by raising his voice and simply talking over her. "As I was saying, I have no doubt that you'll both benefit in many ways from this experience. You should acclimate yourself to your new home before attempting the course." He gestured to the wall next to the waterfall, where there were a handful of room-sized holes in the stone wall.

"You can leave whenever you'd like, but if you leave the way you came in, I'll take that as an admission of defeat."

Eithan turned to meet both of their gazes as he said that. Yerin didn't know what Lindon was thinking, but *she* wouldn't be backing out. Even leaving them a way to escape was soft work, by her thinking. The Sage of the Endless Sword would have backed her into a corner and made her fight her way out.

"Very good, then!" He waved them over. "Away you go! And you'll be spending quite a bit of time in there together, but do keep your hands off one another. I need you focused, not distracted. I will be watching to ensure your...compliance."

Yerin couldn't look at Lindon after that, but she glared at Eithan. "Sacred artists are disciplined. If I got distracted, I'd have been dead and buried years ago."

"You're...sixteen years old, I'd say, give or take a year." He pointed to his own eyes, and then to them. "I'm always watching. Now, in!"

Lindon bowed to the Underlord. "I'm grateful for the opportunity. In the interest of training as quickly as possible, did you happen to bring any pills? Elixirs?"

Eithan grimaced. "We'll be light on elixirs for the next few months, I'm afraid, but I'll come deliver you whatever we can spare. The Jai clan seized our last refinery in Serpent's Grave."

Yerin wasn't about to let that pass. "Hope you don't forget me, once you've got something to spare."

"As I believe I mentioned before, I have something special in stock for you. You'll simply have to wait and see."

On the ground, Cassias stirred, his glassy eyes taking on a spark of awareness. He mumbled something through thick lips, trying to speak.

While Lindon and Yerin were both distracted by the fallen man, Eithan vanished again. Yerin jerked her eyes up, sweeping her spiritual sense out to catch the Underlord, but he was gone.

Eithan and Cassias had both vanished.

Lindon hitched his pack up onto his shoulders. "Does it worry you that he just left before explaining how this course works?"

"Not a special worry, no," Yerin responded. She'd have been pleased with a few straight answers, but she was used to working without them. Her master treated explanations like they were made of wintersteel and crusted with diamonds.

"You get pushed into more than a few impossible challenges, and you start getting used to it," she said. "What itches at me is that he's keeping secrets."

Lindon rubbed the back of his neck. "He can't tell us everything, though, can he?"

She checked the leather-wrapped roll of swords under her arm and marched over to check out one of the caves. No sense wasting time. "When my master told me to do something cracked in the head, I marched in step because I knew he could be trusted. Eithan, though? I don't even know what he wants us for. Won't be much help in cleaning up the city, will we?"

Lindon followed her to the caves, frowning as he pondered. He looked so grim and serious when he was thinking.

The five caves were dug into the back of a little alcove in the shadow of the black cliff. Nearby, the waterfall streamed down into a crystalline pool, and a cluster of scraggly black bushes held berries nearby.

"I'll take what I can get," Lindon said at last. "If he's willing to sponsor me on my Path, the rewards are worth the risk. I just have to hope he's not looking for anything too terrible."

"I've never liked betting on hope," she muttered, but that wasn't entirely true. When you got swept up in the nets of someone powerful, you didn't have much left to your name but hope.

Hope that they were looking out for you, and not just using you as grain in a mill.

Cassias' body had deserted him, and by the time he could move again, Eithan had snatched him away from Lindon and Yerin. They were deep in the caverns now, and Eithan wouldn't let him crawl back.

But his bloodline powers were still working. He'd heard everything.

Eithan still stood there in his fine outer robe, hands tucked behind his back, smiling in self-satisfaction as he waited for Cassias to stir. It was black as tar in the tunnel, but he could still see well enough through his detection web. The Underlord, he was sure, could see perfectly.

"How did they offend you, for you to make them suffer so?" Cassias asked, his voice weak.

Eithan raised one eyebrow. "Offended me? Quite the opposite; they have impressed me again and again. I might actually have placed a winning bet this time."

Cassias had heard Eithan talk about a bet before—one that had gone wrong. Which had resulted in the destruction of the Arelius family main branch, over six years ago.

"They won't win anything in *there*," Cassias said, struggling to his feet. "I can't say why you directed Lindon to this Path at all, but there are safer ways to teach him."

"You think safety is one of the values I hold most dear, do you?"

Cassias stabbed a finger in the direction of the exit, assuming Eithan could see it. "The Black Dragon Trials were designed for a team of *five* Lowgolds, all trained to work as a unit. They were supervised by the elders of the family, who would call off the Trials or order breaks for the participants, as necessary."

"I seem to recall reading about that, yes."

Cassias longed to break something in his frustration, but his training and upbringing only allowed him to grow more stiff. His back straightened, his jaw tightened, and the grip on his sword hilt whitened his knuckles. "The Jai are strangling us. We *cannot* throw away recruits when we're short on manpower as it is. Not to *mention* the sheer time and expense it must have taken to open this place back up and power the Trials. Underlord, this is irresponsible to the point of negligence."

It was the most openly he'd ever contradicted Eithan, but Cassias couldn't say he was sorry. Eithan had finally cleared his way to marry Jing, and Cassias would always be grateful, but he couldn't watch the man run his family off a cliff.

Eithan turned his head, looking into the darkness, and his whole demeanor seemed to shift.

Cassias knew that Eithan had grown up in Blackflame City, but they had never met. He'd never even heard of Eithan Arelius until six years ago, when the man stumbled through a portal to the other side of the world. Already an Underlord.

Life and blood artists beholden to the family had confirmed that he wasn't far past thirty. That was partially what had created such an impact in the Blackflame Empire: Underlords so young were not unheard of, but they were rare as phoenix feathers. Eithan had the potential to advance to Overlord, a stage that only the Emperor, Naru Huan, had currently reached.

During the time Cassias had known him, Eithan had behaved like a child playing with toys, like a rich man indulging his idle whims, like a genius in the grip of his eccentricities, and—very occasionally—like a powerful and dignified

Underlord.

But now Cassias found himself watching a new side of Eithan. He looked weary. Uncertain.

It shook Cassias more than he cared to admit.

"We settle for so little," Eithan said at last. "We protect what we have instead of reaching for more. Even when the door is open, we refuse to walk through it." He clenched a fist in front of him. "Cassias, I can take this family through that door. I can drag the rest of them, *kicking* and *screaming*, into a future better than you or I could ever imagine."

He sighed, and his arm dropped back to his side. "But I can only see so far. I think these two could be the sails that carry us far beyond this empire...but what if I'm wrong? I could squeeze this family dry, betting on a glorious payout fifty years from now, and the Jai could devour us tomorrow.

"I feel blind."

Speechless, Cassias sat with Eithan in the silence. And the endless dark.

CHAPTER TWELVE

The five caves dug into the side of the black cliff were each identical. They were just deep enough to provide shelter from the rain—though not the wind—and they were stocked with a single reed mat and blanket each.

Yerin took the first one they came across, stabbing her row of swords into the soil outside the cave's mouth so that they would start gathering aura. Lindon had no need to do anything of the sort—the vital aura was thick with the power of Blackflame here. He felt like he would harvest it if he took a deep enough breath.

After placing his pack into the cave next to Yerin's, Lindon went into the other three caves and gathered the extra mats and blankets, bringing them back to his cave. Might as well have spares. Then, together, he and Yerin explored their basin.

It didn't take them long. They were restricted to an alcove against the side of the mountain containing the five caves, a waterfall and pond, and twenty-four dark, thorny bushes with black-veined red berries that burned to the touch.

The pond and waterfall were warm and tasted of sulfur, but after a short examination, Yerin said the falling water *should* be safe to drink.

While Lindon took his own turn inspecting the water, Yerin nudged him. "Looks like we won't be alone after all," she said, pointing to the cliff wall.

Mud-brown crabs the size of dogs clung to the rock, so dark that they almost blended into the black rock. At first he only saw the one she'd pointed out, but his Jade sense weighed on him until he could *feel* more sets of eyes on him. He looked more closely, and realized that dozens of the crabs were clustered all over the wall.

As if it had sensed the attention of humans, one of the crabs peeled its legs away and scuttled down the wall, sliding into the pool beneath the waterfall and vanishing.

Lindon scooted away from the water.

"He said we'd find food and water inside," Yerin said. "Guess we have. I'll leave it to you to roast one of them up, when we get hungry."

"Then I'll leave it to you to bring it down, when the time comes," Lindon responded. He thought he could capture one, but he couldn't rid himself of a vision of all those dozens of crabs swarming down the cliff at once, crashing into him like a many-legged wave.

Which made him realize there was no stone to block the cave entrance. He'd have to find a way to keep the giant crabs out while he slept.

Once they had inspected the camp to their satisfaction, they moved back to the red archway.

Yerin and Lindon stood side-by-side, looking through. Beyond was a dense forest of smooth pillars, packed close enough together that Lindon could see nothing else between them but shadows. They stretched up to the height of the rocky cliffs above, where they merged with the black stone.

Just on the other side of the archway, between them and the pillars, there were two other objects.

One, a rectangular slab standing roughly Yerin's height, was etched with writing and pictures too distant to read. The second was a waist-high pedestal holding a gray crystal ball.

Lindon had left his pack back in the cave, and now he slid

off his parasite ring and put it into his pocket next to Suriel's glass marble. His madra immediately moved more easily with the parasite ring gone, the Blackflame power burning merrily within him.

"This is the first Trial, I'd guess," Yerin said.

Lindon nodded to the two characters painted on the archway pillar, above the dragon design: 'Trial One.'

"That, or they're playing a sadistic trick on us."

They traded a look and then, together, stepped through the archway. Sure enough, there was a script embedded between the pillars: he could feel it ignite as they stepped forward. Icy power washed over his skin, and then he was through.

He stood before the stone tablet, which was crammed with diagrams and ancient characters. Lindon examined it for a few long breaths, committing segments to memory and wishing he'd brought paper and ink.

Yerin cleared her throat. "What's it saying to you?"

Lindon scooted over, making room for her at the tablet. He gestured to the outline of a man, filled entirely with intricate loops. "This looks like the madra pattern for their Enforcer technique." He brushed dust from the four characters comprising the name. "Black...fire...fierce...outer robe?"

"That has a nice sound to it, doesn't it? The legendary Black Fire Fierce Outer Robe technique."

"Well, what would you call it?"

With a thumb, she rubbed a scar on her chin. "Couldn't tell you. Can't read a word of it."

She sounded defiant, as though daring him to make a comment about it, but he was immediately ashamed. "Forgiveness. I was fortunate enough to learn the basic characters of the old language as a child. It's not so different from our language, though it looks much more complicated. You see—"

He was about to point out some of those similarities when she interrupted him. "Doesn't make a lick of difference. Can't read my own name."

Lindon stared at her for too long before realizing how

awkward that must be for her, then he shifted his gaze and pretended he'd been examining the stone all along. "That's... ah, I'm sorry. Did the Sword Sage not..."

"Not much writing to be done with a sword," she said, in a deliberately casual tone.

In the Wei clan, everyone learned to read before they learned their first Foundation technique. But it fell to the individual families to teach their children; he'd never considered what it might be like for someone raised outside a family.

"Well, ah...this section at the top is a simple sequence. It explains the history of the Blackflames."

His fingers brushed the vertical lines of writing, each column separated by pictograms: a dragon flying over a human, then a human standing over a dragon, then a human with a dragon on a leash.

"When the humans came to this land, the dragons ruled. They burned through all opposition, ignoring all defenses. No one could stand against them. Finally, a...I think this means 'great disaster'...came to this land from the west, bringing the dragons down from the sky."

That was interesting; Sacred Valley and the Desolate Wilds lay to the west. There were no pictures illustrating the great disaster, to his disappointment.

"Once they fell, the humans began to learn the sacred arts of the dragons. It helped to even the score, but their understanding was incomplete. While they were still studying the arts, the dragons discovered a way to..."

Lindon hesitated. "It says here they leashed the humans, but it seems to imply that the humans were the ones to benefit. Maybe a deal? A *contract.*"

Understanding sparked. The first Blackflames, at least, had bound themselves to the dragons just as he had done with Orthos.

"Some Paths bind their kids to sacred beasts," Yerin said. "It's like gluing a sword to your hand so you don't drop it, if you ask me."

Lindon spent a moment wondering if she was trying to

insult him before he realized she didn't know. He hadn't seen her since making his contract with Orthos...who was drifting around the mountain as the mood took him. If Lindon wasn't mistaken, Orthos would probably check on him before he finished the Trials.

"Not to ask too much of you, but if you happen to see a giant, flaming turtle wandering around out here...please don't attack it."

Yerin stared at him like he'd started babbling nonsense.

"Well," Lindon continued, "it seems that the remaining dragons linked themselves to the Blackflame ancestors for some reason. With the power of the dragons..."

He tapped a picture of a man with a dragon standing over a large crowd of humans, and Yerin nodded. "Yeah, I can figure that one."

There was a line of text just beneath the story, separated from everything else. These words were engraved more deeply, so the passage of time had hardly touched them.

"The dragon advances," he said aloud.

"That's a long stretch better than 'Fierce Robe Burning Fire,' true?"

"It's not a technique name. It looks like their family words, or maybe the philosophy of the Trial."

Yerin looked bored, so he moved down to the next section.

"Now it's talking about the Trials, and the language gets harder. The Blackflame ancestors placed three Trials here for the three basic techniques of the Path, that much is clear. This one is the...you know, the Fierce Fire Robe. It's their Enforcer technique. Seems like it burns..."

He trailed off.

"You'd expect fire madra to burn," Yerin said.

"No, that's...ah, it seems to burn away the body of the user." He searched his mind for another interpretation, but came up with nothing. That would explain why Eithan thought he needed the Bloodforged Iron body to handle the Path, but he wasn't exactly enthusiastic about burning himself from the inside out.

"That's a gem for you, isn't it?" Yerin asked. "If a technique costs you something, means it must be a good one."

Lindon grunted noncommittally and gestured to the smoky crystal ball on the pedestal. "I'm supposed to run the technique through the crystal, and that will activate the Trial. Apologies, but it looks like we can't move on until I'm familiar with it."

She folded her arms. "I'll wait."

He looked from the madra diagram to her. "This could take me days."

"Really?" Yerin tapped a knuckle against the illustration of the madra channels. *"This?"*

The diagram seemed to require him to make dozens of small directions and adjustments to his madra flow with every breath. To use it without thought in a fight would take him months.

"I defer to your experience," he said, "but I think three or four days is reasonable."

Yerin slid her sword around on her belt, then plopped down to the ground. She patted the dirt in front of her. "I'll be buried and rotten if I let you take days for something that simple. Have a seat, I'll walk you through it."

Lindon took one final glance at the diagram and then sat with his back to the stone, his knees against Yerin's. Once again, he wished he'd brought paper and ink; tracing the madra pattern would have helped commit it to memory.

"Do what I tell you, when I tell you, you hear me?" When Lindon nodded, Yerin straightened her back. "Close your eyes."

He did so.

"We're keeping this to a crawl, now. Deep breath in, and picture your madra running like tree roots through your whole body. You inhale, and the roots spread."

It was the same sort of visualization Eithan had mentioned while teaching him the Heaven and Earth Purification Wheel. He followed along, and his madra responded with surprising ease.

"Exhale, and burn it all up. There's a fire consuming those roots, you're burning them, and that fire is the fuel that drives you."

When Lindon focused on the fire, it was as though the Blackflame madra leaped forward like a hungry beast. It spread from his spirit and sunk into his body, but the sensation was painless, just a hot and disturbing tingle as though his muscles were slowly fizzing away to nothing.

He opened his eyes. "As expected of the Sword Sage's disciple," he said, saluting her with fists pressed together. "I almost felt it work. A few more tries, and I think...what?"

She was wearing a smug smile. *"Almost?"* The silver blade over her shoulder inched forward, leaving a polished steel surface in front of his face. "Do it with your eyes open this time."

It was harder to picture his madra flow with his eyes open, so this attempt took him longer. But this time he was watching when his madra flared and the tingling sensation washed through his veins.

The reflection of his face was suddenly blurred by a haze of red-and-black fire.

Lindon almost fell backwards.

Yerin gestured to him. "That covers you all over, like burning smoke. It's got a menacing look to it, I'll tell you true. Jai Long will have to bring a diaper to the fight."

He rose to his feet. "How? So quickly?"

She drew her sword so that she could reach the stone tablet with its tip, pointing to little symbols next to the madra pattern. Lindon had taken them for reading directions in the ancient script.

"Can't read a word, but you'd see these pictures on most old Path manuals. I had more talks about cycling theory with my master than we had hot meals." She shrugged. "You're just moving your own spirit around, aren't you? The *feeling* does you more good than remembering some directions."

She'd left her Goldsign in place as a mirror, so Lindon

flared the technique again. This time, he got a clearer look: a thin aura of black and red rose around him in a haze of power. He would be shrouded in Blackflame madra when he used this technique.

"What does it do?"

"Ask your...stone book, there." She scratched her nose, then added, "But I could take a guess. Looks to me like a basic full-body Enforcement. Works different depending on your madra, but basically every Path has something like it. Your body's protected and powered by madra while you use it, until you run out of madra or have to drop it."

He studied the stone, which seemed to agree with her. As far as he could tell. "If it's so simple, then why did they record it here?"

"You're asking me, but who am I supposed to ask? Not every Path has complicated techniques—sometimes they're stone simple, and it's all about how you use them. Or maybe this was the Trial they gave to Copper kids."

From the tone of the tablet, Lindon doubted this was something so frivolous as a playground for children. And Eithan would never have sent him somewhere easy, he was sure of that.

Lindon flared the aura again, trying to see how long the sensation of painless, corrosive heat would last. He couldn't hold it longer than a blink before the technique fell apart; he'd need to work on keeping his madra control steady and predictable. "It protects me, you say?"

"It Enforces you—figure you know what that means by now. But every Path's madra does something different. You'll have to play around with it." She hopped up, brushing her knees clean. "Hit me."

He looked at her sword.

"Got to try out your shiny new technique, don't you? Hit me."

Not for a moment did Lindon think he'd hurt her. Quite the opposite, in fact: he was worried her counterattack would slice off his arm. "I will do as you say, then. Excuse me."

The technique flared, and as soon as he felt the heat and saw the black-and-red haze around his body, he kicked off from the dirt. He'd been used to Enforcing himself with pure madra, and he had a sense of how strong his Iron body could be.

When he kicked off, it sent a pain flaring in his knees. The ground exploded behind him and wind rushed by his ears as he launched into the air.

Lindon had an instant to scream before he slammed face-first into the packed dirt a dozen feet behind Yerin.

Dirt ground into his eyes, into his lips, between his teeth. His body slapped down to the earth a second behind his head, and a brief moment passed before he could lift his face enough to spit out a mouthful of dirt.

He groaned as he rose to his knees. It hadn't hurt as much as he'd expected, as though he'd taken a hit on a suit of armor instead of to his flesh.

Worse was the internal strain. His knees ached and the bottom of his feet felt bruised.

Yerin gave a low whistle. "Well, isn't that a kick in the pants? You always have to get used to a new Enforcer technique, but...bleed me like a pig, it looked like you strapped a couple of lightning bolts to your legs."

That felt about right. His Bloodforged Iron body had already come to life, draining Blackflame madra to heal his strained knees.

In fact...he hadn't noticed it before, but madra was trickling into every corner of his body for healing. His black-and-red core was already guttering like a spent candle.

Had he really spent his madra so quickly?

After a moment of thought, he realized the reason: the Enforcer technique strained his joints and burned away at his muscles, and his body responded by drawing on madra to heal him. He'd drain himself dry in five breaths.

"What's got your tongue?" Yerin asked, walking over to him. "Didn't bite it, did you?"

"This Fierce Burning Outer Robe costs me more than I thought."

"First thing, we're not calling it that." She chewed on her lip as she thought. "Burning Cloak," she said at last.

He cast a glance at the stone. "The 'fierce' character is core to the reading of the name, and there's a different symbol for a rain cloak than for a sacred artist's outer robe—"

"Burning Cloak," she said, more firmly. "*That's* a real technique name. You want to call it Fierce Burning Clothes on Fire in your own head, that's on your account, but I'll cut you every time you say it out loud."

"It will be an honor to use the Burning Cloak technique," Lindon said with a little bow.

"True enough, it will." She jumped, casually clearing fifteen feet and landing next to the stone. "Now, fire up that crystal ball and let's test the edge of this Trial."

If Lindon spent any more madra, he would be crawling in the dirt instead of fighting. "Lend me a moment to cycle, if you don't mind."

She gave him a wry look, but her scars lent it a sinister, threatening cast. "I'm not throwing you into a tiger's den, I just want a look at the enemy. We don't like what we see, we back up."

She had a point. The arch hadn't closed when they passed through it, and there was nothing preventing them from heading back to their caves at the first sign of danger.

Besides, he was curious himself. There might be prizes to this Trial beyond simple knowledge.

He walked over to the crystal ball, cycling the Heaven and Earth Purification Wheel to replenish his madra. It strained his spirit and his lungs, and he couldn't tell if it restored anything at all—sure enough, the technique was trash for refilling a core.

Lindon rested his hand on the warm, smoky ball that sat on the pedestal. Now that he was close enough, he could see threads of red running through the gray, like the crystals he'd seen in Orthos' chamber.

"The tablet says nothing about what we'll face when I start the Trial," he warned, but Yerin gave a heavy sigh.

"Jabber jabber jabber, we're burning time. Light that candle."

One breath in, one out, and a black-and-red nimbus flared around Lindon's entire body.

When the crystal touched that light, it flared red.

Beneath the ground, a script kindled to life.

Though Lindon saw nothing, he could *feel* it, like a circle of fire ten feet beneath his shoes. He was aware of it in the same way he was aware of his own limbs.

Yerin drew her white blade. "Eyes up."

Cassias followed Eithan, because he had no other choice. The Underlord had seized his Thousand-Mile Cloud, and it was either climb on behind him or be left behind in the tunnel.

As soon as Cassias set foot on the cloud, Eithan took off, sending the construct straight up and out of the valley. Sheer black walls passed them on either side, but with an Underlord's madra propelling them, they reached the peak in seconds.

This was really a secondary peak of Shiryu Mountain. The Jai clan main complex occupied the highest peak with the living quarters for the head family and their subordinates. Cassias could see glimpses of their palaces high above and almost a mile away.

Serpent's Grave proper spread out far beneath them, a mound of bones in an ocean of yellow sand. But Eithan didn't take them down; instead, he flew them around this peak, overlooking the valley where the two children would live for the next few weeks.

There was a temple carved into this peak. Not sitting on top, where it would be visible from miles around, but carved as though to seem part of the stone. Only from the back could you see the stairs leading up, the braziers resting to either side of the entrance, the polished archway leading into shadows deeper within. From any other angle, this place would be invisible.

Cassias ran webs of Arelius power over the whole place, astonished. It seemed that this was connected to the Blackflame Trials below, but while the heads of the family had always known about the Trials, Cassias had never even heard *rumors* of something like this temple.

How could there be secrets on Arelius grounds?

Eithan landed the dark blue cloud at the top of the stairs, hopping out and strolling inside without a word. After taking another few seconds to scan the premises, Cassias followed.

The room inside the temple was small and almost empty. Light streamed in from the far wall, which was made of glass—it angled slightly downward, which meant it wouldn't gleam and reveal its presence to Lindon and Yerin. A massive script-circle was etched into the glass, taking up most of the window, and a broad table of gold and ivory spread out beneath it. Dozens of smaller scripts covered the table, which told Cassias it must be a control array of some kind. A cheap wicker chair—obviously a recent addition—gave the person manning the table a place to sit.

"What is this, Eithan?" Cassias asked wearily.

Eithan turned to face him; Cassias knew it was no accident that he was standing in the very center of the room. "Familiarize yourself with this room, because it will be your sole responsibility for the next...well, quite a while."

Cassias ran strands of detection over the controls, as well as his spiritual perception. "This course operates independently. It doesn't need controls."

"While that is indeed what we have always told the imperial clan when they used this course to train their students, it is not strictly *true*." He looked so pleased with himself that Cassias already missed the uncertain, vulnerable Eithan from the mountain below.

"This—" Eithan spread his hands to indicate the whole room. "—is the control center for the Blackflame Trials. The courses will run themselves, but they will not carry out detailed or advanced maneuvers. With supervision and direction, the Blackflame elders could *truly* test their juniors far below."

"I am to have authority over their training?" Cassias asked. If it were up to him, neither of the children would be here: the course was too advanced for Yerin alone, and Lindon's presence would only hinder her, if anything.

"If you would like the authority to decide between making the course slightly more difficult than usual or *truly sadistic,* then yes. That is entirely within your power."

Cassias continued scanning the control circles. "And if I wanted to deactivate portions of the Trials?"

"That, happily, does not fall inside your purview. You can choose when and how to lend your power to certain constructs, or you can choose to do nothing, at which point the Trials will operate at their standard level of difficulty.

Eithan gestured, releasing some madra, and the script-circle in the glass flared. Suddenly, the view at the window showed Lindon reaching for the activation crystal with Yerin standing beside him. As though they were only feet outside.

Fascinated, Cassias ran a strand of his bloodline power through the glass. Scripts only manipulated madra; they wouldn't be able to change the magnification of glass. Unless...

He found it only a breath after he started looking for it. A light-aspect binding intended to allow vision of faraway objects. The script merely activated it and applied its effects to the window.

That was still an incredible feat of Soulsmithing and scripting, though. How had Eithan managed to restore it? Surely a setup like this one, centuries old, would have decayed by now.

Eithan looked fondly through the glass. "It will rest upon you to test the children. Push them. Hold them in the fire and hammer them, that they might be forged."

Cassias straightened himself, waiting for the Underlord to turn around and meet his eyes. "I will not be part of breaking members of our own family. If you adopted them only to abuse them, I will report to the branch heads and have them removed from Serpent's Grave."

Eithan didn't respond, so Cassias continued.

"Besides, the Arelius cannot spare my absence. Not in times like these. The Jai clan will have free reign of our lands."

Eithan rested a comforting hand on Cassias' shoulder. "I go to deal with the Jai clan myself."

That really *was* comforting, though Cassias didn't say so out loud.

"In the meantime, I will make you a deal. If you manage to push Lindon and Yerin so hard that *either* of them gives up, I will release them from the Trials. And Lindon from his obligation to Jai Long. In that case, you will also be allowed back to your normal duties in the shortest time possible."

Eithan beamed at him. "So you see, the most prudent and merciful course of action is really to come at them with everything you have."

A fist clenched Cassias' gut, but he couldn't argue. There was a fine line between preparing the young for a harsh world and abusing them, but it shouldn't be too hard to get them to surrender quickly. Lindon, at least. Once they did, Eithan would honor his word.

The Underlord patted the ivory table. "Now, it seems we're in luck. They are trying the course for the first time. Let me show you how this works."

CHAPTER THIRTEEN

Lindon hefted the crystal ball in his palm, Blackflame madra swirling around his body, and the crystal flared with a dark, bloody light. He faced the thick forest of stone pillars as scripts ignited all through the ground.

Dark gray shapes started condensing in the shadows, like gravel pulled together by an unseen force to slowly build a larger figure. They gained definition as they formed, until they looked like statues of ancient soldiers: bulky, clad in layered armor, and carrying thick shields and swords or spears.

Three of them were almost finished forming, but there were other half-assembled shapes in the darkness behind them.

Yerin raised her sword.

Lindon bolted for the pillars.

Whether these were constructs or impossibly solid Remnants, his task remained the same. He had to keep the Burning Cloak up in order to keep the crystal active, and his Blackflame core was already on the verge of emptying itself again.

But these soldiers were taking their time to form, so what would happen if he just...skipped them?

He leaped over the first rank of soldiers, pain lancing through his ankles and calves, and the power of his jump almost carried him face-first into a pillar. He stumbled to an awkward landing but kept running, ducking around columns whenever he would run into a half-formed soldier.

It was working. The soldiers at the front formed faster than the ones behind, so he could outrun the Trial.

Even with the enhancement of the Burning Cloak, it took him five or six slow breaths to reach the end of the columns. When he did get past them, they vanished abruptly, leaving him standing in the sunlight again.

Another arch stood before him. It was a twin to the original entrance, with two exceptions.

First, the air between wasn't clear. It was opaque and smoky, so he couldn't see what waited beyond. Second, the paint on the support said, 'Trial Two' instead of 'Trial One.'

A sense of warning shook his soul as he considered that gray area in the center of the arch, which he took as an alarm from his new Jade senses. He slowed, examining the smoke more closely. It was dense aura that sent a shiver through his rib cage.

He didn't know what aspect of aura that was, but he could be sure of one thing: he wasn't touching it.

Lindon scooped up a handful of gritty dirt and tossed it at the barrier between the arch. The dirt sizzled and disappeared.

He turned back to hear Yerin's shout, the sounds of metal clashing against stone, and a roar like rocky plates grating against one another.

Forged gray madra started to gather itself in front of the arch. If the cores of the others had been pebbles, this one was a boulder, and in seconds it had formed into a towering stone giant with a horned helmet and a pair of tridents, one in each hand.

It planted its feet firmly on the ground, and behind it, the aura barrier in the arch flickered and disappeared.

Lindon had a fingernail-thin grip on his remaining madra,

and the crystal in his hand was starting to dim. Nonetheless, when the giant struck at him with its trident, he had to do *something.*

Roots of Blackflame madra slid through his channels, then they all exploded, igniting a shot of blazing hot power. The Burning Cloak flared higher, the air around his body crackling black and red, and he slapped the trident away with the back of his fist.

The repelled trident dug a ten-foot groove in the ground, sending black dirt spraying everywhere, but he barely felt the impact—the strain on his elbow and wrist from moving his arm so quickly was far more painful than the little slap of the weapon.

Lindon was in love. This was it—a power so great it *required* his Iron body to withstand. His elbow blazed with pain as though he'd torn it, but it was already healing.

But he couldn't exult in his power—he had a test to pass. The barrier had opened, which meant he could finish the Trial.

Then he kicked the ground to move forward, and his Blackflame core guttered out.

The crystal ball in his hand went dark. The aura barrier flared to life again in the arch. His legs collapsed, but he switched to drawing madra from his pure core before he buckled to the ground.

And the giant soldier dissolved. Gray madra faded to essence and blew away, half-visible sparks on the wind.

A brassy gong sounded from somewhere, its sound echoing through the canyon, and Lindon had to assume it meant defeat.

Lindon spent a moment regretting that he hadn't passed on the first try, but the promise of Blackflame was like a sun that burned all disappointment away. He turned back to the columns, whistling and tossing the crystal ball in one hand.

He'd already started cataloguing everything he needed to improve the Burning Cloak. It was good for explosive bursts of movement—punching, jumping, kicking—anything where a sudden burst of force would help. But for steady strength, for lifting or carrying or running long distances, he would need a different technique.

To optimize the Burning Cloak, he wanted pills to refine his Blackflame madra base so that he could activate the technique more easily, practice keeping it active longer, and training to answer specific questions: how fast could he move? How much strain could his body withstand? Could he channel the technique through only a single part of his body at a time?

This could be exactly the tool he'd needed to keep up with Yerin. He just needed to master it.

As soon as he had the thought, he realized that he could still hear a battle: shouts, stone on metal, and heavy crashes.

Lindon picked up the pace, jogging through the columns. The back ranks of stone soldiers had started to dissolve, and ignored him, but the ones closer to Yerin weren't banished yet. She was still fighting.

Then he saw her.

He hadn't even reached Copper when he'd watched her fight the Remnant of her master back in Sacred Valley. He had lacked the senses to truly appreciate the fight.

Now, he lost track of his surroundings as he watched in awe.

She fought an army. Two soldiers whipped their swords at her with blurring speed, one fell toward her at the end of a leaping strike, and two pushed at her with shields in one hand and spears in the other. Javelins rained down at her from soldiers in the distance. Stone hands reached up from the ground beneath her, snatching at her ankles.

All at the same time.

Yerin turned them all.

Invisible blades shredded the hands at her feet, churning the earth. Her Goldsign met one of the swords, her free hand the other, and her sword skewered the falling soldier and slammed him down like a hammer on the head of his comrade. He hadn't seen her use her Striker technique at all, but silver slashes of sword-light struck the javelins from the air, and a pair of kicks caught two enemies on their shields and launched them through the air to shatter on pillars.

How long would it be before he could fight like *that?*

An attack he hadn't seen slammed into his skull in a burst of pain and white light. His Bloodforged Iron body drained power, and he rolled to his feet in an instant, pulling the halfsilver dagger from his pocket.

He could feel the presence of the gray soldier even as it dipped behind a nearby column. He would feel its attack coming, but whether his reflexes could keep up was another matter.

And *what* he felt of the construct was even more interesting. In a way he couldn't entirely articulate, the soldier felt... mindless. He sensed no life within it. It was simply a mass of madra, acting according to direction.

But not even the most complex construct ever designed could fight as a living creature without someone controlling it. At least, not as he understood constructs.

The soldier ducked out, avoided his slash with the halfsilver dagger, and struck him a heavy blow on the shoulder with the butt of its sword. His madra drained again to his Iron body, until even his pure core darkened.

The spiritual exhaustion was like a gaping hole inside him, leaving him limp and twitching on the floor. He wanted to squeeze his eyes shut, but instead he kept them wide, watching for the next blow that would land on his helpless body.

Instead, the soldier withdrew. It joined the others in attacking Yerin.

He couldn't see the fight except for an occasional flash of black or silver, but after a few minutes Yerin let out a pained shout and hit the ground with an audible *thud.*

The soldiers retreated, ignoring them both, and dissolved in the shadows of the stone forest. The script beneath them powered down.

Lindon spoke into the dirt. He didn't have the strength

to move, and he knew Yerin would hear him. "At least they didn't kill us."

Yerin groaned.

"In that case," Eithan said, "I didn't have to do much. I could have directed more of the soldiers to stop Lindon, but there was no need."

"Maybe you should have sent more against Yerin," Cassias said, wishing he had a dream tablet handy to record the memory while it was fresh. As a sword artist himself, he was left in awe at the level of skill and control she'd already displayed at the Lowgold stage. He bitterly regretted that he couldn't meet her master.

"She could reach Highgold any day now, if she could let go of that death-grip she's got on her Remnant," Eithan said with a sigh. "She might out-rank you fairly soon."

Cassias watched the girl in the tattered robe as she sprawled out on the dirt, each breath rough and heavy. "Considering what it's costing us to run these Trials, I'd be disappointed if she didn't *at least* take my place in the rankings."

Eithan gently pushed him into the chair in front of the control array. "The course only runs while the sun is up. Tonight, you can go back to your family. If you'd like to retire early, then by all means...push them until they break."

Cassias gave him a wry look, but his spiritual perception was already moving over the console. If he was going to run these Trials, he needed to know the controls like his own sword.

The crab meat tasted like ash and scorched oil. Yerin almost spat it out, but she'd choked down worse food out of necessity. She separated herself from the taste to chew and swallow out of pure discipline.

Lindon *did* spit it out, making a retching noise. "That... that cannot be food," he said.

"It's the fire that's rotten," Yerin said, ripping off another piece of vile meat with her teeth.

It had taken Lindon until well into the night to start the tiny campfire that now smoldered outside their caves. He'd used Blackflame madra to ignite the tinder, and now that power lingered; the aura wasn't the healthy red-and-orange of a natural blaze, but was tinted with bloody scarlet and corrosive black. The flames gave off too little light, too much smoke, and a taste like burnt death.

But Yerin had experienced the consequences of eating raw meat in the wild. Even a corrupted flame like this one was better than nothing—there was no telling what sort of diseases or parasites these wild creatures carried.

Lindon popped another one of those red-veined black berries into his mouth, wincing as he chewed. Yerin had found them even less tolerable than the meat. They burned her tongue, leaving it unable to taste anything...although that might be an advantage, considering the crab.

She was sure the berries must be low-grade spirit-fruits that would burn away impurities in madra, but she didn't have the energy to put up with a burned tongue on top of everything else.

Lindon set aside his cracked crab claw, staring into the flames. "I'm sure we weren't meant to succeed on our first try," he said.

Yerin's grip tightened around her own segment of crab. The shell cracked. "You'd contend so, huh? You think a real enemy would be soft enough to give you a second shot?"

His eyes widened at her tone, but she wasn't feeling charitable enough to apologize. It wasn't fair to him, likely—he may not have grown up on the battlefield, but he'd faced plenty of real enemies just in the few months they'd known each other.

"We'd have some information about a real enemy," he said reasonably. "That's all we were doing—gathering information. We have to know how that construct works if we want to defeat it."

She shoved another strip of revolting crab meat into her mouth, tossing the empty shell in the fire. "Not a construct," she said, around the mouthful of food.

He leaned forward, interested. "A Remnant, then? Compelled by the script?"

"You're Jade now. Did that feel like a Remnant to you?"

"That that exhausts the possibilities I'm aware of, though my experience pales next to yours. If it's not a Remnant, and it's not a construct..."

Yerin gulped water from a hollowed-out crab shell she'd filled at the waterfall earlier, trying to rinse the taste out of her mouth. She spat to one side of the fire. "It's a Forger technique."

"A *technique?*"

"Sure. Probably stole the binding out of some advanced Remnant, strapped it into a script circle, and tied it to that crystal."

Lindon pulled out a brush, dipped it in ink, and began taking notes. What was he even writing down? This was the basic of basics.

"Jai Long does it," she said. "Fought him for a breath or two in the Ruins, and his moves looked like snakes."

He nodded along with her words, still writing. "How can a technique have a mind of its own?" He stopped, brush poised, waiting for her answer.

"Plenty of the *really* powerful sacred artists can Forge something that looks like it's alive. Carries a piece of their Remnant with it, or so they say, but I can't speak to the details of it. My master could Forge a sword that would fly around and chase an enemy until they died or broke the technique."

Lindon's brush dashed over the page. "So all we have to do is break the technique."

"*All* we have to do," Yerin muttered. "Listen. Whoever left that binding behind was at least as powerful as Eithan. Better, more than likely. And it's meant to test your Enforcer technique, meaning you're intended to tear through it. That's a tall order when I've got to fight by *myself.*"

She slammed the shell full of water down next to her so that it sloshed up and over her wrist.

He blinked, eyes wide and innocent as a child's. "You were amazing today; I've never seen anything like it. I would only have gotten in the way."

That was the attitude that scraped her nerves. You couldn't always fight when you had a plan or a secret weapon. Nobody ever waited for you to sleep a full night, have a hot meal, and cycle your madra before they attacked you. No, you were more than likely to fight half-asleep, with a bleeding arm and a gut full of poison.

When she'd fought Jai Long herself, she'd just cut her way through a pyramid filled with dreadbeasts and crazed Remnants. Did he do her the favor of waiting until she was in her best condition? No, and neither would anybody else.

"If I waited to fight until I was ready," Yerin said, "my bones would be rotting in Sacred Valley right now. You have to dive in there, or you might as well scamper back home."

Well, at least he had the grace to look embarrassed. "I didn't expect we would fight right away."

"Yeah, you thought the Blackflame Trials might be testing your foot speed?"

"I was hoping to gather information. If we could just run past it, we might have been able to walk through to the next Trial. Wouldn't Eithan be amazed if we left here only a day after we started?"

Yerin gaped at him. "You think Eithan wants us to run out of here quick? You don't think he'd drop us right back at the entrance if we didn't learn the lesson?"

Lindon flushed, examining his inkwell as though it held

the deepest wisdom of the sacred arts. "No, of course, but surely there's not just one way to solve a problem. If we come up with a solution on our own, then..."

Yerin stood up, brushing herself off. "I'm going to cycle," she said abruptly, cutting him off.

She walked off, storming past the swords thrust into the ground in front of her cave. The vital aura had finally started to gather around them, generating enough sword aura for her to harvest.

Yerin knelt just inside, calming her breathing to cycle the aura steadily. It had the effect of calming her down as well, leaving her alone with her thoughts.

Lindon hadn't lost the fight for her.

Sure, it would have been nice to have a second person fighting alongside her, if only to split the enemies. As it was, she had been on the defensive the entire time, battling as hard as she could just to survive for a while longer. That was no way to win a match, and she knew it.

But she'd had no choice. Her madra was squirming out of her control.

Not due to her uninvited guest—it was quiet and placid for the moment, content without straining against the Sword Sage's knot.

No, it was the Sword Sage *himself* who was causing this problem.

She had to force her Goldsign to defend her when all it wanted was to strike at the enemy. Her master had left her a second, buried set of instincts inside her that kept trying to teach her how to attack. Her master had been a predator for most of his life. It wasn't in his nature to stand back and protect himself in front of an enemy. Ever since she'd absorbed his Remnant, she'd only felt fully in control when she was attacking all-out.

Eithan might be right that cracking open her master's Remnant was the fastest way to Highgold, but that meant there were other ways. Slower ones. As long as she worked hard enough, she could stay a step ahead of her unwelcome guest *and* keep her master's voice around at the same time.

Her master was trying to teach her a lesson. And he was going to keep his hand on her sword, pulling her his way, until she learned what he wanted to teach.

This was her last chance to learn from the Sword Sage. She couldn't waste that opportunity just because Eithan told her to.

Besides....she wouldn't admit this out loud, but if she tapped into her master's Remnant, his voice would go away. It would just be her and her unwelcome guest in her head. Alone again.

Yerin continued cycling, focusing on her breath to calm her frustration. She still had plenty of time to reach Highgold. This impatience could only hurt her progress.

Besides, she'd get another crack at the Trial tomorrow.

ITERATION 217: HARROW

Suriel landed on hard-packed sand next to a lake-sized plate of chrome. In Limit, this had been a piece of a giant machine. In Harrow, a desert.

When Limit lost its grip on the Way and slammed into Harrow, the two worlds merged together and split the difference.

On the horizon, mountains flickered in and out of existence, as they tried to stabilize in one Iteration or the other. Here, Suriel's presence was stability itself. Her connection to the Way anchored the world around her to order.

For the most part.

A fractal distortion in space unfolded into a field of impossible shapes before blooming into a two-story creature of dark glass. It had the legs of an origami centipede and the body of a black mirage, and it strained her human senses just by its proximity.

The creature of corruption reared over an upturned iron wagon, which had been half-buried in the sand. A woman crouched beneath it, filthy and ragged, having sheltered there for the better part of two weeks as reality crumbled around her.

Drawn to her sentience, the monster would have devoured her to remove her connection to the Way and to extend its own existence in the material world.

Suriel drew her Razor, now a meter-long rectangular shaft of blue metal, and blasted the creature apart. It dispersed into hissing shards of chaos that were difficult to perceive—they looked like burning nightmares.

Suriel activated one of the many functions in her Razor and the armored wagon dissolved, leaving a terrified woman huddled in the sand, surrounded by what looked like a nest of garbage.

Something hissed at the edge of Suriel's awareness, trying to get her attention, but she ignored it.

[Mu Bak Ti Yan,] Suriel's Presence said, and the woman's head jerked up at the sound of her name. [You have been chosen to live. You will begin on a new world, where you will work to settle a wilderness. Do you accept this task?]

Mu Bak Ti Yan stared at the Presence, a gray figure of smoke on Suriel's shoulder. Then she stared at Suriel.

In her original world, Suriel had been a pale, scrawny woman with hair like seaweed and eyes that took up half her face. That woman was still there, only...perfected.

Her hair was the color of sunlit emeralds, her skin ivory, her eyes a bright violet etched with vivid runes of Fate. Her childhood friends would have said she had the body of an immortal—flawless and statuesque—which was only appropriate, since they had died of old age more than four thousand years before.

She wore the armor of the Abidan, smooth and absolutely white, as though it had been poured into place. Her correlation lines looked like smoke trailing from the fingertips of her left hand up to the back of her neck, though they functioned more like an instrument's strings. And, of course, she had just used the meter of blue metal clipped to her hip to blast apart an incomprehensible creature of madness.

In Limit, there were beings called Terava, which looked like perfect human men and women but possessed godlike power. The Teravan were natural energy projections that only took human form to feed, but Limit had never learned that.

Mu Bak Ti Yan, born in the dead world of Limit, must have thought she looked like a Terava.

Suriel raised one gauntleted hand in a gesture of peace, but the woman spooked and ran. She kicked up sand and fell to her hands and knees, still trying to crawl.

For the past two weeks, Suriel had been trying to track the human living in this desert. Most of the planet was clear already—its population dead or rescued—and this was the only inhabited planet in this universe.

As the sentient population fell, the power of chaos grew stronger. And the Way more distant.

Which made precisely pinpointing anyone's location almost impossible, at least for an Abidan. She had relied on her old powers, following the trail of Mu Bak Ti Yan's life-force, but the corruption of reality interfered with that as well.

Hunting one elusive prey through twenty thousand square kilometers of madness was more difficult than she remembered. Maybe she relied on the power of the Way too much; she was growing rusty.

Suriel waved her hand, and a blue-edged portal flared into being just in front of Mu Bak Ti Yan. It showed a grassland on the newly formed world of Pioneer 8089, where clusters of crude huts surrounded a great silver bird.

The woman stumbled through the portal, and the silver bird crowed, alerting the rest of the population. A tiny orange moon shone alone in the night sky; none of the stars had formed yet.

That was normal. Iterations started from clustered world fragments and grew outward, like seeds.

Suriel cut off the portal, and the door through the Way vanished, leaving Mu Bak Ti Yan trapped in a world far from her own. She had never gotten verbal agreement for the relocation, which was against Abidan protocol, but people usually only refused resettlement until they realized that *staying* meant horrifying death or mutation.

Of the two-point-one million survivors that had remained human through the merge and corruption of Limit and Harrow, she had saved one-point-four million in the half of a standard year since she'd been working here. The others had either died or evaded her notice long enough that she had no hope of finding them before the end.

On the first day, she'd sent half a million people to Pioneer 8089. They'd had to form orderly lines through the portal. By now, she was lucky to find one a week.

And this world didn't have a week left.

She could feel it: the Way was losing its grip on this Iteration. Before she could locate anyone else, Harrow and Limit would accompany one another into the void.

Suriel lifted herself into the atmosphere, the land below her shifting from continent-sized machine to desert and back again. The atmosphere was even more chaotic than the surface, twisting like six hurricanes at war with one another, but she felt nothing inside the bubble of her isolation shell. She dove into stars under its protection; *wind* was not a worthy opponent.

From above, the world was a rapidly shifting mass of images and impressions, like a nonsense puzzle with pieces that randomly rearranged themselves. It was straining at the Way, ready to break.

And Suriel finally turned her attention to the hissing that had tried to grab her earlier. It sounded like a whisper just at the edge of hearing, like someone trying to call her name from a dream.

[Further contact established,] her Presence reported. [Transmission location still unknown.]

"Best guess," Suriel said. She liked talking to her Presence, and had chosen its form for that reason: it almost looked like a person. She enjoyed conversation, and that simple psychological trick was enough to cut away the pressure from the isolation of her job.

Usually.

[The most recent transmission raises estimate accuracy to fifty-four percent.]

It was better than the last three times she'd tried to find the source of the transmission. It *sounded* like an Abidan beacon, as though someone had left a call for help, but Sector Twenty-One Control would have heard about it before she arrived. And it should have been as clear as a voice in her head.

It was quiet and hidden behind static, which meant that either it was *not* an Abidan beacon, or it had been broken during the violence of the merge.

Suriel blasted through the atmosphere toward the coordinates her Presence indicated, not bothering to keep herself subsonic. No one would notice, and this world no longer had a connection to Fate that could be disturbed by legends of a flying goddess.

She could have bent space and arrived directly there, but direct spatial travel was imprecise, better suited for very short travel—like range of sight—or very long travel where precision mattered little.

Besides, the beacon had persisted for months in the most chaotic environment possible. It would last a few more seconds before she arrived.

The flight brought her to an ocean. It had been an ocean in both worlds, so it was still an ocean, even if the chaos meant that it sloshed like a cup of water on a flying dragon's back.

The whisper did seem a little louder here, though no more clear, so she dropped into the water.

As soon as she did, a signal reached her Razor. This beacon triggered in response to her weapon, then, though she could choose if she allowed the Razor to respond.

Curious, she let it transmit back, and a green light appeared in her vision. Coordinates a few hundred kilometers away, still within the ocean. Though her Presence warned her that finding something specifically keyed to *her* on the surface of a random dying world was dangerously suspicious, she followed it.

There was only one person who would leave her a message here. This might even be Ozriel's hiding place.

That would be just like him: predict where she would end up, and then hide there, waiting for her. Waiting on a dying world would just add style, as he saw it.

She tore through the water, but was forced to stop in less than a second. A spatial crack the size of a finger stretched vertically for hundreds of meters, its edges sputtering with chaos, and its heart looking into the void. Water gushed through it in an endless waterfall, but that wasn't what concerned her.

Cracks like these were often left behind after an Abidan's battle.

Extending her senses as far as she could, she found other cracks, getting wider and wider as they drifted into the sky. With the chaotic interference, she couldn't detect anything further than about a kilometer, but they might very well keep going. If this had been a battle between Judges, the spatial cracks could have gotten wide enough to swallow suns.

There was no testing that now. This Iteration's stars had already vanished—there had only been one inhabited planet in each universe, so it was the last to disappear before the world fragmented.

She flew on, dodging other spatial cracks. If not for the chaos of the merged worlds and Limit's corruption, she would have sensed these the second she landed in this reality.

Finally, beneath a storm of spatial cracks, she found the location of the beacon.

It waited for her beneath a city-sized dome of stone.

There was Abidan technology here, because the dome remained stable and unaffected despite the chaos of the water above and the world outside. She slipped lower, but as she got closer, a hole opened in the stone.

[It would be wiser to alert Sector Control,] her Presence said.

If it really *was* Ozriel down there, and she turned him in before hearing what he had to say, he would never forgive her. She drifted in through the hole.

The inside of the dome was very simple. It was all a single room, its structure reinforced by the Way to add stability, and big enough to swallow a city.

But there were no streets or buildings inside.

Only pods.

Transparent, organic pods in rows for hundreds of kilometers. All filled with people, sleeping and drifting in liquid.

The pods had been arranged in grids with space between them, so the people emerging could leave and walk away, but there were no other facilities. No shelters, no water, no plants. Each pod gave off a slight radiance, but that was the only light.

[Twelve million, four hundred forty-five thousand, six hundred thirty-two people,] her Presence reported. [And some shipping crates containing culturally significant icons.]

"Point of origin?"

[Iteration Two-one-six: Limit.]

Of course. The Abidan had evacuated the elite of Harrow, and she herself had saved a million and a half survivors of the combined world, but no one had saved the population of Limit. Their world was destined to end, so the Abidan had allowed it.

Except for Ozriel. He'd saved enough to preserve the unique genetics and cultures of a doomed world.

But there was one more feature of the space inside the dome: spatial cracks, which buzzed like a storm in the air. The structure of the building and the pods were still intact, but Ozriel must have protected them. Otherwise, the void would have swallowed them by now.

Even so, the chaotic interference was so strong here that

the air crackled with it, and Suriel had to move carefully around each crack. Not that they would threaten her, but she might stick to them like iron to a magnet.

The cracks were thickest surrounding a door at the far end of the compound...a door marked with the image of a scythe.

Well, that was simple enough.

With one hand, she shoved the heavy stone door aside, and the chaos hit her like a stench. The room on the other side of the door was only as large as a one-room office, and positively *black* with spatial cracks, so that it looked like the weapons of two Judges had clashed in here.

Except that a conflict like that would have destroyed this shelter and most everyone else in Limit.

She couldn't see much in the room past the nest of hissing cracks in reality, but half of a desk remained in the center. A fist-sized ball glowed blue on that table: a beacon, though all the chaos in here must have degraded it. And on the far wall, a spray of ancient blood and flesh, as though a man had exploded right before the door was sealed for a century.

[Impossible to identify remains,] her Presence reported. [Chaos and time have destroyed them beyond the point of analysis.]

The beacon was still resonating with her Razor, indicating that it held a message. She reached out to accept it, but hesitated.

Not out of reason, or to buy herself a moment to think. She was scared.

Ozriel had come here to prepare for Limit's death. He had left this message here for her after a battle...or had he prepared the message before the battle began, stretching out past the planet?

Either way, it wasn't good news. This message was *not* about to tell her that Ozriel was safe, happy, and ready to return to work.

She was afraid for herself, afraid for the Abidan, and afraid for the man she'd known even before she'd joined the Abidan Court. He had always been Ozriel to her, but there had been a time before she was Suriel, the Phoenix. They had been friends.

She accepted the message, and her senses were consumed in endless white.

This was a perfectly ordinary way to send a message in Sanctum, headquarters of the Abidan. Sharing senses and experiences was common, and crafting an experience like this would have taken Ozriel seconds. But the world of this message crackled, tarnished by damage and chaos. The world of white was speckled with imperfection, as though she watched it through grainy film, and interference was a constant hiss in her ears.

At least she wasn't alone.

Ozriel stood before her in his polished black armor, the Mantle of Ozriel streaming behind him like a boiling cape of shadow, and the white hair running down his back. But it was all fuzzy, like a half-forgotten dream. His face blurred, though she could fill in the gaps from memory: cold and distant and grim.

In person, he had more of a sense of humor than any other Abidan she'd ever met, but he always wore an expression like a man bracing himself for terrible news.

"Sur...looking lovely...get to the point, because...murdered." He was speaking, speaking to *her,* because he'd known she would find this. Of course he had. But whatever he'd predicted, it hadn't included a battle in this room ruining his message.

The scene congealed for a moment, until she could almost believe he was really standing in front of her. "...didn't abandon you. I've identified the sixteen worlds...a facility like this one..." She could make out his lips moving now, but it was as though she'd gone deaf.

"...sure you'll...quarantine. I sh—...actually kills me."

His expression darkened, and he looked over her shoulder. The Scythe appeared in his hand: a long, curved blade like an obsidian scimitar. At least, that was how it presented itself.

She was sure this was the heart of the message, but she heard nothing but a whisper of static. Finally, his voice faded back in, just on the edge of her hearing.

"...if I didn't act, it would all stay the same. I don't—"

The dream world squealed with feedback, and colors twisted in her eyes as the message's recording was violently cut off.

That wasn't interference. He'd been attacked while speaking, ending the message.

So the battle had *started* here, but continued off into the world. Or had he recorded it elsewhere and the beacon survived the battle?

...survived a battle that he, perhaps, had not.

"Presence," Suriel ordered verbally. "Reconstruct the probable content of Ozriel's message. Authorization Suriel zero-zero-six." The Presence was more than capable of simple predictions, but interactions between Judges usually required verbal confirmation. Sanctum wanted any jurisdictional overlap to be well documented.

[Incomplete information supplemented with standard Ozriel prediction model. Best recreation follows.]

The message was audio-only, but it was as though Ozriel was speaking right into her ear. The voice of her friend, full of weary humor.

"Suriel. You're looking lovely today, I'm sure. I'll get to the point, because I have an unexpected visitor who needs murdered: I did *not* abandon you. I have identified the sixteen worlds that will be corrupted while I'm gone, and I've prepared a facility like this one in each. I'm sure Makiel will send Gadrael, and then you'll volunteer. If I'm still gone, chaotic interference makes it impossible to predict beyond sixteen, so go ahead and initiate quarantine. I shouldn't take much longer, unless this actually kills me."

His voice turned serious. "We have to change, Suriel. If I didn't act, it would all stay the same. I don't—"

The sound cut off.

Of their own accord, her eyes slid back to the blood on the walls. He'd seen her standing here. From hundreds of years ago, he'd seen her.

He was still watching out for her, if not for himself.

Her heart hammered in her ears, her respiration sped up a fraction, and her adrenal glands squeezed hormones into her bloodstream. She chose not to cut off the physical responses.

Let her feel fear for her friend.

CHAPTER FOURTEEN

On the fourth morning since starting the Trials, Lindon slid the Sylvan Riverseed's case out of his pack, holding out a pair of freshly Forged scales.

The Sylvan waved at him, smiling cheerily.

He stared back.

Someone had replaced his tiny, faceless spirit with a miniature woman Forged out of water madra. Until she opened her mouth at the sight of Lindon's scales, waiting to be fed, he suspected it was a different creature entirely.

Where once she had been a translucent bright blue doll, now she was a deep azure woman with long, flowing hair, a dress that swirled around hidden feet, teeth that showed clearly when she smiled, and curious eyes.

Those eyes were now scrunched closed as she held open her mouth, waiting for her meal. Lindon thought he could see her tongue.

She had a tongue now. And eyelids.

Dazed, he ran his eyes along the edges of the case, looking for changes. He found one immediately: a spot in the corner where the scripted glass didn't fit perfectly together.

That was *certainly* a change. He'd spent hours searching the tank for any imperfections, trying to figure out a way to open it without breaking the glass. He ran his thumb along the flaw, and that corner of the case popped open. He repeated the process on the other side, and the lid of the case rose.

The Sylvan was still begging for food, so he slipped the madra coins inside without taking his eyes from the case itself. They dissolved as soon as they reached the Sylvan, flowing down her throat in streams of light.

Eithan. Eithan did this.

Either he had to accept that the Sylvan had drastically changed her form in the week since he'd fed her—and that someone else had figured out how to open her case and then closed it again—or the Underlord had done something. But what? And why?

He was itching to investigate, but he wasn't even sure what questions to ask. If he had a drudge, he could examine the composition of her madra and see what had changed. Fisher Gesha could tell him, but if he left the mountain, he was considered to have given up.

In the absence of any clear answers, he placed her back into his pack. He'd inspect her more closely later, to see if Eithan had left any obvious hints for him.

Putting the Sylvan out of his mind, he and Yerin challenged the Enforcer Trial a second time.

Lindon cradled the red-and-black crystal in his arms, dashing through the stone forest with Burning Cloak active. Every second sizzled as his muscles burned from the Black-flame madra, every step sent dirt flying behind him and drove splinters of pain through his knees, and every breath came slow and heavy, as though he were trying to suck air through a wet blanket.

It was like running through a nightmare: gray shapes chased him from every direction as pain wracked his body. Though he knew he was moving faster than he ever had before, he still *felt* as though he were slogging through mud.

Finally he dropped the breathing technique, heaving a deep breath of pure air that sent sweet life flowing through his veins, but then his madra channels couldn't handle the burden of the Burning Cloak. It flickered and died, the seal dimmed, and a soldier's blade knocked the crystal from his hands.

A silver blade of madra blasted from the woods, slashing the soldier in half, but the gong had already sounded: failure.

The soldiers changed.

They always carried stone weapons, but sometimes those weapons blazed with sword aura until they could take a slice out of the surrounding pillars.

Not all the soldiers ever carried the gleaming silver weapons, but Yerin preferred the ones that did. She could sense them coming thanks to the aura gathering around their weapons, and the Endless Sword technique would mince them. When those showed up, she could eliminate them in a blink, and she and Lindon could make it deep into the columns before a living statue slipped past her and caught him.

But they never made it any further.

The frustration grew until she wanted to take a sword and carve her way out of this valley by pure fury. She could do *so much* better than this. If she could use her true ability, she would split every single sword-carrying soldier open on their own aura and then carry Lindon through to the end like a baby.

Not that Lindon was a burden anymore, which was enough shock for a lifetime in itself. He had surprised and impressed her in the days since they'd started the Trial. The Burning Cloak fit him like a good sheath, giving him everything he'd lacked before: explosive speed, bursts of strength, and enough confidence to stand against his enemies fist-to-fist.

Truth was, fighting next to him was a treat, now that he

could keep up with her. They could only challenge the Trials every three or four days, when they were in their best condition: his spirit didn't recover as fast as hers, and her injuries stuck around longer than his did. She looked forward to the Trial days, because that meant fighting together, as a pair.

If she could have used her full skills, fighting next to Lindon as they learned to train and grow as a team, she'd have been on holiday. It would have been the best time in her life since the Sword Sage plucked her out of the ashes of her childhood home.

But she was hobbled. Weighted down.

Her uninvited guest strained against its seal, gaining on her day after day as she remained stuck at the barrier to Highgold. She had to dedicate half her attention to keeping it under control, so it didn't squirm further into her core. Every night she tied the bow tighter around her waist, trying to reinforce the Sword Sage's seal, feeling the bloodthirst of the red rope seeping into her.

On its own, that wouldn't be enough to cripple her—she'd dealt with this parasite most of her life. But now even her own *madra* was fighting her.

Her Goldsign still slipped through her control sometimes, lunging against enemies when she wanted it to pull back. If anything, it was getting worse; now her own techniques were also trying to defy her. Her master's instincts, buried inside her along with his Remnant, would tell her to Enforce herself and run into battle. Madra she'd been preparing to hurl at her enemies would flow into her sword instead, sharpening her weapon. She had to switch tactics, adapting to her master's lesson and costing precious seconds in battle.

Together, it was like trying to fight with someone else's hands. Some days it felt like she couldn't take two steps without her own body betraying her.

She could tap into the silver Remnant in her core, and sometimes she was tempted. But even when he was stealing her madra, ruining her chance at passing the Trial, it was still another chance at hearing his voice.

She couldn't give that up. And any insight into the Path of the Endless Sword was rarer than diamonds for her; without her master's voice, she would be the only expert remaining on her Path.

She'd cross over to Highgold eventually, even without silencing her master again, she was sure of it.

Every day, the gong seemed to grow louder.

Lindon knelt, driving an Empty Palm deep into the ground. He'd raised his pure core to Jade, and the technique penetrated deeper than he'd dared to hope, almost disrupting the script that powered the Trial. If he could break it, that would disrupt the function of the Trial long enough for them to pass through.

But it wasn't enough. The soldiers swarmed him, beating him until he dropped the crystal. He screamed as the gong sounded.

The cool winter breeze that had once flowed into the valley had long since grown hot. Lindon and Yerin gathered food with wordless efficiency now, choking down the oily, gritty crab meat and retiring to their own caves to cycle.

Lindon cycled Blackflame for two hours every night, drawing aura of heat and destruction into his endlessly grinding stone wheel.

It would burn everything, that aura. Lindon came to think of it as a hungry power: the blazing drive for more, more, more. It filled him as he cycled, until he wanted to tear the Enforcer Trial apart with his teeth.

The dragon advances. That was what the Enforcer tablet had said, and those seemed like the words of the Blackflame madra itself. It wanted to advance like a furious dragon, tearing apart everything before it.

If only he could.

The parasite ring weighed down his spirit. He knew that in the long run it would help his training, but every day he almost threw it into the pool.

The Heaven and Earth Purification Wheel made his breath so heavy and long that it burned his lungs, every cycle of madra so torturously slow that his spirit ached like muscles cramped and trapped. Whenever he caught a normal breath, free of the technique, he almost sobbed with relief.

His own Blackflame madra ate away at his madra channels, leaving black residue like soot in his spirit. If he didn't cleanse it, he'd be leaving injuries and blockages in his soul, harming his future development. After using Blackflame too much, he had to spend several hours cycling pure madra to clean out his madra channels. It was hard to sit there all afternoon, cleaning his spirit, and *not* feel like he was wasting time.

Real Blackflames probably had a method to deal with that problem, but he had no one to ask. Orthos had kept his distance, circling through the mountain but never intruding on their Trial grounds. Sometimes Lindon felt him in the distance, his spirit burning with madness, and other times he was calm as a dying fire. In both states, he stayed away.

The Sylvan Riverseed's appetite had increased since her transformation. She begged him for pure madra even when he was exhausted and could barely push his spirit through a single cycle.

The Burning Cloak had cost him weeks of training before he could use it naturally. The explosive bursts of strength and speed it provided meant he had to learn to do everything over again: run without hurling himself into a tree, throw a punch without breaking his own elbow, cut food without slicing off his own fingers. Yerin had even set him up with a juggling routine until he could keep three stones in the air without losing the Burning Cloak, dropping a stone, or hurling one of the pebbles out of the valley. Every day they spent perfecting his precision felt like a day lost; a day when he could have been challenging the Trial.

Even his body betrayed him, leeching his core every time he was wounded, draining him dry and leaving him limp and powerless on the ground. The Bloodforged Iron body was the only reason they could challenge the course as often as they did, but it also crippled him after every failure.

Over it all, Jai Long loomed like a specter. This Trial was supposed to be the first step to defeating him, but Lindon had tripped and fallen at the first stair.

...though as painful as each day was, as miserable as he felt in those nights when he wept alone in his damp cave, he couldn't deny the results.

After months of work, his Burning Cloak covered him in a thick blaze of red and black. He could keep it active for twenty minutes, so long as nothing cut him and activated his Iron body, and he could drive his fist straight through a Forged soldier.

His cores felt like a pair of lakes now, where they'd once been buckets. They didn't look any larger than before, but they felt *deeper,* like the Heaven and Earth Purification Wheel had drilled down to profound depths. He spent more madra in a single Trial attempt now than his entire spirit could have contained only months before.

The improvement kept him going, got him out of his cave in the morning, kept him from abandoning his breathing technique as a trap, made him pick up the Trial's activation crystal again and again even though he'd sooner embrace a venomous snake.

Continuing meant taking another step forward. Giving up meant accepting death at Jai Long's spear.

Between them, he and Yerin were now destroying fifteen or sixteen soldiers every run, getting closer and closer to the end of the Trial.

But they never made it.

He'd tried every answer he could think of: hurling the

crystal, digging to break the script, building a simple construct out of half-formed soldier parts, running straight through the columns without stopping, altering the script that ran the Trial. Nothing worked. It seemed the Soulsmiths who built this course had thought of everything.

Time blurred and faded away. Only the endless cycle of day and night mattered, because the Trial only worked during the day.

He stopped hearing the gong. When the soldiers caught him or his Burning Cloak flagged, he simply walked away.

It had been four months since Eithan had first opened the temple at the top of the mountain, and Cassias had grown used to his duties.

Since Yerin and Lindon usually needed two or three days of rest between attempts, he could bring his work with him. He'd moved a table up to this peak, writing letters and reading reports while keeping half of his detection web on the children. After sixteen weeks, this hidden temple looked more like an office than his actual office did.

Cassias spent most of his time alone with paperwork or his own training. He found he enjoyed it; letting Eithan handle the bulk of Arelius affairs suited him. He'd needed a break.

In contrast, the children were having the most stressful experience of their lives.

He sipped tea as he watched the children cycle in the morning, through the scripted window. He no longer expected they would give up—if they hadn't done so by this point, they likely never would. They would die in an accident during the Trials before they surrendered.

Cassias had given himself over to that prospect with weary acceptance. In four months, you could grow used to almost anything.

Somewhere in the back of his mind, he still hoped that today would be the day Eithan would grow tired of this project and pull him away. Almost half of the allotted time to Jai Long's duel had passed, and even a blind Copper could see that Lindon wasn't ready.

Certainly, he'd improved during his time in the Trials. Cassias almost couldn't believe a Jade *could* improve so fast. Yerin was straining against the limits of Lowgold, perfecting both her skill and her advancement, but Lindon was reaching the point where he could almost—for a brief breath or two, with the Burning Cloak active—match her in a fight.

That itself was a feat worthy of pride, but he was far from defeating Jai Long. In fact, if Yerin could finally break through that last barrier to Highgold, Cassias would suggest that Eithan pit *her* against the Jai exile instead. She would still be a stage behind him in advancement, but Cassias wasn't sure that would matter.

He could recognize a prodigy when he saw one.

Still, neither of them had received any instruction in the last months, besides whatever was written on that tablet the Blackflames had left behind.

Cassias wasn't sure exactly what date Eithan had in mind for the duel, but Lindon had at most seven months remaining. Even *with* a teacher, Cassias couldn't imagine a favorable outcome for them.

Without one, Lindon would certainly die.

Cassias gave a heavy sigh and sipped his tea. He would have to appeal to the branch heads, get them to rein in Eithan's...enthusiasm about this duel. But he doubted they would go against the Underlord for the sake of a Jade. Cassias himself would have thought the same, if he hadn't spent so much time in the last half a year watching the children struggle. Now, he couldn't help but wish them success. No matter how unlikely it was.

When Yerin and Lindon had finished their morning meal and cycling session, Cassias set down his tea and prepared himself. They would be challenging the Trial now.

But instead of dragging himself through the archway, as he usually did on Trial days, Lindon went back into his cave like he'd forgotten something.

A few breaths later, he dashed back out, seizing Yerin by the arm and dragging her inside.

Cassias extended his awareness, reaching in to watch the cave.

Lindon pulled Yerin inside and gestured to the Sylvan Riverseed, who scampered around the cave, curiously examining his bedroll and the occasional rock.

"Did she break out?" Yerin asked uncertainly.

"No, she's...it's...watch my soul!" Lindon wouldn't have understood what happened if he hadn't seen it for himself. Instead of explaining, he called Blackflame into his channels.

But instead of guiding it, he let it rampage through his spirit. The result was an uncomfortable spiritual pain, like a red-hot iron pressed against his stomach while a bird screeched next to his ear.

It was only a little madra, and it burned out quickly, but he hadn't controlled it at all. His madra channels felt scorched at several points, and a black substance had built up like rubble in a tunnel. This was the effect of Blackflame corrosion, and the reason why he had to cleanse his spirit with pure madra every day.

When the madra was controlled, the blockage wouldn't build up so quickly. But if he slipped, it would happen in seconds.

Yerin glared at him and snatched her arm out of his grip. "Are you cracked? Now I have to burn *my* time away while you sit there and cycle your spirit clean."

Lindon reached his hand out to the Sylvan.

Grinning like they were playing a game, the Riverseed darted up and slapped her palm against his. A blue presence dripped into his spirit, rolling through his madra channels.

Wherever that deep blue light ran, the corrosion of Blackflame vanished. Even his madra channels felt refreshed, as though they'd never been scorched by out-of-control power.

The spirit paled to the color of a summer sky, leaning against Lindon's shin to stay balanced. With one hand, she pointed to her gaping mouth, and he fed her a fistful of pure scales that he'd prepared for that purpose.

After using her power, she grew pallid and weary on her own, and then demanded even more scales. She would sap all the power in his pure core and then beg for more before she was back to her usual state.

In seconds, Yerin went from irritated to speechless, which gave Lindon more than a little satisfaction. He had almost collapsed when the Sylvan had reached up and grabbed his fingertip while he fed her, scrubbing his spirit clean.

Somehow, it felt better not to be the *only* one surprised.

Yerin darted over to the Riverseed, scooping her up in her bare hands.

The spirit squirmed out of her grip, scuttling over to hide behind Lindon's leg. She bared her teeth at Yerin in a threatening grimace.

Yerin's face fell. "She doesn't like me?"

Lindon was as surprised as she was. The Sylvan had never interacted with anyone but him, as far as he'd seen, but she'd always seemed active and curious. Whenever she saw Yerin through the glass of her case, she had pointed and waved.

He extended his perception to the Sylvan. A sacred artist would feel a scan as a light brush, but it usually seemed to comfort her. She was weaker after expending her power, but she had enough madra for a second attempt.

"Go to Yerin," he said, gesturing. "Go on. Do to her what you did to me."

The Riverseed shuffled a few steps forward, but turned over her shoulder to give Lindon a doubtful look.

"It's okay. I'm right here."

The Sylvan dragged herself over to Yerin, keeping her eyes on the stone floor. When Yerin stuck out a hand, the spirit slapped her finger once and then scampered back to Lindon, climbing up to sit on his shoulder. She had lightened some more, and she swayed as though dizzy.

"It's only been a few days since she would come out of her case," he said apologetically. "Did it work?"

"I feel like I should be more than a little hurt right now," Yerin said, eyeing the Sylvan. "Worked, though, true and stable."

Yerin had built up a slight blockage in her own soul—one of the hazards of cycling within such an ocean of Blackflame aura. It was nothing compared to Lindon's, but she took longer to get rid of it.

Lindon patted the Sylvan on the head with a finger. He wouldn't have to control his Blackflame madra so carefully during the Trial, and he could dive right back into another attempt without cycling pure madra to cleanse his channels.

Originally, he hadn't even had enough madra to support one attempt, much less two. But after months of cycling the Heaven and Earth Purification Wheel, he had the madra for two, maybe three attempts if he stretched it. The major bottleneck now was how much time it took for his madra channels to recover after being strained and scorched by Blackflame.

Which, now that they had the Sylvan Riverseed, was no time at all.

"If we don't get hurt too badly..." he began, but Yerin cut him off.

"If *I* don't hurt myself, that's what you're saying. It's true. Long as I'm not cut too deep, I'll be ready for a second try two breaths after the first one. If we don't have to wait for you to coddle your spirit anymore, we can get some *real* work done."

She was grinning by the end, but Lindon braced himself. Two attempts in a row.

Together, they walked through the archway.

Cassias fixed most of his attention on Yerin. She slaughtered the formation's soldier projections, tearing them apart with her white blade, her Goldsign, her mastery of the sword aura. Any soldier he empowered with his own madra was only destroyed faster; their weapon gathered sword aura more efficiently, so Yerin's Endless Sword tore them up.

Without the ability to empower the soldiers, he could only guide them. At the moment, his most efficient tactic was simply to throw projections at Yerin, hoping to bog her down.

When Lindon barreled through the middle, diving through the forest of pillars, Cassias was caught off guard. But only for a moment.

If he could bring down Yerin early today, he could take care of Lindon without much care. So he diverted two soldiers to slow Lindon down.

Cassias was so consumed by his task that he forgot his original goal. He had grown up a genius of the Arelius family, its heir, and he had won virtually every competition he'd ever entered. Even giving up his position in the family to Eithan hadn't felt like a loss so much as a trade.

But he wasn't used to losing. After four months, even the *idea* of letting the children win on purpose had entirely faded away.

He needed to make them give up.

The two soldiers pincered Lindon, each driving a silver-gleaming sword at him from a different direction. On a previous run, they had pierced through his hand, and it had taken his Bloodforged Iron body a week to restore the damage.

But this time, Lindon wasn't trying to reach the goal.

Any formation like this one had to draw power from the local aura, which meant it took time to recharge. The more energy he could draw out of it this time, the weaker the Trial would be for their second attempt.

Well, the weaker it *should* be. The theory was sound, but they'd never been able to challenge it twice in the same day before.

He smashed the seal down on a soldier's head, Burning Cloak flaring around him. The projection burst apart, leaving a Forged sword to dissolve on the ground.

A sword pricked him over the shoulder blade, but with Blackflame madra roaring through him, he barely felt it. He turned with such speed that it wrenched something in his back, seizing that soldier's face in his palm.

Lindon hadn't learned any Striker techniques on the Path of Black Flame yet, but he'd worked with the power enough over the last few months that he'd grasped a few basic tricks. He could kindle a black fire, though it was loose and uncontrolled, only spraying a few inches from his hand.

In this case, that was enough. He gripped the soldier and sent Blackflame madra flooding into it.

This was the most primitive Striker technique possible; it was more like an Empty Palm than a hurled fireball, but red-and-black power surged into the soldier, dissolving it, burning it to gray essence in seconds.

Without hesitating, Lindon advanced. Between his Iron body and the Burning Cloak, his spirit was burning down quickly, and he had to make sure the course spent more energy than he did.

Cassias couldn't project new enemies fast enough to deal with Yerin. She had given up any idea of moving forward, pouring everything she had into shredding her opponents. Even some of the stone pillars had been shattered, collapsing in a pile of boulders.

There were some earth-aspect Ruler constructs built into the course that could rebuild those columns, but they would take even more of the course's stored power. Even if Cassias provided madra of his own, rebuilding the battlefield wouldn't be cheap.

But the Trial had built up enough momentum. Yerin was on the defensive, Lindon was forced back, and they were surrounded by gray soldiers.

Once again, it was his victory. They wouldn't surrender the Trial after this, but they were one step closer.

As Lindon dropped the activation crystal and held up his hands, Cassias leaned back in his chair. They'd given up especially quickly today, despite causing more damage to the course than average. Maybe they really were getting frustrated.

He found himself a little disappointed. They had learned and grown as sacred artists over the last four months, and it really would be for the best if they quit and trained normally from now on...but part of him had been hoping they would succeed.

Cassias sighed and triggered the course's repair function. The stored energy would dip unusually low, but two days of drawing on the mountain's powerful aura would restore it. Even if they tried again tomorrow, he would be able to funnel some of his own madra into the course to make up the difference.

Once it was done, he slid the chair over to his desk and began his paperwork. He'd have the rest of the day to himself, and there were work orders to be filled.

After about an hour of cycling, Yerin walked over to Lindon's cave. He was sitting with legs crossed into a cycling position, breathing evenly. His little pet Sylvan sat on his head, mimicking his posture and playing with his hair.

The spirit grimaced when she saw Yerin, giving her a suspicious look.

That was more than a little unfair, in Yerin's view. She'd never drawn swords on the spirit, nor even said a harsh word. Maybe Yerin should feed her, like a skittish dog.

Lindon hadn't reacted to Yerin's presence yet, his breaths still steady and measured. In her spiritual perception, he gave off the warm impression of a cycling fire artist, with the added air of danger that came from Blackflame. His jade badge hung from a shimmering silk ribbon and rested against his chest.

Now that they'd spent so long running up against the Blackflame Enforcer Trial, he looked like a real sacred artist. He'd burned off the last bit of softness left from his clan upbringing, his frame hardening and filling out. He was covered by a layer of dirt and ash from their run of the course earlier, his hair messy, his sacred artist robes torn, tattered, and singed.

He showed a sharp difference from the boy she'd met in Sacred Valley. He still had a long stretch of road left to travel, but now she could actually see herself fighting alongside him. Not just in the Trials, either; when she thought of her own violent, uncertain future, she could picture him standing next to her.

Nothing but wishful thinking on her part. If odds played out, he'd be killed by Jai Long and she'd end up as a snack for her unwelcome guest. No sense in planning for anything else until the knives weren't quite so close to their throats.

She kicked his knee, and he blinked awake. "Oi. Get Little Blue to scrub me clean, and then let's go."

He was still gathering his thoughts after having broken out of his cycling trance. Now that she looked for it, he was breathing a little heavy, and his skin had a light sheen of sweat. Whatever cycling technique Eithan had taught him, it must have some weight.

"Little Blue?" he asked.

"Can't keep calling her the Riverseed. She's got a face."

Lindon lifted his eyes as though trying to see the Sylvan sitting on top of his head. "Ah, you're right. We should name her."

Yerin rolled up her sleeve and held out a wrist. "Call her what you want, but get her to hop on over here."

It took Lindon almost a minute to coax the Riverseed onto Yerin, and she scurried off as soon as her job was done. Once again, even a spark of her power was enough to scrub Yerin's spirit clean of the Blackflame aura buildup. On top of that, her spirit was peaceful and refreshed, like she hadn't fought in days. Yerin couldn't feel a particular aspect to the madra, but it was calm and soothing.

If only Little Blue didn't hate her so much. Maybe it wasn't her; maybe Sylvans could smell the unwelcome guest inside her.

Yerin adjusted her blood-red belt. Would only make sense, if spirits didn't like *that*. Meant Little Blue had good taste, more than anything.

That was an answer she could live with.

Cassias vaulted out of his chair and over the table, landing in front of the wooden console. The script in the window flared with the touch of his spirit, showing him a heaven-down view of Lindon and Yerin fighting their way through half-formed soldiers. The smoky gray crystal in Lindon's hand pulsed red, and they'd made it further into the course than they had in the morning: most of the soldiers still hadn't formed, including the giant guardian in front of the exit.

It was only a half-hearted scan of his spirit that had let Cassias know the course was active. Yerin and Lindon had *never* attempted two runs of the Trial in the same day, and the ancient training course simply wasn't designed for it. Its power was already running dangerously low, and there were clear consequences: the soldiers were forming much more slowly, and their combat power was weaker. Lindon smashed through one in a single punch, moving into the latter half of the pillars.

If Cassias had been any slower to notice, they would have torn through the unsupervised and weakened Trial, and they might have passed before Cassias realized anything was wrong.

Well, not any longer.

Cassias poured his madra into the correct scripts, the interlocking circles carrying his power down and into the Trial itself. His core, usually shining silver with the light of sword madra, dimmed—transferring his power down through so many scripts was terribly inefficient. He would save more power by hopping down there and fighting them both in person, two against one.

But he couldn't let it be said that Naru Cassias Arelius picked on the weak.

His power flooded into the projections, making the soldiers form faster, Enforcing their weapons. He strained his spirit.

Slowly, Lindon and Yerin's advance ground to a halt.

Lindon turned in midair, kicking off a pillar and launching himself higher. An archer clung to the stone fifteen feet up to snipe at him from above; he grabbed it by the throat and dragged it down to the ground, slamming it into the earth, ignoring the silver arrow that had pierced all the way through his thigh. Blood ran down his leg, costing him a bolt of pain with every step, but the burn of the Blackflame madra and the rush of his Bloodforged body let him ignore it.

The columns thinned, revealing the red arch of the exit.

Three soldiers stood between him and the gateway, spreading out and keeping their sabers level—they were getting smart now, moving to encircle him, to keep him trapped. They knew where he was going.

Or they thought they did.

The fury of Blackflame filled Lindon. He tore the arrow from his leg, hurling it at the nearest warrior, who knocked it out of the air with a gray shield.

But it cost the soldier a moment of its attention. Lindon had dashed after the Forged weapon, projecting a pulse of Blackflame madra into the soldier's midsection. It blew apart like an over-inflated bladder.

The next one closed the distance to swat the crystal from his hand with its sword, but Lindon seized a dissolving blade from the broken enemy, snatching the blade from midair and using it to knock aside the other weapon's attack.

Then he gripped the sword and drove it through the soldier with sheer force, pinning it to the ground.

The third and final enemy dropped its sword and shield for a spear, which it could use to keep him at a distance and poke holes in him until he ran out of madra. If he let it get that far.

Flaring the Burning Cloak, he leaped. His legs screamed at the strain, but the ground beneath him exploded.

At the top of his jump, he twisted to grab the soldier's head with one hand, and his momentum continued carrying him forward. The Forged warrior smashed into a stone column, bursting with the force, dissolving in his hand.

Lindon shouted with the exhilaration of the moment, landing on both feet. Soldiers collected themselves in chunks of gray madra, and he ground his teeth, ready to tear them apart.

The dragon advances.

He could see the exit, and his Blackflame madra was ready to push him forward still, Orthos' core pulsing with the eagerness of a predator before the kill.

But the huge stone giant with the spiked helmet still stood in front of him, a trident in each hand.

Yerin stumbled up next to Lindon, scratched and bloody, panting in the even rhythm of a cycling technique, pale sword clutched in her hand.

He looked at her and they both nodded, turning to face the giant together.

Then Lindon let the crystal ball fall to the ground, and the test ended.

"Looked a lot shabbier that time, that's a truth," Yerin said, resting drawn blade on her shoulder.

Lindon's Blackflame core was down to one smoldering red-and-black ember. "I think I can manage one more."

"Third try," Yerin said. "Let's go."

CHAPTER FIFTEEN

Panting, Cassias fell back against the wicker chair. He'd exhausted his madra so quickly that his soul felt numb, and his limbs trembled.

Four months. The Enforcer Trial was only supposed to take a few weeks, but considering the circumstances, Cassias would find it hard to say they'd failed.

Even after the fall of the Blackflame family, the Naru used this course to train their disciples. But they only ever trained teams.

This Trial had been built to test a single disciple on the Path of Black Flame, fighting with four of their closest protectors. None of the participants would be higher than Lowgold, but the five would have been trained to cooperate since childhood.

The bodyguards would fight as a unit to keep the soldiers away so that the Blackflame could concentrate on holding their Enforcer technique—what Lindon and Yerin called the Burning Cloak—for the duration of the course.

In this Trial, the Blackflame was never supposed to fight. It was a test of teamwork and spiritual endurance.

No one had ever thought to make it a rule that you couldn't challenge the Enforcer Trial twice in one day. Theoretically, it was impossible: the Burning Cloak put too much of a strain on the body to maintain for long, and even the Blackflame family had to cleanse their madra channels after an attempt. When you added in the injuries that a team would inevitably collect during a run of the course, it was a rare five-man squad that could complete a Trial run once a day.

'The dragon advances' was the advice for anyone attempting the Trial: they had to act so that the *dragon,* the Blackflame sacred artist, continually advanced. If they slowed, they would inevitably get bogged down in combat and lose control of the Burning Cloak.

Lindon and Yerin had evidently interpreted that advice differently. They relentlessly advanced until the Trial broke before them.

Any Blackflame Highgold would have had the skill and power to do the same, of course, as would many of the top-tier geniuses from the clan...but none of them would have *needed* a second attempt. Endurance didn't come into it when you blew through the Trial on your first try.

But Lindon and Yerin had challenged the course until *the course gave up.* Yerin was a Sage's disciple, so she should be expected to produce miracles, but Lindon? How did he have the madra capacity to fuel both his Bloodforged Iron body *and* the Burning Cloak? While carrying the crystal and fighting at the same time? Even accepting that, how had he cleansed the damage that Blackflame madra must have done to his madra channels?

What had Eithan done to him?

When Cassias thoughts turned to Eithan, his heart sank. He was *not* looking forward to bringing Eithan the news.

The Underlord would be insufferable after this.

Lindon and Yerin both collapsed after completing the Enforcer Trial, bleeding into the dirt.

Now that they had reached the Striker Trial, they could walk back through the stone columns freely without the Enforcer Trial coming to life and spitting out soldiers. Once Lindon could move again, he resolved to spend an hour doing nothing but walking through the empty Enforcer Trial, just to prove he could.

The Striker Trial itself was an open field of scorched, blasted soil, with another red arch in the distance. Another stone tablet and pedestal waited for them near the entrance, and Lindon wanted to drag his broken body over and start reading the introduction to the Striker technique.

But Yerin had already begun limping back toward their caves, so Lindon followed her. The slab of rock would be there when the wound in his thigh closed.

And now, though Lindon had prepared to challenge the Enforcer Trial for several more days in a row, they were back home so easily.

The Blackflame-scorched crab meat and fiery berries had never tasted so good.

"...they tried to bury me with their bodies," Yerin said, waving a stick in the air like a sword. Her forearm was wrapped in white bandage, as was her entire left eye and her right leg, but none of it affected her motion with the stick. "Had to scrape and claw my way out. Toward the tail end of it, I had my master's sword in this hand, a soldier's sword in this one, and my Goldsign launching every technique I could. My madra's going out like a river, and I can barely see. I think for sure they're going to bring me down again."

She tossed her stick into the fire, grinning. "And then two of them turn like they hear something. They're off like arrows, and that's the straw that tips it. I cut through the rest and come through, looking for you, just in time to see you smack one to *pieces* against a pillar. If that's not a story worth crowing about, I've never heard one."

Lindon's pride helped distract him from the throbbing pain in his thigh and shoulder. He pressed his fists together, looking at her. "I would never have passed without you taking more than your share. Gratitude."

She half-heartedly kicked dirt at him. "I don't need that. Not like it was your Trial alone, was it? Goldsign did what I wanted it to that time, and I'm *this* close to Highgold. I know it. Didn't have to crack my master open or anything."

A drop of rain hissed as it fell into the fire. Another sent up a puff of dirt as it landed nearby, but he was sitting with his back to the cave. An outcropping of stone kept him dry.

Lindon stared into the remaining flames, thoughts growing heavy. Yerin stuck a hand out, testing the rain, and then slipped over to his side of the fire to join him.

She sat with him, shoulder to shoulder, for a minute or two before speaking out. "A worry shared is a worry halved."

Even halved, he had enough worry for both of them.

"Still a long way to go before Truegold," he said, voice dry. "What do I have left, six months?"

"I'd be cracked in the head if I said I was going to hit Truegold in six months," Yerin agreed. "Especially if I was starting from Jade. There are ways to pump you up on the day, just for one fight, but none of them are stable for your health."

"Then...what am I doing?"

She stayed quiet, looking into the fire with him. The rain picked up, slowly dousing the campfire, turning the dark, greasy flames to smoke.

"Back home, they'd have named me heir to the clan by now," Lindon said. "Jade before seventeen summers. They'd call me a genius, or blessed by the heavens. But that's not enough to keep me alive."

She leaned her shoulder into his. "Back in your home, they stacked up pebbles and called them mountains. When you left, you slipped out of a trap. As for dying..." She gave a soundless laugh. "Not your problem alone, is it? Eithan's to blame for dangling you over the fire; he'll have to do his share of pulling you out."

234 O WILL WIGHT

Yerin slipped her hand into his and gave him a squeeze. Her fingers were rough and callused. "I'm here too, for all that's worth. Don't want to see you buried yet."

Lindon's heart hammered, and he had to concentrate to control the flow of his madra. He had lived in this valley with Yerin for the past half a year, but the contact between them had been almost entirely related to the sacred arts—she would give him pointers during practice, or discuss that day's attempt at the Trial, or help him catch food. They had both been aimed at the Trial like a pair of hawks unleashed for the hunt.

Now, this simple contact felt like sinking into a warm bath after a long day working in the snow. He squeezed her hand back without a word, and she left it there as they leaned against each other.

Together, they sat and watched the rain.

...until they heard the scream.

It started as a distant shriek, but rapidly grew closer. Yerin was on her feet with weapon in hand instantly, her silver Goldsign arched and poised.

Lindon rose more roughly, favoring his wounded leg, but he had recovered enough Blackflame madra to begin cycling for the Burning Cloak. If this was a fight, maybe some unexpected beginning to the Striker Trial, he would be ready.

Eithan slammed into the ground a second later, face-first, kicking up a cloud of dust.

Both Lindon and Yerin took a step back, coughing and waving dust away. When the cloud cleared, the Underlord was still lying there spread-eagle, turquoise-and-gold robes settling into the dirt, his yellow hair a mess around him.

He suddenly convulsed, making a choking sound as he sat bolt upright. An instant later he hacked a mouthful of mud onto the ground, grimacing at the taste.

"That was more of a—ah, let's say—*rapid* descent than I intended," Eithan said, rubbing dirt from his face with the heel of his hand.

The top of the cliff loomed over them, scraping the sky.

He had to have fallen over a hundred feet, if not more. "Underlord, are you...are you all right?"

Yerin folded her arms. "Takes more than that to ruffle *your* feathers, doesn't it, Eithan?"

Eithan spat some more mud onto the ground. "I'm not so sure. My feathers might be intact, but my ribs are going to have some complaining to do for the next morning or two." He coughed loudly into his hand, and then inspected his palm.

"It's a pleasure to see you, after all this time," Lindon said. "Are you here because we passed the Trial?"

"You mean, why did I fall out of the sky and onto my face just now?" Eithan asked, rising to his feet and brushing himself off. "A wise question. I've been keeping an eye on you, as I promised, and now that you've cleared the Enforcer Trial—none too soon, I might add—I decided to pay you a visit. And as I was making my way to you, I..." He coughed once more, more lightly this time. "...slipped."

Yerin looked him up and down. "Underlords slip off rocks every day, do they?"

"I don't make a habit of it, but it *was* a steep descent, as you can see." He gestured to the cliff, which was the next best thing to a sheer wall. "Even I make mistakes from time to time. Anyway, I was waiting for the most appropriate time to make my entrance, and...well, it was raining." He held out a hand. "Looks like that's cleared up, and just in time!"

His grin returned in full force, and he bulled forward before Lindon could ask any more questions about his entrance. "Half of your year remains, as I'm sure you know, so I come bearing gifts." He turned to Yerin, giving a shallow bow. "For you, little sister, I have located that greatest of rarities: a Spirit Manifestation pill."

Yerin stared blankly at him. "If you're expecting me to start dancing for joy..."

"The Spirit Manifestation pill is very delicate and expensive, refined from some of the most valuable herbs and blood essences on the continent. It takes decades to finish, and each individual elixir can be considered a refiner's masterpiece!" Yerin didn't seem impressed, but Lindon was leaning forward, eyes wide.

If Yerin's gift was so rare and valuable, he could only imagine what was coming *his* way.

"Each pill is customized to the individual consuming it," Eithan said proudly. "In this case, it will fill you with enough sword madra to help you break open the boundary to Highgold...*without* disturbing your master's Remnant in the slightest."

Now Yerin's face paled, and a hand moved down to the red rope wrapped around her waist. Lindon always tried to avoid looking at the belt; it seemed to *squirm* in the corner of his eye, and in his spiritual senses, the rope felt like it was soaked in blood.

"Light dawns! Yes, you can stay ahead of your...rude lodger, there...and keep your master's memories for as long as you like."

Yerin drifted toward him as though sleepwalking. "Do you have that pill tucked away? No, not unless you've put a veil over it. Where did you leave it?" She looked like she was going to seize him by the collar and start shaking.

He held up a hand. "It has taken me months of hunting, bartering, and begging to secure a half-finished pill, and it has to be completed to your personal specifications. I have the best refiner in the family working on it whenever he's not occupied with *other* matters, but it will still be many months before it is finished. However, when it is complete..." He folded his hands together respectfully. "...well, I regret that the honored Sage of the Endless Sword will not be there to witness your glory."

Yerin stalked away, leaning with one hand against the cave wall, breathing heavily. Lindon wished there was something he could say to her, but he was still wondering about her "lodger."

In spite of himself, he was somewhat disappointed by that. She knew all about Suriel, but she hadn't trusted him enough to tell him *her* secret. It wasn't as thought he had any right to know, but would have been nice.

"And for you, Lindon," Eithan said, interrupting his thoughts. "I've located a Blackflame Truegold's scales. Pure scales are useful to anyone, as you know, but scales from the Path of Black Flame could save *you* months of cycling."

The implications of that were not lost on Lindon, and he dropped to his knees, bowing deeply. "This one cannot express his appreciation, Underlord."

Eithan waved at him irritably. "None of that. I need you with a straight spine, not a bent one. Stand up."

Lindon did so, but he still pressed his fists together in a salute.

"The scales are up for auction in three months' time, after which I will bring them back to you," Eithan continued. "I will hold it as a reward for completing the third Trial. With the aid of the scales, you could reach the peak of Jade in an instant, and then Orthos could take you to Gold. Lowgold fighting against Truegold..."

He rubbed his chin. "...well, it's not as though it's *never* happened. Your Path is suitable, and a heron could technically kill a lion, if it poked the beast's eyes out at exactly the right moment. But, ah, I still wouldn't bet on the heron."

That dampened Lindon's enthusiasm considerably. Judging from the Underlord's words, advancing to Lowgold was the best he could hope for, and it still wouldn't change his fate.

"If you can complete the two remaining Trials in six weeks each—much, *much* faster than this one—you'll have plenty of time to process those scales! So now that you're properly motivated: fight, fight, fight!"

Lindon sat staring at nothing for long after Eithan left.

Suddenly the future looked so bleak.

Lindon knelt in front of the Striker tablet while Yerin stood over him, listening.

"With the power of the dragons, the Blackflames destroyed their enemies. Their allies feared them, but..." Lindon hesitated in front of a group of four characters stacked together. They seemed to be some sort of idiom, maybe a proverb that had once been common.

After he thought he had it, he continued. "A ruthless enemy is a reliable ally. When their enemies were no more, they had peace."

And that was the legacy he was inheriting now: a Path of ruthless destruction. It was a sobering thought.

He ran his finger down the tablet, skipping past the madra diagram and the description of the Striker technique—he would need Yerin to help him decipher those anyway. He landed on the words in the center of the stone.

"The dragon destroys," he said aloud.

The dragon advances.

The dragon destroys.

"Makes you ask what the third stone says," Yerin said. "The dragon dances, maybe. The dragon naps. The dragon takes a break because he already killed everybody."

Lindon skipped to the Striker technique. "Fierce...River of...Fierce Flowing Breath. I'm fairly sure that's what it means. They certainly say 'fierce' twice."

Yerin folded her arms. "It's dragon breath."

She pointed to the pictogram of a man projecting a line of fire from his hands. It was next to a picture of that same technique streaming from a dragon's open jaws. "Maybe they called it Fiercely Fierce Breath, but everybody knows what comes out of a dragon's mouth."

Lindon looked at the loops indicating the madra flow, and at the characters floating over it. "Would you mind teaching me, then?"

She rapped her knuckles against the stone. "I could tell you without reading them. Cycle your madra to the palms of your hands and keep it there. Let it build and build like you've stopped up a river, and when it's just about to burst, *push* it out." She shrugged. "My Striker technique starts the same way, except through a sword. And mine has three more steps."

Lindon looked at his hands, gathering madra into his palms while trying to focus on maintaining his breathing and cycling according to the diagram all at the same time.

Yerin grabbed him by the arm. "Maybe take a step or two back, if you don't mind. I'm not looking to roast today."

Lindon bowed in apology, moving ten steps to the right and contemplating the broad, blackened expanse of hardened dirt that was the Striker Trial. He was itching to see what they'd have to face in the Trial itself, but one step at a time; he wouldn't even be able to start without the ability to execute a Striker technique.

He steadied his breath, focusing first on the madra diagram, making sure that his madra was flowing through the right channels. Then, once he had his madra moving in the right direction, he ignored it.

In the last few months, he'd gotten something of a sense for the nature of Blackflame madra. He could move by feel, without relying on convoluted patterns, gathering power in his palms and letting it pool there. He had done something similar with the soldier earlier, pouring raw power into the projection and letting it explode.

He held both hands out toward the empty space. Nothing visible changed, but he could feel the madra building and building, the pressure growing, until his hands felt like they would dissolve from the inside.

In that moment, he gathered the force of his spirit and *shoved*.

When Lindon had first learned the Burning Cloak, the technique had started thin, weak, and inefficient. He had worked for months to increase its potency, to use its power effectively. He had expected something similar with the Striker technique: this first attempt might produce nothing more than a tiny tongue of flame, but he would build it up to a roaring dragon's breath.

So when the madra burst out of him in a furious, flaming storm of black and red, scorching the air in an explosion that sent him tumbling backwards ten feet and coming to rest in a tangle of limbs, he was...surprised.

Yerin waited for him to stumble to his feet and press his hand to his skull, checking for bruising, before she nodded sagely. "Yeah, that's how it happens."

The dirt was blasted away in a starburst pattern where Lindon had been standing. It wasn't deep—the soil here was packed tight, and had been charred over and over for years—but it stood out. The aura seethed in his Copper sight, the black and red powers boiling, but they slowly calmed.

"It didn't get very far," Lindon noted, steadying himself against the cliff wall. That explosion had singed his hands, even though it came from his own madra—it must have ignited the air. His Bloodforged Iron body was already drawing power to the injury, sapping his core further. That one technique had taken more out of him than five minutes with the Burning Cloak.

"River doesn't get too far without banks," Yerin said. "Out of control, it's just a flood. Spills everywhere. You want it to go where you want it to go, you have to guide it."

She tapped the stone again. "There's a pointer here. Push it outside your body, but keep it under control." She held her hands a few inches apart as though cupping an invisible ball, and swirls of sharp silver energy began collecting in the air between them. They whirled and slashed in bright flashes, as though she'd contained a dozen blades of light.

"Pack it together," she continued. The silver light bunched up into a ball the size of his thumb, but she kept pouring more madra into it. "Then, when you can't keep it dammed up anymore..." A wild, spiraling blaze of silver light whirled between her hands. "...let it go."

The ball flew out of her hands, a silver fist-sized spiral of sword madra. It spun erratically in the air, going no more than a yard or two before it slammed into the ground.

The technique exploded.

A thousand sword slashes detonated in all different directions, slicing the air, carving hundreds of crisscrossing grooves in the earth. Some of them looked deeper than the length of his hand.

The storm of sword energy faded, leaving Lindon stunned. "Have you used that technique before?"

She shrugged. "Pulled that out of thin air. Not really a winner for me; it only goes a step or two, see, and I could do it faster with my sword. Sword madra likes to move, not to be bunched up like that. Should be stable enough for fire madra, though."

It hadn't looked anything like the diagram: she'd fired a twisting ball, not a stream of energy that struck in a line. But different aspects of madra should be expected to work differently, and this technique *had* been developed for Blackflame.

Lindon was expectant as he held his hands about six inches apart. Even if he ended up with an explosive fireball instead of a dragon's breath, that was a more devastating weapon than he had now.

Cycling his madra according to the Striker technique's pattern, he gathered power in his palms. Then, focusing on the space between his hands, he let the power flow out.

The air between his hands blew apart.

This time it wasn't enough to knock him away, but he did stumble back a few steps, his hands scorched. The front of his outer robe had started to unravel, and his belt was singed.

"You've got to keep hold of it," Yerin said.

"That's what I'm trying to—" he said, before his second attempt exploded.

After three more failed attempts, Lindon eyed the far side of the Striker Trial grounds. They were *mostly* identical to the Enforcer grounds, with one notable exception: there was no crystal ball on the pedestal next to the tablet, and no pedestal on the other side. Obviously he wasn't supposed to carry anything across.

Judging by the nature of the Trial, he had to assume he was intended to launch a technique all the way over there. But if he wanted to extend his Striker range from a few inches to over a hundred yards, then he had to hope his talent as a Striker exceeded his talent as an Enforcer.

"I can practice tonight," Lindon said, putting his hand on the pedestal. "Let's get started."

Yerin rubbed a thumb along one of the fresh scars on her jaw. "Looks like you're trying to fly before you grow wings, if you ask my opinion."

Lindon was already gathering madra into his hand. One hand, this time. "We have to see how far we have yet to fly, don't we?"

"Truth." She drew her sword eagerly—he'd known he wouldn't have to do much to convince her. "Light this fire," she said.

It took him a few more seconds to push the madra through his palms, and this time his madra was recognizable as fire. It spilled all over the pedestal, doing no damage whatsoever to the smoky crystal or the stone, and only knocked Lindon's arm back instead of his entire body.

The technique didn't stretch any further, but progress was progress.

As soon as his madra entered the crystal, circles came to life all over the Trial grounds. The ground rumbled, and a field of hazy gray light sprang up in the center of the field.

There was some good news: at least he didn't have to hold the technique this time, as he had for the Enforcer Trial.

The scripts continued working, making more changes, but Yerin reached down and hefted a rock twice the size of her fist. With a casual flip of the wrist, she hurled it half the length of the grounds, into the gray wall.

The rock sizzled and disappeared.

"As you'd expect, they won't let you just walk through." She flicked her sword, and a rippling wave of silver-tinged light sliced through the air. It passed through the gray field intact; Lindon could sense its energy streak past the aura barrier.

So madra passed through, but not solid objects. Fascinating.

Shadows gathered past the gray wall, visible as though through dirty glass, but Lindon jogged up to the transparent wall itself. "Is this a technique, do you think, or some kind of script?"

Yerin had followed him, though she watched the shadowy figures gathering on the other side rather than the wall. "Could be either one, I'd say. Gathers up destruction aura into one place, leaves madra alone."

Lindon opened his Copper sight, and sure enough, the entire wall was a hazy mass of black, twisting lines that carried the meaning of destruction, dissolution. They meant 'the end.'

He focused back on the physical world, looking for the edges of the wall, sending out his spiritual sense to probe for the script that had projected it. "Blackflame has a destruction aspect. I wonder if I could—"

Yerin shoved him aside as something heavy passed through the air where his head had just been.

He caught a glimpse of the weapon as he fell to the dirt: a heavy stone spear.

More spears flew out of the gray wall, flicking out in rapid succession, each aimed at Yerin. She moved quicker than Lindon could follow without the Burning Cloak active, ducking one spear, knocking a second off course with her Goldsign, and sidestepping the third.

The spears flew back to the end of the grounds, clattering to the ground just before the entrance arch.

The instant Lindon started backing away from the wall, a spear struck like a lightning bolt, flying straight at him.

The Burning Cloak ignited, and he shattered the spearhead with his fist.

Chunks of stone started dissolving as soon as the spear broke—Forged madra, then. Just like the soldiers.

That was a relief. Real stone would have been much more difficult to deal with than a Forger technique.

He waited a breath for another spear, but none came. Then he took a step back.

Two spears flew at him, one on top of the other.

Even in the Burning Cloak, he couldn't keep up, smashing one aside but taking a grazing cut to the inside of his arm from the second. And the Cloak would fall any second; he didn't have the madra to maintain it, not after botching all those attempts at the Striker technique.

He froze in place, trying to conserve madra and movement, and no more spears followed those two.

A steady stream of spears flew out at Yerin, who slowly retreated.

"Stop moving!" Lindon called, and Yerin froze after snatching two spears out of the air.

The remaining spears clattered to the ground, blood flowed down Lindon's arm to drip from his fingertips, and Yerin stood panting with a spear in each hand.

The wall remained still.

Cautiously, Lindon let the Burning Cloak drop. The blazing black-and-red energy around his body faded.

Though it was difficult to see through the cloudy wall of gray aura, he could make out a few shapes: three irregular balls of shadow, each floating in midair, clustered in a rough triangle with about twenty feet between them. The balls were only the size of his head—at least, as far as he could tell—but they bobbed and flowed like liquid.

While moving his body as little as possible, Lindon raised his voice. "I see three dark spots. Do you think they could be the source of the spears?"

"Targets, I'd say," Yerin responded.

"Could be both."

Very slowly, Yerin hefted one of her spears. "Let's test it."

In one smooth motion, she hurled the spear.

Another spear shot out at her, but she ducked and let it pass over her head. At first Lindon thought the weapon she'd thrown would dissolve into the gray wall, but then he remembered it was Forged madra: the destruction aura would just ignore it.

But it was also a moving object.

Another spear launched from the other side, striking Yerin's spear with a sound like a tree splintering. They clattered to the ground, slowly breaking apart.

"That's a neat little trick," Yerin said, still crouching with her one remaining spear.

Lindon thought he had the measure of it now. The wall was to keep them from closing the distance, to force them to use Striker techniques, and the spears were to keep pressure on them. They needed to knock the three targets down without attracting the attention of the spears, so they needed to be fast without much movement.

He could see the path laid out for him: he'd have to throw fire quickly and precisely, while still defending himself from the spears. It would take months of rigorous practice to train his reactions, not to mention building up his spirit. But Eithan had only allotted him six weeks for this Trial.

He needed a shortcut.

Lindon wanted to go back to the cave and start working, but he was stuck frozen in the center of the Trial grounds. He hated to ask, but with his madra as weak as it was, he could only think of one way out. "Forgiveness, but...do you think you could cover me as I run?"

"If I can't, worst thing that could happen is a spear through the back."

She said it like a joke, but he was already picturing a spear thick as his wrist impaling him through the ribs. Even his Bloodforged Iron body couldn't keep up with that.

He stayed still. "I'm sure that a spear to the back is nothing to you, but even with my Iron body, I'm not sure if I want to—"

"Start running, Lindon."

CHAPTER SIXTEEN

After a week, Lindon could almost form a ball of Black-flame between his hands. It would explode immediately, so he'd taken to practicing bare-chested; otherwise, he would have burned away his outer robe on the second day.

Their attempts on the Striker Trial had been less than successful, as they had quickly realized that Yerin couldn't destroy the targets. The black blobs floating behind the hazy wall of aura would just re-form if they were cut.

To destroy the targets, they needed Blackflame.

Lindon condensed another blob of dark fire, casting his palms in a deep crimson radiance. His mind and spirit were drawn to a point, utterly focused on his task, as beads of sweat rolled down his face.

The ball of burning madra between his palms swelled, growing until it was almost the size of a fist—a little more, and he could consider the first stage of the technique passed.

When he sent one more pulse of madra into the ball, it exploded.

He flipped onto his back, slamming his skull against the hard-packed earth and staring up into the blue strip of sky he could see through the opening to his canyon. His breaths came heavily as he tried to find his cycling rhythm, pulling his madra together for another attempt.

A red-tinged shadow loomed over him, and blazing red circles on fields of darkness swiveled to meet his eyes.

"Orthos," Lindon panted, gingerly climbing to his feet so that he could bow. "It has been too long."

The giant turtle grumbled something that might have been agreement. "I am not pleased," he declared, snapping up a small boulder.

Lindon hurriedly pulled his sacred artist's robe back up; he'd pushed it down to the waist, which was not a polite way to meet a guest. "Pardon, honored Orthos. I was not expecting a visitor."

He had sensed Orthos' presence growing closer, but the turtle had gotten *close* to the canyon many times over the last few months. He'd never entered. Besides, Lindon's attention was devoted entirely to his half-formed Striker technique.

"With so much attention on your training," Orthos said, "you should be making *progress.*" The last word was packed with such spite and rage that Orthos' eyes went from red to the bright orange of an open flame. Lindon felt the radiance of the anger in his spirit, and he took a step back, instinctively cycling his madra for a fight.

Orthos snapped his head to one side, bottling up the anger again, mastering himself. "You see?" he said at last. "The pure madra I took from you is not enough to balance the corrosion any longer. I need to pour more power into you, and you are not ready. I am displeased."

Orthos' spirit was in better shape than when Lindon had first sensed it; the painful, burning heat was better contained, and now it moved in regular cycles instead of a wild mass of flames.

But it still felt like a volcano on the verge of erupting. "If you need some scales, I've Forged a few more," Lindon said. He'd left his pack a few feet away, and he dug through it for a handful of blue-and-white translucent coins. He tossed them to Orthos, and they dissolved into pale blue streams in midair that sank into the turtle's body.

If they made a difference, Lindon couldn't see it.

"That will not be enough," Orthos rumbled. "If it were, the Arelius family would have healed me already. They can afford more than a few low-grade scales."

"I'm sure they would. They have great respect for you."

Orthos snorted, blowing out a few inches of dark flames. "As they should. They serve me in return for my protection."

Lindon hadn't seen Orthos providing any protection; it seemed more like the Arelius family was protecting *him*. "Is that how you were injured?"

"Any dragon would defend what belongs to them," he said dismissively. "Even if they died for it." Orthos' spirit was usually alight with arrogance, but he didn't seem especially proud now, like he was talking about a usual chore.

"What threat required *you* to act personally?"

"A rogue Blackflame," he said, as though it were obvious.

Eithan had said the Blackflames fell fifty years ago, but it hadn't been so long since Orthos was driven mad by his own power. Were there still other Blackflames out there, struggling with their spirits as Orthos did with his?

If there were, would they see Lindon as a threat, or a potential recruit? Either possibility shook him.

Orthos dug a stone out of the dirt and popped it into his mouth. "This is a waste of time. Show me your ignorance, and I will instruct you."

Before the turtle changed his mind, Lindon hurriedly adopted the basic cycling pattern lined out for this Striker technique, gathering madra in his hands. He held his palms only a few inches apart, focusing on the air between them, pushing madra into a ball.

The black flames flickered into being. They wanted to rush out, but Lindon held them in place, keeping them swirling in the air between his hands. He added another layer, then another, trembling with the effort of keeping the madra contained.

"I've seen enough," Orthos said, knocking his front paw against Lindon's hands. The Blackflame madra went out like a snuffed candle—fortunately not exploding—and turned away from Lindon. "I don't know what the family called this technique, but it was made in imitation of a dragon's breath."

Lindon silently thanked Yerin.

"Watch me, and learn." Orthos opened his jaws wide. Ruddy light gathered in his throat.

With both his eyes and his perception, Lindon focused on the technique. Madra flowed up from Orthos' throat, gathering and stopping in the back of his throat. More and more madra poured into a black fireball that spun, faster and faster, until it grew to half the size of Lindon's head.

Then Orthos compressed it so that it was no bigger than a fist, and poured more power into it.

The whole process only took a second or two, and Orthos packed down the energy three times, always keeping the ball of fire spinning. The turtle was holding the madra with his spirit, but he didn't grip it tightly; he cupped it like an egg until he was ready to pack it down.

With a roar, Orthos released the technique.

Lindon had expected a rough cloud of flame billowing out of the turtle's mouth. Instead, a dense, almost liquid-looking bar as thick as a man's leg blasted into the sky. The Blackflame madra streamed into the air, smooth and compact, radiating heat.

The bar of black fire punched through a cloud, drilling a hole in the middle as it blasted into the sky.

Lindon stared up in awe. "It is an honor to be instructed..." He trailed off as he sensed a change in Orthos' spirit.

The turtle stumbled away, each step thumping against the earth like he walked on a drum. His eyes burned orange, and Lindon felt such a confusing mix of emotion through their bond that he couldn't separate one thread from another: anger, exhaustion, confusion, fear, and pride fueled one another, blazing into a hot mass.

There was a flutter of black robes, and Yerin came to a stop in front of Lindon, staring up into the sky. She raised her white blade to point at Orthos without looking.

"I don't place a heap of bets, but if I had to bet a box of gold against a horse's hair, I'd say that was your giant Blackflame turtle."

"He's not well at the moment," Lindon said.

"You have a leash for him, true?"

Blackflame madra shot out of Orthos' body like sparks from a campfire as he stumbled around, his spirit a mess of confusion.

"It's spiritual damage built up in his channels. If I could get the Sylvan Riverseed—"

Yerin tackled him in the middle and scooped him up, throwing him over one shoulder. Before he could react, his world lurched as she leaped away.

Just in time. His spirit sent him a warning, and he flinched an instant before another wave of Blackflame blasted away a chunk of the cliff. Rocks the size of his torso rained down, and Orthos whirled on them, roaring like they were his ancestral enemies.

They passed through one red archway and into the forest of pillars before Yerin let him down. "Is he going to trail us?" she asked.

"I don't think he remembers we were there," Lindon said. "I'll see if he notices me this time or not."

Yerin's scarred face froze. "You're...turning back?"

"I don't *want* to," he said apologetically. "I left my pack back there."

Usually, there wasn't much for Cassias to do in running the Striker Trial. He could guide the spears to some degree, or empower them with his sword madra, but none of that would significantly increase the difficulty or value of the test.

His real role was going to come during the Ruler Trial, the most difficult of the three Blackflame Trials, so he spent most of his time packing that course's reserves with power. They wouldn't run through *that* like they did through the Enforcer Trial, he could guarantee it.

Cassias was reading reports when he sensed Orthos' arrival. He'd grown up with stories of Orthos, so he was initially nervous, until he reminded himself of Lindon's contract. The sacred beast should be much more stable than before.

That was a relief. If he went crazy, the children's lives weren't the only things at stake: this course was a loan from the Empire, and it was worth more than the Arelius family made in a year. If Orthos ruined it, Cassias would have to answer to the branch heads.

Now that he thought of it, maybe *that* was why Eithan had left him in charge...

Shaking his head, he returned to his reports. The Jai clan had slowed their aggression, giving the family some breathing room at last. It seemed that having Eithan back and working was having some effect after all.

He was still working on the reports when he sensed the power of Blackflame blaze up. Cassias actually shouted and drew his sword, primed for battle, before remembering that the enemy was outside.

He manipulated the window, focusing on the Striker Trial—on Orthos. The turtle was going wild, spraying Blackflame madra in all directions, tearing up dirt and stone alike. He would exhaust himself in a few minutes, but if the contract wasn't enough to restrain him, Cassias needed to call Eithan.

When he saw a figure in dark blue robes creeping closer to Orthos, Cassias first thought the window was malfunctioning. Lindon snuck up right behind the turtle, snatched his pack away—it had miraculously avoided obliteration—and dashed back toward the Enforcer Trial.

Orthos must have sensed his presence, but somehow, the turtle didn't kill him.

Cassias let out a slow, heavy breath and returned to his table. Snatching up a fresh sheet of paper, he began a report to Eithan.

Lindon and Yerin didn't attempt the Striker Trial again for a few days, instead hiding from Orthos. The turtle wandered back into the tunnels soon after venting his anger in the Trial course, but he didn't go far. Lindon could feel him prowling in the nearby tunnels, like a predator waiting to strike.

He'd grabbed the Sylvan Riverseed and tried to use her to heal Orthos, but the turtle had tried to attack him on sight. So he'd stayed away, resolving to try again the next time Orthos regained his sanity.

Though Lindon stayed in his cave for three days, he didn't waste the time. Instead, he tried out an idea.

He didn't have the skill to keep Blackflame madra under control for as long as Orthos had. That was the result of years of practice, and Lindon wanted results *now*.

But it wasn't as though he needed to pierce the clouds with his Striker technique. He just needed to hit some targets through an aura shield. So he asked himself: what was the minimum he needed to complete the dragon's breath?

Lindon explained the process to Yerin as they finally snuck out of their caves and headed back to the Striker Trial. His pack was mostly empty this time, half-filled with a few necessities.

"I only needed something to hold the madra together for a few seconds," he said as they stepped through the arch to the Striker Trial. "Once the madra is dense enough, it's easier to control, and the dragon's breath will go as far as I want it. So I came up with these shells: they're made of pure madra, so they hold the Blackflame power in place *just* long enough before they melt away."

The gray wall of aura boiled up, and Yerin scratched at her neck. "Cheers and celebration for you, but it doesn't sound like you learned the Striker technique."

"No, I did! I did, I'm just using some...props."

She eyed him over one shoulder as she pulled her sword free. "You try out a technique for the first time in battle, and you'll be walking away with your guts in your hand."

Lindon reached into his bag, pulling out half a dozen blue-white globes the size of his hand. He set them on the ground as though they were made of glass; the slightest impact would reduce them to dust. Pure madra was not an effective weapon, even Forged.

"I've practiced," Lindon said, though it had only been a few days. "Keep the spears away, and I can destroy the targets."

"You might recall I don't smile especially bright on cheating," Yerin reminded him. "Don't want you to take the wrong lesson."

"I'm happy to practice the Striker technique when we get out of here. Once I get those scales, and you get your pill."

She nodded to him. "We have a bargain."

He stood, cupping an empty shell of pure madra in his hands, and they both faced the wall of aura. Three black blobs floated behind the hazy barrier, though they had been quiet so far.

The Striker Trial didn't seem to respond to small movements, or the spears would never stop coming. Only large, quick motions attracted the course's attention. Yerin stood perfectly still, Goldsign poised over one shoulder and white blade held off to one side.

Lindon clutched the pure madra shell in his hands and concentrated, sending a ball of Blackflame into the center. A dark stain showed through the semi-transparent madra, growing larger as he poured more Blackflame inside.

Always keep it spinning. Pack more inside. Keep it spinning...

His control slipped once, but instead of exploding, the half-formed technique ate through the inner layer of the shell like it was made of ice. The barrier was thinner now, but he continued pouring Blackflame inside.

After a few seconds, it melted through the outer bubble

of madra, and Lindon was holding a rolling ball of Black-flame madra suspended between his palms. It was stable now, and much easier to keep under control; only while it was forming did it take concentration to stop an explosion.

"You close to done?" Yerin asked him, barely moving her lips. No matter how loudly they spoke, it didn't seem to matter to the Striker Trial, but she had decided to stay cautious.

"Now," Lindon said, and she stepped left. A spear shot out at her, and she slapped it aside, but another streaked through the air.

Lindon held the ball of black fire between his palms, raised it until it was level with one of the targets, and *pushed.*

A bar of Blackflame, thick as his arm, tore through the air. It streamed through the gray wall of aura, passing through the center target and blasting it apart like a wisp of cloud.

The other two targets both sent out Forged spears, and Yerin knocked them away, but more came. It appeared they were speeding up.

Lindon clenched his jaw as he watched the dissolving target. If it re-formed from this...

A gong echoed through the canyon. Maybe the same gong that had announced failure in the Enforcer Trial. And this time, the target didn't re-form.

The spears were coming so fast now that Yerin's motions were a blur. "Two...left...to go..." She forced out, in between blasting Forged weapons apart.

Lindon snatched up the next hollow ball of pure madra.

When the third gong sounded, Cassias stepped away from his paperwork. It had only taken them ten days for the Striker Trial, though he hadn't watched their final, successful attempt; Orthos must have given Lindon some pointers.

Cassias cycled his madra, touched his spirit to the silver aura around his sword, and readied himself. The Ruler Trial was his true test; he would pour everything he had into this one. They would either give up, or he would be forced to admit that Eithan had been right about them.

When he moved to the panel, he left behind the two reports that had arrived today. Both regarded the city's Underlords:

The first message warned him that Jai Daishou had deviated from his schedule today. It seemed that he was going to take care of Jai Long's rebellion personally. That was a relief to Cassias, though Eithan might take it differently; if the Jai Underlord was acting, then Jai Long wouldn't survive to fight Lindon.

The second message said that Eithan had returned to the city. He'd left again only a week or so ago, and Cassias hadn't expected him back for weeks, so Eithan must have received his report about Orthos. Other than the Underlord, there was no one in the Arelius family who could soothe Orthos without killing him.

Both letters contained valuable information, but nothing alarming. If Jai Daishou meeting with Jai Long was cause for alarm, Eithan would know and deal with it. Cassias could focus on his task.

In situations like this, at least, Eithan was reliable.

For months, Jai Long and the Sandvipers had waged a guerilla war against the Jai clan. That mostly meant ambushing them as they tried to sabotage the Arelius family, which was still enough to make Jai Long laugh.

Every time the Jai clan tried to capture another Arelius warehouse, Jai Long was there, gathering food for his spear. Every time they moved against Arelius street crews under cover of night, Jai Long spilled their blood in the streets. And servants bearing the black crescent moon were always right there to scrub it clean.

He was doing a better job of protecting the Arelius family than their Underlord was.

More than once, he'd wondered about the legendary powers of the Arelius bloodline. If they really could sense a speck of dust on a single tile at the top of a hundred-foot roof, as the stories claimed, then Eithan had to know what Jai Long was doing in the city. He could have stopped Jai Long at any time, removing a steadily growing threat to his own adopted disciple.

But he'd been the one to promise that disciple a duel in the first place. Jai Long was glad he didn't work for the Arelius; that family must treat its disciples lives as tinder for the fire.

Thanks to Jai Long and Gokren, the Jai clan had been forced to lighten its grip on its enemies. Jai Lowgolds had a curfew now, and the clan had distributed valuable communication constructs to carry word of any suspicious sightings. Most of the clan had retreated to the very peak of Shiryu Mountain, living as close to their Underlord as possible, and a Highgold had been assigned to every house.

Not that it would do them any good. Jai Long had broken through to Truegold weeks ago.

At this point, draining Lowgolds of their Remnants did virtually nothing but replenish his core. Only Highgolds or better would help him advance, and Truegolds were the best.

Which was why he was here, crouching on the roof of one of the Jai clan's lesser palaces, waiting for the first Truegold patrol of the night. The sun was dropping behind the mountain, casting long shadows over Serpent's Grave, so it would be harder to see now than in the middle of the night.

Ordinarily, the streets outside the Jai clan homes would be packed at sunset, but the curfew required everyone except designated clan guards to be inside a safehouse before dark. None of the palaces in this district were secure, so they would be empty. Defended only by a Truegold at the beginning of a long patrol.

He gripped the case for the Ancestor's Spear. There would only be one opponent this time, so no need to capture a Remnant—he could drain the elder dry right there on the street. No witnesses.

Gokren and two Sandviper Highgolds waited nearby, ready to provide backup if Jai Long encountered any difficulty. He was powerful enough now to rank in the top twenty or thirty of the Jai clan, but a true elder had been practicing the sacred arts since long before Jai Long was born. Who knew what crafty tricks they might have prepared.

As Jai Long slowly cycled, keeping his spirit calm, he felt it: the approaching force of a Truegold soul.

He hadn't needed to scan the target directly to confirm that it was a Truegold, because they weren't bothering to hide their power. There was a slightly muffled feel to it, as though they'd tried to veil themselves but had given up halfway. Maybe it wasn't intentional; nerves could interfere with cycling. Perhaps they feared the attacker in the shadows.

If that was true, they would try to flee and sound the alarm rather than doing battle. Jai Long would have to strike so hard that they never had the chance to shout.

A white-clad figure with pale hair strode by beneath him, hands clasped behind the back. Through the shadows, Jai Long couldn't make out if it was a man or a woman, but the force of a Truegold radiated from them.

Jai Long leaped off the building, Ancestor's Spear shining in his grip. Stellar Spear madra ran through his muscles and bones, Enforcing him for the landing, bracing his body for the strike.

The Flowing Starlight technique settled in as he fell, until the wind seemed to whip past for long breaths of time. The white-haired head tilted, and Jai Long prepared himself for impact.

Then dark eyes swiveled up to meet him, showing no surprise.

An invisible fist gripped Jai Long's heart and squeezed.

Jai Daishou, Underlord of the Jai clan, took a single step to the side and let his rebellious descendant crash to the ground.

Less than half a year had passed since Jai Long arrived in Serpent's Grave; he'd expected to have months more before Jai Daishou personally acted. By then, he would have had more leverage.

He'd underestimated the Underlord's insight, or overestimated his pride. Either way, the bill had come due long before Jai Long was prepared to pay.

Just like that, his revenge was over.

The impact of landing shocked Jai Long's entire body, rattling his bones, and the bricks of the street cracked beneath him. The pure white shaft of his spear was driven two feet into the ground, and he'd landed in a crouch.

But slamming into the earth was nothing compared to the force of seeing Jai Daishou here, staring at him with the icy strength born from a hundred years of absolute rule.

A corrosive Truegold aura moved closer: Sandviper Gokren. He would have heard the crash, sensed the flare of Jai Long's madra, and known that the trap was triggered. He'd never seen the Jai Underlord before; he would assume that Jai Daishou was just a Jai elder who had gotten the better of Jai Long.

He would try to help.

Jai Long's stomach twisted, but he forced himself to meet the Underlord's eyes. "This humble junior greets the Patriarch," he said, his voice firm. He might have been about to die, but at least he didn't have to show fear.

Jai Daishou turned to regard him head-on, his wrinkled face a mask, and Jai Long could no longer suppress his body's trembling. The old man's gaze was placid, like a frozen lake, but Jai Long shook as though he stared down a hungry dragon.

"You have killed sacred artists of your own clan," the Patriarch said. "For quite some time now." His tone remained neutral.

"Let the punishment fall on me alone," Jai Long said, through clenched teeth and a burning throat. The words tasted bitter; he longed to spit defiance and die trying to shove his spear into the Patriarch's heart.

But if the Underlord had known about Jai Long's activities, it was best to assume he knew everything. Including Jai Chen's presence in the city.

If the Underlord grew too irritated, he could wipe her out with a motion of his hand.

There was nothing Jai Long could do to prevent his own execution, but if he had to bow and scrape with his last breath to save his sister, he would shame himself a thousand times over.

Jai Daishou nodded. "Humility is a virtue, when you face a stronger force. I am pleased to know you've learned to swallow your pride." One slow, shuffling step at a time, he made his way over to Jai Long. The pressure built with every step, until he stood only a foot away. It was like being within arm's reach of an earthquake.

The Patriarch extended one hand and waited.

Jai Long knew what he wanted, so he forced his pride to bend even further. As though it weighed a thousand pounds, he slowly extracted the Ancestor's Spear from the earth and held it out, presenting it with both hands.

The Underlord lifted it with a more pleasant expression than Jai Long had ever seen on his aged face. He held it in one hand and ran the other over the weapon, feeling the script. The spearhead looped in one slow arc, tracing a line of white in the air, as Jai Daishou closed his eyes and savored the sensation.

"I have your sister already," Jai Daishou said, eyes still closed, and Jai Long's heart crumbled to ash and blew away. "My men picked her up hours ago. I had intended to use her life to stop you from throwing your life away in a suicidal charge, but you have at least a spark of wisdom."

He had known it was a mistake to take her out of the Desolate Wilds. He had known it, but where could he have left her? Where could an Underlord not reach?

Jai Long prostrated himself, scraping his cloth mask against the sandy bricks. "She knew nothing of my actions. Please."

"You have cost me twenty-three Lowgolds, eight High-golds, and three Truegolds. So far. More importantly, you forced me to stop my actions against Eithan Arelius, which has given a *servant* family the opportunity to surpass our rank and join the great clans of the Empire."

Madra flared like the rising sun, and Jai Long jerked his head from the tiles in time to see Jai Daishou disappear in a flash of white.

An instant later, he was back, holding Gokren from the back of a fur-lined collar. The Sandviper's gray hair was mussed, and his left leg looked broken. He tried to choke out a word, but the Jai Underlord released him, and he collapsed in a heap on the ground.

"You will repay me everything I have lost," the Underlord said, and Jai Long knew neither he nor Gokren were escaping with their lives. He owed the Jai clan three Truegolds, and here were two, ripe to be plucked.

But Jai Chen still had a chance to survive.

Jai Long lowered himself to beg again, but the Patriarch held up the Ancestor's Spear like a scepter. He regarded the weapon, lips pursed as though he'd bit into a lemon. "Regrettably, I do not have much time remaining. Five years at most, they tell me. And in the entire clan, I have found no one else who can replace me in that short span of time."

Jai Long's breath came faster. He'd known the Patriarch was reaching the end of his lifespan, but if he said five years, that meant it was more likely two or three. The old man had always been one to exaggerate facts for his benefit.

"Even with the spear?" Jai Long asked politely. For his sister's sake, he resisted the urge to laugh in the Underlord's face. There were hundreds of thousands of loyal Jai clan members, and he couldn't find *one* among them who measured up to Jai Long.

He hoped the regret *burned*.

"The spear is a wonderful tool, but a tool is all it is. Advancing to Underlord requires an element of insight, of inspiration, that no weapon can provide. Increasing and purifying your madra will take you to the limits of Gold, but no further."

The old man spun the spear at minimum speed, agonizingly slow, but every motion fluid and perfect. Centuries of training engraved their habits deeply.

Neither Gokren nor Jai Long made a single sound between them. Every second he wasted was another breath for them to live.

"If any of my elders could replace me as Underlord, they would have already," Jai Daishou said as he danced with his spear. "The Ancestor's Spear will not allow them to bridge that gap. I once had many possible successors, and one by one, they have failed me. So I come back to you...with my help, you could be Underlord in another year."

A tiny hope joined anger, despair, and humiliation in the war inside Jai Long's heart.

"You will only guard the clan in my absence, of course, you will not succeed it. You are a stopgap measure, a deterrent to keep the jackals at bay until a true heir can be raised from the Path of the Stellar Spear. Swear your soul to my control, utterly and completely, and you are a tool that can be used."

He came to a stop, swung the spear up to rest on his shoulder, and looked down on Jai Long. Waiting.

"My sister," Jai Long grated out.

"As the only sibling of our clan guardian, of course she will have access to the very best treatment the Jai can produce."

Jai Long inclined his head. "On my soul and my power," Jai Long said, "I swear to take no action against the Jai Patriarch or the Jai clan, to follow the orders of the Jai Patriarch absolutely, and to act always in the best interests of the Jai clan."

His soul tightened, restricted by his words, but a true oath always had two sides.

Jai Daishou spoke immediately. "In return, I swear on my

soul and on my power to protect Jai Long and Jai Chen as my own children, so long as their loyalty remains true."

This was a flimsy shield, but a shield nonetheless. Far more of a protection than he and Jai Chen had ever had on their own in the wilderness.

All his madra tensed, as though a knot had been tied around his soul, but then the sensation eased. Jai Long let out a breath.

Though a voice in his head cursed him as a coward, he shook with relief. His concern for his sister had drowned out everything else, but he hadn't wanted to die. At least living as a Jai clan dog would lead to a cure for Jai Chen.

Jai Daishou tucked the Ancestor's Spear under one arm. "You've gotten enough use out of this. It won't raise any Underlords, but I can always use more Truegolds." He glanced down at Sandviper Gokren as though regarding something he'd tracked in on the tip of his shoe. "Now then. That was sensitive information you just witnessed."

A cloud darkened Jai Long's relief. He had been so focused on the discussion that it hadn't occurred to him to think about their audience.

The Patriarch crooked his finger, and Jai Long staggered to his side, pulled up by a compulsion so strong it was almost physical. "Underlords may be blessed by the heavens, but we are far from saints. When it becomes necessary, we must dirty our hands."

The old man clasped his hands behind his back and turned toward the light disappearing over the peak where the sun had died. He said nothing else.

Jai Long gathered his madra and looked down at Gokren. The Sandviper's skin had paled, and there was fear in his eyes.

Fear and resentment. He had never seen his son avenged.

"Let him swear loyalty," Jai Long said. It was a stretch of his luck, and Jai Daishou might strike him down for sheer impudence, but he had to try. It was the least he could do for the man who had risked the existence of his sect to follow him here.

The Underlord half-turned and showed Jai Long a cold smile. "Exercise your own judgment and do as you wish. But *I* will not be burdened by the weight of extra oaths."

Jai Daishou turned his back again, long metal strands of hair swinging behind him. "But hurry," he said. "I have a task for you."

Jai Long spoke before the Patriarch could change his mind. "Sandviper Gokren, I swear on my soul and on my power that I will have you executed...if you repeat a word of anything that happened here today, or betray us to our enemies."

Gokren brightened, straightening his back. "On my soul and my power, I swear not to divulge a word of your conversation with the Jai Patriarch, nor to provide any information or assistance to your enemies. I offer my life as forfeit."

The oath tightened, and Jai Long bowed to the Jai Underlord's back. His role now was to wait for instructions.

"Eithan Arelius' disciples are challenging the Blackflame Trials," Jai Daishou said.

Since the fall of the Blackflame family, their Trials had been used to train students from many Paths. Those with the proper access keys could activate the Trials even without Blackflame madra, and the course would challenge any Lowgold, not just one on the Path of Black Flame.

The Naru clan only permitted a handful of disciples to use the Blackflame Trials each year, but the Arelius family kept the course defended and maintained. It made sense that they would have access, though using the Trials without permission sounded unwise.

Most Underlords would never defy the imperial family, but Eithan Arelius...

"The Arelius Patriarch acts on his own whims," Jai Long said. "Unless...is one of his disciples a descendant of the Blackflames?"

If so, *that* was truly chilling. A new sacred artist on the Path of Black Flame would be a scandal to shake the Empire.

Jai Daishou turned back and regarded his descendant with scorn. "Certainly not. The only Blackflame they have is that insane turtle, and he's too old to form a contract. But the truth is bad enough. If Eithan Arelius thinks it is worthwhile to risk Naru displeasure by opening the Blackflame Trials, then he must believe his student has a chance against you."

Jai Long tried to fit that information into any form that made sense, but failed. Wei Shi Lindon was an *Iron*. Even if they fed him scales instead of food and elixirs instead of water, they could at best advance him to Jade. If the heavens themselves descended on his behalf, perhaps he could make Lowgold. Jai Long wouldn't retreat from a duel with *ten* Lindons.

"I will not risk a future Underlord in a duel that the opponent has any chance of winning," Jai Daishou said calmly. "That would be an absurd gamble with nothing to gain: you earn us no respect if you win, and endless shame if you lose." Gokren's face twisted in rage, but he bottled it up before he got himself killed.

"Patriarch, I am *far* more than—" Jai Long began, but the Underlord cut him off with a smug smile.

"I have another plan. Recruiting you was my final step, and now we can begin." He turned to walk away, gesturing for Jai Long to join him.

Confused, Jai Long walked after him, Gokren trailing after.

The Jai clan built their homes in this position on Shiryu Mountain for the view. A curving wall of stone a hundred feet high blocked the wind and sand from behind them, while Serpent's Grave stretched out before them, far below. From this high up, you could get a sense of the majesty the dragons had left behind, their skeletons stretching from one end of the city to another. A single skull made up an entire residential district, and looked as big as Jai Long's hand, even from this distance.

Jai Daishou walked out past the houses, to the edge of the cliff, looking down at the city. The sun had long set behind the mountain, casting darkness over Serpent's Grave. Cold wind tore at Jai Daishou's robe and blew between the gaps of Jai Long's mask.

"It is difficult to deal with an Arelius Underlord," the Patriarch said. "They see all your hidden weapons, hear all your plans. You can't make any preparations. You can't say a word. Only when the Underlord leaves for months at a time, forcing the one other blood member of the Arelius to go after him... then you can make your plans." He held up a finger.

"But you can't strike. He has left the city defended in his absence, arranged for countermeasures. Your preparations lie dormant for weeks and months, as you wait until all the pieces to fall naturally into place."

The full scope of Jai Daishou's words hit Jai Long like a falling star. The Jai Underlord had collected his family together in safe houses. Not just to protect them from Jai Long, but to gather his fighting power in a way that the Arelius family wouldn't find suspicious. With the clan's forces marshaled, there was only one remaining variable: the enemy who had struck at them over the last several months.

Jai Long shivered. He'd been trying to cut off a spider's legs, only to find himself caught in a web. If he hadn't surrendered instantly tonight, Jai Daishou would have torn out his heart. The plan was already in motion, with no room for delay.

The Underlord raised his white spear into the sky. "And then, having never spoken a word to alert the watchers... you strike."

A bright light burst from his spear. It rose into the newborn stars and exploded, bathing Serpent's Grave in white.

All over the city, Stellar Spear madra flared to life.

CHAPTER SEVENTEEN

When the white light rose like a full moon over the city, Eithan knew where it had come from. He saw the man who had launched the technique, with white metal hair down to his waist, and the young man at his side with the red-wrapped face.

And he heard the screams beginning all over the city as the Jai clan began to systematically hunt anyone wearing a black crescent. They were following a script that had been laid out for them months ago, while his eye was turned elsewhere.

Eithan was on the roof of an Arelius family tower, and he clenched his teeth to stop from crushing the broom in his hands.

He had only returned to the city at all because of Cassias' message about Orthos, and had immediately seen that Lindon and Yerin had the situation in hand. He would give the turtle a few more Underlord scales to keep his burning spirit under control until Lindon was ready to advance to Lowgold and take on a greater burden. It had all been going so well.

He felt so blind.

The Jai clan had played him perfectly: they had continued

to work against the Arelius family, even when they knew he was watching. If they had pretended to cooperate while he was in the city, he would have known they were biding their time. But they had been forced to back off because of Jai Long...and because of his own actions against them, subtle though they had been.

Eithan had been sure he was winning the game, right up until his opponents swept the cards off the table and stabbed him.

An unfamiliar fear flooded him. If they had hidden this from him, what else had he missed? What unseen threats lurked beyond his sight?

With that fear came anger, cold and bright.

He leaped away from his half-swept rooftop garden, broom still in hand. His madra spun the Hollow Armor through his whole body—it wasn't the best Enforcer technique, his not being the best Enforcer Path, but combined with an Underlord's body, the fall wouldn't hurt him.

It would shatter the street, though, so instead he grabbed a windowsill for an instant as he passed, then kicked off the wall, slowed himself for a second on the edge of a nearby roof, snagged a tree branch, and landed without breaking anything. A few loose leaves fluttered to the ground behind him, and he swept his sleeve so that the wind carried them into a nearby trash box.

Servant One-Thirteen sat on a bench nearby, a girl leaning against his shoulder. He wasn't wearing his Arelius robes tonight; instead, he was dressed in a layered red coat that must have been the best he owned. She wore pearl silk, with matching jewelry pinning up her hair. Minutes ago, they'd been having a lovely evening.

Now, they both had daggers in their hands, but seemed too afraid to move; a Jai Highgold was sweeping down the street with spear in hand. Screams haunted the distance.

All three of them froze on seeing Eithan.

He strode up to the unfamiliar woman on One-Thirteen's arm. "You look lovely tonight, madam. The Arelius family will reimburse you for this." Then he pulled a pin from her hair and hurled it over his shoulder.

The dagger would have been sharper, but he didn't want to leave her defenseless. Besides, the pin drove through the Highgold's throat easily enough.

One-Thirteen and his date stared behind Eithan as the Jai's spear went one way and his bleeding body the other.

"One-Thirteen," Eithan said, "emergency drill number one. Ring the bells." He pulled another pin from the woman's hair.

The servant rose and saluted, grabbing his date by the hand and pulling her with him as he ran to sound the alarm. Loose strands of hair fluttered behind her.

Eithan waited another instant for the spiked Stellar Spear Remnant to rise before he sent a wisp of madra flowing into the hairpin and threw it. It blasted through the spirit like a ballista bolt.

He was off again, leaping whole buildings with the power of Hollow Armor. He watched every servant of the Arelius die, heard their pleas for help. They tore his heart.

Eithan was halfway up the mountain when he felt the boundary formation spring into place.

He had leaped up from one cliff to another, ignoring the roads, and he'd just landed on a bare plateau when all the aura around him froze. In his Copper sight, it was like he was caught in an upturned bowl of swirling color, blocking him from the outside world.

It didn't stop the power of his bloodline legacy. His detection web still swept the city, carrying every death to stab him in the gut. And now they'd trapped him here, where he couldn't save anyone.

The six Jai clan Truegold elders who had placed the formation flags waited for him, just on the other side of the barrier. He'd felt them pacing him, but he had expected them to provide backup for Jai Daishou in the fight between Underlords.

Now, he realized, they were meant to keep him in one place until their Patriarch came to join them.

Half a dozen old men were feeling very proud of themselves right now, but they watched him from beyond the boundary formation like mice watching a trapped hawk.

Eithan stood on a shelf of black rock, the white-robed elders surrounding him. He gripped his broom in one hand as the icy wind blew his hair and his robes around him.

He tried to pull up a smile, but it wouldn't come.

"Gentlemen," the Underlord said, "this is a mistake."

As the daylight died, Cassias cycled his madra and waited for Lindon and Yerin to attempt the Ruler Trial. They were inspecting the instructional tablet already, and he knew from watching them that they would try the course immediately afterward.

He felt like Eithan as he grinned in anticipation, staring at them through the scripted window. He would take it easy on them this time, since they'd only be able to run through one time before the sun set completely. They would feel like they had a chance.

And then, tomorrow, he'd pour everything he had into the Trial. He felt like *he* was the one competing, though it was just a break in the routine he wanted. He couldn't admit he was excited about pushing a Jade and a Lowgold to their limits, but he looked forward to seeing—

One of his strands of awareness, stretched out behind him, caught a white light flaring high in the air. Curious, he stretched his perception back into the city.

As the sun fell, Stellar Spear madra took its place.

A whisper of fear threaded its way through him. The clan was probably just confronting Jai Long and his forces, but he focused the entire web of his Arelius bloodline on the city.

Shining white, a spearhead pierced a blue-and-black outer robe, driving a bloody hole through a crescent moon symbol.

"I'm not Arelius, I don't work for them, *please!*" a woman begged.

A door shattered as a Jai Truegold blasted his way into an Arelius facility, and the crowd's murmurs of uncertainty rose to shouts and panic.

...a coordinated attack. All throughout the city.

And these were only the first seconds.

His breathing came so hard that it threatened to throw off his cycling technique. His son was three years old. His wife was a member of the imperial Naru clan and a powerful Highgold, but if a Jai elder was feeling particularly cruel or clever...

Cassias launched himself from the temple so fast he blasted his wicker chair to pieces. The paperwork swirled in a whirlwind behind him, but he didn't spare a glance back.

He needed to get home.

The Silver Step was an Enforcer technique with Striker elements, meant to help mobility in a short-range fight. It was the only movement technique he knew, and all but useless over long distances...but he used it anyway, kicking off the ground and leaving a silver ripple behind. The technique launched him forward with speed that pushed the limits of what a Highgold should be capable of, but it was only one step. His madra might burn out before he reached his home, leaving him helpless.

He stretched his web out toward the bone tower in the distance, trying to get a glimpse of his family, but it was like trying to find someone by running house to house and peeking in keyholes.

His wife was strong, even on an imperial scale. Stronger than he was. Jing would survive.

But there was always someone stronger...

His Silver Steps carried him down into the streets, which were already choked with combat. He rushed past Arelius servants defending themselves with swords and spears, with claws of ice and arrows of fire. He ignored whips of blood and slipped around toxic mists.

It wasn't just Arelius family members dying tonight. The Jai clan were reclaiming their territory with ruthless efficiency. They targeted those in Arelius colors, but anyone who got in their way, or resisted, or looked like the slightest threat...they were blasted apart by regimented ranks wielding white light.

Only the Redflower family was untouched, as expected: a pair of Jai clansmen escorted a group with flowers on their chests away from the chaos of the battle. The Redflowers grew food for the Empire, and if one of them died, the Skysworn would come down on the Jai clan like a hammer.

His wife's family should be exempt too. If a Naru were caught in this crossfire, the Emperor would make the Jai clan pay for it.

But he could see the Redflowers, safe and escorted away by the Jai warriors. He couldn't see anyone with the green wings of the Naru family's Path of Grasping Sky.

Until he saw Jing, he couldn't relax.

He looked up at the tower through a haze of smoke, and something slammed into his forehead with the power of a kicking horse. He flipped backward, his own momentum turned against him, and only years of training let him stumble to his feet.

Blood was in his eyes.

He gripped his sword, though he didn't remember drawing it.

The tower of yellow bone filled his vision, closer now, but still so far away.

Three Highgolds from the Jai clan closed in on him, spears wet, faces tense. Six more were spearing a Truegold Remnant to death nearby; that explained why so many of the Jai clan's mid-level fighters were together.

That couldn't have been an Arelius Remnant; none of their Truegolds were in the city. Someone had tried to intervene.

There were nine enemy Highgolds, most of them with spirits as strong as his own. Nine.

Head still ringing from the blow, thoughts fluttering like a cloud of butterflies, Cassias took one staggering step forward.

A white light crashed into him, but somehow his sword had knocked it away, filled with enough madra to break the technique. A flash of silver and white exploded.

"Highgold," one of them said. "Yellow hair. Arelius?"

"Could be dyed," someone else said. Blearily, Cassias focused on her face.

He recognized her. He knew most of the famous people in the Jai clan. Jai Yu, that was her name. The two hundred and sixty-fifth strongest Highgold in the Empire.

Out of the hundreds of thousands of Highgolds, she was considered to be among the top three hundred. Strong. A strong opponent.

Cassias focused his awareness on the bone tower, desperately sweeping for a glimpse of his wife's face.

A man poked him in the arm. Cassias couldn't get his silver bracer, his Goldsign, up in time to block, and blood spurted. He didn't feel the pain, but his arm gave a spasm and his sword clattered to the bricks.

"There are only two bloodline Arelius in the city," Jai Yu said, "and our Truegolds have them both. If he's an unregistered blood relative, we'll turn him in for the bounty."

"No crescent," the man said, inspecting his clothes.

A crash came from two streets over, and Jai Yu muttered something under her breath. "Forget it. I'm not carrying him around."

Light gathered on her spearhead, and Cassias' breathing sped up, because he still hadn't found his wife. The ringing in his head had sharpened to a scream. He poured all his madra into his detection web, scanning the tower from top to bottom, racing to see that his family was safe.

Then...he saw her.

She wasn't in their rooms, but at the base of the tower, on her way to a shelter with more Arelius family employees. Black hair streamed behind her, and her left eye was dark and furious. Her right was an orange globe of madra, a construct to replace one she'd lost in battle years ago. Her wings spread—one the natural emerald Goldsign of her Path, and the other a matrix of sunset-colored energy. Her second prosthetic.

She was safe. They were both safe.

That was all he needed to know.

...before his mind cleared and the ringing in his ears faded. He thrust his palm into Jai Yu's spear, sending up a pulse of sword madra and slicing it in half.

He opened his eyes afterward, letting the spearhead fly over his shoulder. "Jai Yu. I'm disappointed you didn't recognize me."

Her face paled.

White lines began creeping over her skin as she prepared her Flowing Starlight technique. "We...I'm sorry, we didn't... we thought you were..." She swallowed, and then yelled, *"Run! Everyone run!"*

Two of them took her advice, but one of the more distant Jai fighters gripped his spear as though ready to join the fight. "What is it?"

Jai Yu shouted back while fleeing. "It's Ca—"

Silver Step.

The technique rang like a bell under his foot, launching him behind Jai Yu. He drove his hand into her back, and silver light pierced her heart.

Another Silver Step, and he stood beside the Jai clan Highgold who had asked the question. Cassias hadn't bothered picking up his sword.

The spearhead pointed in his direction quivered. "Number...two..."

Cassias placed a palm on the man's head, and sword madra blasted through his skull and into his brain. He died silently.

Nine Highgolds would have been too much of an opponent, even for him. If they had cooperated. But splitting up and coming at him one at a time...

There was only one Highgold in the Blackflame Empire who could fight with him face-to-face, and she was carrying their child into a shelter.

Naru Cassias Arelius, former heir to the Arelius family, had been allowed to marry into the Naru clan for three reasons. First, the recommendation of his family Underlord. Second, the personal feelings of Naru Jing, star of the clan's young generation.

And third, his personal strength.

Another Silver Step, and he sent a head spinning onto the street, its metal hair striking sparks against the stone. Six more Steps later, he was out of madra, and there were six more bloodstains on the streets.

Of all the Highgolds who had tried to ambush the second-ranked Highgold in the Empire, none remained.

"This is what you get, trying to see new places at your age," Fisher Gesha mumbled. A Lowgold Remnant sank into the flagstones in front of her, and she sheared its head off as she moved. She wanted to collect its eyes and check it for bindings, but her drudge was currently carrying her along the flagstones, and she certainly wasn't going to run on her own two feet.

"Came to get a taste of the Empire, didn't you? Came to teach a promising student. And where is he, hm? Tucked away in a mountain, isn't he, not even *thinking* of Soulsmithing."

A swarm of spider-constructs scuttled over the street around her, escorting her through the screaming city and up to a hatch in the ground.

She pressed a scripted key against the aura lock and used her madra to pull on a catch on the other side. This was a

Soulsmith's underground storehouse, meant to hold volatile substances, but it was the most secure location she knew of outside the Arelius shelters. Forget the shelters; a bunch of victims packed inside like weeds waiting to be plucked.

Gesha hopped down into the cellar, pulling the heavy doors shut behind her with strands of purple madra. She locked them, and then sealed them with layers of invisible threads. Then she Forged a few purple wires and physically tied it shut, positioning half a dozen spider constructs at the entrance.

Finally, she ran to the back of the storehouse and webbed herself to the ceiling.

"Wasting my time," she muttered. "Risking my life. Too old for this."

Withdrawing all her madra, she cycled power in a shell around her core, veiling her power.

Then she waited for the noise to end.

Jai Long and Gokren hiked over to Shiryu Mountain's second peak, a handful of Sandvipers in tow.

Gokren ran a hand over his gray hair, slicking it back. "We'll take the strong disciple together, then move on to the *Iron.*"

This was their task, entrusted to them by the Jai Underlord. Eithan's pair of students would soon sense the uproar in the city, and would emerge from their training. Rather than gamble everything on a duel in the fall, eliminate the Arelius family's new recruits here, in the spring.

Jai Daishou's pride would take a hit if this plan became public knowledge, but Jai Long had to respect the decision. It may not have been the most honorable course of action, but the Patriarch certainly wasn't underestimating his enemies.

Jai Long leaped from one outcropping to another. "Not

together. I'll kill the Lowgold, you handle Wei Shi Lindon." The sword artist could live, but he didn't want Lindon sneaking off.

Besides, she had traded blows with him before, even a full stage behind him. Her advancement could not have kept pace with his; he wanted to see how much stronger he'd become in the past half a year.

They landed by what Jai Daishou had described as the exit for the Blackflame Trials. An aura barrier covered the opening.

Gokren itched to break through—he had a short spear in each hand and was pacing back and forth, barking at his men for being too slow as they arrived.

On Jai Long's orders, they all backed higher up the slope, so they could watch from a vantage point. Gokren had to pull himself away from the entrance, but he ultimately obeyed. Once everyone had spread out enough to cover any possible exit—even if they dashed out of the cave—Jai Long sat on a rock and began to cycle aura.

He could wait.

The sun's last rays were drifting up the canyon as Lindon and Yerin knelt before the Ruler Trial's tablet.

"Blackflame madra burned the body and the...mind, I'd say, although it could be spirit. Or dreams." He tapped a picture of a screaming person grasping at his own head. "The point seems clear. Using Blackflame slowly ruins you, building up damage and eroding the soul, destroying your advancement, your sanity, and your lifespan." He tried not to feel the Blackflame raging inside him, deadly and explosive, instead returning his focus to the ancient symbols.

"That is the price you pay for the...largest hammer? Ah, 'greatest weapon.' Blackflames rule by...one man on the battlefield?" He traced his finger between the symbol and a nearby picture of a man standing alone with flames in each of his hands.

"Last man standing," Yerin said quietly.

Lindon shivered. That was impressively reliable, but somewhat *grim* for his taste. They ruled by virtue of having killed all their opponents. And this was core enough to their philosophy that they engraved it in their basic training course.

Well, he'd chosen this Path for its ability to win duels, not for its outstanding moral values. And he'd want the biggest weapon he could find if he had to fight the creature destined to attack Sacred Valley.

The next phrase was in more modern language:

The dragon conquers.

He said it aloud, and Yerin nodded along. "Ruler techniques conquer. Fits like a good boot."

The dragon advances.

The dragon destroys.

The dragon conquers.

Orthos' core was unsteady and had been for days, but the words resonated with his spirit. He was a sword rather than a shield, a force of destruction, and a jealous king.

That wasn't a comfortable personality to share a soul with, but it described a weapon that Lindon could use.

Yerin nodded to the rest of the Ruler Trial. "Rather than that...these guys tickle your memory at all?"

Lindon had been trying not to look out at the field of opponents arranged for him in the final Blackflame Trial. There were ninety-nine dark, humanoid figures in the field, each clutching different weapons, and he sensed different madra from each of them. Ninety-nine mannequins with faceless heads.

Ninety-nine dummies, arranged in a circle.

The activation crystal was on a pedestal in the center, and Lindon had to use his Ruler technique to some degree before he could power the course. He wasn't looking forward to it. The Striker Trial had only taken them ten days to pass, but based on how long it had taken him to fight *eighteen* dummies, almost a hundred would take...

...very probably the rest of his short life.

Lindon moved on to the technique section. "Dance of the Dragon of Emptiness," he said.

"Not 'Fierce'?" Yerin asked. "Nothing fierce about this one?"

Lindon shook his head, trying to remember a story that Orthos had told him months ago.

"Then I like it. Dance of the Dragon of Emptiness...what about Dance of Emptiness? Plain and stable. Doesn't look like you have to do any dancing, though."

He searched the characters, trying to figure out how else they could be read, before the memory clicked. "Void Dragon's Dance."

Yerin slapped him on the back. "There's the winner. That's a name you'd be proud to put in a manual."

White light flashed in the darkening sky overhead, and they both looked up.

Lindon extended his Jade perception, and was sure Yerin had done the same. He had the brief sense that the light felt cool and sharp, but that was all before it faded.

"A celebration?" he asked. The Wei clan had shone colored lights into the night sky at every festival and most holidays.

Yerin's face went from distracted and curious to deadly serious in the space of a blink. "Get your pack, bring it here. We should put our backs to an exit."

Lindon strained his perception, but he didn't even get a vague sense of the city. "What's happening?"

"Nothing's sure yet," Yerin said, "but it's not a party."

He turned to run back to the cave, but stopped before he'd taken a step. To his surprise, he *did* sense something. Something a lot closer than the city.

Orthos' core quivered like a bomb on the edge of exploding.

His shock and outrage echoed inside Lindon—he must

have felt the same things Yerin did. Whatever that was, it hit the turtle like a gong. His spirit shivered, teetering off balance for an instant.

Then it fell into rage.

"I'll go back later," Lindon said, worrying for the River-seed. "Right now, we need to—"

A roar shook their little valley. Dirt trembled, and the walls shivered.

Yerin's sword was in her hand, and her Goldsign buzzed with sword aura. "That's your turtle?"

"Not at the moment," Lindon said. Blackflame madra swirled within him in furious, explosive bursts, ready to be used.

A deafening series of crashes filled the canyon, and gray smoke rose between them and the Enforcer Trial. The stone pillars were collapsing as Orthos got closer.

He was crashing straight through the forest of columns on his way to them.

"Yerin," Lindon asked, his voice surprisingly calm. "Where would you put Orthos' strength, if you had to rate him?"

She leaned on the balls of her feet, ready to dash into battle. "Hard to weigh sacred beasts, but I'd call him Truegold."

"That's what I thought." He swallowed. "Gratitude, Yerin. I would never have made it out of Sacred Valley if not for you."

Her spirit flared, and silver aura condensed around her like a shell. "Wouldn't make it out of this valley without me, either. Talk when the fight's over. Eyes up."

Lindon had never taken his gaze away from the approaching sacred beast, but he *still* almost missed it when the huge black bulk hurled itself through the arch of their Trial, body blazing with the Burning Cloak, red eyes shining with madness. If Lindon had been any less than fully focused, he wouldn't have made it in time.

But a Burning Cloak of his own sprung up around him, and he dashed off to the side, kicking up a spray of dirt, everything from his ankles to knees screaming at the strain.

His Bloodforged Iron body kicked in instantly, stealing more of his madra and sending it to his legs.

Yerin ducked so low she looked like she'd plastered herself against the ground, slashing up with her Goldsign and her white sword both.

Orthos kicked out, and both of her attacks met burning claws.

Then the turtle's momentum carried him over her body, and he slammed into the earth, roaring and turning in an instant. Yerin was back on him, slamming an aura-assisted blade at his neck.

They traded six blows while Lindon took stock of his options.

He could go back to the cave and get the Sylvan Riverseed to try and cleanse Orthos. It might not work, but he'd intended to try whenever Orthos showed up sane again. But the pack was all the way back in the cave, and by the time he returned, Yerin could be dead.

He could try to lure Orthos out the exit. He could probably get the turtle to follow him, and then Yerin could knock him through the aura barrier to the outside. If he was trapped, he'd be harmless until Lindon could bring the Riverseed to heal him.

Of course, that was assuming he couldn't just drill a hole with Blackflame straight through the stone and come right back inside.

Or...Lindon patted his belt, feeling the weight there. He'd brought his halfsilver dagger along to the unknown Trial. He gripped the hilt in a sweaty hand, flared his Burning Cloak, and dashed into battle.

One cut. If he could stab Orthos at all, the halfsilver would disperse his madra, and Yerin would have an instant to stop him. It might even be enough to relieve the pressure on his spirit and make him sane again.

When Yerin rolled in the air over his shell and came down behind him, Orthos turned to face her.

And Lindon leaped in, striking at the turtle's tail. He

could cut anywhere, with a halfsilver blade, and it would work just as well. The important part was that the metal contacted the madra.

He stabbed Orthos in the tail, and his blade snapped in half.

Halfsilver was a brittle metal, and the turtle's skin was thick as leather armor. He should have seen it coming.

Lindon cursed himself as he tumbled backwards, having been sent flying by Orthos' tail. He eventually rolled to a stop, but hopped straight up to his feet—he'd been hurt worse than that in the Enforcer Trial.

If Orthos was in full command of his powers, they would both have been dead by now. Lindon could feel that in the power echoing through their contract. But fueled entirely by blind rage, the turtle could hardly string two thoughts together.

That was their only chance.

Clutching that possibility, Lindon dashed back into the fight.

CHAPTER EIGHTEEN

In Yerin's view, you never got used to the fear of death, but you could ignore it. It didn't go away, but when you'd spent more nights in swordfights than in soft beds, you learned to shove the fear into the dark corner where it belonged.

But facing the hulking, burning, armored beast that loomed over her and struck with a fury that singed her skin, that fear was creeping out of its corner and showing its ugly face.

Orthos was overwhelming her with the sheer power of his madra. He would smash down with an Enforced paw that cracked the ground, cough up a tongue of abyssal flames, and rush forward to crush her with his body weight, all in the space of a breath. She dodged what she could, but some attacks had to be turned, and it took everything she had to shove one of his blows to the side.

Her master's voice was finally starting to scrape her nerves. She'd learned so much from the instincts bubbling up from his Remnant that she couldn't believe Eithan had ever told her to get rid of him, but *now* he was starting to feel like a burden. Her Goldsign twitched like her master wanted her to cut the turtle in half; well, that would be just fine, if it weren't a *turtle*. There was a big mound of shell in the way.

The Sword Sage didn't see the problem. That was a stable enough move if it were him in the flesh; *he* could cut a mountain in half without a sword in his hand. But she was still a Gold, ten leagues and two oceans behind his stage of advancement. She couldn't cut through that shell if Orthos stood quietly and let her...but her Goldsign was *still* pulling her to try it.

If not for Lindon, she'd be dead already; when she saw him catch a gap in Orthos' defense and rush in to hammer it, she was prouder than a hen with six eggs. Good thing he was there, because he could take hits from Blackflame madra without dissolving like salt in water.

Orthos hadn't gathered himself for a big show like that Striker technique that had pierced the clouds—and a good thing too, or he'd bring the canyon walls down—because he didn't have the presence of mind for it. Best he could manage was belching a few black flames, which Lindon could swat away with his own madra and keep fighting. She had to meet each of those techniques with her sword, or risk losing an arm.

But every time Lindon did that, his power dimmed like a dying light. He was faltering, that was plain to see.

If she didn't win this fight in the next two breaths, he wouldn't get a third.

Smoke and red-tinged light rose from Orthos' shell as he stomped around, swiveling his head to point at Lindon. The turtle's jaw gaped, and his eyes blazed with what she'd call hatred.

There was a mountain of shell between her and Lindon, but there was one last thing she could try.

With all the strength of her Steelborn Iron body, Yerin hurled the sword between Orthos' legs. It stuck into the earth beneath the turtle, buried up to the hilt, and Orthos didn't notice.

Dead on target.

Yerin gathered all the sword aura she could pull onto her Goldsign, and even the edge of her fingernails. Sword aura showed its power in motion; when she swung them all forward, she struck with the Endless Sword technique.

Her Goldsign rang like a bell. Her fingernails echoed, tiny chimes, as they popped and sprayed blood into the air.

All the sword aura resonated in a twenty-foot radius around her, the technique spreading out in a wave and looking for other swords. When it hit her master's blade, the ringing sounded like the gong that announced victory or failure in the Blackflame Trials.

Sword aura burst out of the buried weapon, a wave of dirt spraying everywhere, and blasted the turtle's underbelly. She had been hoping to split Orthos from bottom to top, but she could feel when the aura didn't bite. It slammed into his belly, lifting him six inches off the ground and making him roar...but it barely cut him. She'd gotten worse from sharp twigs.

In that half-second while all four paws were off the ground, she saw one more chance, but she didn't have the strength to follow up on it. If she had her sword, sure. But she was unarmed, bleeding from all ten fingernails, and low on madra to top it off.

She opened her mouth to shout, hoping Lindon would catch this chance before it passed.

Before a sound left her lips, Lindon moved.

The months of training together finally showed their worth. Lindon, heavens bless him, saw the opportunity. He slid closer to Orthos and reached down, fist flaring with the black-and-red light of the Burning Cloak.

His uppercut caught the turtle on the edge of his shell, sending Orthos flipping upside-down.

The sacred beast slammed into the earth a moment later, spraying Blackflame madra from its mouth and roaring. Yerin clambered closer, snatching the hilt of her sword away— only luck had stopped him from landing right on the blade.

Another benefit of working with Lindon: she knew exactly where he'd be without looking.

She tossed the white sword into the air over Orthos, and

Lindon—already at the height of a jump—snatched it out of the air.

His thoughts were the same as hers, she knew. They didn't want to kill Orthos, because they'd have to fight his Remnant, but heaven strike her down if she could see a better way. Besides, Lindon could adopt the Remnant; he might not have been instructed through that process, and he may not have been quite ready for it, but that would be better than another fight to the death.

Lindon landed on Orthos' belly, swaying like a man on the deck of a ship. He reversed the sword, raised it in both hands...

...and he switched cores.

His presence went from a fiercely burning fire to a calm, almost invisible lake. He was a Jade on a different Path.

And before he killed the sacred beast, something caught her attention.

When did he have full strength in both his cores?

She'd never noticed much of a difference, since he'd grown so slowly, and he only switched to his Twin Stars madra once in a blue moon. But he *used* to feel like half a Jade. Now, she'd never know he had a split core without scanning his spirit closely.

His core still wasn't the deepest, but compared to how he was before, the difference was like heaven and earth. Just the core he was showing now wouldn't embarrass a Jade back in Sacred Valley, and she'd eat her sword if his Blackflame core wasn't a notch wider.

His cycling technique. Eithan taught it to him.

Lindon had never made a secret of that, but Yerin hadn't given it two thoughts before. It was just a cycling technique; every Path had one. Lindon had complained about how difficult his Heavenly Whatever Wheel was, but he was new to the sacred arts. Everything was difficult to him.

She'd been jealous of the personal attention Eithan had paid him, but if she was honest, he needed it more than she did. But Yerin had never thought Eithan was teaching him anything great because—to cut right down to the bone—Eithan wasn't treating them like real disciples. He hadn't even told them the name of his Path.

But...what if he *did* think of Lindon as a disciple? What if he was *actually* passing along his sacred arts to Lindon?

Because if that cycling technique had made up for his lack of madra, it wasn't some half-baked technique that Lindon had found in an old scroll. It was on the same stage as the cycling technique her master had passed to her.

She expected a fresh surge of envy, but what passed through her instead was relief. A large slice of a sacred artist's future could be told from the quality of their Path.

You could get to Truegold without a perfect Iron body, but then your flesh wouldn't survive the advancement to Underlord. Same story for spirits: without a solid Jade cycling technique, your soul would get shakier and shakier at each stage until you couldn't advance any further.

The more solid your foundation, the further you could go.

When Eithan told them he wanted to take them all the way to the end, he hadn't just been spitting in the wind.

Of course, they wouldn't take one step out of the valley if Orthos' Remnant killed them both. The fight wasn't over.

Lindon pulled his free hand back for a strike and drove an Empty Palm down into the turtle's midsection, and Yerin could *feel* the creature's madra going wild. It screamed like an earthquake, so loud she had to cycle madra to her ears to stop her eardrums from bursting. It bucked like a ship in a storm, trying to shake Lindon off.

But it couldn't Enforce its body anymore. Orthos' quick, graceful movements were gone, and he was just a big turtle.

Lindon raised the Sword Sage's blade and threw it to one side.

Yerin gaped at him. Every rosy thing she'd thought about him flew away and died.

Lindon's knees almost buckled when he hopped off the turtle and hit the ground, and he braced himself against the side of Orthos' shell for balance. "Forgiveness, but he doesn't deserve to die here. And the Sylvan might help him."

For once, the three voices in her head were all in agreement. Her unwelcome guest, her master's Remnant, and Yerin all told her to kill the enemy before this idiot could ruin everything.

"I'm not saying to gut him for the *thrill* of it. You kill enemies, you hear me? If you don't, they come up behind you and stab you in the back."

Lindon looked ashamed, but he didn't pick the sword back up. "I have to go get my pack."

Yerin marched over and snatched her master's weapon from the dirt as Orthos squirmed to right himself. Her bloody fingernails sent sharp pain up her arms, but nothing she couldn't ignore. "If you were making this mistake alone, I'd let you. But you're not." She leaped over the turtle, landing next to its head, and raised her blade. Her madra flowed into it, gathering along its edge, gathering aura.

The target's black-and-red eyes rolled in their sockets, searching. Not furious any longer.

Lost.

They stared at her as though begging for an answer. A low groan rumbled in the turtle's throat.

"Do...what...you...must..." the sacred beast said, in a voice both ancient and heavy.

Yerin paused with her white blade against the black, leathery throat. Everything in her told her to split the turtle's neck.

She sheathed her sword and jogged back to Lindon. He started running for his pack, and she joined him.

"Not even an enemy, really, is he?" she muttered, as they ran side by side.

"I've never thought so, no."

"The Path makes him crazy?"

"His mind can't compete with the feelings in his spirit." He gave a sheepish smile. "That's the impression I get."

"Well, if it happens to you, I *will* cut your head off."

The Sword Sage taught her not to show mercy to her enemies, but he also taught her to act in a way she wouldn't regret. Well, if his bloodthirsty Remnant and her blood madra parasite agreed on something, she could bet she'd regret it sooner or later.

They spent more than a minute chasing Little Blue around the cave and scooping her back into the tank. Otherwise, packing up was easy as a breath; Lindon kept his stuff so organized it would make a librarian jealous, and Yerin didn't have anything. Everything she owned, she kept on her body.

They returned to the Ruler Trial, Lindon cupping a quivering Sylvan in his hands. He was certain the Riverseed's power could calm Orthos' spirit, but Yerin kept a grip on her sword.

She didn't want to kill someone she'd just spared, but Lindon could be too trusting.

When they returned and found Orthos gone, he tucked the Sylvan away as though he'd expected as much, and she breathed a sigh of relief.

"Nothing left for us here," she said, grabbing him by a shoulder and dragging him toward the exit. When he didn't move fast enough to suit her, she pulled him into a run.

"I doubt we can clear the Ruler Trial now," Lindon said as they ran, looking like a turtle himself with the pack bouncing on his back.

"I'm feeling a little doubt myself," Yerin said, voice dry. A chunk of the ninety-nine dummies had been ravaged by the aftermath of their battle, either destroyed by Blackflame or shredded by the Endless Sword. Good thing for them that the course hadn't activated, or the mannequins might have joined in.

"You think Eithan will understand us leaving early?" He sounded anxious.

Yerin was still picking up flares of chaos from the city. They'd been driven out of the Trials by a wild sacred beast while Serpent's Grave was breaking into a war zone. Eithan was cracked in the head if he expected them to stay where they were.

The exit arch was black, not red, but its script flared at the touch of Lindon's Blackflame madra. It took him visible effort to activate the circle, and his core felt like the spark at the end of a fizzling incense stick.

Not that she was in much better shape herself. Madra sloshed in her core like the last drops at the bottom of a bottle, and her fingers throbbed like she'd run over her hands with a wagon.

They emerged onto a cliff overlooking Serpent's Grave. A path cut into the rock sloped steadily downward.

But they both froze at what they saw. And what they felt.

As she'd expected, war had come to the city.

Streaks of deadly white light tore through homes. The dragon bone held up, but even at this distance, they could see holes in everything else: wood, plaster, and paint showed smoking gaps where they'd been torn apart by the sacred arts.

Gouts of stone, blasts of wind, and flares of color marked sacred artists fighting all through the streets. The ceaseless ringing of bells reached them even up on the cliff, along with the occasional drifting scream. Smoke hung over everything, and the vital aura of blood, fire, and destruction spread through the city like red and black ink seeping into a painting. Here and there, Remnants crawled over and through buildings.

Lindon looked horrified, clutching the jade badge hanging from his neck as though for comfort. Yerin loosened her own grip on her sword, because she was squeezing blood from her fingertips.

"Eithan's not in the city," she said.

"How can you be sure?"

"This wouldn't be happening. There'd be heaps of dead Jai clansmen piled up all over the city."

"We can go back through the Trials," Lindon said, voice low and determined. "Circle around. We'll come out in the back of Arelius territory. Eithan or Cassias will find us first, we can be sure of that."

Yerin patted her pockets, making sure she still had a flask of water, a wrapped packet of dry food, her knife, and the gold badge her master had left her. Those, her robes, and her sword were the only belongings she needed.

"We should get started for the capital," she said. "Never been to Blackflame City, but I've been everywhere else, and a couple of sacred artists with no name, no clan, and decent Paths can find work anywhere."

"Eithan wouldn't be too happy about that, I'm sure," Lindon said carefully.

That was something to chew on. If anyone could track them down in the mass of a big city, Eithan could.

"That's sharp thinking, but he couldn't blame us for striking out on our own after...this." She swept her arm to encompass the ruined city. "Somebody wants to fight with me and mine, you know I'll draw swords. But the Arelius family hasn't given us so much that I'd want to die on their account. Nobody there would shed a tear if they saw my Remnant."

For most of her life, the only one who would remember her at all would have been her master. Now...Lindon would cry for her when she was gone. He'd remember her name.

Even more reason not to go down there.

"We should go back to the Trials," Lindon said at last, though he didn't sound too happy about it.

"Big turtle's somewhere back there," she pointed out. "If it goes crazy on us again, we're—"

Her spirit warned her, and she shoved Lindon back against the rocks.

Two sacred artists landed in front of her, their backs to the cliff, but there were more up above who hadn't shown themselves. One was a man about her height, packed tight like a coiled spring, draped in black fur. His gray hair was slicked back with grease, a pair of spear butts poked up over his shoulders, and he glared at Lindon in a way that reminded her of a snake baring fangs.

Next to him, a head taller and wrapped in red, stood Jai Long. Last time she'd seen him, his spirit felt deadly but contained, like a sheathed sword. Now the sheath had been re-moved—not only was he Truegold as well, with power that pressed against her senses, he felt *dangerous.* Like he'd cut her just by standing near.

The strips of red cloth covered his face, each bandage filled with flowing script. Dark eyes glittered in the center of the mask.

This time, he carried no spear.

Two Truegolds. *'Show me a fair fight,'* her master used to say, *'and I'll show you an opponent who has lost his mind.'* Even so, there were rigged games, and then there was suicide.

The old Sandviper snarled and swept his hand through the air. A handful of finger-length needles, Forged of ac-id-green madra, flew out in a spray.

Circulating the Rippling Sword technique, Yerin stepped forward to meet him.

Her core might have been filled with hopes and wishes and nothing else, but she squeezed out every drop of pow-er she could get. The needles crashed against her arching sword like a wave against stone, but that wasn't the end of her technique.

Her madra flashed out, a crescent-shaped slash of color-less power sheathed in silver aura. For a moment, shock flashed across the Sandviper Truegold's face, and he pulled spears into his hands with blurring speed.

Then Jai Long was there, his hand glowing white and crashing into her technique. The Rippling Sword broke like a bubble, sword aura dispersing into the air.

"Yerin Arelius," Jai Long said evenly. "Disciple of the Sword Sage. The Underlord told me who you were. If you'd told me last time, I would never have drawn weapons, out of respect for your master."

"The 'Arelius' part is still all shiny and new," Yerin said, still channeling the dregs of her madra into her sword. "Guess you might say I was adopted. If you wanted to use words instead of weapons this time, I could show mercy and let you."

The Sandviper lifted a spear, eyes glued to Lindon, and Jai Long started cycling madra. In that blink where they weren't focused on her, Yerin spun.

She kicked Lindon in the chest, sending him back into the tunnel and closer to the Trial. A Sandviper technique shattered into green light on bare rock where Lindon had been standing, and the gray-haired man was dashing past her, a frustrated growl turning into a shout as he ran.

Above her, the other nearby Sandvipers grew closer.

She turned back, and Jai Long had already charged.

Yerin had a clear obstacle. She had a fight. Now, she just had to do as her master taught her...and cut right through it.

In the dark shadows of her mind, the fear of death reared its head again.

Jai Daishou, Patriarch of the Jai clan, stared through the bubble of aura at the blurred figure with yellow hair and blurred robes.

Ordinarily, sound would not travel well through this boundary formation, but Eithan would be able to see him and hear him. He raised the spear of his honored ancestor, displaying it before the enemy.

Then he shook his head, showing sadness on his face to mask the triumph in his heart. "Your path of recklessness led us here, Eleven. You have done as you wished, acting on the whims of youth without respect or consideration. This is a harvest you have planted."

The elders around him nodded along. They'd gathered close to the Underlord, like children gathering around their father.

Well, let them. This was Jai Daishou's moment of victory, and the more people who witnessed it, the better.

Eithan's face was unreadable through the haze of the

aura. He held his broom out to one side; it was hard to make out details, but it didn't seem to be a weapon or a construct. Just a broom.

Jai Daishou's grip on his spear tightened as he grew irritated. "You could hear me if I were on the other side of the mountain, Eleven. Speak like a grown man, for once in your life, and perhaps we can come to an accord."

Eithan spun the broom in a lazy circle, like a staff, and still didn't speak.

Finally, Jai Daishou's self-restraint broke. For the past six years, since he came from the other end of the world, Eithan Arelius had been a walking disaster. He'd disrespected the Jai clan, ignored the words of his betters, and insulted Jai Daishou to his face. In front of the Emperor once, and the honored Emperor had said not a word.

A man could tolerate only so much before patience reached its end.

Jai Daishou leveled the Ancestor's Spear, shifting his stance and letting madra flow freely into his limbs. "Then you'll forgive me for testing the skills of the youngest Underlord in the Empire."

This formation had been designed with Eithan in mind. No one knew what Path he used, but there were no reports of his ever using a Striker technique. Most reports agreed that he used a Path focused on Enforcement, probably focused on the force aspect. He might have even trained with the Cloud Hammer School, though he lacked their Goldsign.

Eithan's hair blew behind him in the wind generated by the force of the boundary formation. He faced Jai Daishou squarely, until the Jai Patriarch was sure they were locking gazes. The Arelius held the broom in one hand, pointing it toward one of the Jai elders.

No, not to the elder. To the boundary flag.

"Whose idea was the boundary?" Eithan asked, and though the words sounded distorted, Jai Daishou could hear them clearly.

"I knew I would need something to prevent you from

running for your life," he said. The truth was, this barrier would allow the passage of madra. He intended to skewer Eithan with Striker techniques while the Underlord couldn't fight back.

Jai Daishou had spent most of his life building up a reputation of honor and respect that anyone in the Empire would envy, but as death approached, he found that saving face in the eyes of his peers had less and less appeal.

What could their ridicule do to him? Ruin his clan? His clan would fall apart the moment he was buried. Now, only results mattered.

The Jai Patriarch's spearhead blazed like a white sun as he prepared a Star Lance. The other elders spread out around the dome, doing the same.

Eithan nodded. "Thank you," he said. "Now there are no witnesses."

A dull gray spark passed from the middle of the broom where Eithan gripped it, washing along to both ends. Soulfire: the signature of an Underlord. Where the blaze passed, the broom's color darkened, remade in the fires of condensed vital aura. It would conduct energy almost perfectly now, and would be tougher than steel. All the best weapons were imbued with a Lord's soulfire.

That was all within Jai Daishou's calculations. And it was still just a broom.

Jai Daishou hesitated before launching his Striker technique. Maybe Eithan Arelius really *was* arrogant to the point of madness. The young Underlord had always seemed brash with the overconfidence of youth, combined with pride in his admittedly high natural gifts, but now...

No Truegold was a match for an Underlord, certainly. Soulfire itself, and the process of weaving it from vital aura, gave Lords powers that no Gold could access.

But it wasn't as though a Truegold could do *nothing*. Where a lone wolf was only prey, a pack of wolves could bring down a tiger. Skilled as they were, these six Truegold elders working together could bring Eithan down on their own. With Jai Daishou added in, the Arelius Underlord was already dead.

He was just speaking out of pride, that was all.

Just pride.

As Lindon stumbled back through the Trial gate, slapping his hand against the script to reactivate the aura barrier, he tried to remember how many times Yerin had knocked him out of danger.

It had to be at least six by now, he was sure. It wounded his dignity, being kicked away like a wild dog, but if he had to choose between wounded dignity and a spear through the chest, he knew which he'd pick.

All those times, and what could he do when she was in danger? Nothing. Just run.

Hating himself, Lindon ran back into the Ruler Trial. His first hope was dashed when he realized Orthos wasn't there; he was still nearby, but he could be anywhere in the Trial grounds or back in the tunnels.

A green flash of light shattered the aura barrier and the gray-haired Sandviper crashed through, a short spear in each hand. Endless Sword madra still flickered outside, so Yerin was fighting, and at least she didn't have to face two Truegold opponents at once.

Lindon ran for the Trial entrance. If he could make it back to the Enforcer course, he could hide in the rubble of the columns that Orthos had left behind. Then—

A nail drove through his calf, and he went down. He caught himself with both hands and rolled before hitting the ground, so the green Forged nail intended to go through his other leg hit the dirt instead.

His Blackflame core was hopelessly empty, and his Blood-forged Iron body was draining pure madra to his calf like a bucket with a hole in it. He pinched the needle with two fingers—the Sandviper madra stung his skin like acid—and pulled it out.

Then he let his pack slide to the ground, turning to face his pursuer.

"My name is Wei Shi Lindon, honored Truegold," Lindon said, spreading his hands. "As you can see, I'm only a Jade, and surely I have nothing to interest an elder of your caliber."

"Sandviper Gokren," he growled. "Kral's father."

When the spear came in, Lindon instinctively tried to form the Burning Cloak. Of course, nothing happened—he was cycling pure madra, and it had to be handled differently. But he clumsily Enforced his arms anyway, managing to knock the thrust off course.

The second spear followed instantly, and he had to step back to stop it. Which meant putting weight on his bleeding calf.

He tried to stop the scream, but when he faltered and took a spearhead to the shoulder, he screamed all the same.

Lindon covered his face with his hands as another technique came in, but the spray of needles covered him from head to hips. At first, he trusted in the power of his Iron body and his Enforcer technique to save him, but the strength of a Truegold overwhelmed him. Every wound burned with poison, and his body *leaked* madra trying to counteract the Sandviper venom.

His lungs locked up. He couldn't get a breath. His madra channels flickered and went dark, the pain overwhelming him as his Enforcer technique broke.

Gokren was shouting something, face purple with rage, but Lindon didn't hear a word of it. He was drifting away, his flesh distant, as darkness crept into the corners of his vision.

Orthos hit Gokren like a landslide.

The turtle's roar shook the canyon. Foreign anger echoed in Lindon's soul, and Blackflame power flared against acid-green light. Rocks cracked, men shouted, and fire crackled.

The fight continued, but all the other details faded with Lindon's consciousness.

Time passed in a haze of pain as the ground shook beneath him. He came back to himself choking on a mouthful of dirt and ash. He was riddled with holes, blood still seeping out of him, and he was starting to shiver. But the Bloodforged Iron body had done its job; at least venom no longer crawled through his veins.

He spat out bloody mud and rolled his eyes in his sockets, craning for a sight of Sandviper Gokren.

Twilight had passed, the stars bright pinpricks against the dark.

He could see no one. He strained his spiritual perception, and sensed...

Nothing.

He tried again, taking deep breaths despite the pain, quieting his spirit as best he could. The world remained dead around him. He opened his eyes, staring beyond what he could see, looking to open his Copper sight and catch a glimpse of aura.

No color. The world was gray and lifeless, and his limbs now trembled with creeping cold.

Calming his panic, he focused on his madra. His core was drained, but he could fix that by cycling. He braced himself for the pain as he tried to push himself up on his elbows.

In the dirt, he saw his arms twitch. He felt nothing.

Panic rose into his throat again, throwing off his breathing, and he tried to picture the heavy stone wheel in his core. He didn't feel anything; not a spark.

His Bloodforged Iron body had drained everything.

Though the pain made his vision swim, and fear weighed him down, he managed to shimmy closer to his pack. It had fallen close to him, and there might be a Four Corners Rotation Pill or some scales inside. At least he could see what he had available, take stock.

He inched closer, seizing the corner of the pack with his teeth. Through pure will, he managed to slide his hand to the hook at the top. The hook held only a loop of cloth; all he had to do was slide that loop off, and the pack was open. He edged his thumb into the gap.

It didn't take.

He tried again and again, despair growing like mold in his chest, until finally he caught the loop. With a limp finger, he pulled it open.

The pack tipped.

Its contents tumbled onto the ground, pelting his face and hand with junk. The pack must have been jostled around during the fight, because even some things that should have been secured in inside pockets had come free: his *Path of Twin Stars* manual, his Soulsmith primer, a sealed inkwell, a handful of halfsilver chips. It all spilled around him like trash.

In his hazy awareness, Lindon could only latch onto one thought: he had to put everything back where it was supposed to go. He pushed his hand, trying to keep his precious Path manual out of the dirt. Without madra, his arm might as well have been a dishrag.

He was empty.

The canyon had always been dark, allowing only a strip of light in from the sky, but at night the darkness surrounded him.

So when the light came, it hurt his eyes.

The blue light seemed blinding at first, even with his eyes closed, but when he swiped muddy tears from his eyelids and squinted into the shadows, his eyes quickly adjusted.

He stared into an azure candle flame, burning steadily at the heart of a glass marble. The flame was smooth and bright, the glass flawless.

As Lindon bled into the dirt, he stared at the ball of glass and fire. Just stared.

In the visions Suriel had shown him, he had died...but not here. Not alone in the dark.

He had a long way to go yet.

Lindon slapped one hand down on the marble, feeling its

warmth. He hadn't been able to cycle before, but given that he wasn't dead yet, he had to think there was *some* power left in his soul. If he bled to death, he'd do it while cycling.

If that didn't work...well, he'd climbed his way up from powerless before. He could do it again.

Lindon tried to draw on his Blackflame core, though it was like trying to inhale wood. There was nothing there. But if he *could* reclaim some shred of power, Blackflame was what he wanted. Pure madra wouldn't do him much good if Gokren came back.

The thought made him shiver with fear, but he steadied his breath again and started cycling according to the Heaven and Earth Purification Wheel. The pain in his lungs almost made him return to his earlier, simpler Foundation technique, but he persevered. Eithan had told him to practice this cycling technique, and at least no one could say he'd given up.

Breath after agonizing breath passed, each one feeling like it hadn't delivered enough air, but he kept going until he started to feel something. An approaching flame, a slight red light, and a tingling feeling on his skin.

His eyes snapped open to find that he was staring straight into black eyes with irises the color of shining blood.

Orthos.

CHAPTER NINETEEN

Yerin dashed up the black slope, headed for the other peak, but Jai Long followed her.

He was playing with her, she could see that clear as glass. Maybe he wanted to hammer out a new technique, and maybe he thought she wasn't worth his best. Whatever the truth, it stung.

She had clawed the last drop of madra from her core, and was running on prayers. But there was a mass of silver power left in her spirit, and she begged it for more power.

Her master's instincts told her to attack.

I can't, she thought. *Give me something, and I'll use it.*

The Remnant had no other advice for her. Just a few wispy memories of running straight at an enemy, weapon and techniques primed and ready.

Someone else had a word for her, though.

Her long-time guest, unwelcome and uninvited, sat there in her core in a knot of deadly power. If she unleashed it, it could save her. If she released it, she could save *herself.*

As always, she reminded herself what would happen if she released her guest. Unless Eithan popped out of the ground, her guest would destroy everything. And everyone, probably including her. Unless it hollowed her out and used her as a husk, which was worse.

No, she didn't need that parasite's help. She needed her master to *step up*.

A twisting snake shot out from Jai Long's palm, and she met it with the edge of her master's sword. Only the sheer quality of the weapon saved her, because she had no madra left to pour into it. Her bloody fingernails drummed with pain to the beat of her heart.

Show me what to do, Yerin begged.

The Remnant still urged her to attack. The unwelcome guest still pleaded for freedom.

And Yerin's heart bled, because she finally accepted the truth: this wasn't her master. Breaking him open wouldn't be a betrayal, it wouldn't mean abandoning him. If she dug into the Remnant and sucked its power dry, she wouldn't be losing her master's voice.

She'd lost that almost a year ago, in Sacred Valley.

So, as Jai Long kicked her body down the mountain with a bored sigh, Yerin reached inside herself. Her master's Remnant was just a mass of silver power in her core, but she visualized it as it had appeared when she adopted it: a ghost of silver chrome, armed with six bladed limbs.

She reached for that ghost and crushed it with the power of her will.

As though she'd lit a beacon, the aura around her ignited. Silver light blazed into the sky, a column of razor-sharp power that turned all the vital aura in the area to sword aura.

Beneath her feet, a thousand invisible blades slashed at the stone, pebbles whipping up to sting her skin. Even the air whistled by her ears as it was cut, the wind lashing at her hair and her robe.

As the power of the sword raged within and without, she was devoured by a memory.

The girl stood before the Sword Sage amidst the wreckage of what had once been a prosperous family.

Her power blazed in his spiritual sense, half of it raw and unshaped, half bloody and murderous. She was only seven or eight and scrawny, and she looked like she'd missed more than her share of meals. Ragged hair hung into her eyes.

She hauled on a rope of blood madra that stretched from her stomach as though the far end was tied to a runaway horse. Her bare feet were planted, her teeth gritted, arms straining against the power of the parasite.

Which stretched out, its end forming into a blade, trying to cut him. She had managed to halt it while the blade was still an inch from his throat.

The world came back into focus as Yerin found herself scraped and bloody and surrounded by a furious storm of silver light. Even the droplets of blood running from her wounds splashed up, sliced by aura, covering her with a scarlet mist.

A column of light rose into the air from her body, like she was a falling silver star.

She grasped at the Sword Sage's memory like the fading edges of a dream; her master remembered that moment more vividly than she did. That moment: their first meeting. When she'd tried to save him from the power of her unwelcome guest.

Jai Long stood over her, and she found enough energy to stare defiantly back. He was far enough back that the sword energy didn't cut him, but he was a sword artist himself—he could fight through the violent storm of her advancement to continue the fight while she was vulnerable.

But he merely crossed his arms and waited.

He could defend himself from this weapon, this seed of a true Blood Shadow, with only a fraction of his madra. He was in no danger.

But she didn't know that. And she forced her body to its limit, muscles straining, blood running from the lip she was biting to keep the parasite from stretching any closer to him.

He was a stranger to her. The Blood Shadow had already consumed everyone she knew. All the others he'd seen in her position had given up—they had lost all reason to live, and thus all reason to fight. Their parasites thrived in such situations, filling their bodies like husks, stealing their power to bring it away.

And here, a little girl fought with all her body, mind, and spirit. She held on, her eyes furious and determined, resisting to the end.

And the fragment of a Dreadgod was no easy foe.

Yerin climbed to her feet, madra filling her, seeping into her weapon. Sword aura was so thick in the air, bright silver even to the naked eye, that it had started gathering on the edges of her blade. With half the effort it normally took, she executed her weapon Enforcer technique: the Flowing Sword. The technique collected aura with every slash and thrust, making the weapon stronger as it moved.

Everything in the Path of the Endless Sword revolved around vital aura. Most sword Paths could be used without a sword—their madra itself was sharp enough to cut old oak, so who needed the weapon itself? You could Forge whatever you needed for a fight.

On her Path, every technique was half a Ruler technique. Made her more powerful, gave her techniques extra heft...so long as she held a sword. If she didn't have a weapon with a sharp edge, she was worth less than any other sacred artist.

That's what her Goldsign was for.

Looking down on her, Jai Long must have felt the power building to a crescendo. He stood just beyond the silver light that poured as a torrent into the sky, and debris scattered by aura blades crashed against his chest.

Still he waited, arms crossed. Obviously, he expected more.

He had come to kill her, but here was a child who stood against a Dreadgod's madra. She had power of her own—otherwise, the parasite would have chosen someone older—and enough resolve to keep on fighting even when the battle was lost, when she had no one left, when there was no hope of victory and nothing to fight for.

She was perfect.

Her master's memories and attitudes soaked into her, washing over her with a palpable sense of his presence. He had chosen her because she fought to the last breath. Because, when backed into a corner and given no path to victory, she would still attack.

The Path of the Endless Sword had no defense. Sword aura could not shield her, it could only cut.

Whether she fought to escape, to kill her opponent, to protect herself, or to save someone else, she had to do so by attacking. That was the one weapon in her arsenal, the one road forward.

She'd studied the Path of the Endless Sword for years, and she knew exactly what it could do, but now she felt it. Bone-deep.

The silver light around her faded from a blaze to a halo and then died. Pebbles and droplets of blood, held aloft by the force of her spirit, scattered on the ground. The vital aura had carved out a smooth crater in the stone beneath her, and many of the rock pieces now drifted in the air as a fine dust.

"Congratulations," Jai Long said, in his flat voice.

Yerin stretched her second bladed arm, which loomed over her other shoulder. With the pair of them, she looked like she'd glued a couple of steel fishing rods to her back and strapped knives to the end.

"Highgold," she said, feeling the new resonance of her spirit. "Well, that's got a kick to it." She pressed her fists together, a sacred artist's salute, and noticed her fingernails had stopped bleeding—Lowgold to Highgold wasn't a big advancement, but advancing always did the body good. "Thanks for waiting."

"I need an opponent," he said softly. "Not a victim."

Madra flooded through her flesh and into her skin, fueling her Steelborn Iron body, sinking into her muscles like water into thirsty soil.

She kicked off, and the leap took her over Jai Long's head. He lashed out with a hand glowing like a star, but her Goldsign blurred and met his technique. They clashed with a sound like steel on steel.

Her second Goldsign whipped out, and he had to turn it with his other hand. When she followed up with a hit from her white sword, he took a step back.

Aura flashed out from her sword, slashing one of the strips of cloth from around his face, and he backed up again.

This time, he thrust a palm forward, and a Forged snake flashed through the air to bare fangs of light in her face.

He was following up with more snakes, defense and offense in one, and his spirit still hummed against her senses. She was far from being able to compete with him in raw power.

At least, as far as madra went.

While she was suffering through the birth of her Steel-born Iron body, her master had painted a rosy picture of its future. *'It grows with you,'* he'd said. *'Our body Enforcement techniques aren't worth a chip of rust, see. So you need a body that Enforces itself.'* She'd seen him bend a steel door in half and crush a rock to powder. *'You won't notice at first, but it'll be sharper every stage.'*

For the first time, Yerin could feel the gift her master had left for her.

Something had changed for Yerin at Highgold, and it wasn't her spirit. Jai Long had fought dozens if not hundreds of Highgolds, and it wasn't that her spirit was so much stronger than usual.

Her techniques became sharper, like she'd spent a month practicing, but Jai Long could understand that. Highgold was a journey through the skills and experiences embedded in the Gold Remnant, so she'd have inherited some insight from her master.

It was her sheer physical strength that baffled him as she crushed his serpents, shoved his attacks aside, and matched his movements even through Flowing Starlight.

She drove his Enforced punches apart with her twin Goldsigns, which now moved as quick as her hands. He ducked her sword stroke, which she'd telegraphed by shifting her weight...but then she caught him in the side with a kick.

The force of it strained his Iron body and sent him rolling; he gathered himself and vaulted over from one peak to another. Now he was on the slopes of Shiryu Mountain's main peak, beneath the Jai family palaces.

When she saw how far she'd kicked him, she looked more stunned than he was.

Jai Long's whole purpose in allowing her to reach Highgold had been to measure himself against her. He was still ahead. The power of his techniques, his precision and timing, his speed: these were all beyond her.

But they should be. He was Truegold.

He *shouldn't* feel any pressure from her attacks, but he did. He *should* be so much faster with his Flowing Starlight that she couldn't keep up, and yet she did. She *shouldn't* be able to threaten him except with her weapon, but that kick had nearly broken his ribs.

There was less of a distance between them now than there had been six months ago. He'd used the Ancestor's Spear to gain power faster than any other sacred artist could, and she was still closing the gap.

Fear crawled up his spine, and for the first time, he focused his full power. He had to kill her now.

If he didn't, then the next time they met, she would kill *him*.

He gathered points of light on the tips of his hands, forming Star's Edge techniques. It would have been more effective with a weapon, but he worked with what he had.

Yerin leaped over to the slope with him, slashing out in a Striker technique. He broke it with one Star's Edge, sending a Serpent's Shadow at her to cover her movement as he leaped up the slope.

She followed, of course. Only when he reached the cliff and stood beneath the Jai clan homes did he turn and wait for her.

When she landed on the cliff, tattered black robes fluttering in the breeze, she sheathed her sword.

"You'll need that," he warned her.

She shrugged. "Still better armed than you are."

A hand-sized Striker technique shot out from one of her Goldsigns, and though he crushed the madra immediately, she'd closed the gap.

He drove a Star's Edge at her throat.

They exchanged a dozen blows in an instant, his Enforcer techniques crashing against her Goldsigns. His core had finally started to weaken, dimming from a bright moon to a fading star, and hers couldn't have been much better. Her breaths were still in a cycling rhythm, but they were ragged.

She flicked her eyes to his hands, watching for his next attack, and he took the opening. He squeezed one last burst of speed out of Flowing Starlight, dashing behind her.

This was his chance. He didn't have the power for a prolonged battle with her, certainly not without a weapon. She wasn't even a priority target; if he'd known she would grow so fast, he would have taken Gokren's suggestion and crushed her with the full power of their numbers.

He had one chance to end the threat she represented, and this was it.

Her back was open and unprotected. In one invisible motion, he slashed a razor-sharp Enforced palm at the back of her neck to sever her spine.

As he moved, his spirit cried a warning. He leaped back as the air rippled, and sword aura tore the space where he had just been standing

Yerin's Goldsign had twisted behind her, launching a Ruler technique in her blind spot.

She spun, face red with anger—at herself for letting him get behind her or at him for trying to stab her in the back, he wasn't sure—and sent another rippling slash at him. With his Star's Edge, he broke that technique, and the next one, but she seemed to be trying to empty her core in one breath. The Striker techniques kept coming.

His Star's Edge shattered too early.

There was still a rippling silver-edged distortion in the air, heading right at his face. He needed a moment to call his Enforcer technique back, but he didn't have time.

Before he had time to think, he acted on instinct.

Jai Long used his Goldsign.

His jaw unhinged like a snake's, tearing the red bandages away from his face. He bared a mouth full of glowing white fangs: his inheritance from the serpentine Remnant that had nearly taken his sister's life. They twisted his face, reshaping his jaw, and anytime he opened his mouth he looked like a nightmare.

He opened his mouth wide and bit down on the rippling slash of energy, his teeth shattering the technique like glass. The shards of madra slashed at his cheeks, tearing the rest of his mask away, and he glared at Yerin with open hatred.

She kept her eyes on his, hand on her sword. Her spirit's power was fading, but she was the picture of resolve, prepared to keep fighting.

Jai Long cast his perception back over the city. The tide was turning against them, he could feel it in the ebb of Stellar Spear madra throughout Serpent's Grave.

Shame overcame him in a moment. The Jai clan had lost a battle in their own city.

But as much as it pained him, he was part of the clan again. His oath tugged at him, pulling him to do the responsible thing, to preserve himself for the family's sake. He was wasting too much time on an uncertain battle, and fair fights were a fool's game.

As soon as the clan regrouped, Jai Long intended to suggest that Jai Daishou kill Yerin personally.

Because Jai Long wasn't sure he was up to the task.

With one last glance at the Sword Sage's apprentice, he leaped off the cliff to regroup with his family.

Even with her core emptied for the second time that evening, and both her spirit and body aching with exhaustion, Yerin tried to follow Jai Long.

"Get back...here, you..." Her voice was mumbled, and she wasn't even sure the sounds that came out were real words.

She staggered after the enemy until her knees buckled, and then she sank to the rock, panting. The energy that came to her from her master's Remnant would return, but for now, it was tapped out. Her brief burst of clarity and insight was already fading away like a dream. There was more to gain from the Remnant, but that sense of his presence had gone.

Leaving only a memory.

She was exhausted in body, mind, and spirit, and saying goodbye to the Sword Sage a second time struck her like a physical wound. His absence tore through her.

And there on the mountain, she wept again for her master's death.

Orthos was wounded. His skin oozed dark blood, and Lindon could feel the pain of venom working its way through the turtle's blood and spirit. His spirit was in chaos, and Lindon couldn't sense whether Orthos' mind was in control or not.

A massive black paw, the size of Lindon's entire torso, smashed down onto his stomach, slamming his back against the ground.

Lindon tried to scream, but it came out as a rush of air. He clawed at the leathery leg, but he might as well have been slapping a tree.

The great turtle stretched out his neck, looking Lindon in the eye. He growled and choked into Lindon's face, as though trying to speak, but no words came. The sacred beast gave a great scream of frustration that tore Lindon's face.

He squeezed his eyes shut. Some deaths had to be faced with eyes open, but this was not one of them.

His core flared with a dark, bloody light.

Blackflame raced through his madra channels, scouring him from the inside out, making him gasp.

Is this what it's like to leave a Remnant? he wondered. He'd always imagined it as a sensation of the spirit tearing itself away from the body, which was exactly what this felt like.

His spirit burned hotter and hotter, Blackflame racing along his channels, until he could bear it no longer. He screamed, and Orthos screamed with him, dark fire racing from the turtle's mouth and scorching stone.

Lindon cycled furiously, trying to digest some of the power—not Eithan's Purification Wheel, but the simplest, fastest breathing technique he could. He ignited the Burning Cloak, which raged around him, giving him the strength to lift Orthos' paw and throw it off him.

But Orthos roared in response. A red-and-black corona flared around *him,* and suddenly the leg was pressed back down like a mountain collapsing, claws digging into Lindon's chest.

Lindon built up power in his hands, *pushing* rivers of Blackflame out through both of his palms. The Burning Cloak raged, and he could feel red and black aura flaring all around him.

The power was too much for him, he could feel it; his channels and his core were stretched to the point of bursting. He hadn't reached the end of Jade—his spirit wasn't mature yet.

So he clawed at his pack, searching for the one thing that might help him: the Sylvan Riverseed.

He tore at his pile of belongings like a man on fire looking for a bucket of water. Tongues of Blackflame licked at the fabric of his pack, scorching away chunks, but he couldn't care.

The glass case tumbled out and the Riverseed rubbed her head, as though she'd knocked a skull she didn't have. Lindon didn't wait to get her attention and draw her in; he felt as though his spirit was shriveling and blackening.

Instead, Blackflame burned through the side of the glass. It didn't melt; it hissed and blew away in a cloud of grit like fine dust.

Lindon stretched out trembling fingers, and the Sylvan Riverseed cocked her head to look at him. For a second, she seemed uncertain, like she didn't recognize him.

Then, firmly, she seized his middle finger in both hands.

A surge of liquid blue flowed through his madra channels, quieting the flow of dark madra and soothing his channels like cool water on a burn. Blackflame madra kept coming, and Lindon kept cycling, but the Riverseed poured all she had into him.

Finally, the flow of fire slackened. Orthos pulled his paw from Lindon's core and staggered away, unspeakably weary.

The Sylvan Riverseed sprawled on her back, chittering like a frustrated wind chime. She had lightened to the blue of a robin's egg, and after a moment she squirmed back into his pack and started digging around for scales.

And Lindon lay there panting, spirit and body aching. Much of Orthos' madra had been diverted into his Blood-forged Iron body, so Lindon's smallest wounds had closed and the venom in his veins had been burned away, but he still hurt like he'd been beaten all over with hammers.

Then Gokren stumbled back through the exit, hair wild and furs burned off. He stared wildly around, fixing his gaze on Orthos, and leveled his spear.

Four Sandvipers entered behind him, moving to flank the turtle.

Lindon's spirits fell like a sack of bricks. It just wasn't fair. Suriel was playing a trick on him—surely every mortal's trials had to end sometime.

"The dragon advances," Orthos declared, eyeing Gokren. Lindon could feel the turtle's spirit, strained to its limits, but he still roared and lumbered toward the Sandviper.

Lindon started to gather Blackflame madra between his palms, but he froze. His pure core was still empty.

He couldn't make a shell around the Striker technique.

Orthos took a hit from the side and screamed, while Lindon hunkered behind the stone tablet explaining the Ruler technique, trying to condense Blackflame madra.

The Riverseed whined, shaking his knee with both her hands and pointing to Orthos, trying to get him to help.

Lindon tuned out Orthos' screams and the Riverseed's pleas, focused on the black fire flickering between his hands. This was a dragon's technique. He needed to think about it like a dragon.

He poured more power into the ball, and when he felt himself about to lose control, he *forced* it into place. A dragon wouldn't try to bend or shape its power; a dragon would make the power submit.

The dragon conquers.

When he finally succeeded, he almost didn't realize it, dripping sweat over a fireball twice as big as his fist. He stumbled out from the shelter of the stone tablet, watching Orthos withdrawing all his limbs into his shell.

Sandviper madra crashed on the outside without leaving a mark, but Lindon knew the fight was over. Orthos would never have hidden unless he was prepared to die. His spirit was a mournful song, an aching wound of injured pride.

There was nothing in Lindon's mind except his desire to push the enemy away from his partner. He shoved both hands forward, releasing the madra he'd stored up into a Striker technique.

If he could knock Gokren off-balance, even a weakened Orthos might be able to kill him. Maybe they could escape. But that assumed that Lindon's pitiful Jade technique could even wound a Truegold.

An arm-thick bar of Blackflame madra streamed toward Sandviper Gokren, the technique dense and liquid smooth. The Truegold condensed a green spear out of madra, slamming his Forged weapon against the spike. Truegold Sandviper madra met Lindon's Blackflame.

The dark fire washed over Gokren's defense, taking his hand off at the wrist.

He stumbled back, eyes wide as he stared at the place where his hand used to be. Lindon stared, just as stunned. He had put everything he had into that Striker technique, to the degree that he was feeling dizzy from the strain on his spirit, but he had only hoped to take some pressure from Orthos. Even the Lowgold Sandvipers stepped back, turning their focus from the turtle to Lindon.

Orthos poked his head out of his shell. In the stunned, frozen moment after Lindon's Striker technique, he extended the remainder of his madra. Lindon sensed what he was doing through their contract, but he didn't comprehend it until he opened his Copper sight.

The red-and-black aura was rising like a tide, spreading to encompass all the Sandvipers.

The Sandvipers came to their senses, running from Orthos' ruler technique, but Gokren bared his teeth and swung the spear in his remaining hand down. It glowed green, shining with toxic madra.

Lindon shouted, spraying Blackflame madra in his direction. It didn't even come close to reaching—he hadn't taken the time to concentrate the technique and keep it under control. But Gokren, who had just lost a hand to Lindon's deadly Path, flinched. His spear wavered.

And Orthos activated his Ruler technique.

Five roses of fire bloomed out of nowhere, centered on each of the remaining Sandvipers. The golden-orange flames flared, spotted with inky black and bloody red, devouring five bodies in an instant.

Not one of them managed to scream as the Void Dragon's Dance consumed them.

The fight was over almost too quickly.

Five minutes later, Lindon still didn't believe his own memories. First, the madra had obeyed him more easily than it ever had before. Then, his technique had worked on someone at the peak of Gold. Based on everything Lindon knew, the force of Gokren's madra alone should have been enough to block anything a Jade could do.

Orthos dragged his massive body over to Lindon, chewing on a mouthful of bones as he went. "You're not a Jade," he announced. "I gave you more of my power than a Jade could handle."

Lindon looked at the turtle, then down at his jade badge, then scanned his own spirit. "I'm stronger, certainly, but I don't feel so different. Nothing like when I advanced to Iron or Jade." The stone wheel at the center of his Blackflame core might have spun a little faster, and his spirit cycled with the force of a raging river instead of a trickling stream.

But Iron had come with a new body, and Jade with a new soul. Compared to those changes, this felt too simple. Maybe if he had adopted a Remnant, instead of taking in power through a contract, he would have seen a real difference.

Orthos gingerly stretched out a leg, wincing at the pain. "Humans make every stage into a legend. A Lowgold is just a Jade with teeth. The only difference between Jade and Gold is a mountain of power." He gave Lindon a look that radiated smug pride. "Now you see the *real* glory of Blackflame."

Lindon was still dazed, but he couldn't argue with reality. Sandviper Gokren's legs—the largest remaining parts of him—lay a few dozen yards away. His skull was sliding down Orthos' gullet.

Lindon was Lowgold now. A real Gold.

This was the power of Gold.

But Orthos' soul still pained him—if his condition went untended, he would lose himself again. That was a problem Lindon thought he could solve.

He placed the Riverseed on Orthos' head and, after a moment of panic, the spirit placed both hands on the turtle's skin. Blue light flowed into a Blackflame spirit, smoothing and calming as it went.

Orthos shouted like a man doused in icy water. The Riverseed gave a terrified peep, scuttling back up Lindon's arm. She stumbled at his shoulder, her skin pale, and collapsed on his head to curl up in his hair. "Forgiveness," Lindon said, bobbing a bow. "I didn't think to warn you."

"The insect stung me!" Orthos said, gnashing his jaws. The Sylvan trembled against Lindon's scalp. He swept his perception through her and confirmed what he'd suspected: the tiny spirit was exhausted.

Orthos' madra already flowed more smoothly, even weak as it was, and his madra channels didn't pain him as badly as before. It looked as though it had calmed his soul without diluting his madra, and allowed his channels to repair themselves.

The damage would have returned in days, if he hadn't shared his power with Lindon. Combined with their contract, the Sylvan's attention might be able to—over time— make some real improvement in the turtle's soul.

"You should feel a *little* better at least," Lindon said, knowing he did.

"I have survived three hundred winters and the fall of the Blackflames," Orthos grumbled. "I would have survived this."

On his behalf, Lindon patted the Sylvan on the head with one finger.

Lindon extended his perception, and it unspooled much more easily than before, his perception floating over the mountain. He caught a trail of sensations that *felt* like Yerin, as though her voice still echoed behind her, but not her.

"While you were out there..."

Orthos finished the thought. "I felt her in battle on the main peak. Not now, but her spirit is likely weak." Laughter rumbled out of his chest like aftershocks. "There is another familiar soul in that direction as well."

Lindon let his perception float, and he sensed exactly what the turtle meant: Eithan was no longer bothering to veil his power, and the full force of an Underlord shone like a signal-fire only a short distance away.

As Orthos insisted he could walk, Lindon slid his pack on

and headed in that direction. Where Eithan was, and where they'd last seen Yerin.

The Sylvan Riverseed rode on his head.

CHAPTER TWENTY

Jai Daishou was living a nightmare.

He and his Truegold elders launched their Striker attacks together, streams of white light that should have pierced the enemy from seven different angles.

Then, to his eyes and senses both, Eithan vanished.

One moment he was standing there on the other side of a distorted aura barrier, holding a broom in his hands, and the next...

...the next an elder's skull was crushed like an eggshell *outside* the boundary formation. His body toppled as Eithan stood over him, broom bloodstained. Jai Daishou reacted before any of the elders could, blasting a Star Lance in Eithan's direction, but he slipped back into the formation like a fish into water.

That was impossible. The boundary stopped everything physical from passing. Pushing through it like that was like pushing through a burning wall. Even if his body was so monstrously strong that he *could* do it, the formation should have crumbled. Only madra could pass.

Eithan's upper body popped out of a different side of the bubble, seizing another elder and dragging him back inside. There came a crunch and a scream, and a spray of blood was stopped by the aura.

Only one possibility made sense: he could be covering his body in a shell of madra to pass through the formation. But it would be easier to Forge a human-sized ball and *roll* through: the amount of power it would take to slip in and out while covering every inch of his body would beggar even an Underlord. Jai Daishou himself might have been able to do it once, if he could control his madra precisely enough, but he wouldn't be fit to fight on the other end.

Either this was a trick, or an illusion, or Eithan had madra reserves that the Jai Patriarch could only describe as monstrous. Maybe he had stolen a ward key, somehow.

Jai Daishou ordered his remaining four men back, adjusting his tactics. If Eithan was using speed and mobility against them, he could compete with raw power.

He had no use for this mountainside anyway.

His spear thrummed with power, a fan of Forged spears hovering in the air above him. Each weapon held the full power of his madra and blazed with sword aura; they would hit like bombs, and even if they missed by three feet, the aura alone could peel meat from bone.

But that wasn't enough. He tapped into the soulfire he'd stockpiled over the past decades, channeling the faded flames into each spear. The power sunk into them until the air around them shook.

These were seven deadly attacks capable of drilling through steel plate, spread out to cover every angle of escape. Each technique launched with a split-second difference in timing, to cover any openings and preventing the enemy from grasping the timing.

Eithan would meet a wall of unstoppable spears, burning heat, and slashing blades. He may as well have been nailed to a board.

The cliff shone with white light like a dawning star, invisible gouges appeared in the dirt from the force of his sword aura, and his spiritual sense trembled with the power of his seven spears. Jai Daishou used this technique to level fortress walls, not to kill individual enemies.

This was the culmination of all the individual spear arts passed down among the Jai for generations. Jai Daishou called it the Fall of Seven Stars.

He thrust his spear forward, unleashing a stream of deadly white madra and six Forged missiles that screamed as they blasted through the air. The pale, deadly lights washed over the cliffside like a shining wave, the air between each light churning with sword aura that chewed up pebbles and spat dust.

Utter devastation scoured the cliff, shredding the boundary flags and dispersing the formation, churning the fallen bodies of the two elders into bloody mist. The technique plowed through stone and soil, and when the cloud of dust cleared, the entire half of the outcropping where Eithan once stood was completely gone. A chunk had been gouged out of the mountain, and a chunk of night sky replaced what had been rock a moment before.

Jai Daishou took a deep breath of satisfaction and let his madra begin to cycle. He had strained his spirit too much for this, but at least—

His spirit shouted at him, and he spun, leaping in the air and readying the Ancestor's Spear in both hands.

With his broom, Eithan had swept a Truegold's ankles out from under him. While the old man was still in the air, the broom's handle crashed down on his back.

There was a *crack* as the man's spine snapped.

The wooden broom stayed intact.

Eithan hadn't escaped the Fall of Seven Stars unscathed: blood trickled down into one eye, which was stuck closed, there was a bloody slash across his left shoulder, and his fine blue robe was half-shredded. But he *had* escaped, and that was frightening enough.

Jai Daishou shouted to draw Eithan's attention, and to give his three remaining elders time to run. He whipped Stellar Spear madra in a line—the Star Lance was the simplest Striker technique possible, but also the fastest. No matter how quickly Eithan could move, he couldn't dodge this.

It was practically instantaneous.

A technique of this degree couldn't kill an Underlord, but it could pin him down, keep him from chasing the remaining Truegolds and butchering them one by one.

Eithan raised his hand like a man blocking out the light of the sun.

And when the Stellar Spear madra came within a foot of his hand, the madra dispersed. It dissolved. It vanished, as though the Underlord were simply *wiping out* his technique.

Jai Daishou landed, his metal hair flogging his back like chains, and began channeling Flowing Starlight. He needed to devote everything he had to speed if he wanted to keep up.

Though if he couldn't figure out Eithan's Path, speed might not matter. The man could *eat* his techniques.

Eithan blurred and moved again, but with the Flowing Starlight running through him, Jai Daishou tracked his movements. He kicked madra behind him and launched, intercepting Eithan's broom with his spear before the man could crush a fourth elder's ribs.

They strained against each other for an instant that lasted three full breaths, the world around them crawling. Even the fastest Truegold elder seemed as though he was moving through water as he dashed madly away, the white lines of Flowing Starlight sliding over his limbs.

Jai Daishou had the full force of his body and his Enforcer technique pushing Eithan's broomstick back, but the blond Underlord pushed against him just as heavily.

Eithan's jaw was set, his one open eye blazing with fury, sweat trickling down his jaw. He trembled with the effort.

But Jai Daishou was using a legendary weapon forged by his ancestor. Eithan was using a broom.

He may have imbued it with soulfire, but every significant artifact had that treatment. The Ancestor's Spear would have been tempered in soulfire many times.

Despite the difference in their weapons, Eithan was still holding him off.

His body is younger, but my spirit is stronger. He channeled a Forger technique, and a fan of needles longer than his forearm condensed over his head. One by one, they launched themselves at Eithan to break the deadlock.

A pulse of madra flooded out of the Arelius Patriarch's entire body. Jai Daishou felt nothing on his skin, but his Forged needles melted like ice in the summer sun.

Finally, he got a good sense of Eithan's power.

Jai Daishou shoved, pushing his opponent away, and spoke in confusion. "Pure madra? Who uses *pure* madra?"

"It has...its uses," Eithan panted, leaning heavily on his broom and flashing a smile.

Now Jai Daishou *had* to make it out alive. He'd read a dozen theories about the mysterious Eithan Arelius' Path, and all of them were wrong. Bringing this information back to the clan was the only way to bring the Arelius family down.

Worse, none of the Truegolds would have heard him. They were too far away.

Even so, despite what his perception told him, he still wondered if it was some kind of trick, maybe a Soulsmith's device hidden on Eithan's body. Eithan had Enforced an ordinary broom—even one washed in soulfire—to survive contact with the spear of an ancient Jai Matriarch. He had suspected madra of earth or force, to be so effective at hardening a weapon.

To do that with pure madra...it would be the least efficient technique possible. He must be *gushing* madra into that broom just to keep it from exploding.

All his senses told him Eithan was ordinary, if any Underlord could be considered ordinary. He was ranked *eleventh,* putting him near the bottom of all the active Lords in the Empire.

His only two extraordinary aspects were his senses—as expected of an Arelius—and, apparently, the depth of his madra.

That shouldn't be enough.

Sudden fear tickled his spine and trembled in his gut.

Fear that he hadn't faced since he transcended Gold: fear of an unknown opponent. Fear for his own survival.

He stiffened his spine and burned that fear for anger.

He was the Patriarch of the ancient Jai clan. He would bow to no man. Not even in his own mind.

Even if it crippled him, he had to win tonight. Jai Daishou unleashed his full power, his core blazing, his Flowing Starlight technique shining in blinding lines on his skin. Even Eithan seemed to crawl now, and the young man's blue eye widened in surprise.

Like every aspect, pure madra had its strengths and weaknesses. It was second to none for attacking and defending the spirit, but it had no ability to interact with the physical world.

Eithan had no power over the forces of nature. So he was helpless before the techniques of a Ruler.

There were no Ruler techniques on the Path of the Stellar Spear, but the decades Jai Daishou had spent perfecting his own sacred arts were not wasted. Stellar Spear madra was a blend of the sword and light aspects, so he focused on his spear, staring into the white-and-silver aura braided along its edge.

He seized that silver power, spreading the aura into a blade the width of an axe. He activated the aura, and it shone silver.

Like this, he could slice through a tree with no more effort than cutting tofu. And there was nothing Eithan could do about it: he had no authority over sword madra, and no way to stop a blade.

The Jai Patriarch had burned through too much of his madra too quickly, but this would end it. He thrust his spear with all his strength, though the aura-empowered blade would slice through Eithan's body even if a child pushed it.

Eithan dropped the broom, which fell so slowly it seemed to hang in the air, and reached into the pocket of his outer robe.

Jai Daishou watched everything as though it played out

for him at half speed: the silver blade of aura sliced through strands of yellow hair, piercing the silk threads of Eithan's robe. The Arelius Underlord was leaning back, away from the strike, but not fast enough.

His hand emerged from the pocket. The silver blade drew blood from Eithan's cheek, spilling red droplets that drifted lazily up.

Eithan sliced open the back of his hand as he slid it in front of his face, holding what he'd drawn from his pocket as though it were a talisman that could ward off the spear's approach.

As Eithan held it into the path of the silver blade, Jai Daishou saw what it was: a pair of black scissors.

Ordinary scissors with long blades, of the sort a tailor might use to cut fabric. He sensed nothing unusual about them whatsoever—they weren't even made of goldsteel. Just, as far as he could tell, iron.

He had to assume they had been washed in soulfire, which would make them stronger and allow them to conduct madra and aura more efficiently, but there was only so much an Underlord's blessing could do to mundane materials.

The aura crashed into the scissors and, instead of slicing them in half, split like a wave running against the rocks.

Jai Daishou was so committed to his attack that he could only watch in horror as the blade of silver light split around the scissors, dispersing, spraying immaterial aura light to either side of Eithan's face. A few more blond hairs fell to the ground, but no more blood spilled.

The spearhead reached the black blade, and Eithan gripped his scissors in both hands, shoving Jai Daishou's full-power strike to one side.

As the Jai Patriarch staggered, the Arelius bent over, breathing heavily, scooping up his broom. "Close one," he said, between ragged breaths.

He straightened with a tailor's scissors in one hand and a janitor's broom in the other, standing over the lord of a warrior clan whose spear had failed.

Jai Daishou wondered when someone would wake him from this nightmare. Even using soulfire, it was impossible to Enforce ordinary iron to that degree using pure madra. *Impossible.* It would empty Jai Daishou's core three times over.

"Tell me how," he demanded, looking up at his rival.

Then black scissors met his throat, and the pain blasted away his Enforcer technique. Time staggered back into focus.

Eithan considered a moment. "I'll tell your Remnant," he said.

Lindon found Eithan sprawled out on his back at the edge of a cliff. Yellow hair fanned out behind him, his blue robe looked like he'd fed it to a gang of dogs, and he was bleeding from half a dozen wounds that Lindon could see. Just out of reach of his outstretched hands lay a broom and a pair of scissors.

"Are you hurt?" Lindon asked, sliding his pack down to pull out the bandages. It almost slipped out of his grip—one of the straps had been burned halfway through by a tongue of Blackflame.

Eithan cracked one eye, though he might have tried to open both; one was gummed shut by a mass of blood. "I am taking a break and enjoying the brisk night air. *You* look like you were beaten with clubs while climbing through an erupting volcano."

Orthos was still picking his way through the debris between the two cliffs, his frustration echoing through the contract, but neither he nor Eithan seemed to expect another attack.

Lindon extended his perception and felt a handful of very alarming spirits on the slopes above him. "They aren't going to attack us, are they?" he asked.

Eithan barked out a laugh, then winced. "Oh, that's...that's tender. No, after the show I gave them, they wouldn't come near me if I had a spear through my chest and was begging for death. Couldn't say if any Skysworn were watching us, but I suspect my ranking among Underlords is about to be adjusted."

A feather's weight lifted from Lindon's head, and the Sylvan Riverseed hopped to his shoulder, sliding down his arm, ocean-blue hair drifting behind her. She jumped off his hand, landing on Eithan's chest.

The Underlord raised an eyebrow. "Why, hello there."

She walked up to kneel on his forehead, looking down curiously. Then she rubbed his head with one hand, whistling like a flute in a way that Lindon suspected was meant to be comforting.

"Your power can't help me," Eithan said, flinching as he sat up. The Riverseed scurried up to sit on top of his head, still making a sympathetic face. "Madra doesn't get any more pure or gentle than mine." He looked to Lindon as though something had just occurred to him. "Speaking of which, I see you're making good use of my cycling technique. Reliable, isn't it? No fun to practice, but there are always tradeoffs."

"Yes," Lindon agreed immediately, "I couldn't be more grateful. Without..." The implications of Eithan's statement caught up to him a second later. "...ah, pardon, but when you say 'your' cycling technique..."

"I mean mine," Eithan said cheerily. "The one I'm using right now. It was in the family library, but everybody else can supplement their cores by cycling aura. Focusing on capacity is inefficient, unless—as you've experienced—you can't add to your power with vital aura. Pure madra Paths aren't as rare as everyone seems to think they are."

"You..." Lindon began to express suspicion, but there was a more polite way to confirm. He extended his perception, scanning Eithan's spirit. This time, the fog that usually covered Eithan's core was lifted.

And he felt a pool of pure blue-white power, just like his own.

"I didn't pick you up because of your impeccable fashion sense," Eithan said, touching two fingers to the corner of his blood-stuck eye. "Hm. I think this is swelling. Anyway, a pure core is one of two ways in which we are similar, so I thought I might be able to provide you with some unique guidance. And that you might help me as well, in the long run."

Lindon was sure he was supposed to ask, but he played his role anyway. "What's the second way?"

"You left it back in the Trials after you advanced to Gold," Eithan said. "It happens. Advancement can play havoc with the memory, especially when the process is traumatic. It should be lying in the dirt, but it followed you. Now it's in your right pocket."

Lindon reached into his pocket, knowing what he would find, and withdrew Suriel's marble. The ball of pure glass sat on his palm, its sapphire flame steady, casting blue light over him.

"Do you know what this is?" Lindon asked, and he wasn't sure if he was afraid or excited.

"I wasn't sure at first," Eithan said, reaching into his own pocket. "Not everything that blocks my senses is from the heavens." He pulled out his own glass marble the size of a thumbnail. "And yours looks somewhat different from mine."

Inside the hollow shell was a ball of perfectly round darkness. It looked endlessly deep, like a bottomless hole suspended in glass.

Eithan held it up to one eye, inspecting it. "Maybe they're like coins," he mused. "This could be the celestial equivalent of tossing a scale to a servant."

Lindon had so many questions that they all tried to exit his mouth at once. They came out together, so they sounded like, "Bluh."

Eithan nodded as though that was exactly the question he'd expected. "Yes. Precisely. Well, let's trade stories while we're *not* surrounded by hostile strangers." He slipped his black marble into his pocket and pulled something else out:

a gold plate slightly bigger than his palm, set with white, dark blue, and a black crescent in the center.

"This is the authority of the Arelius clan's Patriarch," he said, tossing it to Lindon. "You'll need that to run a quick errand for me."

Lindon cradled the ornate emblem in both hands. "It would be an honor," he said, still trying to catch up to the rest of the conversation.

"Above us, you'll find the homes of the Jai family. One of the homes has a decorative tower on the grounds, a tree with pink leaves, and the statue of a crane and a dragon locked in combat. Break into that house and search for a girl named Jai Chen."

"Should I bring her back here?"

Eithan's grin widened. "That's Jai Long's sister, held captive by the Underlord to ensure his cooperation. In all the confusion, I'm afraid she's been left alone."

"Really," Lindon said, and Blackflame surged in him.

Eithan snapped and pointed to him. "That! When you are stopped by Jai clan members, show them the emblem, look them straight in the eyes, and do *that.* If they don't listen to you then, I'll come kill them."

"I'm...sorry, look them in the eye and do what?" Lindon asked. He'd done nothing but cycle.

"You don't need a Remnant to have a Goldsign," Eithan said, then lifted the Sylvan Riverseed on his palm. She hopped back over to Lindon, who settled her on his shoulder. "Now, go. Go!"

When Orthos felt that Lindon had changed direction, his spirit surged with irritation, and he reluctantly turned to follow.

Jai Chen was trapped in a room nicer than any she'd seen since she was a child. The Patriarch had locked her here, but he hadn't bothered to tie her—there was no need. She lay in bed as though a great weight pressed down on her limbs, focusing the full force of her spirit just to breathe. As always.

She'd considered killing herself. Jai Daishou had to be using her against her brother, or she wouldn't be here, and killing herself would burn one of the cards in his hand.

But it wouldn't change anything. Jai Daishou was an Underlord; he would get what he wanted with or without a hostage.

Instead, she focused on cycling. Some of the medical experts who had examined her over the years had suggested that she might eventually regain partial function in her spirit if she diligently exercised, so she spent most of her day attempting to cycle. It was like jogging on broken legs, but she persevered, shoving madra through shattered channels.

If the cracked madra paths were the only problems, she would have been thankful. But her power squirmed away from her direction, fighting every cycling technique, slithering against her will. The same power that brought her brother's techniques to life polluted her spirit, keeping her core out of her control.

She tried anyway.

A wave of heat washed against her face, and her eyes snapped open in time to catch the door to her room dissolving.

Jai Chen pulled sheets up to her chin as though they could protect her from enemies, rooting under her pillow with a half-asleep hand. She only found the knife when she cut her finger on its edge.

She held out the weapon with both hands as dark fire consumed her door. It dissolved the painted wood like black acid, sending a cloud of dust and ash billowing over her.

A massive black shadow blackened the area past the door, its eyes burning circles of red. She let out a squeak, arms trembling as she held out the knife.

The shadow passed, moving away from her door, and she almost let out a breath of relief.

But it had left someone behind.

A man stood in her room, and he had eyes like a death Remnant. They were black all around, with rings of blood red shining in the center. With those eyes, he could be nothing but a monster, come to kill her...and black fire still played around his fingers.

Her arms were too heavy to keep holding in the air, and it was taking all her focus to gasp in enough air to breathe. All she could see were his eyes.

The man bowed at the waist. "Forgiveness, please, I thought you were deeper in the house."

The fire faded from his hands, and the darkness from his eyes bled away like paint in water. They were perfectly normal eyes now, staring at her intently.

Now that he didn't have the gaze of a soul-eating monster, she got a look at the rest of him. He was a tall young man, about her age, broad-shouldered and wearing a bulky pack that must weigh more than she did. His outer robe was smudged and stained with mud, ash, and probably blood, until she couldn't make out its original color. A jade medallion hung on his chest from a dark silk ribbon, etched with the image of a hammer.

He seemed like a perfectly normal sacred artist, though he stared at her like he never intended to blink. With his *other* eyes, the look would have given her nightmares.

But her bed shook, and a growl echoed around the hallway. There was something else in the house, not just him: something with the silhouette of a giant beast and another pair of evil eyes.

"I'm *so* sorry I frightened you, that was not my intention. I'm here to take you out of here."

Jai Chen's breath was finally catching up with her fright, but she still couldn't respond.

"I assume the Jai clan is keeping you hostage so your brother will cooperate," he went on, looking a little pleased with himself. "I can take you away."

"Eyes," she said at last. "Your...eyes."

After a moment of confusion, he picked up a nearby hand-mirror. "My eyes?" He glanced into the mirror, saw they were normal, and turned his gaze back on her.

She didn't take the time to explain. Maybe it was just his Goldsign.

Jai Chen shook her head to signal a change in topic. "Can't...leave. They...will...kill...him." Not that she would go with this stranger and his demonic beast anyway.

He seemed stumped by this response, but sighed and moved toward her anyway. "I know you don't know me, but you're in more danger if you stay. Excuse me for my rudeness, please."

Before he could grab her, she slid out of the bed—embarrassed for an instant, as she realized that she was wearing only her bedclothes—and stood on her own shaky feet. With both hands, she drove the dagger into his chest.

It pierced his outer robe and then fell, bloodless, to the ground.

That was all the strength she could muster. Another instant and her knees gave out, though he grabbed her under the shoulders before she could collapse.

Instead of throwing her over his shoulder, as she had expected, he gently lowered her to the floor. His gaze was still wide and intense, but now he looked concerned.

An instant later, as she was trying to gather enough madra to stand, she felt a shiver in her spirit as his scan passed through her.

"Pardon my curiosity, but what happened to your spirit?"

CHAPTER TWENTY-ONE

She took a few heavy breaths before answering. She considered refusing, but it wasn't a secret. "Remnant...fed on... my spirit." A few more gulps of air. "Brother...killed him... halfway."

He nodded, chin in his hand, frowning like she'd given him a riddle. "You had to have seen healers. What did they try?"

Was he some kind of...traveling spirit-healer? With eyes that could turn black, and a beast rattling around in the other room?

Or was he trying to get to know her so that she would agree to leave?

She debated for a long moment, but eventually told him. If he meant her any harm, he could have killed her without lifting a hand. "Channels...core, need...repaired. Expensive... elixir. Then...pure madra...for core."

Jai Long usually gave her longer breaks between sentences, and he and Sandviper Kral were the only ones who ever talked to her. She cycled madra to her lungs as best she could, though the energy tried to squirm out of her grip.

He knelt in front of her, pulling his pack off and setting it down. This close, she could see black scorch-marks on the canvas.

In a low, crooning voice she couldn't hear, he murmured to something inside the pack. Was there an animal in there? She flinched back against the bed, imagining the sandvipers from the Desolate Wilds. They would crawl into packs sometimes. Or boots. Or beds.

A moment later, a girl the size of a hand popped out of the pack. She looked like a Remnant of water madra, blue the color of a sunlit lake, but far more solid and detailed. Her head bobbed as sapphire eyes scanned Jai Chen from head to toe.

Cute. For a moment, she wondered if this man would let him pet the little Remnant.

"What do you think?" he murmured, and it took Jai Chen a breath to realize he was talking to the spirit. The miniature woman pulled herself entirely out of the pack, her legs flaring into an azure dress—Jai Chen wasn't sure if she was *wearing* a dress, or if her bottom half just fluttered out.

The spirit considered her for a second, then jogged up to Jai Chen. They locked eyes for a moment, and she lowered a hand to pat the little woman on the head.

The Remnant hopped onto her palm and scurried up her arm. Jai Chen barely had time to gasp before the spirit slapped her on the cheek. It was like being slapped by a raindrop.

But the real surprise came from her spirit. A deep blue power rolled through the madra channels in her head, sliding through her like mercury. Her madra tried to squirm away, but it couldn't escape: the blue power slid through it...

...and where the tiny spirit's azure power passed, she regained control of her madra. She must have jerked like a spooked horse, because the man looked concerned, but she couldn't explain. Her power still moved, it still slithered in a way that normal madra didn't, but it was *hers* again.

Then the liquid blue spark ran into a broken madra channel, and Jai Chen slammed against the floor. Her consciousness dimmed, and a sharp pain rang through her spirit. The foreign light faded as it tried to push through her broken channel, like it expended something of itself to drill through.

Her limbs started twitching, but she was afraid the blue

light would stop. *Go,* she urged it. *Break through.*

"I need another one," the man said distantly, and there came a sound like muffled bells. "I know you're tired, and I'm sorry. I'll feed you scales until you explode."

Jai Chen cracked an eye to see the spirit returning to her, tiny blue fingers extended. She looked more pale than earlier, like a winter sky.

A second sapphire light joined the first, then a third. They drilled through her channels, shaking her limbs until he had to hold her down, but they were *doing* it. They were drilling new connections through her madra channels. Where they passed, the loops of light were connected again, healthy and free.

The first light was soon extinguished, but when the second and third converged on the core, she blacked out.

...only for an instant, it seemed, because she woke up to the same situation and a man's voice saying, "Forgiveness. I only know how to do this as an attack."

She braced herself before a hand struck her in the stomach.

The blow itself was light, but a rush of madra flooded into her, scattering her core, forking like lightning through her channels in reverse. Her madra was scattered, her circulation broken, and even her living madra seemed stunned.

But more madra came in behind it, like a tide. The first pulse had broken the damage, and now his energy filled her, settling into her new channels. It filled her, stretching her core, soaking into her spirit. This must be pure madra, because her soul accepted it gladly, even her serpentine power not resisting at all.

As a test, she cycled madra to her lungs, trying to Enforce herself as she usually did to breathe.

Opening her mouth, she took her first *full* breath in years.

Her spirit was weak, her core tiny and dim, and her madra channels felt tender as burned skin. Her entire soul ached, and spiritual pain was deeper than physical.

But she could cycle now. Madra ran from her core in loops, flooding her body, bringing life, and returning to the core unobstructed. She lifted her hand, and it didn't feel like trying to lift a brick with a willow switch. She could move.

The blue spirit curled up on the man's shoulder like an exhausted dog. She was shivering and almost white, and the broken door was visible through her body.

The man rose, standing over Jai Chen. He scanned her again, letting out a breath of relief. "My name is Wei Shi Lindon. I can leave you behind, *if* you tell your brother what happened tonight. Will you do that?" She was focused on breathing. How much sheer joy could be packed into a single breath?

"*Lindon,*" he repeated. "Will you remember that? Do you want me to write it down?"

"Wei Shi Lindon," she said, and she didn't have to pause to gulp down air between each word. "Yes. I *will* remember, and I'll tell him, I..."

She trailed off as she realized her hair was a mess, her bedclothes were askew, and she was huddling on the floor in front of him. They were back in the real Empire now—appearances would matter to this young man.

Jai Chen straightened, hurriedly smoothing out her clothes, but her legs were still unsteady. She caught herself on the edge of a desk, and avoided his gaze; she didn't want to see him judging her. "My name is Jai Chen. I've never hosted a guest, so I'm not sure what I can...but I don't want to be rude to..."

Lindon held up both hands to stop her. "No, please. I can't stay long anyway; I told the old men outside I was on Arelius family business, but they could come in here with spears at any time."

But he didn't leave. He paused awkwardly, as though he meant to say something else. Her spirit shivered again.

Jai Chen risked a glance up at his face and realized he was staring intently, almost glaring, at her stomach. Which was only covered by a thin layer of silk.

She didn't want to be rude, but...Slowly, she moved her hands to cover her stomach.

His head jerked up. "What? Ah, excuse me." His eyes climbed away from her until he was staring at the ceiling. "I was looking at your core. This might be a rude question, but is your madra *alive?*"

Her madra was still as animated as before, but this time it was on *her* side. Her spirit didn't fight her anymore; it was almost as though it fought *for* her, slithering along according to her cycling technique.

"It used to fight me," she told him. "I think your Remnant brought it under my control. Thank her for me, if you would."

He returned to looking at her stomach, realized what he was doing, and jerked his eyes to the side. "Her madra cleanses and restores, I think. She helped me too." He patted the sleeping spirit on his shoulder.

"Ah, I have to go. Please tell your brother: I'm Wei Shi Lindon, and I'd be much happier if we didn't have to fight."

She felt dazed, wondering if this was somehow a trick and her spirit would collapse into wreckage again. If she didn't, then she owed him a debt she didn't know how to repay.

Because she didn't know how else to express that, she bowed. "Thank you," she said at last.

Lindon was staring at her again, but at least it was at her face this time. "This may sound terrible, but have we met before? If I've forgotten you, I apologize, but you seem familiar to me."

Jai Chen had heard about *him* from her brother, but she'd never seen him in her life. "Maybe I look like..." She cut herself off before realizing what she'd been about to say.

"No, I've never seen his face," Lindon said. He shook his head. "Anyway, if you'll excuse me." He gave a little smile, bobbed his head, and started to walk out.

Without knowing why, Jai Chen spoke to his retreating back. "Um...did you kill young master Kral?"

He stopped, hitching up his pack. The heavy monster in the other room growled again.

"It was a pleasure to meet you, Jai Chen," Lindon said,

without turning around. "If I've done anything wrong, or if you need her help again..." He patted the sleeping woman on his shoulder. "...then you can find me at the Arelius family. I'm sorry for disturbing your night."

He walked out, pausing briefly in the dusty wreckage of what once had been the door to her room. A moment later, he opened the front door, and she got a glimpse of the outside world through the hole in her bedroom wall.

A Jai clan warrior in blue held a spear at Lindon's chest, while an elder to the left looked nervous.

Lindon turned his head, meeting the elder's eyes, and the old man flinched visibly. Jai Chen could understand; if his eyes had turned black and red again, the elder could be forgiven for thinking he was a death Remnant in human skin.

Then Lindon dipped into a bow, his pack bobbing behind him. "Thank you for your patience," he said, and walked away.

A giant turtle followed him, big as a horse, munching on a chair as it left—a couple of painted legs disappeared into its lips as it rounded a corner. The doorway was already damaged where the sacred beast passed through earlier, and the frame shattered further this time.

Smoke rose from the giant turtle's shell, and the cracks between the plates smoldered red. The sacred beast growled in Lindon's wake, snorting black fire at the elder on the outside. The old man yelped and hopped back in time to avoid burning his toes.

After a moment of debate, the Jai clan members shut the remainder of the front door without asking her a word.

Jai Chen sat down on the edge of her bed, stunned. So much had happened in such a short time that she felt like she'd been slapped in the face. Now that she thought of it, she *had* been slapped in the face.

But she could move again.

Ordinarily, she had to be careful when she opened her wardrobe, so she didn't strain herself. Now, she opened and closed the door. Open and closed. Open and closed.

Her brother found her half an hour later, standing on her own two feet and opening and closing her wardrobe.

His mask had torn, exposing the lower half of his face. His skin was pale and tinged with blue, his jaw swollen and misshapen, and light leaked from between his lips as he spoke. "What did they do to you?"

He sounded ready to find someone to murder.

Jai Long was standing in the ashes of what had once been her doorway. She must have looked insane, standing in her bedclothes with her wardrobe door in one hand.

And tears were running down her cheeks. Her eyes were swollen, her nose stuffed, and she'd been sobbing. When had she started crying?

Jai Long walked over to her, gently guiding her closer to bed, but she pushed back against him. He noticed her strength and his eyes widened between the remaining strips of his mask. "Tell me what happened," he demanded, and her spirit shivered at the touch of his scan.

Her voice was quivering, and she was still uncertain about many of the details.

But she told him.

Jai Daishou woke on a crumbling, icy cliff inside a pile of moon-white Remnant parts. They were already dissolving in streams of essence, so he must look like he was bathed in stars.

Which was no comfort to a man who had just died.

His limbs trembled as he hauled his way to his feet, his joints screaming like he'd packed them with broken glass. Every breath was agony, and his vision blurred.

He pushed the palm of his hand against his aching head, trying to shake loose his memory.

An image snapped into place: Eithan Arelius, standing

over him with face bloody, hair blowing in the wind, scissors held against Jai Daishou's throat.

Snip.

Pain, blood, absolute exhaustion...and something breaking in his soul.

He ran a thumb over the fresh, tender scar on his throat and shivered despite decades of self-control. Without his good fortune years ago, he would have lost his life tonight.

The Underlord plunged his awareness into his spirit, looking for a black-and-red ornate box that usually floated above his core. The Heartguard Chest was a spiritual object, a treasure he'd plundered from an ancient clan of Soulsmiths, but it had an invaluable function.

It contained enough blood and life madra to save you from death once. And only once. He'd thought it might prolong his lifespan for a few months, when time eventually claimed its due.

Sure enough, the box was open, and the Chest itself melting away to nothing. Jai Daishou had spent months filling it with a decoy Remnant, one convincing enough to fool—it seemed—even Eithan Arelius himself.

He coughed heavily into his hand, the force rattling his bones, and he was surprised when he *didn't* find blood in his palm. Even with the healing of the Heartguard Chest, his body was finished. He was held together by little more than hope and wishes.

If he lived out the year, it would be because the heavens smiled on him.

He cycled what little madra remained, his channels burning, his core throbbing like a bruised muscle. He needed his remaining elders to find him alive.

Before Eithan Arelius did.

Because Jai Daishou was the only one in the Empire to know the truth about the Arelius family Underlord. *Pure madra.* He'd always thought of Eithan as nothing but an overgrown child, and he was more right than he could have known.

He wouldn't die until he could plant that knowledge like a dagger in Eithan's heart.

ITERATION 216: LIMIT
ITERATION 217 HARROW

TERMINATED

As Harrow and Limit dissolved and crumbled away into the void, Suriel witnessed once again the death of an Iteration.

The endless darkness of empty space had peeled away first, like black wallpaper peeling away...only to reveal an even deeper hole. The void surrounded them, infinite nothing dotted with swirling balls of color, like a rainbow of fireflies dancing in the night.

The planet itself faded away like a ghost, leaving fragments: pieces of the planet with a strong enough identity to hold together even in the chaos of the void. There, a disc of earth holding a forest spun into the distance, its trees frozen in a wind that no longer blew.

Time worked strangely in the void. Fragments tended to either live the same moments in a loop or to freeze entirely, waiting to join back into an Iteration. Fragments with inhabitants crawled along, their time drifting slowly forward, but the inhabitants tended not to fare well.

She had sent Ozriel's population shelter straight to Pioneer 8089. With a population of over thirteen million, they had good odds of surviving until their world stabilized into a true Iteration.

Of course, if the Abidan didn't survive Ozriel's absence, it wouldn't matter.

Iterations were like fruits, and the Way was the vine. So long as the worlds were healthy and connected to the

Way, they enjoyed luxuries like causality and existence. As a world's population shriveled, that strained its connection to the Way, which invited infection.

Whenever a corrupted world—like Limit and Harrow—broke into fragments, those pieces still contained some of their corruption. Corrupted fragments were like parasites, drifting up and down the vine, looking for healthy fruits to infest. When that world was corrupted, it broke into diseased fragments as well, and the corruption spread exponentially.

A few thousand standard years ago, the Abidan could only care for two hundred and fifty Iterations. That was as far as they could stretch their forces, because they had to protect each world from the chaos-tainted fragments that hunted the edges of the Way.

When Ozriel appeared, someone who could dispose of a corrupted world without breaking it into toxic pieces, the Abidan went through a period of explosive growth. They stitched healthy fragments together into new Iterations, spinning out new universes that they could protect.

Without infected world fragments flying around, they could expand without worry. And they did.

Suriel and her predecessor had known the danger of putting the weight of their entire system on a single component—Ozriel—but they were *saving lives.* Every Iteration under Abidan protection was another reality not left to the ravages of chaos or the Vroshir.

And everyone agreed: they would replace Ozriel as soon as they found another candidate.

The problem was, they had never found one. And they'd kept expanding.

They held ten thousand worlds now, with only enough Abidan to secure two and a half percent of that number. If any of the other Judges had gone missing, they could have found someone else to fill their function, but not Ozriel. He was irreplaceable.

And now, in all likelihood, dead.

[The probability of Ozriel's death is unknown,] her Presence said, its voice robotic and cool. [If he is capable of hiding from the Court of Seven, he is capable of faking his own death.]

He had left a fractured message behind with *just* enough information to allow her to reconstruct its contents. And a body's worth of unidentifiable blood and decay staining the walls. And evidence of a battle that had conveniently *not* spilled over into the room where the rescued inhabitants of Limit lay sleeping.

But there was no reason to fake his death. Makiel wouldn't believe it, so Suriel couldn't call off the search. And if he were pretending to be dead, he wouldn't have left her instructions on what to do in his absence.

He had most likely been attacked while preparing to disappear, and either been killed or driven deeper into hiding.

She had to assume he was dead. If he *was* still alive and hiding even from her, she'd never find him until he wanted her to. The only logical step was to proceed as though he *had* been killed here.

His death was another weight on her soul. She had known everything: the pressure they put on him, his desire to change the restrictive rules of the Abidan, Makiel's refusal to listen. She could have joined him, lobbied for change.

Another chunk of the planet crumbled to nothing, leaving a loose collection of fragments drifting in an ocean of nothing. A slice of city spun away, all but frozen in time. A great machine of springs and copper gears kept pumping away as it tumbled into the distance, and a hundred-kilometer mass of flesh and limbs drifted away.

Ozriel had finally taken matters into his own hands, as he always did. He'd manipulated Fate so that no one could see his departure coming—if anyone could twist the future to such a degree, Ozriel could. He'd prepared to minimize the damage of his absence, but he'd been caught in the middle of that work.

But who had caught him?

[Entities confirmed capable of killing Ozriel, while he is

fully armed and aware: NOT FOUND.]

Well, that was telling.

[Entities possibly capable, though not confirmed:]

The possibilities spooled out in Suriel's consciousness, a mix of images, text, and memory.

INFORMATION REQUESTED: JUDGE KILLERS

BEGINNING REPORT...

VROSHIR:

Our information on Vroshir worlds is limited, so the capabilities of the Vroshir themselves are largely unknown. Only a handful are projected to possess combat power that rivals a Judge.

The Silverlords gather armies from the worlds they conquer. Between them, they may have found a combination of specialists and assassins capable of catching Ozriel unaware.

The Horseman rides from world to world, gathering energy systems and replicating their effects. He has demonstrated capabilities from at least thirteen dead worlds, and under certain conditions, he could have bypassed Ozriel's protection.

The Mad King hosts an entity that has killed Judges before, but the Court would have been notified if he had left his Iteration. If he has found a way to cross the Way without alerting Sector Control, then he represents a Class One threat.

The Angler has stolen six weapons from Abidan Iterations, and she remains at large. Her confirmed arsenal holds nothing that could threaten the Reaper, but certainly possesses other weapons beyond the knowledge of the Court.

FIENDS OF CHAOS:

True Fiends defy classification by nature, and the only individuals known capable of threatening Judges remain imprisoned in Asylum. Also, no Fiend has ever demonstrated the ability to pass into existence without disturbing the Way, and the Spider Division has reported no such violation near Harrow or Limit prior to Limit's expiration.

If a Fiend capable of doing battle with Ozriel has passed through the Way undetected, current quarantine levels are insufficient. Contact the other Judges to prepare for system collapse.

ABIDAN:

For security reasons, each Judge's combat potential is not available for access. However, inferences can be made from publicly available data.

Razael, the Wolf, has expressed a personal grudge against Ozriel since the creation of the Reaper's office. She was capable of depopulating an Iteration even before her first conscious contact with the Way, and Razael's Sword was designed for the execution of Judges and Class One threats. The Wolf Division contains many destructive powers that are not public record, and Ozriel may have underestimated them.

Makiel, the Hound. As the Judge of Fate, he is the only individual whose prediction skills rival Ozriel's. In combat power alone, he was once considered capable of assuming the role of Razael, though he declined the mantle. He has attempted to replace Ozriel many times, fought to deny Ozriel the rank of Judge, and led the opposition to all Ozriel's proposed modifications to the Eledari Pact. With the Reaper gone, he will propose an imperfect replacement within the standard year, and unofficial reports suggest he has been developing his own Scythe.

Due to the personal biases involved, an encounter between Makiel and Ozriel is virtually guaranteed to end in conflict.

REPORT COMPLETE.

As the report faded away, so did Harrow. Suriel drifted in a black nothingness like the darkness of space, with swirling balls of color instead of stars. They were world fragments—one of the closer spots carried the fractured black tower from Harrow. Another fragment was a shining blue bubble with an island floating inside; water streamed down from the island and hit the bubble, looping up the inside to fall as rain.

The power of the Way was weak here, where chaos thrived. Each fragment was a little pocket of order and energy, which could someday be combined once again into a new Iteration.

With Gadrael's isolation gone, her information requests arrived from Cradle one after the other:

Lindon and Yerin, together, left Sacred Valley and went into the Desolate Wilds.

He was trained by a local Soulsmith in the very basics of the art.

They encountered the Transcendent Ruins, where they were the first to retrieve the treasure at the top.

Lindon killed a Highgold, initiating a rivalry with a young man named Jai Long. Good. Pressure would help him grow. His sister was more interesting: she would have met Lindon in a few more years, if not for Suriel's interference.

The exact nature of their relationship would have changed depending on several factors, but the destiny between them must have been quite strong to survive Lindon's divergence.

A minor point of interest, nothing alarming. Fate adjusted for such small variations as a matter of course.

After a few moments of reviewing her Presence's predicted future for Lindon and Jai Long, Suriel noticed a handful of gaps. She reviewed the data, pulling up extra information, comparing the reports.

Finally, she found what her automated requests had overlooked.

The Arelius family.

A young Underlord had found Lindon and Yerin, adopting them, and taken them back into the Blackflame Empire for training.

Suriel frowned. *That* could be a problem. She was familiar with the Arelius family—or rather, their ancestors—and they hadn't come anywhere near Lindon in any of her projections. Why would they? He was a weak child from nowhere.

She tore open a blue hole in the void, stepping into the Way: the power of order washed over her, soothing and empowering, soaking her body and mind in comfort.

Here, she was close to every Iteration of reality. She could get some answers.

Through her Presence, she reached out to Cradle, requesting information on Wei Shi Lindon.

[Significant deviations detected,] her Presence announced. [Entity Wei Shi Lindon has deviated from primary course. Any analysis of current conditions or projections of future activity will have a low degree of accuracy.]

She'd made a mistake somewhere, but a quick review of her actions found nothing to account for this degree of change. She'd altered his *future,* true, but she should still be able to call up information about his current status.

If her Presence couldn't even connect to the fate of Cradle, then something was badly off-course. None of her assumptions were reliable any longer.

And all of her predictions were wrong.

Irritation growing, she requested general information about the status of Iteration One-one-zero.

[Iteration One-one-zero has deviated from primary course. Any relevant information will have a low degree of accuracy. Direct contact with Iteration is recommended to ensure precision.]

Suriel cut off her physical reactions before she could feel irritation, anger, and uncertainty.

Abidan were allowed a certain degree of autonomy when responding to a spatial or temporal violation, especially Judges. She was permitted to alter the course of many individual lives, so long as the fate of the world remained intact.

Nothing she'd done should have violated those restrictions. Even if Wei Shi Lindon defied all odds and transcended Cradle, it would only mean one more potential Abidan recruit. On a cosmic scale, that was virtually irrelevant. Cradle wouldn't notice when he was gone.

Something else had changed.

The Hound Division would have seen this. She had to go back to Cradle and determine the origin of this deviation before—

An eyeball the size of her head popped into being in front of her. A human eye, in appearance: pure white sclera, black pupil, purple iris ringed with symbols like a Cradle script-circle.

It looked very much like one of *her* eyes, in fact, only larger.

[Judge designation zero-zero-six, Suriel,] Makiel's Presence said, by way of greeting. [Please travel to the following coordinates. Judge designation zero-zero-one, Makiel, requests a meeting.]

CHAPTER TWENTY-TWO

Years ago, when Renfei had first earned her way into the Skysworn, her instructor had congratulated her with these words:

"You'll stop rebels, rivals, and runaway killers all over the empire, and you'll do great service to the emperor. But somewhere, someday, you'll run across somebody trying to revive the Path of Black Flame." He'd chewed on a straw as he spoke, tapping the burned half of his face. "When the Blackflame returns, *that's* when you'll really stretch your oath. Can't help but wonder if you'll fight, or if you'll leave your honor behind."

The challenge had hovered over her, unanswered, for twelve years. She had fought with the Kotai clan against walking sharks on the beaches of the Trackless Sea, executed exiled criminals trying to sneak in across the eastern border, and returned runaways to the Stonedeep Mines. But, though she had kept her spirit open in special vigilance, she had never encountered a Blackflame.

Until a week ago.

She and her partner had been patrolling near Serpent's Grave, keeping an eye on the battle in the city with their spiritual perception. They wouldn't interfere in the battle;

a clan was well within their rights to pass judgment on citizens in their territory. But conflicts led to crimes, so they remained vigilant wherever swords were drawn.

Of the many things they sensed that night, one in particular had drawn them to Serpent's Grave like flies to rotting flesh: the power of Blackflame.

The Arelius turtle, Orthos, was known to them. His madra had flared during the battle, which was to be expected, but what they *hadn't* anticipated was a second source of the Path of Black Flame.

As they had for the past seven days, Renfei drifted next to Bai Rou over the dragon-bone city, dodging horned skulls and yellow ribs that clawed the sky. They flew on emerald green Thousand-Mile Clouds: the symbols of the Skysworn.

Over this week, they'd sensed occasional flares of Blackflame through the city, but not much they could track.

"South-southeast?" Bai Rou asked, his voice coming from the shadow beneath his broad bamboo hat. His great bulk was shrouded by a huge, heavy coat that covered him from shoulders to toes, and his eyes—his Goldsign—shone yellow from within the shadows over his face.

She extended her own perception and checked. Not a Blackflame, just a fire artist practicing. "No. Two more days, and then we confront the Jai Underlord."

Renfei had come to her own conclusion: their mysterious source wasn't a sacred artist at all. Rather, it must be a Blackflame weapon that one of the two Serpent's Grave Underlords had unearthed for their battle. The hints they'd gotten since then were only the weapon being transported throughout the city.

They had planned to confront both Underlords once they had evidence of the weapon's existence, but thus far, they'd found none. And the Arelius Patriarch had fled the city before the Skysworn arrived. That suggested a guilty conscience to Renfei, but she needed more than suspicions to pursue claims against a Lord.

So if they found no more trace of the weapon soon, they

BLACKFLAME ⬡ 349

would take Jai Daishou's testimony anyway.

Bai Rou wordlessly agreed—he was only twenty-eighth among the Skysworn Truegolds, while she was rank thirteen *and* a disciple of the prestigious Cloud Hammer School. While they were assigned together, her opinion would override his.

Deadly heat flashed in the direction of the great black mountain that loomed over the city, and she started to call its position to Bai Rou.

Then flames blasted into the sky from Mount Shiryu's peak.

The fire was streaked with red and black, and Blackflame aura gushed into the sky. All over the city, scripts flared to life, as sacred artists scrambled to defend themselves from another attack.

Renfei and Bai Rou streaked toward the dark peak, their clouds leaving green trails behind them.

"Testing," Bai Rou said, voice hollow.

She agreed. Someone had decided to test the weapon; it must be based around a Ruler binding, based on the vital aura and flame that erupted from the mountain.

As part of standard procedure, the Skysworn each veiled their spirits, suppressing their power so they wouldn't be detected as they approached. An Arelius would see through it, but Naru Cassias Arelius was with his family at the moment, and Eithan Arelius was gone.

They hovered over the mountain until they looked down into a canyon. The same narrow canyon that contained the Black Dragon Trials.

Renfei had checked this location as soon as they had arrived, finding no extra lingering Blackflame power, but obviously someone had managed to hide the weapon from her. It was their own foolishness that they had revealed it so soon.

She and Bai Rou flew over a circle of ninety-nine black, scripted dummies. The Ruler Trial. No better place to test out a Blackflame Ruler weapon than the course that taught them to use their Ruler technique.

Warm air still gushed from the canyon, buffeting their clouds, but it only took a minor expenditure of madra to stay steady.

There were two people inside the canyon, neither of whom Renfei had seen before. One, a shrunken old woman with gray hair in a bun crawling around on spider's legs. She had a goldsteel bladed hook on her back, and she was tinkering with one of the dummies, exposing the construct inside. A Soulsmith, then, in charge of the course's operation.

The other must be the one using the weapon, but his hands were empty. He was tall and looked stern despite his age, and a *very* careful scan of his spirit didn't pick up anything of his madra.

She couldn't check him more thoroughly without alerting him to their presence, but he must be very skilled to have veiled his spirit from even a cursory scan. His madra almost felt *pure,* which was a testament to the power of his veil.

Currently, he was sitting in a cycling position, a tiny blue Remnant on his lap.

"The weapon?" Bai Rou asked, but she shook her head. There was no way to make Blackflame madra look so much like pure water. If she had to guess, she'd say that was a natural spirit. Maybe it helped activate the weapon.

"We'll wait until they draw it again," she said, as the young man stood up. "It shouldn't be too—"

The young man's spirit changed.

His veil must have dropped, because his soul suddenly burned like a hungry flame. His eyes turned black with shining blood-red irises—that wasn't the Goldsign from the Path of Black Flame she remembered, but otherwise his power felt just like a black dragon's.

"A Blackflame in the wild," she muttered.

Bai Rou's yellow eyes flared. "Who would be this *stupid?*"

Aura gathered like clay, wrapped around the activation crystal for the course, and then flared to black-and-red light. The Ruler Trial began.

One dummy came to life, drawing an orange bow and firing a blast of light at the young Blackflame. A lance of sword energy followed, and then a fireball, then a crystal of dark ice stabbed up from the earth beneath his feet.

The course was designed to keep its participants on the defensive, pressuring them so they couldn't hold on to their Ruler technique. When the Blackflames had taken these Trials, their guardians had countered the techniques while the one on the Path of the Black Flame readied the Void Dragon's Dance.

But *this* boy...

Black-and-red madra covered him like blazing fog, and he dodged the arrow of light, took a cut from the sword energy, shattered the fireball on his fist—which must have left burns on his hand—and broke the ice with a kick.

All the while, his madra was still gathering vital aura, scooping it up like piles of gold. He took control of all the Blackflame aura he could, building a mountain over the dummies.

He fought as the attacks continued, dodging with his Enforcer technique active, blasting projectiles from the air with short bursts of dark fire, and taking cuts to the body that should have stopped him in his tracks. He was a bloody mess, and his core should have gone dry in seconds—he only felt like a Lowgold, and not a strong one.

But he kept going. In Renfei's Copper sight, the canyon looked like a seething mass of red-tinged darkness.

Finally, long after she thought he should have collapsed, he ignited that pile of aura.

The entire top of the mountain rose in a column of black-spotted fire.

Renfei had never considered taking shelter. Her Cloud Hammer madra spread into a haze around her, shielding her from the heat and the impact.

The shock hit her harder: this was a real Lowgold on the Path of Black Flame. One of the living weapons that had carved out an empire using sheer power. Even though he wasn't much yet, the Schools and sects and clans would fight to control his future.

The firestorm had died almost as quickly as it was born, but for a moment, it had looked as though Mount Shiryu were transformed into a volcano.

Even this wasn't enough to pass the Ruler Trial. A true Void Dragon's Dance should have devoured the dummies and nothing else; the tower of flame rising into the air was just wasted energy.

But he was sitting on the ground with his legs crossed, and his spirit was veiled again. She sensed madra flowing to his flesh, his wounds drinking it up...and closing. Visibly healing before her eyes, no life madra required.

"Someone," Bai Rou said, "is making a monster."

Renfei released her aura and flew down into the canyon, her partner flying with her. A raincloud hovered over her head: the Goldsign of the Cloud Hammers. Her actual hammer rested at her side, and if the Blackflame boy showed the slightest intention to resist, she'd draw it.

The old woman scurried up to the young man, and they both looked up in shock. The boy's eyes weren't dark anymore, Renfei noticed. They were ordinary, human eyes.

A clever deception.

The two in the canyon were bowing and sweating by the time the Skysworn landed. That showed wisdom, but Renfei still considered striking the Lowgold Blackflame dead.

It would certainly simplify matters in the future.

But in the end, her honor won out: Truegolds did not strike down Lowgolds to make their lives *easier.*

"Name, sect, and rank," she demanded.

"I am Gesha of the Fishers," the old woman said. "A guest of the honored Arelius family. As for my rank, I—"

"Not you," Bai Rou said, his burning yellow eyes on the boy.

Sweat dripped from the young man's forehead, and he didn't dare to glance up at the two Skysworn. "This one is Wei Shi Lindon, an adopted disciple of the Arelius family. This one apologizes, but he can't be sure of his rank. Among the outer disciples, this one believes he is ranked second, but he is only aware of two in total."

"The Arelius family has thousands of outer family disciples," Renfei said, her voice dry. If he was trying to deceive her by saying he didn't know his rank, he wasn't working hard enough. "Who is your master?"

"This one is honored to be the disciple of Eithan Arelius, though regrettably, this one's master is not in the city at the moment. He has gone to the capital. This one would be honored to lead you to—"

She interrupted him. "Wei Shi Lindon Arelius, in the name of the Emperor, the Skysworn are taking you into custody. You will not be tried or punished until a representative of your clan can be found to speak for you." That was the end of what she was required to say, but she added, "Eithan Arelius has no authority in this matter—we speak with the voice of the Emperor himself. A Blackflame cannot be allowed to run wild."

Lindon looked distinctly uncomfortable, like a child caught in a lie, and only then did Renfei remember how young he was. Not even eighteen, she was sure.

Which made him all the more dangerous.

"Excuse me if this one misled you, but this one has only recently begun learning the Path of Black Flame, with the guidance of the Patriarch. This one is not a member of the Blackflame family."

"You might as well be," Bai Rou muttered.

They shackled his spirit, reducing his power. He was more cooperative than most of Renfei's prisoners, though he did repeatedly insist that they tell his family what happened to him.

He might as well not have bothered; the Arelius family never needed to be informed about anything. Renfei's only report would go straight to the Emperor.

The Blackflames had returned.

Emperor Naru Huan spread his wings as he walked through an ornate doorway. He had a fifteen-foot wingspan, but all the doors in the palace were made to accommodate the Goldsign of the Path of Grasping Sky. Etiquette dictated that he brush both sides of the frame with his outer feathers, demonstrating that anyone else would have to give way. When two members of the Naru clan met in a doorway, the lower-ranked had to defer.

No one had walked past Naru Huan in almost twenty years.

Servants closed the door behind him as he entered his home, a luxurious complex of black wood, red paint, and golden dragon statues. He had three joined towers within the imperial palace, all for himself, his wives, and his servants. Palaces within palaces.

He still remembered a time when it had been his job to scrub these floors.

Naru Huan paused on the inside of the doorway. Ordinarily, three servants were stationed here to take his robes of office, his slippers, and the heavy circlet woven into his hair in lieu of the imperial crown.

He opened his Copper sight, which was tuned to wind after his long years on his Path. The entire complex was a placid lake of pale green.

The air was still. No one moved inside.

Madra spun within him, faster and faster. He had no need to call his guards; anyone who could sneak into his home was a greater opponent than they could handle.

Green swirled as the wind stirred. He raised a hand.

A man walked around the corner, where he'd been seated and still a moment before. Long, yellow hair streamed behind him, and his outer robe was threaded in intricate patterns of blue silk. He was fifteen years younger than the

Emperor, though they both looked about thirty: Overlords aged even more slowly than Underlords.

Eithan Arelius grinned and plucked a grape from a bunch that he must have stolen from Naru Huan's table. He popped it into his mouth.

"Welcome home," Eithan mumbled through a mouthful of grape.

Naru Huan glared at him. "Where are Our loyal servants?"

He usually had people to ask questions for him—Emperors were never supposed to demonstrate a lack of knowledge.

"*Someone* altered the schedule last night," Eithan said, shaking his head. "It seems everyone believes it is someone else's shift."

The Emperor had never expected his security to hold up to Eithan Arelius; it had been a joke for generations that if the Arelius family wanted the throne, they would have it. Their bloodline gifts were so dangerous that, if they hadn't shown such a complete lack of ambition, one of the Blackflame Emperors would have exterminated them centuries ago. Total awareness combined with access to the Empire's maintenance facilities gave them the keys to all secrets on the continent.

But the Emperor should never be left unattended because of a *shift change.* He'd have to order some adjustments to security.

"We are not pleased at the disrespect you have shown," Naru Huan announced, his tone a dire pronouncement. "Our office is nothing—"

"No one's listening," Eithan assured him, eating another grape.

Naru Huan's eyes flicked to the nearest bedroom, where he still saw no movement in the air. Which meant anyone inside was either unconscious or dead.

His calculated anger started to turn real, and the air of the hallway began to thicken.

Eithan held up his hands, the bunch of grapes dangling from one thumb. "Wait, wait, wait! She's shopping, you hear me? *Shopping!* She's with your sister, who owed me a favor."

Naru Huan let out a breath, finally relaxing. He tugged the replacement crown out of his hair, tossing it onto a nearby table that existed solely for that purpose. "You could have warned me, Eithan. You can't just pop up anywhere you want to."

"It's better when I don't explain how I do it," Eithan said, sighing around another grape. "Explanations ruin my all-knowing mystique."

"If anyone knew you had entered the palace without my permission, I would have to take action against your family. When a Patriarch acts recklessly, he is not the only one to pay the price."

"If I thought an official message would get me an invitation in a timely fashion, I would have sent you a message," Eithan pointed out.

Every message the Emperor received became common knowledge in Blackflame City within a day. Every message he *responded* to became a political talking-point. "Inviting the Arelius Underlord to the palace would be a rebuke against the Jai clan," Naru Huan said, struggling out of his heavy robes of office—never easy, thanks to the wings. "For now, we still need them to hold the west."

"As long as you don't need them to have an Underlord," Eithan said, pulling a grape off with his teeth. "He initiated an open attack against me in Serpent's Grave, and I was forced to take out *the broom.*"

"I've never heard that expression. I assume you mean an actual broom."

"Of course I do. What better weapon is there for an Arelius Patriarch?" He squinted into the distance, thinking. "Maybe I could have the Soulsmiths make me a better one..."

"Well, if you had to fight him, you should have killed him," Naru Huan said, sliding out of his slippers and walking around Eithan to get to the dining room. "I could have assigned you as the temporary guardian of the western territories while the Jai dissolved to infighting." He stopped as he realized Eithan hadn't followed him, turning on his heel to see what had happened. "What is it?"

The bunch of grapes hung forgotten from Eithan's fingers. His smile was gone, and he stared at the Emperor as though ready to do battle on the spot.

Which would result in nothing more than a dead Underlord, so Naru Huan folded his arms and waited.

"I *did* kill him," Eithan said.

The Emperor raised both eyebrows. "I have a dream tablet from him that arrived yesterday, demanding I punish you for your insolent actions in Serpent's Grave, and requesting imperial assistance in establishing his authority over the city."

Eithan looked like he'd accidentally killed his own mother. He paled, braced himself against the wall, his eyes distant and unfocused.

"Am I to understand that I just received accurate information *before* the Arelius Underlord? Let me just..." Naru Huan took a deep breath. "...breathe it in. This is a good day."

He continued walking to the dining room, where a table was laden with fruit and delicacies. Eithan staggered after him like an animated corpse. "I killed him, Huan. I killed him myself."

"You left an enemy alive," the Emperor said in disbelief, pouring himself a glass of wine. "Do you know how to tell whether someone is dead? Would you like me to teach you?"

Eithan dropped the grapes, snatched the pitcher of wine away from Naru Huan, and started pouring it into his mouth. He only stopped to come up for air.

"I haven't made a mistake like that in...no, it's never happened. Well, I'm going to need a new plan now."

That reminded Naru Huan of another matter—one he had planned to visit the Arelius family to address personally. His mood instantly soured.

"What part of that plan involves reviving the Path of Black Flame?" the Emperor asked, his tone dark.

Eithan waved a hand. "Oh, that."

"*That?* I need an explanation, if only to know what you could *possibly* have thought you were doing. You had to realize I would take him from you immediately."

"Teaching someone the Path is not illegal."

"Neither is hanging yourself, but that doesn't make it wise. He's going to be isolated both for his own safety and to stop him from causing a *panic,* Eithan." Naru Huan slammed his glass down, remembering at the last second to cushion it in wind madra so it didn't shatter.

Eithan sighed and replaced the pitcher on the table. "That does bring us around to the reason I'm here. I have a request."

That was about as surprising as the sun rising in the east: no one ever came to see the Emperor without a request. "The Skysworn already have him in custody. I can't let a Blackflame go, Eithan. He'll cause a riot."

"Let him go? No, no, not at all." His smile returned. "I want you to make sure he still has to *fight.*"

THE END
of Cradle: Volume Three
Blackflame

LINDON'S STORY CONTINUES IN

SKYSWORN

CRADLE : VOLUME FOUR

BLOOPERS

Tears glistened in Jai Chen's eyes as Jai Long held her hand. "Kral died fighting beside me," he told her. "He went quickly and courageously. He died a hero."

"The Underlord...killed him?" his little sister asked.

Jai Long squeezed her hand a little harder. "A boy the Underlord brought with him. Just an Iron."

Jai Chen's eyes opened wide, and her arms fluttered as though she'd tried to raise them. "An Iron?"

"He struck like a—"

"Amazing!" she cried. "An Iron, striking down a Highgold... that's incredible!"

"No, wait, you don't understand. He stabbed Kral in the back from behind with a stolen weapon."

"So resourceful! If he can defeat a Highgold, maybe I can too!"

"Don't admire him! He's a weakling and a coward."

"When *you* were an Iron, how many Highgolds did *you* kill?" She stared at him innocently, waiting for an answer.

Jai Long cleared his throat but couldn't answer.

"You said his name's Lindon, didn't you? Do you think you could deliver a letter to him for me? I'll write him right now! Dear...Lindon..."

Jai Long closed his eyes.

"Your unworthy servant greets the Underlord," Gesha said.

"Underlord," Lindon said, hurriedly sketching a bow of his own. "Forgive me, I was...startled."

Eithan brushed that away with a gesture. "There will be no forgiveness. To the blood pits with you!"

Gesha trembled on her knees, and Lindon laughed awkwardly.

"Why are you laughing?" Eithan asked blankly. "I said, take her to the blood pits!" Two Highgolds appeared from the crowd, dragging a struggling Fisher Gesha away.

"Let this be a lesson to you, Lindon," Eithan went on. "The second anyone disrespects you for any reason? Blood pits. Blood pits are the cornerstone of good rule."

"Apologies, honored Underlord, but did the Fisher really—"

Eithan shook his head. "Lindon, *Lindon*. You know what I have to do to you now."

"Blood pits?"

"Blood pits."

[The probability of Ozriel's death is unknown,] Suriel's Presence said, its voice robotic and cool. [It's most likely a mystery we'll never solve.]

Suriel let out a breath. "You're probably right, so let's stop trying."

[Yes,] the Presence went on, [we will probably never hear any more about this Ozriel fellow. I don't think he's even that important, really.]

"Agreed."

[Let's assume he's dead, and never try to find his killer or unravel the mystery of why he ran off in the first place.]

"Sounds like a plan to me. I'll report our intentions to Makiel at once."

And so, Ozriel's death remained unsolved, one of the great questions of the cosmos, and his name was never spoken again.

Jai Daishou was living a nightmare.

He and his Truegold elders launched their Striker attacks at Eithan together, streams of white light that should have pierced the enemy from seven different angles.

Then, Jai Daishou's pants vanished.

He stood shivering in his underwear as all the Truegold elders pointed and laughed. When he tried to run away, his childhood teacher stepped out from behind a nearby building and told him it was his turn to present his project to the whole class.

But he didn't have a presentation, he had never prepared one, so he was forced to stand in front of his peers and stammer out some nonsense words as everyone continued to laugh at him.

Abruptly he forced himself awake, panting and sweating.

He saw all his Truegolds dead and Eithan Arelius holding a blade to his throat. He sighed in relief.

"All things considered," Jai Daishou said, "this could have been much worse."

Lindon read the tablet aloud as Yerin nodded along.

The dragon advances.

The dragon destroys.

The dragon conquers.

"Fits like a good boot," Yerin said, but Lindon had noticed more at the bottom. He brushed dust aside.

"There's more writing...a lot more."

Beneath the third line were more sayings in the ancient script.

The dragon is respected.

The dragon is cool.

People like the dragon.

"That's really what it says?" Yerin asked.

"It's the best translation I can come up with. And there's still more."

The dragon isn't scared.

The dragon wins all the time.

The dragon could beat you up.

The dragon left his ex-girlfriend, not the other way around, and she's a liar so you shouldn't trust anything she says about it anyway.

"This dragon was working through some issues," Yerin said.

Lindon slowly covered the tablet back up with dirt.

"This Fierce Burning Outer Robe costs me more than I thought."

"First thing, that name's growing on me." Yerin chewed on her lip as she thought. "Yeah. Fierce Burning Outer Robe. I like it, I think it'll stick."

"All right, Fierce Burning Outer Robe it is!"

Lindon ignited the Fierce Burning Outer Robe and dove into combat.

"I am to have authority over their training?" Cassias asked.

"If you would like the authority to decide between making the course slightly more difficult than usual or *truly sadistic,* then yes," Eithan said.

"Good." Cassias immediately cranked the course up to Truly Sadistic.

The screams of the two children rising from the training course were nothing compared to Cassias' manic laughter. "Dance, my puppets!" he cried. "Dance!"

Lindon looked at the simulation showing him the Blackflame Path. It really *was* perfect for him.

But he wanted another one.

"Path of the Broken Star," Lindon said firmly.

Eithan hesitated. It looked like he was about to pull some kind of key out of his outer robe. "Are you...are you sure you don't want Blackflame?"

"Nope, Path of the Broken Star. You told me I could choose, and that's the one I want."

"Well, I—hm."

"What? Can you not do it?"

"No, no, we can do it, I just...I had this whole presentation prepared, I already had a subordinate of mine make preparations. I was going to introduce you to a turtle..."

"A turtle?"

"Are you *sure* you don't want the Path of Black Flame?"

"Broken Star."

"Okay, fine." Eithan sighed and tucked the key back into his pocket. "Fortunately, I know another turtle."

"There's a turtle for this Path, too?"

"Oh, Lindon, Lindon, Lindon. There's a turtle for *every* Path."

When the moon rose on their thirty-second night of traveling, Cassias Arelius walked away from the control board of *Sky's Mercy.* The script didn't need constant maintenance, but he felt better with someone watching the sky. If a Three-Horned Eagle rose out of the clouds, they would be in trouble without someone close enough and quick enough to steer out of the way.

From deep in the house, Eithan shouted: "Heaven save us, watch out for that Three-Horned Eagle!"

A horrifying screech came from the sky around them, and then metallic talons the size of oak trees seized around *Sky's Mercy* and tore it apart.

"If only someone had been watching the sky!" Eithan cried. "Your carelessness has doomed us all!"

Moments later, the cloudship crashed to the ground in a fiery explosion. There were no survivors.

Now that he had a Path, Lindon felt like he had finally taken a real step toward saving his valley.

Eithan threw an arm around his shoulder. "You're making good progress! If I had to put a number to it, I'd say your journey is about...twenty-five percent done. Three parts out of twelve."

"That's not bad!"

Eithan's eyes gleamed. "But it doesn't have to end there! I say, your journey can be longer than that! Much longer!"

"I don't know if I want—"

"Why not fifteen parts, Lindon? Or twenty? How far can this road take us? Lindon and Yerin and Eithan, marching on into the future, forever! A hundred years, and two hundred installments! Let us all turn old and gray and keep marching, until all joy and wonder has left our lives! Forever, Lindon! This could be us forever!"

"...nah," Lindon said. "Twelve is good."

WILL WIGHT is the *New York Times* and #1 Kindle best-selling author of the *Cradle* series, a new space-fantasy series entitled *The Last Horizon*, and a handful of other books that he regularly forgets to mention. His true power is only unleashed during a full moon, when he transforms into a monstrous mongoose.

Will lives in Florida, lurking beneath the swamps to ambush prey. He graduated from the University of Central Florida, where he received a Master of Fine Arts in Creative Writing and a cursed coin of Spanish gold.

Visit his website at *WillWight.com* for eldritch incantations, book news, and a blessing of prosperity for your crops. If you believe you have experienced a sighting of Will Wight, please report it to the agents listening from your attic.

Want to always know what's going on?

With Will, we mean.

The best way to stay current is to sign up for
The Will Wight Mailing List™!
Get book announcements and…

Well, that's pretty much it.* No spam!

SIGN UP HERE!

Made in the USA
Middletown, DE
30 November 2023

44140527R00209